JERKWATER
TOWN

JERKWATER
TOWN

A Historical Novel

F. James Greco

JERKWATER TOWN
A HISTORICAL NOVEL

iUniverse books may be ordered through booksellers or by contacting:

iUniverse LLC
1663 Liberty Drive
Bloomington, IN 47403
www.iuniverse.com
1-800-Authors (1-800-288-4677)

ISBN: 978-1-4917-4351-5 (sc)
ISBN: 978-1-4917-4352-2 (e)

Library of Congress Control Number: 2014914937

Printed in the United States of America.

iUniverse rev. date: 09/11/2014

For my grandparents and all the immigrants who, like my grandfathers, faced the uncertainty and tribulation of seeking opportunity and prosperity in the new world.

For Donn, who has worked diligently to preserve the best of our grandparents' traditions.

There is too much energy going to waste organizing locals in jerkwater towns of no industrial importance. A town like San Diego, for instance, where the main industry consists of catching suckers, is not worth a whoop in Hell from the rebel's point of view.

—Joe Hill
Songwriter, itinerant laborer, union organizer

History has a long-range prospective. It ultimately passes stern judgment and vindicates those who fought, suffered, were imprisoned and died for human freedom, against political oppression and economic slavery.

—Elizabeth Gurley Flynn
IWW "Rebel Girl" and civil rights activist

One

1

But for the litany of a bare foot tapping drum-brush rhythm on wood flooring, silence hung in Michelle Gallo's office like the cumulonimbus cotton balls stacked over the peninsular mountain ranges of San Diego's east county.

Michelle's sister, Maria, thumped the floor with the heel of a foot that bore evidence of a multitude of miles traveled unshod. Long strands of matte-brown hair—interwoven with paintbrush strokes of auburn and gray—framed her oval face as it flowed over the shoulders and back of her flannel shirt. She scanned the walls of Michelle's office with gunmetal-blue eyes, harder in reflection than the warmer, indigo orbs of her sister and unwilling or unable to settle on the younger sibling who sat across from her.

The walls' array of diplomas, family portraits, and photos of Michelle with various civic leaders demonstrated the distinction between the sisters and the choices they had made. Maria might easily have envied her sister. She had chosen not to succumb to that temptation; one of a few good choices, she thought, like the decision—made with no lack of trepidation—to approach her estranged sister about helping to free a wrongly convicted former lover.

1

As Michelle continued to peruse a stack of documents, Maria nibbled at a hangnail—a sapling that dared give rise in a forest of devastated cuticles and ragged-edged fingers. Eyeing a sister who could just as easily be a movie starlet perusing a script, Maria was reminded of the last days she had spent in Michelle's company. Their mother had conducted an obsessive search for meaning at the bottom of a bottle until, on a predawn morning in February, when Maria had just turned thirteen, she left—her good-byes spoken between the lines of a rambling note about needing to find herself. By the time their father, Lou, remarried—to a younger woman who offered solace and guidance to Michelle—Maria had fled.

Now, two decades later, Maria gazed at a face—framed by wavy auburn hair cascading from center part to bodice—that defied the passage of time. *Thirty-one years old*, Maria thought, *and she still could rock a catwalk. Only two years older, but people checking us out together would take me for her mother. I guess I could look like that too, if I wanted to flush a load of shit through the bourgeois sewer system of high fashion and personal care.*

As she perceived Michelle peering over the rim of papers clasped in her hands, Maria shifted in her seat, folded her statuesque legs yoga-style, leaned forward, and placed her elbows on her sister's desk.

"It's all there, *Michela*. Just like I told you on the phone, right?"

Maria tensed as her sister let the bundle of documents fall loosely to her desk and dropped her hands onto her lap.

"It's *Michelle*. I dropped the Italian version many years ago, but then you wouldn't know since you chose to disappear long before that."

Maria sat back, planting her bare feet on the hand-loomed area rug covering the central portion of Michelle's office. She clutched the arms of her chair and dropped her head briefly before raising it to gaze out the window, where, from her vantage point, she could see beyond I-15 and the nearby Rancho Bernardo rooftops to the San Pasqual mountain ridge—an undulating line along the eastern horizon emboldened by puffy clouds that rose behind it. Maria turned her head, focusing her eyes on the top of Michelle's desk as she spoke.

"Shit. I've—I've never been good at …"

"Communicating or being a sister?"

"Neither, I guess." Maria reached for the tattered handbag that she had placed on the floor at her side. "I guess this was a bad idea after all."

"Resurfacing after twenty years as though you had just returned from a quick trip to the market, or asking me to help overturn your former lover's murder conviction?"

"You've never been one to mince words."

"At least I use them. It's called communication."

"Look, *Michela* ... Michelle. I'm fucking trying."

"It took me a long time, but after the events of three years ago, I get why you couldn't live under the same roof with Dad. But why did you stop writing? Why not pick up the phone?"

"It's a long story." Maria dropped her head and wrung her hands. "You wouldn't understand."

"People tell me I can be very understanding, so try me."

Maria raised her bag to her lap and wrapped her arms around it. She rose from her chair and cast her eyes once again to the floor as she turned toward the door. "I'm sure you're really busy and ..."

"No, you can't just walk into my life for a few hours, ask me to help this Vito Erbi, and then disappear again. I cleared my calendar, so I have all morning. Sit down, Maria, please."

Maria paused. She gazed at the office door, dropped her shoulders, and turned back.

"I'll buzz my secretary to bring us some coffee, okay?" Michelle smiled thinly.

"Thanks. I guess I could use some caffeine."

As Michelle called her secretary for an urn of coffee and two mugs, Maria turned her focus back to the window; her mind's eye, tumbling like the swirling dust particles suspended in the morning's sunlight, took her back to May 1974 and the last time she had seen her sister.

May 7, 1974
Tuesday, 4:20 p.m.

2

"How dare you challenge my authority?" Maria's father screamed. "You are not leaving this home braless and in a skirt exposing half your ass. You look like a slut."

3

"At least your impression of me has improved," Maria taunted, gesturing down the length of her sheer blouse, suede-fringed mini, and knee-high boots like a used-car rep ascribing the hand of Leonardo to the finish on a tenderly used sedan. "Just yesterday you called me a filthy putana."

Maria heard the whistle of air before feeling the crack of leather against her bare skin. She stood against the open door stunned, caressing a welt rising on her cheek. Lou Gallo stood waving the belt he had drawn from the loops of his trousers. His lips were pursed in a snarl; his eyes bore into Maria like torches. At that moment, Maria became aware of her sister scrambling up the porch stairs.

"Daddy, don't!" Michelle shouted as she stepped between her father and sister. "Please, stop."

The timbre of his younger daughter's plea brought Lou up short as though he had just received a lash from his own belt. He gathered himself, face muscles relaxing and his eyes brightening as he addressed Michelle.

"Hi, honey. I'm sorry you had to walk in on Maria's shocking behavior." The corner of his lips turned slightly upward. "Please go to your room, dear. This is between your sister and me."

"But Daddy ..."

"Michela." Vertical crevices appeared above and between Lou's arched brows, and his lips thinned. "Go to your room now."

Maria reached out and touched Michelle on the shoulder. She spoke in a whisper.

"Do like he says, Michela. It's just the same old shit, and I was just leaving anyway."

Maria wiped a tear from her cheek, offered a cheery face to her sister, and turned to leave. In a single motion, Lou pushed Michelle out of his path, dropped his belt, and grabbed Maria by her hair as she stepped onto the front porch.

"You get in here right now," Lou demanded. He took a quick glance up and down the residential street, while his daughter yelped in defiance and struggled to free her hair from his grip. "What will the neighbors think of me if they see you standing on the porch half naked?"

"If they're looking at me, I doubt they will be thinking of you."

Lou scowled, grabbed Maria by the shoulders, and shook her. She squirmed out of his grasp and squared her stance.

"I told you that you're not going anywhere dressed like that."
Lou's voice grated on her ears like gravel ground beneath a boot.

"I'll go where I like dressed any way I please, asshole."

Lou's eyes flared and his cheeks flushed as he yanked his daughter inside the doorway and clasped the low, rounded neckline of her blouse in both hands. His single downward jerk tore the blouse to her navel.

"Now you can't wear that, and you won't be going anywhere, will you?"

Maria crossed her arms over her bared breasts and admonished her sister—who stood quavering, hands covering her eyes.

"Don't worry. You'll be okay. It's me he hates." She then ran to her bedroom and slammed the door behind her.

May 3, 1990
Thursday, 10:50 a.m.

3

Once their coffee arrived, the sisters moved to a plush sofa within the Gallo Development Enterprises office, which bore no evidence of the father who was forced to vacate it three years ago.

"But we have better things to talk about," Michelle told Maria after dismissively summarizing the aftermath of their father's arrest and conviction for pandering and solicitation of prostitution. "I want to know what happened to you after you left."

Maria craved a cigarette, opting to gaze into her lap and wring her hands as though struggling to remove indelible stains.

"I didn't have much of a plan." Maria paused, raised her head, and took a sip of coffee. "I just robbed my piggy bank, emptied my bank account, and grabbed a bus to San Francisco. I knew the Haight was fucked by then but figured—even at that—it had to be better than living another day with the old man."

"That couldn't have lasted very long ... your savings, I mean. But then you landed that waitress position you wrote about."

Maria evaded her sister's glance and turned her eyes to the floor. The room grew quiet.

"I didn't want you to worry. I ... I never got that job."

"Then how ...?"

"I earned a street degree in panhandling and groveling—you'd be proud of my should-have-been-Oscar-nominated performance. I eventually stumbled onto a decent gig in a homeless shelter in the Tenderloin, where I filled food trays in exchange for a room."

"Oh, God, Maria. So, no job means there was no Camaro or cute Downey Street apartment either?"

Maria dropped her head, remaining silent while running her fingers nervously through her tresses.

"I see." Michelle said, then paused a beat. "You know I bought all that bullshit you wrote. How long did you live among the addicts, con artists, and prostitutes?"

"About a year ... until ... until I met Vito."

"Your former lover who's been rotting in MCC for gunning down this mobster Bompensiero?"

Maria nodded hesitantly and fidgeted with the hem of her skirt.

"Before that, though, why on earth didn't you cooperate with the PI that Dad sent looking for you?"

"That greasy asshole? No fucking way he had a legit license. I may've been loaded as hell ..." Maria realized her error. "I'm sorry, Sis, but yes, I dabbled ... well ... a lot. Mostly booze. Some acid and shrooms. A little coke, but I'm clean now."

"No more heroin?"

"Heroin? Who said ...? Oh, shit, Dad's little messenger boy? What fucking pack of lies did Daddy tell you?"

Maria straightened, reached for her cup, and then set it back down on a nearby coffee table. Tears welled in her eyes. Michelle's eyebrows rose; her pupils widened; her mouth opened slightly.

"Do you mean the detective didn't find you stumbling down Geary Street strung out, arm-in-arm with a big, tripped-out African dude?"

Maria shook her head; the dams at the rims of her eyes breached; rivulets trickled down her cheeks.

"But Dad told us the PI offered you a plane ticket home and told you that we were worried about you and how much I missed you. That you just blew him off. I tried to understand, but it really hurt when you never wrote me after that. A few years later, he told me he'd received news that you had ODed."

"The goddamned bastard. All this time, you thought I was dead?"

"Of course, I mean Dad said …"

"Dad said?" Maria's eyes had become puffy. She wiped her nose with the back of her hand and stared down into her lap. "Dad's shithead PI—giving that rat bastard the benefit of the doubt—came up to me on the sidewalk one night and strong-armed me into a dark alcove. He put a knife to my throat, shoved a thick envelope into my hand, and told me to do what I was told to do. Then he just walked away."

"What was in the envelope?" Michelle slid closer to her sister and placed an arm over her shoulder.

"There was a wad of cash inside the envelope with a handwritten note from Dad. His note said I had dishonored the family, that I could no longer call myself a Gallo, and to never contact anyone in the family again, especially you. The knife at my throat supplied the 'or else'."

Maria slouched as she watched Michelle attempting to hold back her own tears.

"Dad showed me the typed report from the PI. It said you—I'll never forget the smarmy prose—'had become betrothed to a drug-addled lifestyle consisting of daily rites along San Francisco's seediest curbsides.' You allegedly treated him with disdain, shoved the envelope filled with cash and a plane ticket back in his hand, and told him to go fuck himself—and Dad, too."

"A typed report, Sis?" Maria rolled her eyes; her lips turned upward.

"Oh, my God, Maria. That conniving son of a bitch. How could I have been so gullible?"

"We were both really young, you know?"

"What happened to you after that? You must have fallen apart."

"It didn't take long to run through my savings, so I … I did whatever it took to survive short of violence … or, for Christ's sake, shooting up." Maria picked up her coffee cup, took a sip, and stared out the office window again.

"You mean …"

"Yes. All of it: petty theft, B and E's, lifting wallets, dealing pot and coke, hooking." She continued glancing out the window, unable to meet her sister's gaze. "In the midst of all that, I met Vito."

7

"Vito, the knight in shining armor, who saved the damsel that now wishes to repay the debt?"

"You make it seem so goddamned trite." Maria met her sister's gaze. "It wasn't like that at all."

"Then why come all this way, after all these years, to beg me to believe he's an innocent man and seek my help to reverse his conviction?"

"He … he got me off the street. He took care of me."

"This guy Vito, who must have been in his midforties around then, just takes in an eighteen-year-old waif—with no strings attached?"

"I … he …" Maria's voice weakened, her upper lip trembled, and her face turned pale. She drew her hand to her mouth and gnawed at a fingertip.

"Maria! What is it?"

"Vito doesn't know, but … he's the father of my son—your fourteen-year-old nephew."

"You have a son? Where is he?"

"He's in good hands with an older couple that befriended us several years ago: Donna and Steve Molina. Steve was in construction and retired early with a good pension; Donna's a teacher. They're making sure Evan gets to school and stays out of trouble while I'm here."

"My nephew's name is Evan?"

"Yes."

"You've been a single mom for fourteen years? Let me guess, this scumbag you want me to help left you both high and dry?"

Maria jumped to her feet, grazing the coffee table and tipping the coffee cups.

"No. No. No. Michelle, how can you be so insensitive?" She spoke between sobs.

"I'm a former prosecutor and criminal defense attorney." Michelle rose and took her sister's hands in her own. "Cynicism comes free of charge with the job. Sit down."

As Maria settled back down on the sofa, Michelle retrieved a box of tissues from her desk and offered it to her sister. She buzzed in her secretary to blot up the spill and provide fresh coffee. Michelle then returned to her sister's side.

"Let's start from the beginning. Okay?" When Maria nodded, Michelle continued. "How did you meet Vito?"

Maria tugged a proffered tissue from its container, blew her nose, and sighed.

"I was boarding the trolley on my way back to the Tenderloin after …" Maria paused. "I had just left the Franciscan from an outcall."

"Outcall?"

"Jesus, Michelle, you can't be that naïve." Maria let the corners of her mouth rise briefly. "Anyway, I tripped on the step and dropped my purse. The trolley was moving, and I was afraid to step off. This kind man—Vito, as it turned out—picked up my bag and ran after the car until we reached the next stop.

"I offered him a reward, but he refused; said he'd accept a cup of coffee with me instead. I was still doing drugs, soaking up liquor like a sea sponge, and … well … the other thing. So in that state of mind, I figured he just wanted a freebie."

"Which, of course, he accepted?"

"Michelle, no. But when I offered, he got all serious. Said when he was much younger he had been involved in a business relationship with women like me. He said I reminded him of some girl from that time, and so he just wanted to help me."

"Assuming he wasn't pimping, what kind of business was he in when you met him?"

"He told me real estate management at La Costa Resort. When I mentioned my ties to San Diego and Dad's development business, he grew reticent. I thought it a little odd, but he was so charming and sweet."

"How did he help you?"

"After coffee, he took me to an SRO, paid for a two-week stay, gave me a little cash, and told me he would be back before I had to check out.

"No quid pro quo?"

"No what?"

"Lawyerspeak. He didn't ask for anything in exchange?"

"That was the fucking weirdest part. He said the only condition was that I get clean and look for a real job. Of course, I promised, but—in my state—had no intention. I didn't think I'd ever see him again anyway."

"But of course he did come back."

"He was so fucking pissed. Christ, I'll never forget that scene. He grabbed me by the shoulders and shook me; then he slapped me. The only time he ever laid a hand on me. Once things calmed down, he detailed all these stories from his past. Scared the piss out of me. After that he took me to lunch, said he didn't think I had it in me to change, but he'd at least try to make it safer for me by supporting me while I earned a CMT license."

"CMT?"

"Certified Massage Technician. He said I could make good legit money, if I were licensed, but if I couldn't find my way out of the life, at least I could work under better conditions."

"At a *rub and tug?*"

Maria's face brightened.

"Not as sweet and innocent as I've been led to believe?"

"You can't practice criminal law in San Diego as long as I did and not get tangled up in a Red Light Abatement, anti-massage parlor case or two. I just choose not to ..."

"Lower yourself to my level?"

"I didn't say *or* mean that.

"It's okay. Just a little defensive about my not-so-enchanting career choice." Maria shook her head slowly. "Anyway, long fucking story short, we started seeing each other—dating—and then I got pregnant. No way I was going to tie a noose around Vito's neck and force him to care for a child I'm sure he didn't want, so I dropped out of sight and made sure he couldn't find me again."

"You didn't consider an abortion?"

"That was my plan."

"But?"

"I couldn't go through with it. Blame our Catholic upbringing, but being pregnant made me rethink what I was doing with my life. I stopped using and boozing cold turkey, finished getting my CMT— through a different school, so Vito couldn't find me that way—and got a straight job as a massage technician in a hotel spa."

"I still don't understand why you didn't contact me sooner. I mean, you must have known—after I moved out and had my own career—that you could've contacted me without fear of Dad."

"I could only guess what Dad had told you that caused you to stop writing me as well." Tears filled Maria's eyes again. "I figured you felt the worst of me and would be really pissed if I tried to reconnect."

"So, then, why now? Why after Vito's sat in prison for the better part of a decade?"

"I didn't know. I'm awful about following news. When I did learn about the conviction, it took time to verify that he was *my* Vito Erbi. The whole scene just didn't fit the man I had known, you know? I started going through old newspapers and magazine articles. Read books about the Mob and as much about this Frank Bompensiero as I could. When I became convinced that Vito had to have been wrongly convicted, I wrote him."

Maria paused, gazed at the floor, and drummed her foot. She raised her head to meet her sister's gaze.

"Then I had to work up the courage to contact you. I knew I couldn't … wouldn't … do it unless it was in person. I actually thought that when you heard my voice or I showed up on your doorstep, you'd …"

"I haven't exactly done anything so far to alleviate that fear, have I?" Michelle took Maria in her arms, hugged her, and between mutual sniffles, whispered, "I'm so sorry, Maria, and so disgusted with the man who is our father."

"*Was*, Sis. It's time for you to start thinking of him in the past tense, too."

TWO

1

A gaunt-faced Vittorio Erbi clasped a knee with one hand, using the other to support himself as he twisted to look out the narrow windows of his cell. The muscular fifty-nine-year-old sat on his cot on the nineteenth floor of the twenty-three-story San Diego Metropolitan Correctional Center, built in 1974 as the nation's first high-rise urban detention facility. From his southwest-facing vantage point, his deep chocolate eyes peered through his cell's two thin, rectangular windows at a couple walking their dog in Pantoja Park, the Trolley as it turned northward toward the old Santa Fe terminal building, a naval vessel temporarily moored at the G Street Pier, and then the Pacific as it undulated eastward from the horizon.

The patchwork stubble on his buzzed scalp accentuated an oblong face marked by two large coffee-bean orbs diminished by thick-lensed, horn-rimmed glasses. His lack of facial wrinkles belied his age.

Vito often gazed out his windows in an effort to retain a semblance of contact with the outside world, but this morning he had become obsessed once again with how the legacy of his family's nearly eight decades in America might conclude within this dank structure.

13

At least when I croak, he thought with dark humor, *my name won't be listed among a bunch of punk amateurs stewing in county lockup.*

He learned soon after being incarcerated that MCC had housed several high-profile inmates prior to his arrival, including Patty Hearst, one of MCC's first guests; Black Panther leader Eldridge Cleaver; spy Christopher Boyce; and, ironically to Vito, Jimmy "The Weasel" Fratianno, a mafioso turned informant.

Vito had kept Jimmy's company—as well as that of other mob toughs—at La Costa Resort, a Mafia-designated "hit-free zone," where Vito had worked after leaving the employ of his family's Erbi Realty. Beyond its legitimate purpose, the business had been established as a front for money laundering and drug running—activities that brought Erbi family members in contact with numerous Chicago-, East Coast-, Las Vegas-, Los Angeles-, and San Diego-based gangsters. It had been through these associations that Vito came to know Fratianno and Frank Bompensiero.

Fratianno wore the mantle of interim don for the LA family prior to becoming an FBI informant, author, and talk show guest. Vito was convinced Fratianno knew who took out Bompensiero, but his efforts to make contact had been stymied—likely, Vito thought, because his family had not been welcome in the primarily Sicilian-led inner circles of the LA, Vegas, and Chicago branches.

So I pay the price for my family's heritage, Vito thought at the time of his arraignment. *What can I do but shut up and take my medicine like I was told?*

Erbi reluctantly did as advised and was convicted in late 1980 following the acquittal of the LA family leadership triumvirate—Dominick Bruccoleri (Dominic Brooklier), Samuel Orlando Sciortino, and Louis Tom Dragna—in a 1977 trial for charges related to Bompensiero's death. Vito's cooperation, at least, had garnered a transfer to a single-occupant cell shortly after his incarceration. Yet, even that reprieve came at a price.

2

Vito leaned forward toward the television as UCLA quarterback Rick Neuheisel dropped back to pass. Under pressure from a USC blitz, Neuheisel scrambled until he spotted JoJo Townsell streaking across the middle about fifteen yards downfield. A group of about twenty convicts were gathered in the common room watching the game with him. Bets had been laid and sides taken on the annual game pitting the two Southern California rivals.

As UCLA advanced down the field, the intermittent chorus of cheering and jeering grew louder. Just as Freeman McNeil took a handoff from Neuheisel, an inmate shoved Vito hard in the back, causing him to pitch forward and sideways into the lap of another convict. The behemoth on whom Vito had fallen pushed him to the ground and cursed as he rose to his feet.

In the ensuing melee, a convict hoisted the television overhead and tossed it across the room. Inmates grabbed chairs and heaved them at perceived foes. In the chaos, Vito found himself being shoved, punched, and dragged into a far corner of the room, away from the primary fracas. He flailed and kicked at his two assailants, until they were joined by three more. At this point, and despite his size and strength, he could only curl into a fetal position and hope to withstand the barrage of kicks and punches.

Just when Vito was convinced the five thugs would kill him, a guard arrived, pointed to a ceiling-mounted camera, and shouted at the brawlers, "You're on camera." Vito's attackers quickly dispersed among the other scattering rioters, but not until one of them slammed a chair upside his head.

Vito staggered to his feet. Blood trickled down his face. His insides raged with fire; his head spun; his legs buckled. The officer who broke up the beating bent low and whispered in a coarse voice.

"Your friends, pal, they send their apologies for this and a reminder to keep your mouth zipped, if you want soft time from

15

now on." The guard called over his shoulder for medical assistance, and then turned his attention back to Vito. "I'd take the advice, my friend. Otherwise next time no one may be around to save yah."

After a brief recovery period in the hospital ward that occupies the institution's third floor, Vito was transferred from his 220-bed dormitory-style pod—one of ten within the San Diego MCC—to the facility's eleventh pod, which consisted of single-occupant cells on a split-level floor housing nonviolent convicts.

May 3, 1990
Thursday, Noon

3

Vito paced the few steps required to cross his cell, stood in front of a makeshift desk he had crafted in the prison woodshop, and picked up an envelope he planned to post on his way to lunch. The thin packet contained his most-recently completed missive to a woman from the Bay area, whom he recalled as being a nice piece of tail.

Holding the envelope to verify the address he had scrawled upon its face, he thought: *Maria, my dear, I ain't got a clue why, after all this time, you've developed pangs of guilt for dumping my ass fifteen years ago, but if you really think you can work a little magic, well, who am I to look a gift horse in the mouth?*

He had thanked his Savior for thwarting an impulse to tear up her first letter and considered her correspondence a blessing beyond serendipity. Then Maria, in a follow-up letter, wrote that her sister was a successful, well-connected criminal defense attorney and that Maria planned to approach her about his case sometime in the near future. Although, by outward appearance, Vito had adhered to the prison guard's advice, he had never reconciled serving his full thirty-years-to-life sentence.

If the Weasel can snitch and become a fuckin' talk show guest, he had thought since early in his incarceration, *there ain't no reason why I can't just patiently bide my time, wait for the right opportunity, and turn that screw that secures my freedom.*

The Erbi family had established a long—if not always honorable—history in San Diego. The family patriarch, Vito's grandfather Emilio Erbi, a Calabrese emigrant, had died of a heart attack in late 1954. Emilio's wife, Rosabella, lingered in a nursing home, suffering from dementia until her death in 1961. His mother, Tina, and his uncle Ilario had met with violent death long before that. His father, too. Their early passing—all as the result of a prideful, misguided feud—left Vittorio the lone survivor. Regardless of how the Erbis had lived and died, Vito vowed that an unjust conviction would not become the coda to his family's American legacy.

Can you believe it? Vito thought as a guard approached his cell to escort him to the dining hall. *I've been sweating about turning the right screw all this time, and I just may have screwed it long before I could've known she might turn out to be my guardian angel.*

Three

May 3, 1990
Thursday, 12:25 p.m.

M aria and Michelle sipped iced tea under an umbrella on the Veranda fireside lounge patio overlooking the eighteenth hole of the Rancho Bernardo Inn. The setting, warmed by temperatures in the midseventies, spoke of villas, gardens, and olive trees that occupy the Mediterranean coastline. The sisters were joined by a lunchtime clientele clad in fashionable golf wear and natty business attire—bragging about the morning's round; anticipating the market's push toward a record 2,900; celebrating agreement on a deal; sharing gossip.

While Michelle perused the menu, Maria assessed her surroundings and then shifted to a furtive evaluation of her sister's wardrobe: ivory, long-sleeve top; leg-hugging stirrup pants in a complementary hue; narrow-toed, midheel shoes; heart-shaped earrings, brushed gold like the finish of her Raymond Weil watch. Maria noted that her sister's attire looked professionally tailored, and her auburn tresses—unlike Maria's own—revealed no signs of premature gray.

No doubt weekly trips to a high-end salon, if she inherited the trait, account for the difference, Maria thought. *But Jesus, two kids later, and she's still got a figure to die for.*

When Michelle glanced up from the menu, Maria reached for her iced tea and took a sip. She shifted in her chair, rotated her torso away from Michelle, and rhythmically drummed her foot on the terrace floor. Her face tensed, and she avoided making eye contact.

"It's okay, Sis," Michelle said with a wide smile. "Relax."

"This place ..." Maria's eyes blinked rapidly. "I don't exactly fit in."

"You're *my* guest. If anyone doesn't like flannel shirts and torn jeans, they'll just have to deal with it. Have you decided what you want?"

"I'll just have whatever you're having."

"Did you even look at the menu, Maria?"

Maria cast her eyes downward once again and fidgeted with her silverware.

"Do you think you can help Vito?" Maria asked in a timorous voice.

"I paid only passing attention to the news about the hit on Frank Bompensiero. I knew he'd been the San Diego crime boss for the LA family, that he pissed them off when he became a rat. I've never had reason to question whether the accused had been unjustly convicted."

"I know he's innocent. You can tell from the letters that Vito and I have exchanged that he's a kind and thoughtful guy who wouldn't purposely hurt anybody."

Michelle's lips turned downward reflecting her concentration; she squinted as she met her sister's eyes.

"The arrest and conviction record, which I've had only moments to review, scream to the contrary."

"Yes, he had some run-ins with SDPD when he was younger, but none of the incidents involved a weapon or violence," Maria protested. "Besides, what would have been his motive?"

"Not sure it mattered. Based on my quick perusal, the DA *and* the jury thought an eyewitness account placing him at the scene and his lack of an alibi established a basis for conviction. Did you know about his apparent ties to the mob?"

"Through his father and uncle? Yeah, I came across that, which explains why their *business associates*, as he cautiously refers to them in his letters, provided for his defense."

"Hmm." Michelle paused. "I assume his 'business associates' fronted his appeal as well, which, maybe not for me to say, evidences a less than conscientious effort."

"Meaning the mob made sure their patsy went down?"

"No, I can't make that call from the scant time I've had with the files."

"But you'll help Vito, right?"

"It's not whether I will or won't, Maria. I can't. I haven't practiced criminal law in three years. Besides, I've got a development company to run, two little kids to raise, and a husband who's about to head out on tour with his band. And he's adamant that I join him for at least part of it."

"So an innocent man who wasn't properly defended is going to spend the rest of his life in jail?"

"Maria, let's not jump to conclusions. We don't know that he was wrongly convicted nor whether he had inadequate counsel."

"But you said ..."

"I've had only a few moments to review a lot of documents. Will you give me a couple of days to digest everything in the file?"

"That would be so kind of you. But if you find anything, who'll help him, if you can't?"

"Let's take this one step at a time, okay? Does he know that you're here?"

"No. I realize I already may have raised his hopes falsely by telling him about you, but it could make things worse for him if he knew I was here and wanted to see me." Maria paused and glanced at her hands, which she had folded in her lap. "And honestly, worse for me if he didn't."

Maria raised her head and met her sister's gaze.

"I guess that's selfish of me. At this point, I need to concentrate on finding someone to help Evan's father, if you can't."

"As I implied, Maria, let's proceed in a logical order. If the facts warrant going further, an old friend who moved up to Portland a few years back might just provide the perfect answer. Assuming we can convince him to return. He didn't leave under the best of circumstances. But let's worry about that if and when the time comes."

Their waitress arrived, took their orders, and then strode to an adjoining table. Maria watched her walk away and then turned her attention back to Michelle, who Maria realized had been staring at her.

"What, Michelle?"

"Where did you stay last night?"

Maria looked away again, dropped her chin, and mumbled.

"I ... I have a friend that moved down from the Bay area a couple of years ago and ..."

"The truth, Sis."

"I stowed my stuff in a locker at the bus station and caught a few zees here and there."

"And you didn't check into a hotel or at least a motel because ...?"

"The spa shut down two months ago, and ... well, there hasn't been much demand for upscale masseuses in this economy."

Michelle's eyes widened and became moist. Her forehead furrowed as her eyebrows arched.

"Right after lunch, Maria, we're picking up your niece and nephew from day care and then driving to the station to get your things. I'm taking you to my house. We have a lot of catching up to do."

Four

August 5, 1909
Thursday, 4:00 p.m.

1

Butterflies and spiders had chosen this moment to cavort in Emilio Erbi's stomach. A crowd of about fifty fellow Italians joined him as they pressed against the bow rail of the 580-foot SS *Canopic* for a view of rapidly approaching Boston harbor. His golden-brown eyes widened and his jaw lowered as the outline of the city came into view. He had never seen such an accumulation of buildings—far greater in mass and stature than he could have contemplated during his nearly two weeks at sea.

As the oldest of nine Erbi children living hand-to-mouth on a small sheep ranch in the hills of Spezzano Piccolo at a time of extensive famine in southern Italy, Emilio had become beneficiary of an invitation from his uncle in America to live with him, his wife, and his daughters in Spokane, Washington, a thriving center of commerce in the Pacific Northwest. His uncle Giuseppe Erbi, who operated an employment agency on Stevens Street in downtown, needed an assistant, but his profit margin would not support a new hire.

When he received a letter from his brother Pasquale enumerating the family's woes, Giuseppe hatched a plan to have Pasquale send his oldest son, who would work for Giuseppe for a pittance but for free room and board. Emilio had been delighted when informed of the prospect. Like the millions that fled Italy during the diaspora, Emilio would be escaping the poverty and overpopulation that plagued this region.

The gangly nineteen-year-old clutched the ship's rail with fingers that may have destined him to become a pianist had he been born to a family of greater wealth and social stature. With his other hand, Emilio firmly grasped the strap of his patched and hand-sewn canvas bag. It bore all his possessions. Freeing his hand momentarily from the bag's lash, Emilio removed his *berretto* and grasped it tightly in order to prevent a sudden gust from blowing it overboard. He leaned as far forward as he dared and strained to look around the others crowding in front of him. Now that he laid eyes on America, he could not contain his compulsion to step on its soil.

As the *Canopic* neared the dock, Emilio repeatedly reached into his second-hand suit coat pocket so as to assure himself that his train voucher and the letter from his uncle that had accompanied it remained safely tucked inside. The letter contained detailed information about what to expect as he departed the ship and passed through customs, how to reach the train station, and the address of the Erbi home in Spokane. To Emilio, this correspondence was as dear as his travel documents.

The *Canopic* had pulled into the Commonwealth dock, one of three immigration sites situated in Boston's harbor equipped for immigrant inspections by federal officers. To Emilio, it seemed an eternity before the disembarkation process began. He had memorized Giuseppe's instructions but still struggled to keep his anxiety in check. Not able to understand directives given in English, he meekly followed his fellow immigrants through customs inspection.

Only immigrants and transfer company representatives were allowed to enter the general waiting room, which had been segregated according to the service class under which they had sailed. As Emilio's family could afford only a steerage fare, he followed the third-class passengers to the area assigned to them. Giuseppe had warned Emilio to be leery of the transfer company agents, who were allowed into the room to provide guidance to confused immigrants. Unfortunately, most of these representatives employed connivery to swindle unsuspecting immigrants. Emilio, however, had the good fortune to encounter an Italian-speaking representative of a local merchant bank. The merchant banker verified that Emilio's papers had been properly stamped, signed, and approved by steamship company officials before converting Emilio's travel documents into a valid US train ticket.

Once Emilio had been cleared, he found himself among a crowd of ship passengers—none of whom spoke Italian. As his anxiety and bewilderment rose, Emilio's stomach began growling, reminding him of how hungry he had become. He had not had a meal in hours, and he had not found hot food or even coffee on the dock. The sole vendor he encountered wanted a quarter each for a dime bottle of sarsaparilla or a ten-cent pack of canned meat. The vendor wanted another dime for a stale loaf of five-cent bread.

Emilio chose to endure the increasing pangs until he reached the Boston Terminal Company's South Station, where he stumbled upon a banana stand. He could not express how many he wanted nor make change in American currency, so he handed the salesman a few coins from the front pocket of his ill-fitting pants. In return, he received a bag filled with three dozen bananas.

I can't possibly eat all of these by myself, Emilio thought. *They will rot before I complete my journey.*

Unable to explain his predicament and not wanting to offend the kind peddler, Emilio took the bag and hurried to board the Boston & Albany train that would take him through New York City and on to Albany—but not before claiming a banana, peeling it, and stuffing it in his mouth as he ran.

Once he reached Albany, Giuseppe's letter told him, he would need to switch trains before rolling to Chicago. The total trip from Boston to Chicago would take him thirty-six hours aboard an all-steel passenger train that featured—to Emilio, an awe-inspiring invention—electric lighting. Having safely reached Chicago, the harried young man employed his wits and his uncle's instructions to transfer from his arrival depot to Grand Central Station in downtown Chicago, which served the Northern Pacific Railroad line that would take him to Spokane over the course of another fifty hours.

2

Emilio sat transfixed by the sight of a two-story, red brick structure dominated by several chimneys rising from a pitched, green roof, like redwoods rising from the forest floor. He gathered from the mounting commotion that his train was nearing the city's Northern Pacific Depot, where his uncle was to meet him. His heart thumped against the walls of his chest. Despite countless occasions during his journey when whistles blew, braking wheels ground against steel, and railcars lurched and jangled as though in rebellion, this stop represented a singular occasion: he finally had arrived in Spokane.

After countless hours of sequestration, Emilio's legs wobbled beneath him as he swung his bag over his shoulder, staggered to the exit, and stepped to the depot platform. His eyes blinked in protest at the August sun's brilliance. While shielding his eyes with the bill of his cap and squinting, Emilio tried to discern that one person in the waiting crowd he thought he could recognize.

He shuffled forward along the gangway, his eyes gaining purchase over the glare, until he caught sight of a figure attired like a businessman—dark suit, white waistcoat, dotted necktie, and lace-up boots—waving his hat above his head. This shorter-but-equally-slim version of his father—elongated nose, charcoal hair, receding hairline, and eyes the color of rich earth—*must be Giuseppe*, Emilio thought. *He recognizes me from the description I sent in my letter.*

Emilio returned his uncle's gesture with a horse-tail swat of his cap, pulled it back to his head, and picked his way through fellow passengers. Giuseppe sauntered toward him and then paused at arm's length in front of his nephew. He smiled broadly, doffed his bowler, reached forward, and embraced his nephew.

"*Caro mio, caro mio,*" Zitzi Giuseppe cried. "*Benvenuti in America.*" Giuseppe pulled back and stared up at his nephew as though checking off features described in Emilio's letter: tall and slender with a prominent jawline, high cheekbones, full lips, topaz-brown eyes, and locks the color and coarseness of a sorrel horse. Apparently satisfied with his appraisal, Giuseppe opened his mouth broadly. His eyes glistened like glazed chocolate drops.

"*Vene ca. Vene a conoscere la famiglia.*"

Giuseppe insisted on carrying Emilio's bag as he led them into the southern side of the arid depot, where trains arrived, and down to the lower depot area. They approached a trio of women assembled in a knot near the front entry. Speaking in his native tongue, Giuseppe introduced his family.

"This lovely woman—*qi bella, no?*—is your aunt Augustina."

The corpulent woman's lips broadened in an upward curve, causing the cheeks of her round face to rise like red rubber balls. Her linen walking skirt and hand-embroidered shirtwaist clung, moist with perspiration, to her bulky form. Her straw bonnet, riding precariously on curly sable hair piled like a dark thundercloud, slipped to her shoulder as she embraced her nephew.

"Welcome to Spokane," she said in broken English, employing her amber eyes to enhance her intention to communicate joy. Giuseppe translated for his nephew, and then nodded to his oldest daughter, who stepped forward.

"This young beauty, who already cooks and sews better than her mama," Giuseppe continued in Calabrese, "is my eldest, Gabriella. She has nineteen years; just like you."

The squat, equine-nosed girl curtsied stiffly, keeping her lips pursed, as was the custom of the day. Emilio noted a hint of upturned mouth at each corner, but her eyes—the same hue as Augustina's— revealed no emotion. Gabriella wore a green, ankle-length skirt and white waistcoat. She had tied a bow around her neck and cinched her skirt with a belt that bore a locket as a buckle. Her dark brown hair was parted in the middle and drawn back severely in a manner that reminded Emilio of pictures he had seen of a Sikh's turban. She offered her cousin a slim, weathered hand that clutched a white handkerchief.

While Emilio greeted his aunt and eldest cousin, he fought the impulse to stare solely at Giuseppe's youngest daughter, Rosabella, who wrung her lace-gloved hands, toed the floor, and stared at her feet—except when stealing surreptitious glances at Emilio. Each time their eyes met, Emilio experienced the captivation of smoky jade

27

orbs enticing him as surely as *la voce della sirena* lured her legendary victims into the rocky shore of Castelluccio.

Rosabella, though two years younger, stood several inches taller than her sister and wore her hair down, framing her oval face—boldly flaunting a fashion that would not become popular for several more years. Also, unlike her mother and sister, she wore a summer-weight dress in a slightly narrower and straighter line with a hemline that exposed her ankles. Her bodice cut a vee that terminated just this side of modesty.

Giuseppe bristled when he noted their exchanged glances.

"*Uarda, walyun*. Rosabella is too young for you and off-limits, *capesce?*"

As he spoke to Emilio, Giuseppe's eyes narrowed; then he turned to Rosabella, whose coquettish expression had transformed into a smirk.

"*Figlia mio*, take the carriage back home with your mama and help her prepare for supper. Your sister and I will call a hack and give Emilio a little tour of downtown. *Si?*"

"*Si*, Papa." Rosabella glared at her father before casting her eyes downward in obedience. As she strode away, Rosabella cast an evocative glance at Emilio.

"See you later," she said in English. "I can't wait to get to know you better."

She let her wink serve Emilio as a translation.

As Gabriella, Giuseppe, and Emilio hailed a horse-drawn cab to take them westward on First Avenue, Rosabella and her mother wheeled by in a Democrat spring wagon. Emilio watched until Rosabella guided the carriage out of his sight and eastward toward the family home in the nearby Union Park neighborhood.

Emilio turned his attention to Giuseppe, who was speaking in English to a hack holding the reins of a Mike O'Shea's Spokane Cab. When his uncle concluded what Emilio gathered were directions to the driver, who sat above and outside the glass-enclosed carriage, Emilio obliged his uncle's request—given in Italian—to sit between him and his daughter. Once underway, Emilio noted that Giuseppe seemed intent on drawing his nephew's attention to Gabriella.

"Emilio, you will be surprised at the number of *paisani* living here, especially in our part of town." Giuseppe looked across to his daughter and asked her to tell Emilio about the city's history. "And, *figlia, para in Inglese* the important words. He must start learning the new language."

"All these buildings we are passing are fairly new," Gabriella said in Italian. "Twenty years ago about this time, a fire destroyed the downtown commercial district. It is thought that it started near the depot that we just left. Although thirty-two blocks were destroyed, only one person died."

Gabriella paused as she spoke in order to translate the Italian for buildings, fire, died, and the numbers twenty, thirty-two and one. She had Emilio repeat them before proceeding.

"It's funny, I think, but it was the Dutch mostly who paid to rebuild our city. A company owned by a man named Van Valkenburg rebuilt the burnt wooden structures with granite and brick."

After traveling a short distance farther, Giuseppe directed Emilio and Gabriella to exit the cab and board a streetcar—powered, Gabriella told Emilio, by hydroelectric dams on the Spokane River.

"For a small city, we are quite progressive," Giuseppe boasted as the streetcar rolled westward on Riverside. "It's because of the railroads. We have four transcontinental systems, making Spokane one of the most important centers in the Inland Northwest."

"How big is this town?" Emilio asked his uncle.

"We have over one hundred thousand people now, making us the largest city west of Minneapolis."

"*Si*, Papa," Gabriella chimed in. "We also have the greatest water power west of the Niagara."

They rode the streetcar to Post, where Giuseppe indicated they should stop. Once on foot again, Emilio's uncle led them south on Post to Sprague Avenue. At the intersection of these two streets, Emilio learned from Gabriella about a forthcoming visit by the American president.

"*Caro*, Emilio." Gabriella's face flushed with the unintended word of endearment. "The president, Mr. Taft, will be here next month for our National Apple Show. He will visit Davenport's Restaurant, which is right over there."

She pointed to the southwest corner of the intersection. The trio then walked eastward on Sprague, walking briskly for three blocks until they came to Stevens Street. As they strode along, Emilio realized that Giuseppe had fallen back, allowing his daughter to walk beside Emilio and continue translating common English terms. As they reached Stevens, Emilio gestured with his index finger to his cousin.

"Teach good you, *si?*"

"No," Gabriella responded, her cheeks flushing. "You just learn quickly."

They proceeded along Stevens Street, where Giuseppe pointed out window and awning signs proclaiming the proprietors' ability to provide work. They stopped at the entry to one of the larger spaces on Stevens, and Giuseppe pulled a key from his pocket.

"This is my office, Emilio," he said. "It will be yours, too."

Five

June 6, 1990
Wednesday, 3:45 p.m.

1

A banquet of emotions wrestled for attention as Nick strode through Terminal 2 of San Diego's Lindbergh Field, rode the escalator down past the life-size replica of the Spirit of St. Louis (the original he knew had been manufactured here in 1927 by Ryan Airlines), and headed toward baggage claim. His mind and his mission had been clear when he kissed his wife Laura at the front door of their home near the Reed College campus, drove to Portland International, and boarded the one-stop flight to San Diego.

When Michelle Gallo called to convey a tale about a middle-aged man possibly being set up to take the fall for the murder of Frank Bompensiero, Nick Lanouette's latent reportorial juices flowed like proverbial printer's ink through a dedicated journalist's veins. He sensed his skills had grown rusty in the three years since he and Laura had migrated to Portland, where Laura opened a photo studio and Nick taught English Lit. But his writer's instincts had been difficult to ignore.

This could lead to a series of magazine articles, he told himself after Michelle's call. *Or if Michelle's skepticism proves righteous, I can use what I dig up as fodder for a second novel.* The idea of a second novel brought to mind the circumstances that led to his first,

31

published shortly after he and Laura had relocated to the Northwest. That book, based on events that had led to his departure from San Diego, nearly cost him his wife, his career, and his life. *Time may heal a lot of wounds, but I'm kidding myself if I start thinking it can cure an addiction. Then again …*

As he waited by the baggage carousel, he recalled the career he had left behind three years earlier:

What did the Reader *article call me? Brash? Relentless? Arrogant purveyor of the region's underbelly? Guess I was all that. But hey, my work helped spring Holly's husband from those trumped-up charges. And we forced SDPD to finally pursue the link between forty-eight mostly unresolved slayings of young women here and the Green River killings up in the SeaTac area.*

Holly? Finally stopped dwelling on her. If I had kept my obsession in check and not fallen ass-over-tea-kettle, would she be alive today? Certainly Laura would never have been victimized by Lou Gallo's protégé. Can I ever forgive myself for letting my addiction nearly lead to Laura's death in that plunge off the Ardath Road access to I-5?

Nick felt his muscles tense. His booted foot impulsively tattooed the rail of the baggage claim conveyor belt. He swiped at the beads of sweat gathered on his brow, then ran his hand through his chestnut brown hair, recently transformed per Laura's urging from mullet to a casual, fuller, and front-facing Caesar cut. He craved a Camel. *Hell, any cigarette*, he thought.

The sudden urge to rekindle a defeated habit made him anxious about whether other impulses—ones that had driven him to adultery and betrayal—would resurface now that he had returned to face the people and places that had been a part of his hellish past.

At least one inducement won't be around to tempt me. Nick shuddered as a clip of Holly Damkot's naked body pressed against his played vividly on the movie screen of his mind. Nick struggled to push the recurring scene out of his head. *Man, I'm so glad I never told Laura about Holly or how my relationship with her got Laura entangled in the mess her best friend's father created.*

He had reasoned it was enough for Laura to know Lou Gallo's aide-de-camp had tried to kill her because she came too close to learning about the sex-for-hire galas in which Lou entangled his wife, his business associates, civic leaders, and, of course, Holly.

Nothing to be proud of, but I did man up to the rest, what could have—should have—cost me my marriage: the peep show treks, rub-and-tug sessions; strip club lap dances; all those prostitutes.

Nick had measured out the revelations about his uncontrolled compulsions as though he were sifting ingredients into a mixing bowl: a teaspoon here, a cup there. He had been tempted to divulge nothing about his sordid obsession, but begrudgingly—a Sexual Addicts Anonymous tenet weighing on his conscience—came clean; his confessions tempered only so as not to threaten Laura's own recuperation from the brain trauma sustained in her accident.

The first few months had been agonizing and painful. Nick focused first on a day-by-day regimen for *staying clean*—drug vernacular he adopted because it seemed apt. Eventually, he regained Laura's trust, and together they decided to relocate to Portland, where Nick could pursue a less angst-inspiring career and continue professional counseling. Another tacitly acknowledged benefit of the move had been Nick's diminished exposure to sources of temptation.

As Nick carried his valise from Baggage Claim and walked through a crosswalk to hail a shuttle to his rental, the familiar warmth of San Diego's afternoon sun restored his tranquility. He stood at the shuttle stand and gazed through dark umber eyes toward downtown San Diego. Intervening terrain and structures obscured sites his memory painted in detail: Uninhibited nudes bathing in Sergio Benvenuti's Two Oceans at the foot of Wells Fargo, Emerald Plaza's green neon halos, the Marriott Hotel ensconced next to the convention center, Seaport Village, the dilapidated former SDPD headquarters ...

He closed his eyes and recalled how he had covered his beat from a musky space within the old complex and how he had met his friend and dedicated homicide detective William Buck Jarrett there. How Buck had met him in the headquarters parking lot one night with the intent of sharing a few beers and listening to the blues at Patrick's. And most vividly, how the lead Buck offered him that night set off a course of events that Nick likened to a rainstorm rill, engorging as it flowed down a Banker's Hill gutter until its escalating volume engulfed him like a day-old newspaper tossed into curbside runoff.

This time, he pledged to himself, *I won't tempt fate by stepping off a curb into a puddle of my own creation.*

2

After picking up an onyx Lumina at the airport's Budget outlet, Nick steered toward downtown, where he embarked on what he tabbed "the nostalgia tour." His journey took him by *The Daily Journal*, where he had been a reporter in what now seemed like a lifetime ago; a place that harbored too many ghosts to be revisited—at least for awhile. He then turned down First, where he paused in front of the Victorian home Laura and he had leased shortly after they married; idled in front of Patrick's II, where he had spent many evenings listening to live blues; then motored south to the old police headquarters, a sad tumbledown complex that reminded him of the what, where, when, why, and how of his involvement with Holly.

With his memories darkening like June gloom over the nearby Pacific, Nick pulled away from his old haunts. He drove north on Kettner to Broadway, then bumped along with the traffic eastward to Eleventh Avenue. He drove a short distance on Eleventh until he reached a Burger King, where he grabbed a Double Whopper, fries, and a Coke to go before entering Highway 163 North to Mission Valley and into the parking lot at the Travel Lodge in Hotel Circle. Once settled into his room, Nick made a call to a local SAA member he had contacted before leaving Reed in satisfaction of a promise he had made to Laura. Leo Talega, whom Nick contacted before leaving Portland, had agreed to be his sponsor during his time in San Diego.

After arranging an introductory meeting with Talega for the next day, Nick took a quick shower, toweled off, and sprawled across the bed, where he began examining the material Michelle had mailed him. He wanted to thoroughly acquaint himself with Vittorio Erbi's case before he met with Michelle and her sister. He had told Michelle that he would devote a couple of days after he arrived to "kicking tires," not commiting his services until he had conducted his own research.

As he leaned against the bed's headboard, a nagging thought floated like the gloom wafting over Mission Valley from the bay: *Erbi. I've come across that last name somewhere in the past.*

June 6, 1990
Wednesday, 8:00 p.m.

3

Maria pulled her '88 Tempo into an open space at the curb in front of a two-story stucco apartment complex in North Park. The unit she sought fronted on a side courtyard and was reached by a metal stairway that provided the sole access to the second-floor units of the L-shaped building. She killed the engine, scrunched her cigarette into the ashtray, and glanced at her makeup in the rearview mirror before exiting.

Wanting to establish her independence and not be a burden on her sister, Maria had used the majority of her limited funds to buy the used car, a necessity in Southern California for job hunting—and just about everything else. A three-week search through want ads and drop-ins at hotel and shopping center day spas bore no fruit. In recognition of her diminishing options, Maria reluctantly implemented her contingency plan—one that brought her to her destination this evening.

Her platform shoes click-clopped up the stairs. She adjusted her oversized neon tank top to prohibit her ascent from exposing her otherwise bare breasts and straightened her raw-hemmed jean shorts. She turned left after reaching the top and strode by a large curtained window before reaching the front door, which stood open behind an old but serviceable screen.

"Come on in," a female voice beckoned in response to Maria's rap. "You're right on time."

A well-endowed woman in her late twenties with full face, pink cheeks, bright ruby lipstick, and flaxen hair rolling to her shoulders opened the screen and ushered her in. She stood barefoot; an inner

35

tube of bare midriff—flaunting an advanced state of pregnancy—
floated between halter top and miniskirt.

"I'm Naomi. We spoke on the phone."

Naomi greeted Maria with a hug.

"We picked a perfect time to meet. It's been as quiet as a fag in a
whorehouse." Naomi took a step back and gestured to a living room
sofa. "Please—make yourself comfortable while I take a quick pee."

Maria watched Naomi plod across the room through an archway
leading into a hall with an open door directly opposite the sofa and
then surveyed the premises. To her right, she noted a galley kitchen
that exhibited evidence of use as makeshift office space: a phone, pad
and pen, folded-over romance novel, nail polish, an acetone bottle, and
cotton balls. White cabinetry topped with robin's egg blue Formica
bracketed a stove, refrigerator, and enamel sink. Dark blue linoleum lined
the floor, and where it ended, worn wooden planks covered the living
room—barren but for the sofa, an overstuffed armchair, and a stripper's
pole mounted ceiling to floor in the corner farthest from the couch. The
walls had received a pastel periwinkle wash that stood in contrast to
the cottage cheese ceiling. Two red spots had been ceiling mounted and
trained so that they would illuminate anyone undulating on the pole.

Naomi returned and leaned on the arm of the overstuffed chair.

"Thanks again for dropping in, Maria." As she spoke, her open
mouth revealed orderly rows of pearls set in an oyster bed of gum line.
Naomi peered at Maria through aquamarine eyes that swathed her in
an amphierotic aura that Maria might have pursued had Naomi not
chosen to then embrace her swollen belly as she continued to speak.

"You said on the phone you had seen my ad in *Swing*?"

"Yeah." A pink blossom opened over Maria's cheeks. "I guess
I've just admitted to frequenting the Hi-Lite Theater … at least once."

"No harm in that, hon. Hell, lost track of the times my man
Ronnie and I fooled around in one of those peep show booths." Her
face brightened as she patted her stomach. "I couldn't try that in my
present state, of course, which also explains why we ran the ad."

"And why I'm here." Maria paused and briefly scanned the
premises. "As I told you on the phone, I'm experienced, reliable,
and … ah … I can be most accommodating: males, females, couples."

"And pretty, too." Naomi leaned forward, caressed Maria's cheek,
and ran her fingers through her tresses. "Who does your hair?"

"I ..." Maria faltered. *Might Naomi have felt a connection, too?* "I don't ... Does it look that obviously unkempt?"

"Not at all." Naomi ran her eyes the length of Maria's body and back to her face. "I like that you're natural *and* perky in all the right places. You'll have no trouble attracting *and* keeping clients—of *all* persuasions."

Maria let a perceived nuance float for a beat.

"I understood that you would help with that, at least, in the beginning."

"Sure thing. But why don't we start from the top? Would you like a Coke or something?"

"I'd love a Coke."

"Great. Come along while I fetch it."

Maria followed Naomi into the kitchen.

"Ronnie thinks,"—Naomi looked over her shoulder at Maria and rolled her eyes—"of course, that he runs the place just because he does maintenance and banking. Meanwhile, I do the scheduling, problem solving, handholding, lecturing, admonishing, nurturing, mothering, and guidance counseling."

"You can be sure I won't require any of that, except scheduling, of course."

Naomi retrieved an ice tray from the upper compartment of the fridge, took glasses from a nearby cabinet, and worked a few cubes free, which she dropped in each glass. After handing one of the tumblers to Maria, she opened the lower compartment, withdrew a soda can, and handed it to Maria. She poured iced tea from a pitcher into her glass.

"When you're here, you have your own room with doors that lock. Inside you'll find a massage table, a sofa, towels, and other supplies you might need. I'll show you around in a minute. We've some oils and lotions, but you'll probably want to bring whatever *potions* and toys work best for you."

"And condoms?" Maria queried.

"If you want 'em, you buy 'em."

"On the phone you said my shift fee would be seventy-five plus the first ten."

"That's right. You're free to set your own rates for services, but we get the first ten bucks for half-hour appointments; twenty for an hour. Customers pay me or Ronnie up front, so there's no quibbling later about who owes what."

"That's good. When this was all new to me, I had a couple of assholes who got rubbed, then claimed they didn't have enough money. I like not having to deal with it." Maria took a sip of soda. "About referrals?"

"Until you get your own regulars, we'll direct drop-ins or guys who don't request a favorite to you. There's a twenty-five-dollar finder's fee for that. Of course, it's up to you and your charms to retain repeat customers."

"What type of client should I expect at first?"

"We prescreen every customer, which mostly eliminates drunks, junkies, and assholes. I highly recommend you do the same before arranging to service a new client. As you might imagine, we rarely get single ladies, but you'll likely see the occasional couple."

"What about bottled water for my customers, Naomi? I like to make sure they're hydrated when they leave."

"That's a question I've seldom gotten, if ever."

"Just my training. I'm a certified massage therapist." Maria's mouth opened, exposing her upper teeth. Her eyelids lowered slightly, revealing crescent-shaped, stratus cloud eyes. "About the water ...?"

"You'll need to provide that or any other beverages, including alcohol. You can put your name on anything you want to keep in the fridge. Our honor system seems to work okay."

"What about San Diego's finest?"

"We keep a very low profile and instruct our guests on how and where to park so as not to attract unnecessary attention. If you join us, Ronnie or I can go over our dos and don'ts of solicitation.

Maria gazed at the young woman's protruding stomach.

"Are you still working while ...?"

"Too far along now," Naomi responded as she slowly brushed her fingers across her protruding stomach. "You might be surprised, though, at the number of guys who get off being with a woman in my condition."

"Maybe it's just you. I do sense a certain aura." Maria moved a hand toward Naomi's midsection, then pulled back.

"You wanna feel the kid? You're welcome to give it a go."

Maria offered no resistance as Naomi clasped her hand and placed it palm down on her stomach. She looked to Naomi for a signal, understood Naomi's sigh as one of consent, and initiated a slow, methodical massage. In response, Naomi placed a hand on the nape of Maria's neck and lowered her lips toward Maria's shoulder. The phone jangled. Maria and Naomi started. The moment passed.

Naomi told Maria to have a look around while she answered the call. Maria watched her toddle toward the phone, then began her self-guided tour. She peeked first into the bathroom. *Clean and well-maintained for a forty-year-old place*, she thought, then surveyed the first bedroom. The powder-blue room had been outfitted with a massage table, love seat, space heater, and a cabinet with glass doors that exposed a stack of folded white towels. A small radio, a scented candle, and a variety of oils, lotions, and powders sat on top of the cabinet. Sunlight entering the room through its two windows could be controlled by white blinds, which were shut. A serviceable fixture provided overhead lighting.

She retraced her steps, then proceeded to the other end of the hall, where she found a second but smaller bedroom, a duplicate of the first, except for the presence of incense sticks and an unhinged closet door.

Not much, compared with what I've become accustomed to, she thought, *but at least Ronnie and Naomi keep it clean, simple, and comfortable.*

When she returned to the living room, Naomi had taken a seat on the sofa, her right elbow placed on an arm for support, a hand cupped to her chin, her eyes wide open and turned upward to the side.

"Is there something wrong?" Maria asked.

"That call," Naomi responded as she bobbed her head toward the phone. "A corporate exec I met outside of work who shits money. He's in town on a brief business trip and wants ..."

"Some TLC immediately, but you don't have an available masseuse, right?"

"I didn't want to lose him, so I lied." Naomi cast her gaze downward and sighed. "He told me he had only a short window and needed to have an appointment in half an hour. My best provider is home sick, the other girl who is supposed to be here now called

39

in with car trouble, and I'm certainly in no condition to meet his expectations."

Naomi framed her face with her hands and sighed.

"Shit. I've gotta come up with some way to deliver, or he'll never call again."

Maria, who had been standing arms akimbo, moved closer to Naomi and squatted so as to be at eye level.

"I didn't come prepared to work today, but maybe I'd do in a pinch."

Naomi's eyes brightened. She clasped Maria's hands.

"Do? Sweetheart, you'd blow him away."

"Then?"

"Of course, and because you're saving my ass, you keep the full fee."

Maria stood. Her hands and arms fell loosely at her side.

"Okay if I take a quick shower?"

Six

September 6, 1909
Monday, 5:45 p.m.

The Erbi family sat around the dinner table, finishing a meal that Emilio knew Gabriella had spent most of her day preparing: a side of pasta with meatballs—part of Giuseppe's daily regimine; roasted chicken; boiled fava beans; and a green salad, served as the last course. As had become the nightly custom, Giuseppe sat at the end of the table with Augustina directly across from him. Emilio sat at his uncle's right, and per Giuseppe's insistence, Gabriella sat to Giuseppe's left. Rosabella's place had been set between Augustina and Emilio. Although the two men had doffed their overcoats and suit jackets after arriving from the office, they had not removed or loosened their ties.

The dinner conversation had been unusually subdued. Although anxious to discuss a troubling event from work, Emilio understood that such topics were to be addressed only after they had eaten, and the men had taken leave to the parlor. Despite the restrained discourse, Rosabella creatively enlivened the main course.

As Giuseppe expounded on his process of selecting grapes, separating the juice with his homemade press, and aging the scarlet liquid to self-proclaimed perfection, Emilio risked a glance at

41

Rosabella, who stared at her father attentively. Emilio paid little notice to her placing her hands under the table, until her fingers lit high on his thigh and strummed the inside of his leg. Had this been Rosabella's first flirtation, Emilio may have flinched or vocalized incredulity. Accustomed now to her playful indiscretions, Emilio—without perceptible change in expression—lowered his arm, traced his fingers over the back of Rosabella's hand, and interlaced his fingers with hers. Though he failed to appreciate the time and place, he wanted Rosabella to know that her touch pleased him.

As Rosabella and Augustina rose to clear the table, Giuseppe cleared his throat, took a sip of his homemade wine, and then leaned forward to Emilio.

"Pour yourself another glass of wine, Emilio. We'll relax in the parlor, *caro mio*, while the ladies clean up."

In the parlor, they pulled up chairs and sat across from each other at the fire. Emilio declined a cigar proffered by his uncle, who took one for himself. Before speaking, Emilio waited for Giuseppe to moisten his smoke, strike a match, puff to contented ignition, and gyrate the parejo to the corner of his mouth like a maestro's baton.

"*Zitzi*, I must speak-a you about after tailor you go."

Giuseppe furled his brow, grunted, and clasped the cigar in his fist as he leaned in.

"*Dimmi*."

"I do as you say, *Zitzi*." Emilio employed a mix of his new language and native tongue. "I do-a da paper for da *paisano*. He come after you go. He want job in-a da con- ... da *costruzione*. He-a there maybe ten *minuti*. I hear da noise in da street."

Emilio then related how a group of about a thousand angry workers had assembled outside the office, up and down the street. Emilio had learned previously that Stevens Street served as the hub for businesses like his uncle's, which charged transient workers a dollar to be placed with employers at logging camps, construction sites, or in one of the other flourishing local industies. The employers typically retained an agency-placed worker for a day—maybe two or three at most—sacked him, and then used another agency to sign up a replacement. A displaced laborer had to return to one of the agencies and pay again for the right to continue the merry-go-round ride.

"I get-a worried da mob, so I lock da door, shut lights, and go to da back, to alley. *Che cosa si tratta, Zitzi?*"

"It's those Wobblies. *Vaffangul* I say to the Industrial Workers of the World. They should be happy we find work for people. Instead, this *unione* incites the *bastardi* into calling us sharks and leeches to our very faces."

"Wobblies *e unione, Zitzi?* What these?"

Emilio reached for his wine glass, but stiffened as Giuseppe's face reddened and his forehead furrowed.

"This union organizer come here a year ago when things were even worse in the streets. At first, we think this man come from the heavens. He got the workers off the streets. Convinced them not to destroy our businesses. He said they should join his union instead, and let the IWW leadership negotiate for them."

Giuseppe paused, dragged on the cigar like a starving countryman slurping pasta from his plate, and washed it down with a mouthful of wine.

"Things got quiet for a while. This organizer, you may hear his name sometime—James Walsh—got a union hall built. It's quite *un prodezza*: meeting space, library, news and cigar stand. His Wobblies even created their own newspaper, the *Industrial Worker*. They have meetings and lectures there all the time. Still the mobs gather in the streets, so a group of us go to City Hall and demand that the city ban speaking on the streets. Our mayor, a fine lumberman himself, signed a new law as soon as the City Council approved it."

"They still meet in-a da *strada, no?*"

"Just after you came here, the City Council watered down—*indebolito*—the law for the Salvation Army. This was not acceptable to the Wobblies, so now we live with the results." Giuseppe took another tug of wine. "Mark my words, *figlio*, today I fear is just the start of something much bigger."

Seven

June 7, 1990
Thursday, 9:10 p.m.

1

Flo Bingham, a contemporary of Billie Holiday and Count Basie, took the stage at Patrick's just after Nick and Buck Jarrett arrived. Nick knew Bingham had played in town since the 1950s, when he gigged at the Creole Palace, a club within San Diego's Hotel Douglas that locals of that era tabbed the "Cotton Club of the West." Although Nick's musical interests slanted heavily to blues and edgy rock, he had shared with Buck on an earlier occasion his appreciation for "tasty jazz as a side dish."

"Here's to the good times, old and new." Buck, displaying teeth that reminded Nick of piano ivory, raised his longneck Bud and tipped it toward his companion. Nick reveled in how Buck wore his SDPD homicide detective "uniform"—Men's Warehouse suit; loosened tie; wrinkled dress shirt with top button undone—like a schoolboy poured into last year's Sunday's best.

Buck's stature could pass for that of a former Charger or nightclub bouncer. *Emphasis on the past tense*, Nick thought, because portions of Buck's hair—which he cropped short on his square head—appeared to have been dipped in fireplace ash. His large, deep-set eyes glistened like tumbled obsidian, especially when he smiled, which was often.

"And, none of the bad." Nick winked, kissed the proffered Bud with a peck from his Heineken, then shifted his unlit pipe from mouth to table. "It's great to see you again, Buck."

"Likewise," Buck responded before quaffing his side of the toast and then running a paw across his mouth. He nodded toward the half-bent taper Nick had set on the table. "So, what's with the undersized branch you've been rooting around that new patch of facial weeds? A professorial affectation?"

Nick raised the pipe from the table and pointed the tip toward Buck.

"This helped me break one of my nasty old habits—part of fulfilling a promise to Laura to quit smoking. And this"—Nick rubbed the beard he had acquired since moving to the Northwest—"I did for myself."

"A gift that keeps on giving, huh?" Buck grinned and took a swig of Bud. "Seem strange visiting the old haunts?"

"Yeah, just a little weird, especially considering the circumstances surrounding my departure." Nick reached for the pipe, hooked it in a corner of his mouth, and nibbled on the tip.

"But you came back for more."

"A favor to Michelle."

"Haven't seen her since her father's trial. She doin' okay?"

"Seems to be." Nick paused, casting his eyes upward as though viewing a photographic reminder. "Got over the rough spot in her marriage and the embarrassment of her father's conviction. I think counseling helped a lot, and reuniting with her sister after so many years seems to have brightened her spirits."

"It was her sister—*Maria?*—that whetted your appetite for that can of offal labeled Erbi, right?"

"Like I said on the phone, Vito Erbi had some kind of thing with Maria. He's not kin of any kind from what I gather. But you know Italians: every countryman is related in some way." Nick slipped his pipe back to the table and took a long tug from his bottle. "You got anything good for me?"

"In this case, good is like manure." Buck's jowls shook. The corners of his lips rose as though animated by a puppeteer. "You really don't want to put your hands into it, but if it makes the garden grow ..."

"What the fuck?"

"From what I've seen in his jacket, Mr. Erbi carried a broom and shovel behind his family's business. I'm not sure you want to be poking into that dung heap. Definitely *not* the kind of manure you want for nurturing that growth on your face."

"Jesus, Buck. And to think I'm the one who encouraged you to write because you had a flair."

Buck's eyes brightened. His mouth widened, exposing twin snow-capped hogbacks.

"Nah, pal. You know I'm more comfortable bein' Easy Rawlins than his creator."

"Easy Rawlins?"

"Brother in the Walter Mosley book. Easy's a detective in 1948 LA. You should pick it up: *Devil in a Blue Dress*. It'll bring a little more *color* into your life." Buck took a drink and paused to relish Nick's groan. He waited a few beats before continuing.

"As I was saying, your boy Vito's record—prior to his conviction—paints a picture of a guy trying to tiptoe around family underworld dealings that date back to near the turn of the century. The family dabbled in bootlegging, bookmaking, extortion, and large-scale pimping. Apparently never had a big piece of the action, but that may not have been by choice. Being local and Calabrese instead of LA-, Chicago-, or Vegas-based Sicilian offered little opportunity to amass real power."

"I got that general impression back in the day from one of my sources. He led me to believe that non-Sicilians pretty much got the cold shoulder from the Little Italy community. I understand it goes back to the early days in San Diego when Italian immigrants were primarily Sicilian fishermen."

"History and ethnicity, however, hasn't stopped them from doing business together when it's been perceived as mutually beneficial." Buck paused, squinted, and pressed his lips together. His eyebrows slanted slightly, and a wrinkle gathered between them. "You may have heard that the Erbis ran a quasi-legit realty company, and of course you know about the mob and Teamsters' joint ties to a lot of land around here, right?"

Nick nodded in reply and gazed at Buck as if to say: *and so?*

"Vito's family had a long history as gardeners in my metaphorical manure pile, but the playground gets a little more crowded in a dicey way. Erbi Realty, the Teamsters, and GDE—Lou Gallo's old firm now headed by his daughter"—Buck raised his right hand and crossed his middle digit over his index finger—"used to be like that."

June 7, 1990
Thursday, 11:30 p.m.

2

Nick sat on the edge of his bed, sipping coffee and perusing a copy of the rap sheet Buck had given him. Vito's part of manure cultivation could have been published on a single square of toilet tissue, he thought, at least until the Bompensiero hit. Nick discovered that the DA had conducted an investigation into Erbi Realty's alleged participation in money laundering, numbers running, tax fraud, and merchant shakedowns. The files indicated that the grand jury had focused on the activities of Emilio Erbi and his son, Ilario "Ari" Erbi, but failed to indict for lack of sufficient evidence. Vito's name appeared only tangentially.

He had been arrested and convicted for petty theft in his teens; been a person of interest in a grand jury investigation of La Costa Resort during his employ there; and been tailed by SDPD briefly in 1955, then in his early twenties, regarding potential involvement in a prostitution ring. The file indicated no ensuing arrests or convictions related to that investigation.

I wonder, Nick thought, *might our boy have been on a procurement mission when he took an interest in Maria?*

Nick rubbed his eyes, stood up, stretched, and then briefly paced the room. He glanced at his watch and briefly considered calling it a night. His interest had been piqued, however, by a mob-related thread he'd unraveled while conducting research in the downtown library prior to meeting with Buck. He decided to brew an in-room cup and plod the palpable trail of Erbi Realty's mob-linked associates and *consigliore*. Therein, he thought, may lay the "manure pile" to which Buck alluded.

Nick sipped his coffee and outlined working hypotheses in his mind. As a seasoned reporter, he knew better than to make assumptions or draw premature conclusions. Yet, he had found it helpful when launching an investigation to establish an initial set of theories to direct his work. He had developed one prime scenario already: Vito Erbi, an organized crime outsider, had crossed the mob, which determined the price for his intransigence would be going down for Bompensiero's execution. Nick's second theory, one to which he gave more weight at this point: the jury had convicted the right man.

Nick assembled a "top ten" list of mobsters by focusing on Vito's likely interactions with Bompensiero, the Nevada-based mobsters that developed and controlled La Costa Resort; Bompensiero's LA-based family members; and, by extension, its San Diego–based operatives, including: Joe Adamo, Biaggio Bonventre, Joe Li Mandri, Tony Mirabile, the brothers Joseph and Gaspare Matranga, and their cousin "Big Frank" Matranga. Nick gathered his rogues' gallery from clippings and other resources located in the second-floor Newspapers room of the Central Library, where daily issues of national and international newspapers and indexes to the *Los Angeles Times*, *New York Times*, and *Washington Post*, among others, could be reviewed by the public.

After perusing the indexes, Nick switched to scanning microfiche reels and then thumbed through a bank of vertical files that stood shoulder-to-shoulder along the room's western wall. The vertical files contained a haphazard collection of clips from local publications that disclosed a few kernels of data. Though he considered the effort mind-numbing, Nick pieced together a sixty-year history of Mafia presence in San Diego County. He was surprised to learn that Frank Bompensiero began his career in San Diego in the early 1920s as an apprentice bootlegger under Jack Dragna, an LA-based mob capo and Frank's eventual mentor. After Frank earned his stripes and a brief incarceration for a Prohibition violation, Dragna designated him a *caporegime,* placing him in charge of all LA family interests in San Diego.

Bompensiero skipped town in the 1930s to skirt an ongoing SDPD investigation, but came back in 1941. Shortly thereafter he owned and operated a music store with Matranga; a wire service company; and a downtown café, the Gold Rail. When not expanding his culinary outlets, Frank conducted loan-sharking and rub-outs for Dragna. A second run-in with authority came in 1955, when Bompensiero went down on a bribery charge and illegal liquor license scam.

While serving his time, Jack Dragna died, whereupon Dragna's successor demoted Bompensiero. Frank did his best to stay tied in while he stewed behind bars until he earned parole and returned to the line of work he knew best. When arrested again in 1967, Bompensiero worked a deal, after rotting for nearly three weeks in a sweltering El Centro jail, to have the charges dropped in exchange for becoming an undercover informant. Nick took interest in the fact that Frank, while and despite serving as an informant, had teamed with Anthony Spilotro, a notoriously violent Chicago enforcer based in Vegas. Frank later helped his new partner murder Tamara Rand, a San Diego millionaire real estate broker and naïve investor in Vegas casinos.

Although San Diego had been host to a smattering of organized crime, the city had skirted the mob violence and mayhem common to Chicago in the 1920s and Las Vegas in the mid-1970s until November 1975, when Rand's body was discovered in her upmarket San Diego home riddled with .22-caliber gunshot wounds—an execution-style hit the clippings had linked to organized crime. The coverage Nick perused suggested she had filed suit against her mob-connected partner after she discovered he had bilked her. Nick guessed that a trial accompanied by sensational headlines might have uncovered the mob's veiled interests in Vegas casinos. Avoiding that risk would have supplied the motive, he thought, for the mob-directed hit on Rand by Bompensiero.

Despite the copious copy inches on Bompensiero and his activities, Nick had discovered no direct link between Frank and Vito. He turned next to uncovering any documented ties Vito had established with mob members associated with his employer, the operatives of Rancho La Costa. Rancho La Costa, Nick learned, became feasible as a result of a mob-dominated, Las Vegas–based development company, Paradise Homes, which had successfully leveraged its crime syndicate connections to obtain the rights to build a new Vegas hospital. When the small-time development entity fell short of the necessary capital to complete construction, Paradise Homes turned to mobster Moe Dalitz and his partner Allard Roen, who joined the company and saved the project by swinging a million-dollar loan with the Teamsters Union.

The latter fact had not shocked Nick, especially in the context of his earlier conversation with Buck. Rumors had abounded in San Diego about mob links to the Carlsbad resort's land and Teamster control of a large tract of land in Rancho de los Peñasquitos. Nick realized that before spending another day on the Erbi affair, he would have to undertake the uncomfortable task of querying Michelle about dealings her company allegedly had with Erbi Reality, the Teamsters, or its underworld associates prior to her taking over GDE.

Nick returned to his notes. He found that Paradise Homes, flush with success after the hospital opened, refocused its operations on San Diego. Roen, who owned a ranch house nearby and patronized the Del Mar racetrack, had been drawn to a two-thousand-acre parcel in Carlsbad that adjoined a tranquil lagoon. After buying the land in 1962, the development partners told the *San Diego Evening Tribune* that they were avid golfers. After constructing a golf course, they added tennis courts, horse stables, a hotel, and a spa. The land deal had been brokered by Erbi Realty, and development had been financed, at least in part, by the Teamsters.

La Costa Resort opened in 1965 and began attracting Hollywood elite and moneyed executives like Allen Dorfman, the Chicago insurance magnate who ran the Central States pension fund branch of the Teamsters. Although local media chose to brush over the fact, the crime syndicates had designated La Costa Resort a safe haven for mobsters—regardless of the price on their heads.

By piecing together his research, the file Buck provided, and the data Maria acquired, Nick determined that after Emilio Erbi and his son died, Vito kept the realty business operating—though at a much-reduced scale—for another four years, until he became an employee of La Costa Resort and treated the brokerage as a side project.

Nick thought, *Once I'm past the nasty business of querying Michelle about the extent of GDE's dealings with the Teamsters, I've got to find someone who can brief me on Vito's duties at the resort. Could one have been committing murder? And if not, why tag Erbi as the trigger man?*

Eight

1

Emilio pulled an Old Mill cigarette from its tin foil packaging, lit it, and then pushed himself back from his desk. One foot steadied the wheeled chair; the other he rested on the toe of his boot as his heel jabbed in dissonant cadence. He rolled up the sleeves of his dress shirt, loosened his tie, and took the cigarette from his mouth, rotating it rapidly between his fingers. He sat alone with the responsibility of managing the office while his aunt and uncle rode the train for a weekend jaunt to Coeur d'Alene. Outside, men and boys rustled past as a threatening sky roiled in gunpowder gray, casting an aphotic opaqueness to his topaz eyes as he stared out his office window.

What is wrong with me? Emilio knit his eyebrows and gnawed on his inner cheek as he conducted a silent soliloquy. *I have good roof over my head, plenty good food, people who care for me, even a little pocket change. It would be so irrispettoso to tell my zitzi that I don't like this work. He would not understand, and how could I tell him I think these poor bastards he exploits deserve better?*

Emilio interrupted his train of thought as he slipped the cigarette between his lips and dragged rapidly, inhaling tarry smoke with each tug. As the cigarette danced in the corner of his mouth, he experienced another chilling thought.

And what do I do about Gabriella? Ah, Dio mio, *has my father already sent* a'mbasciata *to Zitzi Giuseppe, or do they intend to box me in so I ask for Gabriella's hand first?*

Emilio began cursing under his breath, a litany of Italian profanity that would be interrupted only by the rattling noise that arose at the rear of the building, startling him from his reverie. He leaped to his feet and rushed behind his uncle's desk, where he knew he would find a loaded Italian-issue revolver holstered inside the bottom right drawer. Giuseppe had instructed him on how to use it the day following their discussion about the street disturbance that had frightened Emilio.

The next series of sounds alerted Emilio that someone had entered the premises. Beads of sweat gathered on his brow and his gun hand shook as he heard footsteps tread the wooden floor toward him. Straining to maintain his wits, Emilio pointed the quivering weapon toward the approaching sounds and strode slowly out of his uncle's office toward the likely intruder.

"I didn't know you could so deftly handle a weapon, dear one," Rosabella proclaimed in Calabrese as she stood in the hall, her round cheeks flush from the cool October air. She pressed a large, covered basket against her chest with both arms. A parasol dangled from the crook of her left arm. "And you have such a big *pistola*, no?"

Emilio lowered the gun. His eyebrows rose; his eyes widened; his mouth dropped open.

"I thought you were ... I could have shot ..." Calabrese streamed from Emilio's mouth in a frantic burst. "*Che cozz?* What are you doing here?"

"Emil," Rosabella switched to English. "Watch your mouth and *parla inglese* like we have been teaching you." Rosabella fluttered her long lashes and giggled. She stepped toward him, setting her basket on a nearby desk. "I thought you might be hungry, so I brought lunch. I got most of it fresh at the farmers' market."

She chose to omit that she would have to creatively explain to her parents when they returned about the disappearance of goods from the family pantry.

"You surprise, *si* ... I mean the yes. Come, come. *Siediti* ... ah ... sit. I get-a da basket."

Emilio freed Rosabella of her burden and led her to a bench provided for waiting job seekers.

Rosabella set down her umbrella, removed her hat and gloves, and slipped out of her coat, revealing a white tea dress with lace inserts and contrasting linen panels. She shook out her curls and sat, permitting the hem of her dress to rise above her ankles—an arousing sight lost to Emilio, who had become preoccupied with staring into Rosabella's dusky eyes.

"What-a you brang, Rosa?" he inquired as he hefted the basket from her arms.

"*Bring*, Emil. The correct word is *bring*, not *brang*." She switched to Italian again. "The tenses are the worst in this American language, I know."

"Yes, hard. So, you *bring* ...?"

"Set the basket here by my feet, and I will show you." She carefully removed the linen covering and splayed it like a tablecloth on the bench, then withdrew a loaf of bread, a quarter round of cheese, and two apples. "I snuck a bottle of Papa's wine, too."

"This surprise is-a good, yes?" Emilio helped her remove plates, glasses, napkins, and utensils from the bottom of the basket.

"I hope so. Let's eat. *Mangia*."

They each occupied an end of the bench, with the center serving as a makeshift tabletop. Emilio left his suit coat off, but had cinched his tie knot back to the apex of his stiff collar. They eyed each other between bites and sips of wine like competing bidders at an auction—neither wanting to reveal interest to the other's advantage.

"You no in-a the school this day, Rosa?"

"I didn't feel like going."

Emilio sat up and leaned forward; his eyebrows raised and lips slightly pressed together. He squinted as he gazed at his cousin.

"I no like," he said. "It is important, yes, the school?"

"Why?"

"If I go-a school more, I make more of myself."

"But of course; you're a man. What does a woman need of math and science?"

"Important to know the things; even for the woman."

Rosabella shrugged and giggled.

"You are much too serious about life, Emil. You remind me of my sister."

The corners of Emilio's mouth drooped; his eyes perused his boots.

"We finish the lunch, no?" He then raised his head to gaze at Rosabella. "Not good to waste."

They completed their meal in silence. As Rosabella reached to clear the detritus of their lunch, her napkin slid from her lap and sailed to the floor. Moving simultaneously to retrieve it, Emilio and Rosabella bumped heads and fell to the floor. He rose, helped her to her feet, then clasped her shoulders and drew her near. He gazed into her eyes—at such proximity that he thought he might drown in the depths of her emerald seas—and trembled.

When she in turn gave no ground, Emilio cupped his hands around the nape of her neck, lowered his head so that he might press his lips to her cheek, and astonishingly to Emilio, Rosabella turned her face so that his mouth met hers. The touch of her pliant lips aroused him as though they had set his heart afire. Then Rosabella abruptly broke the spell.

"Forgive me, Emil." Rosabella's cheeks flushed. She cast her eyes to the floor and wrung her hands. "We must never allow this to happen again."

Emilio took a step back, his eyes expanding in unison with his gaping jaw.

"Cara mia, non ti piace il mio bacio?"

"No, Emil. I *love* your kiss. I love *you*, and that is the problem."

"Is no problem. I love you, too."

"It is not right, *caro*. I am the youngest, and my sister is to be … must be … the first."

"But Rosa …"

"Basta. We shall speak no more of this silliness." Rosabella stood stiffly and dabbed at the corner of her eye. She forced a thin smile. "You must get back to work, and I must go—now."

Rosabella gazed into Emilio's eyes briefly and then ran to the back door and out to the waiting family carriage. She jumped aboard, bidding her horses to hie as she slapped their reins.

2

Several shabbily attired young men had filed documents at the Erbi employment agency during the course of the afternoon, hoping to find employment after being terminated from lumbering or construction work earlier in the day. Emilio had heard Giuseppe demean such migrant workers as bindle stiffs and timber beasts. Having himself risen from poverty so recently, Emilio took umbrage with his uncle's cavalier attitude.

Zitzi shows such little compassion for these poor bastards and their loved ones, Emilio thought. *And should he not at least respect them as the source of income for his business?*

After the day's last client completed the application process, Emilio accompanied him to the door and and scanned the Stevens Street sidewalk north and south. Now what to do, he thought, mindful that the procession of applicants had kept him distracted from thinking about Rosabella.

Darkness had begun to fall. Shopkeepers were closing up. Groups of unionists and underemployed workers had begun to mill about, and a small cluster of them just outside Emilio's office. Emilio pulled the door shut behind him and edged closer to the men in hope of overhearing their conversation. He lingered, struggling to grasp the meaning of their rapidly spoken English, when a young, compartively well-dressed man—a unionist from what Emilio could gather—called out to him.

"Hey, *paisan', vennacá*." The muscular gentleman with angular handsomeness said good evening to the men around him as Emilio hesitantly approached. He then offered his hand and greeted Emilio in Italian.

"I am Giovanni Rosso." The slim redhead gave Emilio his business card. "My people are from Firenze originally. And you?"

"Emilo Erbi. I am Calabrese."

"I've seen you among the workers before, haven't I?"

"Only in passing, I assure you, Mr. Rosso."

"It's getting chilly out here. May I come inside for a moment? I'm pretty new to Spokane and haven't made many aquaintances, especially of fellow countrymen. Perhaps you have some questions about our union."

"No questions, really, and ... well ... you must know my work." Emilio gestured toward the sign above his uncle's office.

"Yes. Of course. My job is to find common ground among the workers, the employers, and agents such as yourself. Your curiousity suggests that you are open-minded, no?"

Emilio shrugged, and then examined his shoes for a moment.

"I tell you I may be awful company, but you are welcome to come in. My afternoon has not been a pleasant one."

"Something we did here in the streets?"

"No, no. It's a personal matter."

Emilio locked the entry door behind him, in consideration of the sporadic melees that continued to erupt in the streets, and guided Giovanni into Giuseppe's office. Emilio positioned himself behind his uncle's desk, in which he had returned the handgun withdrawn when Rosabella's arrival had surprised him. Rosso removed his coat and cap, revealing a rusty steel-wool pad of hair, and folded them over his arm. Emilio pointed toward his own head as he took Giovanni's coat and hat and hung them on a nearby rack.

"Fittingly named, I see." His eyes squinted, and two large dimples formed next to the corners of his mouth as his lips widened. "Please, make you comfortable," he said, switching to English as he gestured to a chair in front of the desk. "You speak English ... slowly. I need to learn. Yes?"

"Thank you, and I will. Just let me know if I need to translate," Giovanni said, speaking the second sentence in Italian.

Emilio followed Giovanni's gaze as he scanned the premises through moss-hued eyes set narrowly on his round face. To Emilio, his visitor's stern assessment of his surroundings belied his round face and jovial countenance.

"A large space for such a young proprietor," Giovanni told Emilio as he brought his focus back to his host.

"This my *zitzi*'s business. I work-a for him."

"With your type of work, I would think you would be disturbed by all the ruckus on the main stem."

"Main stem?"

"Stevens Street. You know—here, where all the hobos congregate."

"I no like-a name the hobos. They just poor sons-of-bitches look ... looking ... for da money for da food."

"So I read you right."

"What-a you mean?"

"When I've seen you out on the street, watching the protests, or listening in on conversations like tonight."

"I no want-a be rude."

"No offense taken." Giovanni waved his hand over the pack of Old Mills Emilio had set on the desk. "Mind if I have a smoke?"

Emilio nodded toward the pack, and Rosso picked it up, offering one to Emilio, who obliged, and pulled one out for himself. Emilio struck a match and lit their cigarettes.

"So how old are you, Milio?" His query arrived wrapped in a cloud of smoke.

"Nineteen. I be twenty soon. And you?"

"I'm only twenty-one, but everyone says I look much older." Giovanni took another drag before speaking again. "So what do you think of Spokane?"

"I be in America only the month. It is-a nice, but cold. The cigarettes help." Emilio raised his smoke between thumb and forefinger.

"I hear you. I'm up from Southern California, myself. I'm of the first generation in my family not of the old country."

"You like the California?"

"It's paradise, Milio. Good weather; plentiful fish; *belle bambole*." Upon the mention of attractive women, Giovanni's face—Emilio noted—brightened. "You got a girl, Milio?"

Emilio straightened in his seat, tossed his cigarette to the floor, and crushed it with a boot heel. He felt a flush rising upward from his neck like flame rising in his uncle's parlor fireplace.

"I ... I think maybe, until the afternoon. Maybe ... I no got."

"The personal matter?"

Emilio cast his eyes downward and nodded.

Giovanni's eyes absorbed the details of an Italian estate on an oak-laden hillside portrayed in a print mounted on the wall just above Emilio's head. He dragged on his cigarette, then rested his hands on the back of his head, leaving the Old Mill to dangle at the corner of his mouth. He panned the painting for several moments, and then withdrew the cigarette from his mouth. The corners of his lips rose, accentuating the roundness of his face.

"I think I have just the remedy, *amico*. Would you like to join me for dinner? My treat."

"I should go the home." He stopped and looked away, dismayed by the thought of facing Rosabella without his aunt and uncle as a buffer, or worse, having to spend time with Gabriella, especially if Rosabella had confessed to her sister.

"We can swing by the union hall, and I'll have a runner take a message to your family not to expect you until late. Come on. We both could use a little fun, and I know just the place."

Giovanni paid the bill as Emilio sat back. Emilio rubbed his stomach in acknowledgment of his pleasure with the fare served at the restaurant Giovanni had chosen. The eatery, located within the three-story Colonial Hotel, a three-story brick building near Main and Post, shared the first floor with a billiards hall and saloon. The two upper stories housed a popular brothel.

"You allow me pay share," Emilio said as he slid a hand into his trouser pocket, hoping to find more than the few coins he remembered putting there in the morning.

"No, I promised this would be my treat, Emilio, so take your hand out of your pocket."

"But is no fair."

"Milio. It's okay. I'm …" Giovanni lowered his voice and switched to Italian. "My family has experienced good fortune in business. I work as a union organizer, because I want others to have a chance at getting ahead, too. Promise me you will work hard and put your own money to good use. That's all I ask of you, *amico*."

Emilio nodded. A blush chased up his cheeks. Giovanni stood up.

"Come on, *paisan*. Let's play a little snooker."

"Snooker?"

"Billiards—the game they're playing at the tables over there."

They played a few games, and Giovanni plied Emilio with several shots of whiskey. They were taking a break and smoking cigars when Erbi's eyes were drawn to two young women clad in lingerie escorting an overweight, gray-haired man down the lobby stairs.

Reacting to Emilio's wide-eyed expression, Giovanni turned his head and gazed in the direction of the prostitutes. His mouth widened and his eyes rolled like ball bearings adrift in ponds of bloodshot oil. He wobbled slightly as he turned his gaze back to Emilio.

"Ah, so you've discovered my remedy?"

"*Cosa?*" An eyebrow shot upward over Emilio's right eye, mirrored at the corner of his mouth on the opposite side.

"A little poke for dessert. I guarantee it will make us both forget our woes—at least for an hour or two."

"A *poke?*"

"*Una scopata piccolo, amico.* Come."

Nine

June 8, 1990
Friday, 1:15 p.m.

Maria and Nick stood at a third-story window in Michelle's office as they waited for her to join them. After being ushered in and offered coffee by her secretary, they fell into casual conversation—interspersing questions shared by people meeting for the first time with observations about traffic snailing along the I-15 just beyond the building's parking lot and the gap-toothed ridgeline demarking the distant, East County horizon.

Maria leaned against the glass, drawing a hand through her hair and twisting her upper torso to face him while she responded to a query about the Bay Area. Her movement splayed her unbuttoned Pendleton, affording Nick a glimpse of perky, unharnessed breasts that rose against an off-white Henley as starkly as the distant peaks prodding the hazy horizon. Nick brushed his blazer aside so he could hook a thumb in the pocket of his pleated trousers, sipped coffee, and compiled an initial impression of his friend's sister.

Her approach to fashion—or lack thereof—brought to mind Mr. Blackwell, a fashion critic Nick met during his stint as a Hollywood reporter, a role that later generated ascerbic cuts from his editor and mentor at *The Daily Journal* in San Diego. As he evaluated Maria's appearance, he wondered what Blackwell might say of her: unkempt hair sweeping like broom bristles over the untucked shirt; tails flagging over baggy, stonewashed denims; bare flesh peek-a-booing through slashes at a knee, thigh, and buttock; tattered Chuck Taylors enveloping her feet? Nick could hear Blackwell dusting off one of his quips to aptly describe her: "She looks like an apple turnover that got crushed in a grocery bag on a hot day."

Nick thought, *If it's true, as Desmond Morris attests, that every costume tells a story about its wearer, and a guy like me succumbs to fashion in order to mask a lack of self esteem, what should I make of Maria's disregard for appearances? Does she just not give a shit, or could she be disguising a stronger disposition than first impression might suggest?*

Nick decided to probe Maria in search of an answer.

"Michelle told me that you're a licensed masseuse. Do you enjoy that line of work?"

"I was doing fine working the kinks out—pun intended—until the spa where I last worked closed. Except for the plasticized, gaudy-jeweled, uppity bitches, the clientele was fun to work with, and I liked knowing I played a part in relieving accumulated stress."

"Do you think you've found a career then?"

"I'd rather go back to school so I can become a physical therapist." Maria drew a pack of cigarettes from her purse and offered one to Nick, who scrunched his nose and wagged his head.

"No more tobacco for me, thanks." Nick gazed toward the office door and tsked playfully. "You know your sister is likely to have your head if you light one of those in here."

"Shit." Maria tucked the pack back into her purse. "Does my goddamned sister enjoy any vices?"

"Privately, I'm sure. And, you—care to reveal any of yours?"

"You've neither the time nor the patience." Maria let her comment hang in air before addressing the purpose of their meeting.

"You truly are a good friend to my sister for volunteering to help us prove Vito's innocence."

"It's what good friends do. But please understand that if I do choose to proceed with the investigation, my motives will not be solely altruistic."

"Michelle told me you write as well as teach, and that you hope Vito's travails create fodder for a magazine article or book."

"Yes, I ..."

At that moment, Michelle entered her office and rushed to Nick, kissing him on the cheek as she enfolded him in a lengthy embrace.

"Nick, I'm so happy to see you again." She then placed him at arm's distance. "Let me look at you. I like the furry face; it adds distinction and a certain professorial air. You've lost weight, too, but not your flair for fashion—a penchant Maria does not share with us, as you may have noted."

Michelle batted an eye at Maria, exposing teeth and gums as her upper lip retracted broadly.

"Just give me an hour or two in your abundant closet, Sis, and I'm sure I could match up—*if* I wanted to." Maria gave Michelle a playful poke in the arm. Michelle returned her attention to Nick.

"My building industry luncheon droned on longer than I planned. I hope you two got to know each other while you waited."

"We have, Chelle. And your physical resemblance is stunning, sans the style-war redux of the Thrilla in Manila."

"Careful, Nick," Maria interjected, her expression mimicking her sister's like a mirror. "It's okay for Michela and I to fuck with each other, but we don't take shit from outsiders."

"*Michela?*"

Nick's nonplussed response illicited a groan from Michelle, a giggle from her sister.

"Oops."

Nick watched Maria cover her mouth in feigned apology, then looked to Michelle.

"It's old history, Nick; a chapter of my life you will *never* reference."

The response more than piqued his reporter's curousity, but Maria ensured the topic went no further.

"I'd heed the warning if I were you, Nick. I remember from when we were kids that she throws a nasty punch."

"I, too, bear witness." Nick tipped his coffee cup to Michelle in jest—an unspoken acknowledgement of Maria's assertion dating back three years, when Michelle and he had come to blows over the way he had been treating her *and* his wife.

They now gathered in casual meeting space, drinking coffee and nibbling on bakery-fresh pasteries served by Michelle's secretary. Michelle noted that she had spoken with Laura on the phone earlier in the day.

"She's sounding almost like the old Laura again, Nick. I so miss her, and I know Zach and Tony do, too. I wish she could have joined you so you both could meet Tony's sister, Marie."

Michelle caught Nick's brief glance at Maria.

"Yes, Nick, *Marie*. An *Americanized* version and, as usual, I can sense the wheels spinning in your head. You've drawn the association among our family given names. Just remember not to give it voice." She raised her fists in a mock boxing stance. "Shall we move on?"

Nick raised his arms, palms open to Michelle, and shrugged, while Marie stifled laughter behind her cup of coffee.

"So, tell me, Nick, will Laura be coming down to visit while you're here? If you decide to help us with Vito, you could be in San Diego quite awhile."

"We already agreed that I would fly home on weekends as often as feasible if this turns into something. And it's supposed to be a surprise, but I've still got my gossip columnist mentality—Laura will be coming down to join us once the working part of this visit is completed."

"She never said a ..."

"Like I said, she wants it to be a surprise, so please keep it that, if for no other reason than to spare me Laura's ire."

The room grew quiet. Nick assigned the lapse to one of those "twenty-minute-in" conversational pauses, what he had read some human behaviorialists call a *protection postulate*, a trait passed down by prehistoric ancestors who required a brief break in conversation to listen for approaching danger. *An apropos time*, Nick thought, *to break the silence with a leap into potentially treacherous waters.* Nick took a sip of coffee, placed the cup down, reached into an inside pocket of his jacket, and withdrew his well-gnawed pipe. As he placed the empty half-bent between his lips, Michelle straightened in her chair.

"I take that as a sign it's time to get serious." Michelle turned her gaze to Maria. "Nick used to smoke Camels as though his IRA's survival depended on the rising value of RJ Reynolds stock, a habit the pipe seems to have helped him break. Knowing my *fondness* for tobacco smoke, you can imagine how pleased I am with this part, among others, of the new Nick."

"Thank you, Dr. Gallo, for your veiled reference to my many foibles, past and present." Nick paused, sucked on his unlit pipe, glanced out the office window, and then turned his focus to Maria. "May I assume, Maria, your sister shared at least the abridged edition of my encyclopedia of wanton proclivities?"

Maria's face flushed. She twisted her hands around each other as though reenacting the workings of a washing machine agitator and then glanced at Michelle.

"I'm not sure ..."

Nick waved his hand as though swatting at a troublesome fly.

"No worries, Maria. Makes it easier for me to know you're up to speed—rather than have it crop up at a less propitious time." Nick turned his eyes to Michelle, exhibiting a mask intended to convey comfort and ease. "Thanks for saving me the need to further illuminate my dark side."

Anticipating Michelle's response, he reached across the narrow span between them and placed an index finger to her lips.

"Really, Chelle, it's good that you did. I need to be open about my past—part of dealing with my addiction. And it's reassuring to know that knowledgeable friends are around to keep me on the wagon if or when I should teeter too near the tailgate." Nick's lips vaguely suggested the outline of an upturned horseshoe. "Let's get on with why you dragged my ass down from Reed."

Nick began with an admonishment that a man with Erbi's family history might have been convicted rightfully. On the other hand, if Vito had been framed, poking into old *family* secrets could irritate violent men who had diligently buried the actual shooter's identity.

Nick paused before proceeding.

"This brings us to another dimension of the case that Buck brought to my attention."

"Who's Buck?" Maria queried.

Nick explained his relationship to Buck Jarrett and summarized their recent conversation. As he spoke, he reached into his wallet—Nick had disposed of his trademark backpack several months ago—and took out Buck's card.

"He's reliable," Nick said as he handed it to Maria, "and very trustworthy."

Michelle confirmed Nick's assessment of the detective. Then Nick opened the line of inquiry necessitated by Buck's comments.

"Chelle, does GDE have any current dealings with the Teamsters or any of their affiliated development funds?"

"No. We get most of our acquisition and construction funding through CalPERS."

"Do you know of any such dealings that may have occurred in the past, before you became involved in GDE?"

"I suppose it's possible."

"I'm sure you'd have said something, if you had knowledge, but I have to ask: Are you aware that the Teamsters and Vito Erbi did business with GDE?"

The inner corners of Michelle's brows knit; the right one rose; the left corner of her mouth simultaneously lifted, pushing her cheek upward.

"Where are you headed with this? Nick, you're not suggesting ...?"

"You obviously know about the garbage that historically tied the mob and the union." Nick looked to Maria. "Your sister, like many other San Diegans, is aware they built La Costa Resort and aquired most of what became Rancho de los Peñasquitos together. Vito worked at the resort for a short period of time, and his family's real estate brokerage did a number of Peñasquitos land deals."

"I see," Marie said with an expression that belied her response.

"What Nick is so delicately implying, Maria, is that Dad may have pumped a little sewage through the mob pipeline. He's concerned whether, beyond any Teamster loans or an Erbi brokerage relationship, this firm had mob ties."

Nick raised the coffee cup to his lips and feigned interest in the container's muddy contents.

"We just all need to understand the potential consequences of my wading in untreated mob waste water." Nick paused, ran a hand through his hair, and then stared briefly at the floor before continuing. "I can hide behind a press shield, but ..."

"If the shit hits the fan, you're worried about the company catching the raw sewage. I'm not worried about GDE, Nick."

"I understand. That isn't my concern. If your father had any mob ties and one of the capos gets wind that I'm snooping in their cesspool on behalf of either of you ..."

"I've got some powerful old connections on the legal side, Nick, so I'm not concerned. Maria?"

Michelle's sister glanced at Nick and then out the window. She continued to take in the parking lot as she began her response.

"I'm thinking of my son. I want to someday tell him that his father is not a fucking mob hit man." She turned her head toward Nick. "Whatever crimes Vito may have committed in the past, he didn't kill anyone. I owe it to him and my son to prove that."

Nick's eyes widened. He glanced at Michelle and then back to Maria.

"Your son?"

"Shit. I thought Michelle told you. Evan is a beautiful boy. He deserves the truth, and he needs his father."

"That explains the question I've been struggling to voice since I first entertained this trip."

"You mean why your friend Michelle's spacey, grunge-clad sister would appear out of nowhere desperately seeking the truth about Vito Erbi?"

Ten

October 18, 1909
Monday, 11:40 a.m.

1

It would be rare for passion to merely smolder like fireplace embers within most Italian families, and the Erbis were no exception. As Emilio sat at his office desk this morning, he thanked the heavens for allowing his brief flirtation with Rosabella to remain a secret, but grimaced at how Giuseppe continued turning up the flame under Emilio's feet regarding his intentions toward Gabriella. Just the evening previous, as he sat with his uncle in the parlor, Giuseppe cajoled him about the need to initiate the *trasciuta*—steps required in the Italian custom to determine the precise rules and conditions under which the marriage would occur.

As a defensive measure, Emilio had increased his time at work and evenings spent away from the Erbi home. He had volunteered to work overtime at his uncle's office, filing paperwork and using his strength with math to balance the business's books. In furtherance of self-improvement and his goal to diminish time around his uncle, he also—at the suggestion of Giovanni—had enrolled in English and accounting courses at nearby Gonzaga University.

Maybe I buy time and keep Giuseppe off my back, he thought, *if Zitzi believes his perceived future son-in-law is dedicating himself*

*to acquiring the experience, skills, and financial acumen necessary
to properly provide for Gabriella. In the meantime, I can work to
become self-sufficient.*

When not at work or in class, Emilio joined Giovanni at the IWW
Hall, an activity he undertook cautiously. One evening he confided to
Giovanni, "Can you imagine what my uncle would do if he learned I
was involved in such traitorous behavior?"

"Relax, Milio. You can always tell him you've been spying on us,
which really isn't a lie, based on how I've seen you keeping an eye on
Miss Flynn whenever she's in town."

"*Stagitto*, you flame-headed fool! I learn much about America and
workers when I listen to dis-a Elizabeth Gurley Flynn."

"If that's the case, then how come you don't pay similar attention
to Jimmy?" Giovanni retorted in reference to his boss, James Walsh,
the man Giuseppe had told Emilio about. "You know how skillful
he is at enrolling new unionists, and it's because of him alone that
the City Council banned public meetings on our streets, sidewalks,
and alleys."

"That is true, *amico*," Emilio said with a jovial expression
intended to set up a punch line. "But now no one worry about da
fire-a wagons not getting by."

"That's not funny, Emil. You know Walsh risked personal
injury when he carried that chair to the middle of Stevens Street and
defused a mob of over two thousand set on destroying the Red Cross
Employment Agency. He always puts public safety and that of the
workers first."

"And in thanks, you tell me yourself, da city fathers reward Mr.
Walsh a plush room in da Spokane jail."

"Emil, you are impossible."

As he now hunched over his uncle's books, Emilio let his mind wander
to the evening ahead, when he planned on playing a game of billiards
with Giovanni and other union hall associates.

*It's fun drinking and now beating Givovanni consistently at his
own game,* he thought in Italian. *And winning means I collect enough
in bets to visit the young ladies in the hotel rooms above the table.*

Recollections of his sexual exploits with Colonial Hotel prostitutes
brought him back to thoughts about Rosabella.

Getting the poke, as Giovanni calls it, yes, that is much fun in the moment, but it will never do as long as thoughts of Rosabella fill my head. I know she was frightened by our intimacy, but does she mean to now ignore me? Dio mio, am I to be the reason she dropped out of school, that she has taken this new job at Murgittroyd's to become ... what did she call her position when she announced at dinner that night of her hiring ... assistant pharmacist?

If only she would reach out to me for comfort. I could cry when I think of how her parents and sister badger her about quitting school and—of all things—gaining employment outside the home. Maybe because of my lengthy absences from home she thinks I am trying to avoid her. Dio mio, how do I approach her about all of this? If I don't do something about it soon, I will go mad.

October 18, 1909
Monday, 4:00 p.m.

2

Emilio strode down toward the intersection of Post and Riverside on an errand to purchase supplies for the agency that would require him to pass Murgittroyd's. As he approached Rosabella's place of employment, he mulled the pros and cons of entering the drugstore as though he were his fictional Italian counterpart Romeo weighing life without Juliet. He took a step toward the entry, fell back, walked several strides up Post Street, then reversed his direction. As he paced past Murgittroyd's front door again, he tugged an Old Mill pack from his jacket pocket, tapped out a smoke, and struggled to light it. He muttered angry Italian admonishments to himself for not being able to control his shaking hands. After successfully setting the cigarette aglow, he embarked on another stroll, plodding up Riverside Avenue and back while continually dragging on his smoke. Arriving back at the pharmacy's entry, Emilio took a quick drag, tossed the cigarette to the ground, and pushed open the front door.

He walked slowly up and down the aisles, pretending to search for items he wanted to purchase and hoping to *accidentally* cross

Rosabella's path. As he surveyed the shelves, he realized why Spokanites were increasingly frequenting the shop.

I've never seen such business, he thought. *Store-made medicines, gifts, housewares, fishing tackle, watches, photo processing, a place to hang my coat at no charge, parcel check, even free delivery.*

Emilio started, his musings vanishing, at the sound of a familiar voice.

"I assume, *if* you needed something, you would've found it by now," Rosabella said with arms crossed, an icy film coating her words. "Or, *if* you wanted to continue avoiding me, you wouldn't have come in at all. What *do* you want, Emil?"

"I ... Rosa, it is-a you avoids me." Emilio straightened and took a step toward her. His tight lips, raised eyebrows, and focused eyes displayed a sense of confidence belied by the pangs that tormented his stomach.

"That is not true, Emil." She met Emilio's gaze briefly. Her mouth closed as she bowed her head and studied the floor wide-eyed. She looked up again. "You could've approached me."

Rosabella's mouth and eyes opened wide in unison; she lowered her eyebrows and wrinkled her nose.

"Couldn't you see how troubled I've been?"

"I could ask-a you da same," Emilio bellowed, bouyed by newly cultivated mettle.

Rosabella surveyed the store and surrounding customers before turning her gaze back to Emilio.

"Keep your voice down, Emil. You embarrass me."

"Then we go where okay da talk."

"I can't just leave. I'm working."

"Ask-a da boss man for da break. Tell him family thing come up. That not da lie."

Rosabella raised her palms toward Emilio and shook her head.

"Wait here. I'll be right back."

3

Rosabella and Emilio sat across from each other at the Silver Grill, a more upscale locale than Emilio would have frequented, but chosen for just that reason. They warmed their hands around freshly poured cups of coffee in an attempt to circumvent the effects of an open-air cab ride from Murgittroyd's. They spoke little during the ride, and now seated inside the Spokane Hotel restaurant, used a perusal of the menus to further defer serious conversation.

As Emilio completed a scan of the menu *and* its prices, he raised his eyes and watched Rosabella sip coffee and survey her surroundings. It was evident from her expression that she, like he, had never dined in such a finely appointed establishment. There were brick floors and a hewn-log ceiling; smartly framed English country scenes accenting the walls; china designed in Chicago; the aroma of two turkeys and a goose wafting from a spit in the fireplace.

Emilio, seated in an oversize black oak chair, picked up his coffee cup and brought it to his lips, keeping his eyes rivited on Rosabella, who apparently had become enchanted with a ferned grotto located in the center of the room and serving as a sanctuary for goldfish and baby turtles.

"Restaurant is charming, no?"

As Rosabella turned her gaze to him, Emilio once again became mesmerized by the depth of her eyes. He thought it pure folly to even consider resisting the magnetic draw of the black flecks that floated within her dark jade orbs.

"It is so elegant, Emil." Her mouth widened and turned upward as she looked at him. She then lowered her voice. "Can we afford this?"

"Not we—I. Such-a da *bell' angelo* deserve such fine place."

"Oh, Emil." Rosabella flushed with color. She dropped her head slightly and swept her eyelashes down. Emilio reached out and took her hand, but Rosabella drew away. Her face paled, her upper lip trembled, and she clenched her hands together on the table.

"I … I'm so confused, Emil."

Emilio looked down into his coffee cup, and then took a deep breath as he prepared to speak.

"I hope to wait until after the meal to say …"

"What, Emil?" Rosabella's expression revealed her anxiety.

"I am think it time to move. Make it easier … for you."

"No, you can't leave because of me, Emil. Where would you go?"

"I go what you call the Single Resident Occupancy first. Maybe later I go da California with Giovanni, when his work finished here. There, I not anger you Papa and Mama. I no wanna hurt you sister, da one I cannot marry, and I no longer bring you da pain."

Rosabella's eyes filled with tears and her shoulders sagged.

"Oh, Emil. I am the one who is hurting you."

"But …"

"You really don't want to marry Gabriella?"

"No. I say you that before."

"Would you stay in Spokane if I … if …" Rosabella reached for Emilio's hands, cupping them in hers.

"For you … with you … I stay. You say you cannot, no?"

Their eyes met. Emilio raised Rosabella's hands to his lips and softly kissed each one. They sat motionless for several moments, silently holding hands across the table until a waiter's arrival dispelled their rumination.

"Would you like to order now?"

"We need little more da time," Emilio said without taking his eyes from Rosabella's face. The waiter sighed and stepped away from the table.

"Wait, sir, please." The waiter pivoted at Rosabella's call.

"Yes?"

"I'm sorry, but I'm suddenly not feeling well. Would you please bring the bill?"

The waiter nodded, then shrugged and walked away. Emilio sat upright in his seat. His eyes widened and his mouth fell agape. Rosabella stared into Emilio's eyes as her lips turned upward, revealing her teeth. She briefly played with the strands of hair that graced her bodice before putting a finger to her lips, leaning closer to Emilio, and whispering.

"I have a better idea. Pay the bill while I freshen up, and then I will explain when I return."

4

At Rosabella's direction, Emilio hailed a cab and gave the driver the address Rosabella had provided him. Once aboard, Emilio drew a blanket over her and himself to shield them from the night air. Under cover of darkness and the blanket, Rosabella brought her hand up to Emilio's cheek, brought his head down to hers, and kissed him. He huddled closer and savored the moment.

The cab stopped at the Pennington, which adjoined the heralded Davenport Hotel, but acquired a reputation for boarding hostesses that lunched with gentlemen at the Davenport before escorting them via a direct link to their private chambers in the Pennington. Knowing this about the lesser hotel, Emilio gazed at Rosabella in wonderment.

"Just pay the fare," she told Emilio as she waited for the driver to assist her.

"What we do here, Rosa?"

"I made an acquaintence with the proprietor through my work at Murgittroyd's. She won't say anything to anyone." Rosabella grabbed Emilio's hand and pulled him into the foyer. "Come on, unless you'd rather stand out in the cold."

The brazenness of Rosabella's behavior at once alarmed and captivated Emilio. He skulked to a far corner of the lobby at her command, picked up that morning's copy of *The Spokesman–Review*, and worked at blending into the wallpaper. Rosabella returned a few moments later and guided him to a back staircase, where she bounded up to the second floor, tugging Emilio behind her. As she inserted a key into the room assigned her, Rosabella turned to Emilio, kissed him hard and long, and then told him in Italian, "Emil, you may have me tonight, tomorrow, and all of my days to come. Please, just never leave me."

Eleven

November 2, 1909
Tuesday, 7:30 a.m.

1

The Industrial Worker, a Wobbly rag published in Spokane, had broadcast a call for union members and agitators to come to the city and get arrested by making protest speeches in defiance of the street-speaking ban. Swarms of migrant laborers, heeding the appeal, descended on the city and now milled about on the street. Emilio and Rosabella shouldered through the itinerants in order to meet at a nearby bakery for an Italian pastry and coffee, as had become their practice since he had moved into his own apartment.

The couple had learned from Giovanni that later today IWW members would mount an overturned crate in the middle of the intersection, daring the police to enforce the anti-speech ordinance. Rosabella told Emilio that she wanted to attend the rally.

"Streets today no place for lady." Emilio placed his hands palm-down on the table, squared his shoulders, and trained his eyes on his companion.

"You told me yourself that women would be there, too. That girl you told me about, Elizabeth Gurley Flynn, she is only two years older than me. If she speaks today, I want to see and hear her, too."

"Today be different. Da men are da angry. Da shopkeepers, da Papa even, want police to make da fight. You get hurt maybe. Or, if da Papa sees you, he disown-a you."

"So what if he sees *you*?"

"He no can throw me out da house, no?"

Emilio's mouth turned upward, revealing the crowns of his teeth. His butterscotch eyes sparkled as he jabbed Rosabella's shoulder. Rosabella crossed her arms, fixed her gaze at Emilio, opened her mouth as though to lodge further protest, then clamped her lips and dropped her stare to her coffee. She jabbed a spoon into her cup and whirled it through the brew like an egg beater.

November 2, 1909
Tuesday, 2:50 p.m.

2

Emilio stood, his cap pulled down to his eyebrows, at the curbside of Stevens and Main among a queue of unemployed workers, union members, and protesters. While waiting for Giovanni to join him, as they had planned, Emilio staved off the cold, wrapping his arms around himself, tucking his gloved hands in his armpits, and stomping his booted feet. In anticipation of standing in the cold for several hours, he wore long underwear, woolen socks, and his winter-weight suit, over which he had drawn a dark woolen overcoat.

The contingent of Spokane police Emilio watched amassing on horseback and afoot gave truth to Police Chief Sullivan's pledge to call in every available officer to deal with the anticipated protest. Although no one had risen on a soapbox yet, Emilio stood in silent protest as Spokane's finest made their presence felt, charging at people who ventured into the street and forcing them back to the sidewalks. As the gathering intensified, he stepped back from the curb, positioning himself next to a lamp post two rows deep within the milling and boisterous crowd. Using his height to his advantage, Emilio peered over the protesters' heads in search of Giovanni.

As he scanned the street, Emilio took note of a second wave of mounted police in apparent pursuit of a ragtag group of men and women progressing southward on Stevens from the direction of the IWW union hall. Emilio noticed the group hastening its pace, no doubt, he thought, in response to the arrival of officers on foot drawing their billy clubs and waving them menacingly. At this point, Emilio watched the union hall marchers peel off as they approached the intersection, taking places along the sidewalk and among those who had gathered to participate in or listen to the procedings. A breathless and perspiring Giovanni approached Emilio from behind and clasped his shoulder. Emilio wheeled, pressing his back against the light post and striking a boxer's pose.

"Milio, it's me." Givovanni took a step back and raised his arms to fend off any forthcoming blow. Emilio dropped his fists to his side.

"You scare me."

"Sorry, comrade, but you won't believe it."

"What?"

"The bulls hauled off several hall cats; clubbed them right in front of the branch. I don't think we'll even hear any angel food today."

"Angel food? What this?"

"You know, mission preaching about the bread of life. Even the exempted Salvation Army won't test the cops today."

At that moment, the crowd hushed as though they had been congregating for services and their minister had just stepped into the apse. Giovanni and Emilio, like all those assembled, turned their attention to the center of the intersection. A man with the attire and physique of a lumberjack strode forward carrying an apple crate. As he set his impromptu stage to the ground and stepped up, several police officers rushed toward him.

"My fellow workers," the lumberman's voice boomed over the crowd, who at first welcomed him with cheers. Their mood changed swiftly as a mounted officer charged the speaker and clubbed him. Several foot police joined their mounted colleague, hitting the speaker with their clubs as they dragged him off the crate.

The crowd jeered and cussed the bulls as they dragged the protester away. Then several voices called for quiet as a second speaker, a young woman, mounted the crate. She raised her arms in welcome and began to speak.

"Fellow workers ..." Sullivan's men fell upon her before she could utter another word. As they pulled her from the podium and arrested her, the crowd surged toward the intersection. Police on horseback and foot soldiers with raised clubs forced them back to the curb. Undaunted, the assembled agitators and protesting workers pushed forward, as one speaker after another rose upon the crate, only to be beaten and hustled off to waiting paddy wagons.

Pandemonium erupted. Giovanni and Emilio tried to hold their ground, using the light post as an anchor. At the same time, the two men continued to scrutinize the flurry of activity unfolding before them. Giovanni raised his arm, pointed toward the center of the intersection, and yelled in Emilio's ear.

"Milio, is that your cousin, the shark's daughter? What is she doing?"

"*Dio mio.*" Emilio crossed himself and then catapulted through the crowd toward Rosabella, who had stopped a few strides short of the soapbox. Giovanni sprinted after Emilio and arrived by his side as Rosabella neared the next speaker in line. She hesitated at the soapbox's threshold as the stymied protester ahead of her fell victim to a rain of clubs.

"Rosa, stop!" Emilio shouted as Giovanni dashed past him.

"Get her out of here, Milio," Giovanni commanded over his shoulder as two officers with raised cudgels approached Rosabella. Giovanni set his body between the police and Rosabella, shoved her into Emilio's arms, and turned to step on the podium. As Emilio led Rosabella to the safety of the sidewalk, he looked back to see Giovanni cave at the knees. Emilio winced at the site of Giovanni's blood dripping down the side of his face as the bulls wrestled him away.

Twelve

June 16, 1990
Saturday, 10:00 a.m.

1

Vito Erbi had showered, shaved, dressed, and eaten breakfast, yet it seemed like only moments had passed since he had risen from his cot. As he paced his cell, he was reminded of one of the many quotes his Nanno Emilio would rattle off in what Vito thought was a vain attempt to impress the family with his command of the English language.

He failed to recall the context in which Emilio had shared this particular axiom, one his grandfather had credited to a guy named Van Dyke: "Time is too slow for those who wait, too swift for those who fear." Vito thought, *Shit, I'd love to be fearing my freedom right now rather than waiting for some punk writer to show his fuckin' face. You'd think Maria could've at least dug up a decent attorney.*

The echo of four federal-issue leather heels approaching his cell disrupted Vito's reverie. He clasped the bars and watched a pair of screws parade to a halt in front of his cage like the toy soldiers his grandfather would display on the mantle at Christmas.

"Step away from the bars," the taller of the two commanded.

Vito shuffled back a few steps, then stood in place as the guards shackled his feet and cuffed his wrists.

"We'll be your escorts to the visitors' room this morning."

"Yeah, buddy, I know the drill. Let's take our time and enjoy the view."

June 16, 1990
Saturday, 10:15 a.m.

2

Nick waited in visitors' quarters, where he had been led after announcing himself to the front lobby officer. The visitor flipped through a reporter's pad, one he had squirreled away in a moving box when he relocated to Portland, and scanned his prep notes. Prior to being allowed to enter the room, which was located on Vito's floor, Nick endured a barrage of procedure and policy delivered in monotone by a chunky, short-haired female officer.

"Welcome to San Diego Metropolitan Correctional Center," the twenty-something staffer droned with an expression that told Nick she would rather be plopped in front of her TV watching a soap opera and spooning ice cream into her face. "I see from the Request for Visitors form and Visitor Information form BP–629 that you received from the inmate, dutifully completed and returned in timely fashion, that you are scheduled to meet with inmate Vittorio Erbi. Because you are neither a relative nor his legal counsel, you have been granted a special media pass.

"It is mandatory that you understand and abide by the visitation policies of this institution. For your convenience, a restroom has been provided here in the front lobby and across the hall from the visitation room. Neither you nor Mr. Erbi will be allowed to use restroom facilities during your visitation. Should you or Mr. Erbi request use of restroom facilities during that time, you will not be readmitted.

"Pursuant to your request, the two tables placed in the visiting room for attorney use have been left in place. For a social visitation, such tables normally would be relocated to the elevator lobby. Your visitation may extend no more than one hour."

After withstanding her recitation, showing proper identification, and clearing the metal detector, Nick gained monitored access to an elevator that took him to Vito's floor. Heeding the obese diva's advice, he obediently paused during the allocated time period to empty his bladder.

Like pugilists tapping gloves at the beginning of a match, Vito and Nick took inventory of each other. Nick felt an immediate dislike to the surly convict, who slouched in a chair across from him dressed in a white T-shirt and regulation trousers. He fiddled with his glasses, breathing on them heavily before swabbing them with a shirttail. Nick took special note of the inmate's haute detachment—exacerbated by his penchant for avoiding eye contact.

An innocent man in Vito's position could hardly be more inappropriately disinterested, Nick thought. *Even someone far less jaded than me would be struggling to empathize with this clown.*

As Nick concluded an explanation of his professional background, why the Gallo sisters had solicited his help, and initiated his first line of questioning, Vito doodled on a notepad he had brought with him.

"You and your family operate or operated a realty firm here in San Diego, right?"

"Yeah. My grandfather started it."

"Are you aware of any illicit operations—bookmaking, extortion, protection services, that kind of stuff—coming down behind Erbi Realty's legit front?"

"You sayin' my family operated a shady business?" Vito's face reddened and his fists tightened. Nick raised his arms, palms forward.

"Whoa, Vito. I'm not accusing anybody of anything. I'm just asking questions."

"Then ask about something else."

Nick glared at Vito, then dropped his eyes to his notebook.

"Okay, then, how well did you know Frank Bompensiero?" Nick raised his head and looked at Vito as he made his inquiry.

"Who says I knew him at all?"

"My research indicates that you were known to have associated with him or at least been in his company, say maybe when you worked at the resort?"

"If I did, they weren't memorable occasions."

"He allegedly had a friend—if he could be called that—up in LA, Jimmy Fratianno?"

Vito's pupils slid upward and left, as did the same side of his mouth.

"Yeah, I know about him. Got a rep as quite the vocalist back in the day."

Nick tossed his notes on the table, then clicked his mechanical pencil closed and slid it into his shirt pocket.

"Being a wiseass doesn't cut it, man. You won't discuss the family business; claim you don't recall your contacts with Frank; allege you only know of Fratianno from the media coverage. Really?"

Vito shrugged. Nick's eyebrows knit, his forehead wrinkled, and his lips pressed together.

"Last chance, asshole: Moe Dalitz?"

Vito sat up in his chair; his expression appearing to Nick as though the inmate were channeling Sugar Ray Leonard reacting to a Roberto Duran insult. Nick glared back, as if to say: *Don't expect me to plea no más.*

"As for an asshole, only ones I know is the one I'm sitting on and the one across from me." His face twisted from anger to a smirk. "As for Dalitz, the name sounds familiar. Yeah, I think he's a Vegas guy that financed the resort."

"The La Costa Resort and Spa, where you worked in realty management?"

"Yeah. That's it."

"How many times did you associate with Dalitz?"

Vito pursed his lips and rubbed his chin.

"Gee. Can't say."

"What can you tell me about your dealings with the Teamsters and Gallo Development Enterprises for the purchase of Teamster land in Rancho Peñasquitos?"

"My family company brokered a sale once, as I recall." Vito stiffened. "And that was a straight-up commission deal."

"Should I have thought it involved anything else?"

Vito glared, then looked away.

"Okay, what can you tell me about any of Bomp's crew here in San Diego: Adamo, Bonventre, Mandri, Mirabile, the Matranga brothers, or their cousin, Big Frank?"

"Some of those names seem familiar, but I might of read about them in the papers."

"I gotta say, Vito, this tough guy act's grating on my patience."

As he spoke, Nick's facial muscles tensed. His lips protuded upward and firmly set; creases gathered at the corners of his mouth. His eyebrows canted downward, and a furrow gathered between his eyes as he stared across the table. He straightened in his chair and tucked his legs in, one hand held close to his stomach while the other rested atop his discarded notebook.

"Look, Mr. Erbi, I'm trying to do you a favor here, but if you aren't willing to cooperate, there's nothing much I can do."

Vito appeared focused on more doodling, his face a blank page. Then he yawned, nudged his chair closer, leaned forward, and extended his arms along the tabletop. He splayed his fists, as though stretching his fingers, before withdrawing an arm to rub his index finger under his nose. In the process, his other hand had brushed Nick's noteook.

"Guess like maybe I'm coming down with somethin'." Vito glanced at Nick's pad as he spoke. "Makes me a little irritable."

Nick followed the direction of Vito's glance and noticed a small piece of paper lying on his pad. He retrieved the pencil from his pocket and pretended to be studying his notes, which afforded an opportunity to scan the handwritten content of Vito's scrap of paper: *Can't appear cooperative. Camera. Mics.*

"Irritable, huh?" Nick said as he palmed the note and dipped his head. "Unless you want me to leave now, I just have a few more questions for you, from the court record, okay?"

"No harm in listening. I'm sure not going anywhere." Vito shrugged, his eyelids drooped, and he yawned again.

"In his opening statement, your attorney stated that evidence would show you were nowhere near Pacific Beach at the time of the shooting, that there were witnesses who could testify to that. Yet, no witness testified, and no evidence was presented to that effect."

"Nope. Sure as hell wasn't."

"Is there a witness who could prove you weren't at the scene?"

Vito interrupted his intermittent doodling, lowered his pad, and raised his palms face up at chest height. He stared at the pad as he responded to Nick's inquiry.

"Lawyers tend to exaggerate sometimes. No witnesses I know of."

Nick once again followed the trail blazed by Vito's gaze and read five words: *Tala, Filipina tender, Star Bar.* Nick's face, which parodied a freshly erased chalkboard, offered Vito no acknowledgement.

"Okay, so no witness, despite your attorney's opening remarks." Nick paused before speaking again. "You ever own, rent, drive, or ride in a black '76 Impala with a gray-primed right front fender?"

"Sounds like lowrider shit to me. Wouldn't be caught dead in one."

"The case record indicates you were identified as the person entering that car at the scene and shortly after shots were fired at Frank Bompensiero."

"Well, if the record says it ..."

"Then, you *do* recall a car like that?"

"Could be. I'm not a car nut, and my memory's not so good after all the time I've stewed in here."

"Have you ever owned a firearm?"

"Nope."

"Ever been on a firing range?"

"Not my thing."

"Ever taken any lessons in the use of a weapon?"

"No, no need." Vito straightened in his chair, and his eyes widened as his eyebrows and cheeks rose. He glanced down at his lap. "Lotta broads have told me I got one big *pistola*, but I never needed no lessons for using *it*."

June 16, 1990
Saturday, 5:40 p.m.

3

Nick arrived early at Scow's—one of those surfer, down-on-your-luck musician, stoner bars hanging a sign on Mission Boulevard—and took a seat at the weathered bar. Michelle suggested the Pacific Beach hangout when Nick called to arrange a meeting, and he had recalled that her husband Zach had frequented the place often back in the day. He sipped a Heineken, his back to a thin crowd of daily regulars that belied the tavern's nighttime popularity, and flirted with a blonde bartender sheathed in tight shorts cut off significantly north of her thighs and a body-hugging top that left nothing about the contours of her breasts to his imagination. She batted an eye, swept her tongue along her upper lip, and leaned in toward Nick as she set a freshly opened bottle on the bar.

Whoa, he thought as the sight stirred his loins. *That cleavage might as well be a welcoming sign to a Grand Canyon vista, and if I stare any longer, I'm likely to tumble over the edge, down those slopes, and into a shitload of trouble.*

Nick wheeled on his barstool to avoid further temptation and sipped on his second Heiney. He feigned interest in regalia haphazardly adorning the walls—surf posters, one featuring a local pro; old concert flyers; skateboard decals; a large color photo signed by lead guitarist Danny of Bedtime for Jack, an East Coast band that gigged at Scow's recently, and a triptych montage consisting of the Monroes in a promo photo, their 45 "What Do All the People Know," and Rusty Jones's autographed guitar.

A glance over his shoulder indicated that the well-endowed keep apparently had gone on break. Nick turned back to face the bar. As he did so, his peripheral vision alerted him to a figure approaching in an odd but familiar gait. As he hunched over the bar, his back turned to the looming man and his brain working to convince him that the tall blond could not be who he thought it was, a large paw clasped Nick on the shoulder.

"Shouldn't ever turn your back on a stranger in a place like this, buddy."

Nick looked up at a familiar face bearing closely set hazel eyes, thick eyebrows, a broad chin, and an equine nose, all framed by a flaxen mane wafting like wheat in an Oregon field.

"Zach. Zach Watson." Nick bolted off his stool and hugged his friend. "What the hell are you doing here?"

As Zach and Nick broke their embrace and held each other at arm's length, Nick reflected on how one of the last times they stood this close, Zach had stumbled into a meeting just in time to save Nick from the gunman that had killed Holly Damkot and forced Laura's Mustang off the road. Zach now broke Nick's brief reverie with a tug on his whiskers.

"The hirsute professor look, I see."

"Keeps my face warm during the winters up north."

"Isn't that Laura's job?"

Before Nick could reply, Michelle came up beside her husband Zach and wrapped an arm around his waist. She then leaned into Nick and buzzed his cheek.

"Chelle, you told me Zach was on the road with the band."

"He was. Still is, technically."

"Yeah, we got a little break in the schedule, and I couldn't wait until Chelle could join me on the bus. I flew down from Boise this morning."

"Wow, Zach. What a great surprise."

"So you're not disappointed that I'm cutting in on your one-on-one time with Chelle?"

"No matter how I answer that question, I risk pissing off one or both of you." Nick grinned and gestured to the bar stools. "Sit down. Have a beer. We won't be discussing business until Maria gets here."

"Maria may not be joining us." Michelle pushed back her hair as she spoke, pausing for a downward gaze, before looking at Nick and continuing. "She told us she doesn't want to be a burden, so she found a job and plans to move to her own place as soon as she has saved enough for the rent."

"You don't seem very pleased."

Michelle sighed. "I'm fine with the idea in principle."

"But?"

"She took a job as a masseuse at ... ah ... shall we say, a questionable location."

"You mean ..."

Zach cleared his throat and leaned forward so he could catch Michelle's gaze.

"Hon, I don't think we've enough facts to be jumping to conclusions. Let's just give it a little time. Besides, I think at the moment we've got some catching up to do with Nick."

Michelle rolled her eyes and started to speak when Nick cut her short.

"Yeah, Chelle. Zach's right." He called out to the blonde barkeep, "Would you please serve my friends their choice? And I'll have another Heiney."

After the first round, the threesome shifted to a table near the front door, where they ordered bar nuts, fried calamari, another round for the men, and a vodka tonic for Michelle. They bantered briefly about the Gallo-Watson toddlers, GDE, music, touring, teaching, and life in Portland, until a harried-appearing Maria arrived. She apologized for her tardiness and, when the waitress appeared, ordered an Anchor Steam. She then looked to Nick.

"Have you already told Michelle and Zach about your meeting?"

"You're just in time to hear it from the top. Want a drink or something to eat first?"

"Good idea. I'm parched."

As Maria accepted the drink she ordered, Nick plucked his pipe from a shirt pocket, clinched it in the corner of his mouth, and gnawed on the mouthpiece. When he thought she had settled in, he removed the pipe from his mouth and cradled it in his hand.

"Shall we get started?" Hearing agreement, Nick cleared his throat and began his summary. "First off, Maria, your—may I call him 'former boyfriend'?—will never be nominated for a congeniality prize. Seemed quite full of himself."

"That's not the man I knew," Maria protested.

"Great." Michelle raised her cocktail glass above her head. "A toast to another lovable Italian male." She took a long drink.

"He made it quite clear that he did not want to appear cooperative. I'm guessing the same party that coerced him into taking the fall—assuming he's innocent—doesn't want him getting chatty. He slipped a note to me about cameras and microphones in the room."

"Or, maybe it's just all a dodge so he doesn't have to answer questions that would remove any doubt about his guilt."

"Funny you should say that, Chelle." Nick took a swig of beer, and then briefly scanned the room. "I gave him a number of chances to clear himself or at least give me something to chase.

"I asked him about the alleged getaway car—a black '76 Impala—and when he claimed never being near one, I reminded him that a witness had put him entering such a vehicle at the scene of the murder. He had the opportunity to deny it, but demurred.

"I queried him about his association or contacts with Bompensiero, his crew members, and other major organized crime figures. Wouldn't cop to dealing with any of them.

"I asked him about his experience with firearms. He denied ever owning one or being at a firing range, but never outright denied having shot one."

"His attitude doesn't help his case any," Michelle said. "Were you able to get anything of substance from him?"

"It's a long shot. And yes, I purposely buried the headline. He passed me a a second message with the name of a woman and a bar. The implication is that she works or worked there and may be of some help."

"A witness with a possible alibi?"

Before Nick could respond to Zach's question, Michelle posed her own.

"How come he never mentioned that before?"

"Given a choice between keeping his mouth zipped or taking a plunge in the Pacific wearing concrete booties, a guy like Vito would know what he had to do to stay out of the ocean."

Thirteen

July 15, 1910
Friday, 11:50 a.m.

1

Joel Barnes King, proprietor of King Grocery, hovered over his cashier, ensuring that the young man had mastered the register, a scenario that had transpired several times over the last month. King, whose market had been established around the corner from his home in the Union Park neighborhood near where the Erbis also lived, was anxious to join his wife and four daughters for lunch.

"You remember how to ring up a no sale?"

"Yes, Mr. King. I do it many times now."

"Mrs. Schindler will want her usual order when she comes by to pick it up later this afternoon."

"I fill her order, Mr. King. I know what to do."

"Okay, then, I'll be back by two. If you need anything ..."

"Lock up and come get you. If I know customer, let watch store."

"Yes. That's it."

As Joel King slipped out the back door, Emilio wondered whether he had been too hasty in his decision to accept the grocer's offer of employment. He recalled how quickly time seemed to pass following the free speech battle and how, during that time, he walked a high wire, balancing the charade he maintained at his uncle's agency against his increasing empathy for the Wobbly movement or, at least, the workers it claimed to represent. His precipitous relationship with Rosabella served to further test the flappable young man's footing.

Pangs of responsibility for Giovanni's beating and subsequent jailing and Emilio's maturing interest in improving the working man's plight had compelled him to volunteer early evening hours to serve as the IWW branch accountant. During the work day, Emilio schemed to find his uncle's clients meaningful, long-term work. The economic impact of his efforts had begun to be reflected in the books that Emilio diligently maintained for Giuseppe.

He understood that he could not continue these combined efforts for any sustainable period without piquing his uncle's curiousity or, worse, endangering the agency's business viability. This realization hastened his resolution to leave his uncle's employ nearly four months ago now.

Emilio took a seat behind the register and began eating a lunch he had prepared at home. As he sat gnawing on his prosciutto and provolone sandwich, his memory painted a detailed recollection of the confrontation that morning in early March, a week before he had started operating the cash register and restocking shelves with the understanding that he would become the store's bookkeeper when Joel King deemed him reliably trained.

Giuseppe seemed to be in a particularly even-tempered mood, and no clients were milling in the agency's offices as Emilio paced the length of the office, halting at times to adjust his tie, tug at his ear, or fiddle with a pen that he removed from its station behind his ear.

"Ma che cozz'u fai?" Giuseppe rose from his chair and stepped out of his office in order to query his nephew about what he was doing. "This pacing and fidgeting is driving me crazy."

Emilio stood, his heels knocking and mouth agape. His eyes darted about the room, unable to meet his uncle's gaze. He tried to speak, but merely croaked. After clearing his throat, he tried again.

"Zitzi, I am the sorry. I have made with-a da new job."

"Maronna mia! What the fuck are you talking about?"

"I most grateful for all da good you do me. But da time ..." Emilio paused and tried to look into his uncle's eyes. "I think it da time I make my own way. I mean you no da disrespect."

"You are serious, aren't you?" Giuseppe switched to their native Calabrese. His face reddened and his chest rose.

Emilio nodded, hung his arms loosely at his side, and stared at the floor. Emilio mused later that Giuseppe's eruption might have put Mount Vesuvius to shame—after escaping the agency in a frantic gallop, his uncle chasing him out the door at full throttle.

"Stanna mabaych! You *fucking little* bastardo. You *ingrate. If I get my hands on you, I will kill you," Giuseppe fumed in a frenzied mix of English and Italian as he gave chase down Stevens Street. "Don't let me set eyes on you again. I and my brother—your father—disown you."*

After running past several doorways, Giuseppe paused, bent over, and gasped for breath. Then he raised his right fist—his forearm perpendicular to the sidewalk, his upper arm parallel—and placed his left hand over his right bicep. "Te fugo and everything you touch from now on."*

July 15, 1910
Friday, 12:15 p.m.

2

As Emilio finished eating lunch in an otherwise unoccupied store, he began reading a high school American history book. An Italian-English dictionary lay open to the side. He heard footsteps approaching and thought that Joel King had returned early or came to fetch something he had forgotten. As Emilio rose and walked around the counter, his eyes widened and his mouth parted; yet he stood passively, arms held firmly at his side.

Rosabella approached hesitantly, then rushed to embrace him. Emilio brushed his lips along her cheek and then to her ear. She trembled at the rush of his breath.

"What a grand surprise, Rosa," Emilio whispered. "I have missed you much."

Rosabella turned her head so that she could press her lips against his. Emilio savored her taste on his mouth; the warmth of her body against his. She broke the kiss; then gasped.

"Since you left the agency, Papa, Mama and even Gabriella keep a constant watch to make sure we are not meeting secretly."

"I thought after the fight with da Papa you no wanted to see me."

"I am so sorry." Her eyebrows arched upward as her eyelids and the corners of her mouth sagged. "Papa made me quit my job, and they never let me go anywhere for more than ten minutes without one of them joining me."

Emilio's lips parted slightly, his brows rose, and his eyes widened as he scanned the store's entry.

"Then how …?"

"I went with my sister to her doctor appointment, and when she was called in, I came here straight away."

Rosabella stepped back from Emilio, placed her palms facing outward on the checkout counter, and lifted herself into a sitting position, running her tongue slowly along her upper lip as she did so. Her eyes flared, branding Emilio with her gaze. She combed her fingers through tresses that fell like a russet skein over her ample breasts, and then scanned the premises.

"Where is your boss?" A mischievous radiance transited Rosabella's face as she queried Emilio.

"At lunch with his family."

"Will he be back soon?"

"Not for one, maybe two hours. He love to eat; then take da nap."

Rosabella leapt from the counter, glided close to Emilio, and ran a hand through his slicked-back hair. The sweep of her fingers dislodged several thick strands that she left dangling over his left ear.

"Then we have time."

"Here? Now?" Emilio sputtered, his facial expression rivaling that of the cat Alice encountered in the Duchess's house. "What about Gabriella?"

"I'll be back in the waiting room before the doctor finishes."

Rosabella clasped the ends of Emilio's bowtie and pulled it loose.

"But … customers may …"

She put a finger to his mouth, hastily removed his studded shirt collar, and freed the first few buttons of his shirt.

"Then they will see today's surprise special."

Emilio placed his hands around the base of Rosabella's neck as he kissed each corner of her mouth and chin before fixing his open mouth to hers. He emitted a low moan as Rosabella swept her pliant tongue through his parted lips.

Emilio broke the kiss, interlaced his hand in Rosabella's, and guided her toward the rear of the store. They fumbled at each other's clothes as they made their way. When they reached the back wall, where they were out of direct sight of anyone entering the market, Emilio pinned Rosabella against the wall and covered her lips and neck with kisses. Then he lowered the collar of her ivory shirtwaist so that he could nibble at her collarbone. As he did so, Rosabella slipped Emilio's suspenders from his shoulders and loosened the rest of his shirt buttons, exposing his heavily forested torso.

As she ran her hands through Emilio's chest hair, Rosabella stared into his eyes and then shifted her gaze downward to the crease between her breasts. Emilio followed her eyes and sighed as he ran his fingers along the small pleats that lined her blouse. He tugged at the garment in order to free its tails, then worked frantically to free the small fasteners on the cuffs. Their tongues explored each other's mouths as Emilio parted the blouse, letting it drop to the floor before raising her chemise over her bosom. Emilio then cupped her breasts, brushing her nipples with his thumbs.

Rosabella worked to unfasten the fly of his straight-waist trousers and, having gained entry, nudged aside his underwear to free his tumescence. They stroked and caressed each other while continuing to share urgent kisses. Emilio felt he would burst as he pulled her skirt and petticoat to her waist, allowing one hand to seek the moistness of her loins. While exploring her wetness, he traced circles around her nipples with his tongue.

"Oh, Emil. I've missed you so," Rosabella panted as she slipped off her drawers, reclaimed him in her hand, and breathlessly guided him inside her. She clinched her legs tightly around Emilio's waist, meeting his rapid thrusts as he pressed her upper torso to the wall. Their mutual moans grew in stature, masking the sound of the front door opening and the clop of heels moving steadily down the aisle.

"Hello?" Emilio recognized the earnest voice of an elderly woman, who was a regular customer. "Is there no one tending the market?"

Rosabella gasped, and then she and Emilio grappled with each other's clothing in a vain attempt to regain an orderly appearance. The woman came upon them as Rosabella buttoned her shirtwaist and Emilio his pants. The heavy-set dowager's eyes spread wide as though replicating the enlarging circle of eggs she broke into her frying pan that morning. Her plump lips, at first agape, merged in a firm downward curve before she spoke again.

"Oh, my Lord. Oh, dear God. I ... I cannot believe ..." she sputtered, turning on her heel and then waddling down the aisle and out of the market as rapidly as her short, corpulent legs could churn.

Fourteen

1

The Sun had enjoyed significant growth since Mrs. Charles P. Taggart published her first edition on July 19, 1881, in a small frame building next to a plaza. Emilio felt fortunate to have attained his position as an accountant with the newspaper, which employed one of the most complete publishing facilities in the United States to produce news from within a modern building at the corner of Seventh and B Streets.

Though he counted his blessings, Emilio had higher aspirations in mind. At the relatively young age of twenty-two, he had come to understand that despite its vast opportunities, America engendered two classes of people: those who worked at the will of the rich and relied on unions to protect their fragile rights, and those who used their wits, guile, and passion to amass the power and wealth necessary to control their own fate.

I will prevail, Emilio thought as he sat in *The Sun*'s business offices balancing January's books. *And when I secure my family's place on the highest rungs of the economic ladder, I will reward those that have been loyal better than any toothless union could.*

He set his Wahl-Eversharp mechanical pencil, an extravagant birthday gift from Rosabella, next to an open ledger, raised a hand to the bridge of his nose, and with thumb and index finger pincered his recently acquired pince-nez. He rubbed his eyes briefly and then gazed out the second-story window that abutted his desk. He watched two gentlemen in long overcoats and hats, a black bowler and a brown trilby, standing at the corner, smoking and conducting an animated conversation. A late model Imperial touring sedan slowed to turn the corner near them. Its four-cylinder engine belched a cloud of acrid smoke and coughed at a decibel level that interrupted their discussion. The bowler wearer removed his hat and shook it at the passing motorist.

Just up B Street, Emilio spotted two women on bicycles, each of whom bore a basket laden with groceries. Across Seventh he noted a young mother walking with a small boy in hand. The sight evoked a daydream of his beautiful Rosa guiding, in the not too distant future, their nearly nine-month-old son Ilario. The thought of Ilario learning to walk heightened Emilio's sense of how quickly life's affairs unfold.

Could it be almost a year and a half since Rosa and I gathered our possessions and rode those interminable rails southward for all those unending hours?

Images of those months as vibrant and colorful as a kaleidoscope flashed through his mind:

I see you now Rosa, lying back on the blanket that late summer day at Natatorium Park, looking so beautiful. We had just finished the picnic lunch you had made. I remember the brightness of your eyes and the glow about you as you struggled to tell me your news. Why would you have thought at that moment that I would be anything but elated when you whispered that you were going to make me a father?

His reverie continued with the recollection of holding Ilario for the first time and learning just two weeks ago that Rosa had become with child again. Among these pleasant memories, other disjointed and grainy images tumbled through his mind like scenes from a flicker he and Rosa recently viewed at the nickelodeon:

Giuseppe casting his daughter's belongings into the street when he learned of her condition.

Emilio frantically running to King Grocery, emptying the store safe, and pocketing a giant red gorni that he affixed around his beloved's neck to ward off the malocchio *Augustina cast upon her and the baby.*

The couple frantically seeking a priest who would marry them once they had arrived in San Diego.

100

Emilio falling to his knees in a pew within Our Lady of the Rosary shortly after arriving in San Diego, promising to repay Joel King for the ill-gained nest egg that had funded their escape to San Diego, the purchase of a home near Cortez Hill, and a number of subsequent frivolous acquisitions for his beloved Rosa.

February 7, 1912
Wednesday, 12:15 p.m.

2

Emilio glanced sporadically out the window of a restaurant at the foot of H Street on the waterfront. Although no one would be able to identify the diner by its illegible sign, locals knew it as The Greasy Spoon. When not watching for the sight of Giovanni, Emilio feigned interest in the menu or toyed with the glass of red wine the young waitress had served. As his wait continued, he gathered snippets of repartee among the restaurant's clientele, which was as diverse in race and ethnicity as in levels of employment and class.

A group of longshoremen who had tromped in from the warehouse at the end of Railroad Wharf held forth at the rear of the eatery. A party of square riggers, whom Emilio assumed from their accents hailed from Europe or Australia, swilled beer and traded off-color tales about their excursions. Clerks, businessmen, and common laborers, originally of European, African, Asian, and Mexican descent, could be seen clustered throughout the rest of the dining area.

The waitress returned to inquire of his needs. He reminded her that he was waiting on a friend and took a sip of wine. As he set the glass down and peered once more out the window, he spotted his friend crossing the street toward the restaurant's doorway. He rose as Giovanni entered and gestured him toward the table. They embraced and exchanged kisses on both cheeks before sitting and engaging in animated conversation.

"It is good to again see you, Giovanni," Emilio enthused as he signaled the waitress over and asked for a refill and a fresh glass of wine for his friend.

As the waitress left to fulfill his order, Emilio profusely thanked Giovanni, despite having done so in every letter they had exchanged over the past year and a half, for suggesting the move to San Diego and his helpful employer recommendations. Giovanni's long-standing relationship with owners of *The Sun* had helped Emilio secure his post. He also had dissuaded the young couple from settling in San Diego's Little Italy.

Emilio remembered Giovanni cautioning, "You won't find many Calabrese in Little Italy. The community consists mostly of Genovese, Marchigiani, and Sicilians, and they choose to live in a relatively confined area, not associating with anyone outside of the neighborhood. Though you will feel welcome at Our Lady of the Rosary, I suggest you locate your home in a friendlier community."

When the Erbis arrived in San Diego, they experienced firsthand the Little Italy culture Giovanni described, so Emilio used a portion of the proceeds from his King Grocery theft and bought a twelve-hundred-square-foot Spanish-influenced arts and crafts bungalow on Second Avenue just south of Redwood Street. The Park West residence afforded Emilio easy access between home and work via San Diego's electric railway. Each evening he boarded the *hobble skirt* two blocks west of *The Sun*'s office and rode a little more than a mile-and-a-quarter to Spruce, where he disembarked for the short walk home.

The waitress returned, delivering a refill and a full glass for Giovanni. Emilio raised his tumbler in toast.

"*Grazie e salut*, Giovanni. I thank you again from the bottom of my heart."

"Enough. Enough already, Milio." Giovanni raised his arms in faux surrender. "You must tell me how your lovely bride and son are faring. I want to see them as soon as I'm settled in."

"They do very well. Rosa sends her regards and is bursting with the news."

"And?" Giovanni's lips turned upward and his eyebrow rose in interest.

"She swears me to the secrecy, *caro amico*." Emilio glanced at the wine glass he clasped with both hands on the table, and then looked at Giovanni with wide eyes and a broad grin. "You no tell her I drop the ... *fava?*"

"Spill the beans?"

"Yes, yes, that is the American saying. Sorry, my English ..."

"Has become quite good. You needn't apologize for not knowing these strange colloquialisms. Now tell me this secret news, please."

Emilio beamed. "My Rosa honors me with another child."

The two friends ate hurriedly and spoke between mouthfuls of their meals and sips of wine. Emilio dabbed a napkin at his mouth and pushed his plate away.

"I eat too fast. The food is better ..."

"Better than you thought considering the appearance, atmosphere, and the fact that there is no pasta on the menu, huh? I told you the look of the place was deceiving."

"I trust you ... as always, no?" Emilio raised his glass and drank more wine. "Now, Giovanni, tell me about the work that brings you to San Diego."

"It's like Spokane all over again, my friend. Just like three years ago up there, the City Council here passed an ordinance last month prohibiting public speeches. We're going to rally against it despite what the California courts ruled."

"Yes, I read the paper." Emilio reached into his coat pocket and extracted a neatly folded clipping. "I save the article—an *editorial*, you call it—when I hear you be coming."

Emilio withdrew his pince-nez from a vest pocket, placed them on the bridge of his nose, cleared his throat, and read it:

> The Industrial Workers of the World (IWW) are dead wrong if they think San Diego requires their socialistic brand of unionism. Unlike other areas of interest to the IWW, we have neither an important agricultural nor industrial based economy. A class struggle—such as the IWW would like to conjure—does not exist among our upstanding 40,000 residents.
>
> Those in our community who have been fortunate to do well continuously display a strong civic conscience, and the rapid growth of our middle-class incomes makes class disparity nearly nonexistent. The IWW

seeks to bring mayhem and mischief to our fine city for no legitimate ends.

The IWW leaders know that we have tolerated their attempts to sell their radical views and con our young men into joining their ranks. The unionizers' actions continue to chip away at our citizens' ability to remain indulgent.

Our fine City Council members have reacted wisely to the IWW brand of rabble-rousing, and we strongly support their decision to ban public speaking in the six-block area defined as Soapbox Row and concentrated at Heller's Corner at the intersection of Fifth and E Streets.

Emilio handed the clipping to Giovanni, removed his glasses, and gazed at his friend.

"I have learned to read the English well, no?"

"Indeed, you have, dear friend." Giovanni refolded the paper Emilio had handed him and tucked it into his coat pocket. "Now that you hold a first rate job, have you begun to share the beliefs of your employer?"

Emilio slid his wine glass closer and studied the contents' red hue as though it might offer an ocean's depth of wisdom. As Emilio's silence loomed, Giovanni's jovial expression sagged momentarily, and then brightened.

"That's okay, Milio. Even our brother Joe Hill thinks the movement is wasting its time in what he calls this *jerkwater town*."

"I read the term in the paper. I look it up at the library. I find this means a city without the water tower. When steam engine need *l'acqua*, the train crew must 'jerk' water with buckets from a well. But we *have* plenty the water towers here, no?"

"It is another of those Americanisms. Hill meant that San Diego lacks enough industrial workers for the movement to make a difference, just like your clipping argues. My brothers and I disagree. You should come to soapbox corner tomorrow night and listen to us. It will be just like old times in Spokane."

"I do not like these old times, if they go the same way."

Fifteen

As he strode in the door and scanned the scene, Nick discerned that no one could righteously contest that the Star failed to meet or exceed its reputation as one of San Diego's more bizarre dive bars, but—as he perceived it—in a good way. Making his way to a red Naugahyde-covered barstool, Nick took note of the scattered clientele that, he thought, could have been a gathering of the United Nations.

The diversity he observed varied in age, sex, social status, race, and ethnicity. Serving the current crowd were two Filipina aunties, who worked the proprietor's dual bars. The barkeep along the eastern wall of the narrow space appeared to be in her midthirties and seemed to Nick like she never missed a meal or any snacks in between.

Nick chose a seat at the bar opposite, worked by a Filipina in her early forties. From Nick's perspective, her Fender-guitar-shaped figure, graced by form-fitting attire—a green spaghetti-strap tank-top tucked into a pair of tight black jeans secured by a wide leather belt—proffered an unanticipated benefit.

He rested his elbows on the oak Chicago bar rail and cringed as Geddy Lee screeched from the jukebox standing against the wall behind him. Lee employed his trademark voice to prattle about planes flying over constellations and swimming out to sea. Nick wished for the magic wand the song referenced, so he could cast Rush out of Star Bar's playlist. Mercifully the song transitioned—after the pause required for the jukebox to load a new disc—to an Elvis Costello number Nick liked.

A couple of battered and forlorn seating areas that might be described as booths sat at either side of the main entry to the long, narrow establishment, the front of which featured six equal-sized panes of mullioned glass on either side of the door. An additional eight panes crossed over the establishment's frontage at door height.

The bar Nick chose stretched to the rear of the building, where the floor space opened into a storage area and restrooms. Red stars and strings of holiday lights adorned the white cottage-cheese ceiling of a lean-to-like overhang, fronted by neglected faux-wood paneling. A similar bar—*sans* overhang—operated on the eastern side of the space, but ran only about half of the length of the west side bar. Each bar displayed various varieties and qualities of hard liquor on two parallel shelves. Unlike the eastern bar, Nick's side featured a mirrored surface between the shelves.

Nick ordered a Heineken, congratulating himself for developing the taste to step up from the longneck Buds he once craved, took a lengthy swig of cold brew, and vocalized his satisfaction with a drawn-out *ah*. He squelched a burp as he scanned his surroundings. He noted that the bar's primary ceiling—unlike the one under the overhang—had been painted red and decorated with intermittently placed ceiling fans and faded, circular paintings of clipper ships at sea.

He took a stroll to the men's room and on the way observed a vertical tattoo sign surrounded by framed colored prints of some long-gone artist's ink work on one side of the jukebox and a modest pin-up collection on the other. A billiard table sat unused at the rear of the space.

Upon his return, Nick ordered a second beer and studied the barkeep with more care: angular cheekbones, a round chin, and almond-shaped espresso eyes defined her narrow face. Porcelain skin graced her countenance and flowed like cream down her neck and over the upper and inner curves of cleavage revealed by her low-cut top.

As she stepped away to fill Nick's order, a forest of verdant onyx extending to mid-back washed over her shoulders. Her tresses swayed in counterpoint to a firm, round bottom that swung like a metronome as she glided away on low heels. When she returned with his beer a few moments later, Nick tried chatting her up while she worked a church key on the bottle. He clasped the proffered refreshment, took a swig, and tipped the bottle's head toward her before setting it down.

"Thanks, honey. My friend was right. Damned, coldest beer ever."

"First timer?" the barkeep asked. "Haven't seen you 'round before."

"Just heard about this place. Only been in town a couple of weeks." He took another drink; then offered a well-practiced line. "I'm Nick. What should I call you?"

"How about a cab, sweetie? It's been a long day." The dark-haired woman squinted, collapsing the almond shape of her eyes to slits, wrinkled her nose, and parted her lips, exposing an even row of yellowing enamel. "I'm Chesa. Nice to meet you, Nick."

"Have you been working the bar here for a long time, Chesa?"

"Long enough to know when a handsome young man is hitting on me."

She batted an eye and smiled before picking up a bar towel and gliding it along the countertop as she sashayed away. Nick chose to bide his time and people-watch. He had been told that the Star Bar's regulars consisted mostly of older men. Younger clientele, he was advised, tended to frequent the place sporadically, for a quick predinner drink or while on bar-hopping treks. This evening's crowd confirmed his scouting report.

At the rear of the bar, a towhead kid with an SDSU sweatshirt and his stout, Asian buddy had taken up a game of pool, exchanging tequila shots between turns. A foursome gathered on stools around a belly table attached to the wall between the east side bar and the jukebox. A graying ponytail swished along the back of one of the men, who wore a well-manicured beard, plaid shirt, blue jeans, and boots. He stood with his arm draped over a buxom, garishly clad brunette, who laughed with a donkey bray. A middle-aged African American man dressed from tam to loafers in black clasped the firm backside of his significantly younger and petite Caucasian companion.

They were sharing a pitcher as they debated—with factual discourse that belied appearances—whether the proposed terminus of Highway 56 should be constructed closer to Sorrento Valley. By the end of the bar nearest the entry, a scruffy drunk with crusty Rasta locks, tattered and faded long-sleeved tee, soiled baggy pants, and torn low-rise sneakers carried on an animated, unintelligible conversation with himself.

"You doin' okay, sweetie?" Chesa had returned. "Want another?"

"I'm good for now, Chesa, but I do have a question for you. My friend said I should inquire about a barkeep here about a dozen years or so ago. Said her name was Tala. Ring any bells with you?"

Nick discerned recognition flash across Chesa's face like lightning slashing the night sky. It vanished just as quickly; replaced by an arched eyebrow, an upward turn of one corner of her pressed lips, and a cautiously spoken question.

"Who is this friend of yours?"

Nick contemplated spreading a little bullshit, but went with candor.

"A guy named Vito. Italian. Lanky but athletic-looking guy with a muscular upper body and a face women might find attractive in a rugged sort of way. Would've been in his mid to late thirties back then."

Chesa's eyes widened.

"And, what's his interest in this woman?"

"So, you know her." Nick paused for a response or look of recognition, but getting none, proceeded. "I gather Vito and Tala knew each other pretty well back then. He's indisposed these days, and I think he just wanted to know if she was doing well."

"Hmm ..." Chesa tapped the bar with a brightly colored fingernail and gazed upward to her right. "Can you imagine how many guys I've seen in here that could fit this Vito's description?"

"Yeah, I see your point, I guess." Nick picked up his bottle and took a sip. "But what about the barkeep Tala?"

Chesa cast her gaze to the bar's oak countertop, where she employed a fingernail to dislodge a nonexistent ort. Then she looked up at Nick.

"I'm sorry, but I don't think I can help you."

"*Can't*, Chesa, or *won't*?"

Their eyes focused on each other in a frozen duel before Chesa drew her eyelids and the corners of her mouth down, breaking the standoff. She turned away and walked to the far end of the bar.

After paying his tab and leaving Chesa a sizable tip with his Reed business card slid under it, he finished off his Heineken and vacated the bar. He trod to a nearby pay phone, placed a call to Buck, gave him a rundown on what he had been up to, and asked Buck if he would do the favor of seeing what SDPD might have on Chesa and Tala. Then he placed a second call to his local sponsor to request a meeting later that day. The exhilaration of his investigation and Chesa's braless cleavage had stirred desires Nick needed to squelch.

Sixteen

1

Giovanni and his IWW colleagues had recently formed a group they dubbed the Free Speech League, which counted as members an improbable coalition of businessmen, church groups, members of the single-tax movement, and trade unions. Their plan this winter evening, Giovanni had told Emilio, was to test the month-old anti-speech ordinance. The protesters would march from Second and G Street near the city jail to a vacant lot at Sixth and B via a city-approved route that would bypass Heller's Corner at Fifth and E.

Despite its knowledge of the approved parade's course, a large crowd, gathered in anticipation of a confrontation between the protesters and the law, assembled at dusk at the off-limits Fifth and E intersection that bore the moniker Heller's Corner. Out of a sense of loyalty, Emilio had agreed to march with the group, even though his taste for such activity had soured since the incident with Rosabella in Spokane.

"Worst case," he told himself in recognition of the fact that the building that housed his employer stood across the street from the approved route's terminus, "I avoid problem by going into *The Sun*."

111

The Free Speech League marchers, led by mounted SDPD police, stepped off promptly at seven thirty. Emilio fell in with the mass of protesters, who strode four abreast, attired in winter coats and hats and, in some cases, waving banners. Anticipating a violation of the parade permit, a twenty-member SDPD barrier blocked the western crosswalk at Sixth and E. While the assembly of truncheon-bearing police massed at the crosswalk, the Free Speech League contingent continued its slow cadence to the planned termination point.

Emilio became anxious when the marchers failed to disband at the vacant lot. Instead, they broke into song, chanting Joe Hill's "We Will Sing One Song" and, to Emilio's consternation, kept marching. To avoid immediate arrest for blocking the public street, the group formed single-file lines on both sides of the sidewalk and proceeded to the center of the Fifth and E intersection.

The organizers hastily moved two box platforms into place, setting one in the street about halfway between Fifth and Sixth Streets and a larger one in the middle of the intersection. Cops immediately surrounded the smaller box as the first speaker made his way through the tightly massed crowd. Holding a Liberty sign over his head, the protester stepped to the rostrum.

"Fellow workers," he began, "the working class and the employing class have nothing in common."

Before he could utter more, two policemen yanked him down from the makeshift dais and tugged him off to jail. Laura Emerson followed and received the same treatment from the men in blue. The third speaker, seventeen-year-old Juanita McKamey, also acquiesced to her arrest, one so forcefully imposed that the surging three-thousand-member crowd screamed with outrage. In response, more of Chief Wilson's boys bullied their way to the soapbox, waving nightsticks as they rushed forward.

Shortly thereafter, the well-groomed E. E. Kirk, an attorney retained by the League to represent the arrestees, and therefore not scheduled to speak, became so outraged over police behavior that he stormed the box. Standing defiantly atop it, he glared over the crowd. With arm raised and in midgesture, he, too, was dragged from the dais.

Emilio watched in horror as one officer, who stood over six feet and weighed at least two hundred pounds, battered Kirk as he was hauled away. When Emilio turned his attention back to the makeshift rostrum, Giovanni had stepped forward.

"My people, like many of yours, came to America drawn by its freedoms. Today a brutal arm of this city has shown us that this is not the America ..."

Two burly officers heaved against Giovanni, forcing him face-first to the ground. They grasped him by his upper arms, jerking him to his feet. Emilio could not contain his shock and disgust. Charging forward, he jumped on the back of the larger of the two officers and tried to ride him down.

February 9, 1912
Friday, 6:10 a.m.

2

Emilio, who fretted about the concern he must have caused Rosabella, and Giovanni spent a sleepless night among the other male arrestees in what police dubbed the jail's "sobering-up room." Women arrested at the rally were detained in a "female ward."

E. E. Kirk, who had negotiated with arresting officers to keep his comb so that he would look presentable to reporters in the morning, gathered the jailed men around him. He thanked the men for their sacrifice and noted with dismay that their arrest for conspiracy would force them to change their strategy of using the courts to attack the city's ban on speech.

While he and other leaders vowed to fight on once they were freed, a thousand people gathered outside the jail. Among them, but at a safe distance, stood a young mother clasping her toddler's hand. Tears streaked her cheeks as she heard the prisoners, led by the men in her husband Emilio's cell and quickly joined by the female detainees, break out in song. The crowd cheered. Rosabella clutched Ilario's hand more firmly and drew him closer. She inhaled deeply, quivered as though an electric charge had coursed through her, and then emancipated a burdened sigh.

Seventeen

1

Maria paced the sidewalk outside the Star Bar. She began her morning with a quick trip to Victoria's Secret inside Horton Plaza, where she selected some revealing undergarments for work. She had completed her mission more quickly than anticipated, so spontaneously decided to exit the mall's east entrance and stroll down E Street. She attempted to convince herself that this morning's journey along this particular roadway had been impulsive. After all, she thought, with Michelle and the kids on tour with Zach, I've got plenty of free time on my hands.

In truth, Maria had become dissatisfied with the progress of Nick's investigation. She found his approach too time-consuming and methodical. He relied—too heavily in her view—on his cop friend, Buck, and seemed to obsess on verifying every iota of information he unearthed.

After completing one more circular journey, Maria, guided by a description given by Nick when he briefed the sisters about his progress, strode into the Star Bar and scanned the premises for Chesa. Maria stepped toward a woman who fit Nick's narrative, delivering a beer to a customer at the eastside bar.

"Good morning," Maria said as she took a stool at the bar. "I'll have a Bloody Mary with a vodka back. When you get a chance."

The barkeep acknowledged the order with a nod and a thin smile. Maria placed her purse on top of the bar and began rustling through it. She found her lipstick, which she opened and quickly passed over her lips. As she finished, her drink and shot arrived.

"Thank you." Maria clasped the shot glass and threw the contents back, savoring its bite before taking a sip of her Bloody Mary. "Mmm. Nice and spicy BM, the way I like it, Chesa."

The woman stiffened. Her eyebrows lifted into an arch at the center of her forehead, where wrinkles formed like plowed rows. Her eyelids rose as her jaw slackened.

"Do I know you?"

"Not until today. My name's Maria."

"How do you know my name?" Chesa's expression morphed into a press-lipped, squint-eyed note of inquiry.

"My business partner came by the other day and spoke with you. Left his card under your tip. He's the one that described you to me."

"What's this about?" Chesa took a step back and scanned the room with a look that expressed hope that a customer would be flagging her.

"My partner is kind of a putz, so I'm sure he gave you the wrong impression." Maria casually raised her glass and took another sip of her drink.

"I still don't understand." Chesa's expression defused; her lips rose at the corners briefly. She moved closer to Maria.

"My associate came in a few days ago asking questions about Tala."

"I have to get back to my work." Chesa turned on a heel as Maria reached into her bag.

"Wait, Chesa, please." Maria spread five bills on the bar, each prominently displaying Andrew Jackson's likeness. Chesa eyed the money, and then the young woman. "It's very important that I speak with Tala. She's not in any kind of trouble, and no harm will come to either of you."

"How do I know that?"

Maria reached into her purse again, this time removing a business card. She cast two unwavering rays of gunmetal at Chesa through a slight squint. Her eyebrows simultaneously slanted inward, and a wrinkle gathered between her brows, further conveying her sincerity. She pointed to the card.

"The detective is standup, a friend of my associate Nick, and further evidence that you have nothing to worry about."

"If I have nothing to worry about, why the cop?" Chesa stood squarely now, feet planted wide and hands on her hips. She pursed her lips into a tight, closed circle that slanted to the left side of her face; an eyebrow rose like a crescent moon over her right eye.

"Think of him as your insurance. He'll vouch for who I am and what you have been told about our interest in Tala."

Chesa eyed the twenty-dollar bills that remained arrayed on the bar, and then raised her gaze in order to slowly scan Maria's face one more time.

"Pitchers in Peñasquitos. Weekends and Mondays." Chesa scooped up the bills from the counter.

"It's a deal." Maria picked up her glass, tipped it toward Chesa, then put the rim to her lips and drank.

June 21, 1990
Thursday, 2:00 p.m.

2

Nick sat in a pair of Levi's, white guayabera, and Vans on a concrete bench overlooking the bay just north of Grape and Harbor Drive. He had donned a pair of shades to protect his eyes as he leafed through the morning's edition of *The Daily Journal*. He felt a momentary pang of guilt about not yet dropping by his old place of work.

Nothing seems right about doing that ... at least not yet, he thought. He peered over the harbor, glancing at passing boats and the rare pedestrian or skateboarder passing by. *Just looking like a guy with nothing better to do than take in some urban rays*, he told himself. This, of course, was by design.

A few moments more passed before a portly man with a cane and a book lowered himself with apparent discomfort to the end of Nick's bench. Waves of senatorial white hair were combed back on the sides and top of his oblong head. He wore large, plastic-rimmed spectacles that rested on a bulbous nose with a deeply indented bridge. Eyes the color of fireplace soot rose above shallow cheekbones. They were crowned with bushy salt-and-pepper eyebrows that arched inward.

Nick noted the old man's demeanor and his attire: a pale blue shirt, cream trousers secured tightly with an oversize belt, and a lightweight brown sweater in a hue that complemented his belt and shoes. The man hooked his cane over the back of the bench, sighed, and then pawed his book open with a massive hand. He rubbed his thin chin with the other hand. His glance at Nick revealed dark circles under eyes set like focal points on a relief map of pale, olive-hued skin that traversed his face like rivulets carving a sunbaked desert. The ends of his thick lips struggled to turn upward.

"Nice day at da harbor, huh son?"

"You're looking good, Carlo."

The old man cleared his throat several times. Phlegm-coated words tumbled from his lips like boulders rolling down an embankment.

"Shit." Carlo spat on the sidewalk. "Used tah say I was good-lookin' back in da day, but I guess I can't complain. I'm still breathin'."

Carlo "the Torch" Tacchino continued to peruse his book. Carlo had been a background source for Nick while he was at *The Journal* reporting on a Mafia fencing operation. As the suspected ring leader had crossed Tacchino in the past, he gladly assisted Nick in a manner that would bring his rival to justice without endangering Tacchino himself. Having his enemy distracted by an arrest and prosecution also had coincidentally given Tacchino an opportunity to move in on his competitor's cut.

A few years later, Nick investigated and brought to light a mortgage banking scam that coincidentally victimized Carlo's son-in-law and daughter. As an expression of his gratitude for Nick's indirect assistance in helping Carlo's daughter recover her funds, Carlo began sending holiday cards, birthday remembrances, and gifts consisting of Italian wines, boxes of homemade torrone, brine-cured black olives, flowers, and recipes for Laura. Carlo protested when Nick, pleading a need to retain all appearances of his reporter's objectivity, attempted to return the gifts. After much discourse, Carlo agreed to forward his offerings to charity.

Nick had grappled to juxtapose this caring, grandfatherly side of Carlo Tacchino with his acknowledged membership in *Cosa Nostra*. Carlo had once told Nick that he served the syndicate as an *insurance specialist*, which Nick later learned meant he employed his skills on behalf of the mob torching property so masterfully that his "artwork" never raised suspicion of arson.

Carlo's retort had made Nick grin. He continued feigning interest in the newspaper as he spoke.

"You seem to be in good enough health for a man in his midseventies *and* with your career history."

Carlo set his book on the bench, reached into his sweater pocket, withdrew a clear plastic bag filled with nuts, and cast them to an assembly of pigeons and gulls milling nearby.

"*Canta ca*, kid."

"Did you finally retire, Carlo?"

"I'm *only* seventy-seven, sonny, and in my line-a work, you don't never retire, if yah going to live long as I have." Carlo's lungs rattled as he hacked up more rheum and cast it to the ground like a spent round. "And flappin' my gums with the likes of you ain't likely tah improve my health none. What yah need besides a shave?"

Nick ignored Carlo's reference to his hirsute face.

"Just a little history lesson about Frank Bompensiero and the guy fingered for rubbing him out." Nick turned a page of his paper and glanced around as he spoke. He lowered his voice. "I think the wrong guy's stewing in the pen."

"Holy Mother of Christ, kid, yah gonna give me the *agita*." Carlo rubbed his stomach to emphasize his allegorical malady. "Yah don't wanna be steppin' in that pile of shit. Besides, I ain't playin' canary for that *cafone* Vito Erbi."

"Kah-phon-ay?"

"He's a little nothin'." Carlo gestured toward a gull leaving a deposit atop the seawall. "Just like dat pile-a guano."

Carlo cast the empty bag to his feet, picked up his book, and reopened it with newly discovered interest.

"Carlo. Listen. To sing on his behalf implies that you know he didn't do it."

Tacchino dismissed his book, dropping it into his lap. He stared out into the harbor.

"Didn't say that."

"Then, what did you mean?"

"I didn't mean nothin'. We done, kid?"

"Cut the bullshit. I've never burned you before, and I won't now."

"At my age, I ain't worried 'bout dem kind of consequences."

"Come on, Carlo. You know *something*."

"What I know 'n' what I don't … that's *my* business this time, Nickie. Let's just say it's personal."

Nick folded his newspaper, set it under his leg, and ran a hand through his hair. He bent over and began retying a shoelace.

"Carlo, an innocent man could be rotting away in that tower just a few blocks from here."

"That little *bastardo* ain't no fair-haired boy."

"Then he was involved?"

Nick's query received no response. He allowed the silence to continue while he went to work on his other shoelace. When he had finished, Nick sat up and tried a different course.

"Jesus, Carlo. What if I ask yes-and-no questions? You can nod if the answer is yes. Scratch your chin if it's no. Okay?"

The old man let several beats pass and picked up his book without a word, nod, or scratch. Nick sucked in a deep breath and exhaled before speaking.

"Come on, Carlo. Do you know who killed Frank Bompensiero?"

Carlo looked up from his book, turned his head in Nick's direction, but focused his gaze toward a harbor tour boat tied off at a wharf just south of Grape Street.

"I'll try this one more time. Was Vito Erbi involved in any way?"

A passerby might have thought rigor mortis had overtaken an old man who had come to read on a bench by the harbor but wouldn't be leaving. Nick rose abruptly and positioned himself between Carlo and the sun. He stood, arms held stiffly at his side, hands coiled in fists, and a snarl curling his lip.

"Shit, Carlo."

The old man raised his head so that he could stare into Nick's eyes.

"Not here, young man. That's why they's got toilets." Carlo sighed and placed his book in his lap. Nick glared at Carlo one last time and turned on his heel, but stopped when Carlo called to him.

"Nick, wait. I'm guessin' yah gonna keep stirrin' up dis shit pot no matter what I say." He raised a hand to his brow to shade his eyes. "Don't be stupid 'bout dis. You could end up wasting more than your time."

"That's all you got, Carlo?"

"That and a second piece of good advice: yah really should scrape dat rat's pelt off yer mug."

Eighteen

June 15, 1929
Saturday, 12:30 p.m.

1

Emilio fidgeted with his fork as he sat in a booth inside the Grant Grill, a men's-only retreat situated within the U. S. Grant Hotel on Broadway in downtown San Diego. During the previous decade, he had advanced significantly toward obtaining his goals of wealth, power, and family security. Through Giovanni's contacts and his own determination, Emilio and Rosabella had been afforded an opportunity to hobnob with San Diego's elite.

These associations led to business contacts—from civic leaders at one extreme to denizens of the city's underbelly at the other. Dipping his toe in the cesspool inhabited by fellow Italians composing the latter—*prendendo un po 'di nuoto*, as Emilio called his venture—had allowed him to dabble in real estate and eventually fund the establishment of a family realty company.

Erbi Realty, he had confidently predicted to himself, will become—through hard work and time—the engine that delivers us. With Congress's enactment of Prohibition, however, Emilio had chanced upon a more direct mechanism for accomplishing his objectives. As part of a land brokerage deal, Emilio came in contact with Charles Mulock, a bootlegger, who took a liking to the Erbis and offered

Emilio employment as Mulock's accountant. Over the next few years, Emilio became a trusted advisor, often traveling to Mulock's LA headquarters to do the books and offer advice when it was solicited.

San Diego, like the rest of the nation, had endured nine and a half years of Prohibition, but through resourcefulness, alcohol could be acquired from Tijuana and Agua Caliente. Or, as the rumrunners had learned, it could be shipped by sea. As one local writer later chronicled:

> The Prohibition era dried things up, but cops would often look the other way if a big convention was in town. The law was the law, of course. But soused tourists liked to spend money, and a wink and a nod wouldn't hurt anyone unless someone squealed.

Joining Emilio and Mulock at the table were Mayor Harry C. Clark's top aide, J. D. Reynolds; Chamber of Commerce head Stephen Hall; banker and civic leader Lawrence Knowles; and Mulock's newest employee, Ilario Erbi—Emilio's son.

Knowles, Reynolds, and Hall represented the "irrigation committee," which had been formed in response to the securing of an American Legion convention set for mid-August.

"We need to ensure the vets get good liquor," Reynolds was saying now. "Good booze means good times and lasting affection for our fine city. Our friend Emilio here has vouched for you, Mr. Mulock, as you know. He's told us we can rely on you to deliver."

As Mulock responded and the others began discussing deal points, Emilio gazed at his eighteen-year-old son, who wore his hair slicked back with pomade and had recently nurtured a pencil-thin growth on his upper lip. Like the other men in the room, he wore a dark suit, his jacket a handmade, Navy blue, double-breasted model, along with matching, eighteen-inch-wide cuffed trousers, a white shirt with a deep pointed collar, and a patterned tie.

Taller than me already, Emilio thought, *but with my jaw and sorrel hair. The rest of him, though ... all his mother.*

Despite excellent progress in school, aided by a doting father's insistence that his son read classic literature and master math, he possessed a penchant for mischief that flabbergasted his parents.

"Ari," who had been engaged in his parents' business from a young age, when his duties were to sharpen pencils and run errands, recently insisted he was quitting school. In response, his parents had warned of dire consequences. When Ari ignored their admonitions, his parents felt compelled to employ him.

"If our *scimmietta testardo* will not do what is best," Emilio told Rosa, "better to have our son under our thumb than running with *il diavolo ignoto*."

Regardless of their strategy to shield Ari, the headstrong teenager had wiled his way into Mulock's graces and, without his parents' sanction, accepted an entry-level position with the bootlegger.

June 15, 1929
Saturday, 1:45 p.m.

2

Charles Mulock charmed the committee, which warmed to his style, methodology, and assurances of timely delivery. His price had shocked them, especially compared to the bid they had received from local bootlegger Frank Bompensiero. The committee, however, had decided Bompensiero's high profile and a conviction the previous year for a Prohibition violation would risk public exposure. They also knew that individual drink sales and the long-term benefit of conducting a successful event would outweigh the cost.

With a deal in hand, the committee members and Mulock lit up cigars. Mulock would deliver 3,500 to 4,000 gallons of liquor worth $27,000 to a building on Seventh Avenue, where it would be stored until the event.

"What 'bout protection?" Mulock asked.

"Never you mind," the mayor's aide Reynolds assured him. "I've got two grand ready to make sure Police Chief Arthur and his deputies cause no trouble."

Mulock seemed satisfied, but the committee had a question for him.

"We know Emilio here," Lawrence Knowles said. "Hell, I've entrusted him with my books a long time. But we've never dealt with you. Can you assure us that the shipment will make it safely to our warehouse?"

"As I said before, I ain't worried 'bout hijackers. My boys will be well armed."

Mulock paused, took a puff on his cigar, and squinted as the exhaled smoke wafted upward past his eyes.

"If it makes you feel better, you can appoint a local to accompany the load up from the border. He'll need to be savvy, though: somebody who ain't just a ride-along, who knows where to find spare truck parts if they're needed, and quick-witted enough to convince some nosy bastard to mind his own business without raising any eyebrows."

Reynolds looked to Hall, who looked to Knowles. They all focused their gaze on Ari.

"Why not Emilio's son, then?" Reynolds ventured. "We've known him since he was a young lad, and he's in your employ."

Mulock nodded to Ari.

"I'd be happy to do it, Mr. Mulock, that is, if you and my dad agree." Ari leaned forward and placed his hands palms down on the table. "I know my way around, and Dad can vouch for my educated way with words."

"*Caro mio*, are you sure about this?" Emilio's brow knit with concern as he met his son's gaze. "It could be dangerous."

"I know Mr. Mulock's boys can watch out for me just fine, and I can get them directly to the drop-off."

"Well then, Mr. Mulock, it looks like we have come to a profitable agreement for all," Reynolds said before Emilio could object. He raised a coffee mug which, like those of his companions, had been laden with bootleg whiskey. "Here's to making our cups run over with a brew as satisfying as what fills them now."

3

Ari slipped aside an edge of the drapery that covered the window in suite 209 of the U. S. Grant Hotel and stroked his moustache as he peered out to the street, where pedestrians plodded or sought out shade in an attempt to escape the near eighty-degree heat. Perspiration saturated the armpits and lower back of his white dress shirt, which he had opened at the top when he loosened his tie. The ceiling fan offered no relief from the stifling conditions inside the room, being exacerbated by the nature of the meeting that was unfolding.

Ari's father, Emilio, along with Mayor Clark, his aide Reynolds, Hall, Knowles, and a most perturbed Charles Mulock had assembled on the bed and a small sofa or stood. Ari had successfully guided delivery of the 116-proof hooch without incident, but just yesterday somebody had snitched to the cops, who raided the Seventh Avenue storehouse and confiscated the liquor. Ari knew how *he* would deal with these city leaders and thought Mulock was being too soft in his response to the mushrooming scandal. Ari looked out the window, daydreaming about being anywhere else at the moment, when the sound of Stephen Hall's gruff voice dissolved his reverie.

"So what now?" Hall grumbled as he poured himself a glass of contraband smuggled into the room by Mayor Clark, who apparently had convinced the police to place a few bottles under his personal protection.

As Hall focused his gaze on the mayor, Clark lowered his head, yanked his bow tie loose, and stirred his glass with a finger.

"This is one damned pickle," Clark said, still avoiding eye contact. "What can we do?"

"You better come up with something, Harry, 'cuz I ain't doin' no time for this," Charles Mulock snarled, his face flushed with anger and alcohol.

J. D. Reynolds studied his shoelaces as Larry Knowles cleared his throat before voicing a comeuppance to Clark.

"You know we all pulled in a lot of campaign cash for you, Harry."

"Oh, hell." Clark slammed his drink down on an end table. "Guess I'll have to go down in person to see Chief Hill and impress him with the importance to the city's future that our booze be released. Arthur promised me months ago that he wasn't going to bother any of the conventions. He owes us."

Nineteen

June 22, 1990
Friday, 7:00 p.m.

1

Maria and Nick agreed to meet for dinner at Khyber Pass on University Avenue in Hillcrest. Nick made the journey up the hill from his motel in Mission Valley with a stop in between to visit Leo Talega. The previous evening, he had become frustrated by his investigation's lack of progress and resorted to an old crutch. The Jack Daniels bottle he bought at the liquor store that afternoon had been drained by eleven that night. The Frustration and Jack tag team had exacerbated yearnings fueled by his absence from Laura and a lapse in his twelve-step program.

Just prior to midnight the previous night, Nick had tumbled out of his room to Hotel Circle, where he hailed a passing cab. He directed the driver to the Body Shop, a nude strip joint located at the western end of Mission Valley and the foot of Point Loma. Like a dog instinctively finding its way home in the dead of night, Nick took a seat at a table three rows back from the main stage. He ordered cranberry juice from a scantily clad waitress—no alcohol service in California's nude cabarets—and checked out a full-figured brunette as she worked a group of sailors seated at the stage rail.

"Hi there, sweetheart." A svelte, copper-haired stripper approached Nick from behind and placed a hand on his shoulder. "May I join you?"

She caressed his neck and ran her hand through his hair in response to Nick's nod, then pulled up an adjoining chair. Once seated, she combed her hair with her fingers, pausing to coil the ends as she spoke.

"I don't think I've seen you here before." She ran her free hand along the inside of Nick's thigh. "And I'm sure I'd remember a hunk like you."

"First time in a long while. I'm sure you didn't work here the last time I was in."

"Lucky for me then that you came back tonight. Would you mind buying a girl a drink?"

"Well, nothing changes, does it?"

"Pardon?"

"Nothing. What would you like?"

"A Coke would be great."

Nick flagged the hostess as she passed and ordered the stripper her drink.

"My name's Harmony. What's yours?"

"Ni ... Neil."

"No worries, Neil, I won't be telling anyone I saw you here."

"Okay. Got me, but we both know Harmony isn't your real moniker either." Nick placed a hand on her thigh and raised his glass. "So here's to tonight's mystery duo."

"And to a good time." After clicking his glass with hers and taking a sip, Harmony leaned in closer, drawing her hand further up his inner thigh and placing her lips next to his ear. "I know just how to make it a good one for you, too. Would you like to start with a lap dance?"

"We could, but if you can assure me that you really know how to show me a good time, I'll go for at least the minimum in that private space I remember from the last time I dropped by."

Harmony trailed her hand over Nick's crotch and cupped the growing bulge she found there.

"Trust me, hon, you won't be disappointed."

After a lengthy session with his sponsor Leo Talega to assuage his guilt and a telephone conversation with Maria, during which she told him she had found Tala, Nick waited with a brightened disposition. He sipped a glass of pinot and admired a mural of a beautiful, young

Afghani woman. His thoughts drifted to his earlier conversation with Maria, pondering how and if she actually learned Tala's whereabouts, when a distinctively transformed Maria arrived.

Maria's face radiated with what Nick deemed salon-applied makeup—lengthened lashes, subtle eyeliner, pink lipstick—and a new coif: shorter, parted high on the left side, a sweeping wave. *A brunette version of Michelle Pfeiffer playing Susie Diamond in* The Fabulous Baker Boys, Nick thought as he rose to greet Maria. She had donned a wine velvet and lace baby-doll dress suspended on bare shoulders by spaghetti straps, black leggings, and pointy black, high-heel boots.

"I almost didn't recognize you," Nick told Maria as she sat.

"I'll take that as a compliment while pondering what your impression of my previous look must've been."

"I like them both—equally as much." Nick took pleasure in his glib recovery. "I was merely commenting on what you must agree is quite a metamorphosis."

"From moth to butterfly? I decided it was long past time for a change."

A waitress approached. Maria ordered a Syrah and an appetizer to share consisting of *borta* and *naan*. In between nibbles, Nick addressed the elephant in the room.

"I'm dying here, Maria. You've got to fill me in."

Maria took a sip of wine and ran a hand through her hair.

"Please don't be pissed, but I got frustrated."

"I know that feeling all too well."

"I went to Star Bar."

"What?"

"It was worth another try ... and a hundred bucks."

"Shit. Chesa spilled the beans for a payoff?"

"Not exactly. She just led me to believe I could find Tala any weekend at Pitchers in Peñasquitos. Do you know where that is?"

"It's a bedroom community up the 15 about twenty minutes to half an hour from here—depending on traffic. You may remember I referenced it at our first meeting. The actual name is Rancho de los Peñasquitos or Ranch of the Little Rocks."

"A place known for its pebbles. Sounds just charming." Maria's voice oozed like thick syrup. "Anyway, I thought we should meet before I went any further on my own."

"How thoughtful of you."

Maria stopped spooning *borta* onto a piece of *naan*.

"So, you *are* pissed at me."

Nick waved off her notion.

"No. No, it's not you, Maria. I'm just frustrated, because I got nowhere with an old, reliable source." Nick accepted a piece of flatbread laden with the eggplant-based concoction from Maria and took a bite. "He's someone in a position to know what happened back in '77."

"And?"

"Total stone wall. That and a veiled threat of consequences for continuing to dig into whether Vito had anything to do with Bompensiero's murder."

"A threat?"

"Nothing I'm taking seriously. His warning and his demeanor, however, make me think he's covering for somebody or, worse, for himself."

The waitress returned and took their orders. Maria ordered the *aushak*; Nick the *sambosa*. They also requested a second glass of wine each. When the waitress departed, Nick took a quick glance at his watch, which caught Maria's attention.

"Are you thinking what I'm thinking?" Maria lowered her chin and cocked her head slightly to one side. Her eyes slid to the corner of their sockets as they focused on Nick. One side of her mouth rose impishly.

Nick grinned.

"No harm in taking a drive north for a couple of after dinner drinks."

June 22, 1990
Friday, 9:20 p.m.

2

Maria and Nick crafted a strategy for approaching Tala—assuming she would be working that night—as he drove them in his Lumina up the freeway to the Peñasquitos Boulevard exit about half an hour to the north. At the end of the ramp, he took a left, passed over the freeway, and then turned right on Carmel Mountain Road. After a distance of about two football fields, Nick took a left into the driveway of a strip mall.

The buildings in the northwest portion of the center were constructed in a faux Spanish style with white adobelike walls, red awnings, and red barrel-tiled roofs. The awnings were supported by squared-off, bowling pin-shaped, white columns festooned with red brick around the shoulders and base and a rectangle of colorful tiles between. Nick pulled into a parking slot under a rectangular sign that proclaimed "Pitchers" in white capitals against a black background.

He opened one of the glass double doors, allowing Maria to enter first. Players mingled around the three pool tables arrayed to their right and a date-night crowd occupied most of the barstools. Maria and Nick turned away from the pool tables and took a table across from the long bar that dominated the northeastern wall. Banners, beer signs, and televisions dominated the décor.

They were greeted by a stout, middle-aged man with a ruddy complexion, slicked-back charcoal hair, and a belly that advertised his enjoyment of an abundance of the bar's wares. Nick and Maria declined menus, asking instead for a draft Heineken for him and a Wyder's Pear Cider for her.

They scanned the premises as the portly keep resumed his station behind the bar, retrieved two frosty mugs, and poured their drinks from two of the twenty tap handles stationed shoulder-to-shoulder like colorfully uniformed soldiers standing at attention.

As Nick returned his gaze to Maria, he was reminded of Mary McCarthy's apt description of a child who has just had "a treat wafted away." He assumed his expression mirrored hers. The only other employees they saw in the bar were a blonde Caucasian woman, who appeared to be in her late twenties, and a young, rusty-haired busboy. This turn of events would require the development of a new plan, which they discussed over the drinks the bartender delivered.

They agreed not to approach the bartender, who seemed like a seasoned manager that might be wary of two first-time customers asking questions about an employee. Nick thought Maria should query the waitress, who, he contended, would respond favorably to questions posed by a woman about her same age. Maria convinced Nick that a third option portended the best result.

She waited until the busboy busied himself with clearing a table nearby, then reached for the purse that she had tucked by her feet at the foot of her squat stool. In the process of raising it to the table, she knocked her glass to the floor. The busboy responded to the clatter, taking a towel to the cider pooled on the table's surface.

"I'll be right back with a broom and dust pan for the broken glass," the young redhead told them. "And I'll have Ben bring you another—no charge, of course."

He gestured to the bartender, who had been observing the scene. Ben reached down for a new mug and turned to pour a replacement cider. As the busboy hustled away with the armful he had balanced while wiping the table dry, Ben approached with Maria's replacement cider.

"Here you go, young lady." Ben placed his hands on his ample front porch. "As my friend Chick Hearn would say, 'No harm, no foul.'"

"Thank you so much," Maria said, feigning a Marilyn Monroe gush that she hoped had not been over the top. "I'm such a klutz sometimes."

"Don't you worry a bit." Ben passed his gaze briefly over Nick before focusing his attention back on Maria. "Is there anything else I can get for you?"

"Why don't you order another Heineken, Nick, while I catch up?"

"Good idea." Nick nodded to Ben.

"Another Heiney it is then. Will that be it?"

"Well ..." Maria paused. "I'd like to properly tip the busboy for being so quick and efficient. What's his name?"

"No need for that, miss. I'm sure Tommy will be fine with just a thank-you."

Ben returned to his station, and Tommy scurried back with cleanup equipment in hand. He busied himself sweeping the shards into a dustpan, and then applying a dry rag to mop the floor. As he was finishing, Maria took a five from her purse and called to him.

"Thank you, Tommy," she purred. "Please, take this for saving me from further embarrassment."

She handed him the money, which he slipped into a front jean pocket.

"Thank you, miss. That's very generous."

"You seem to be a dedicated employee, unlike my lazy-ass friend Tala. Is she goofing off again instead of working her shift?"

Maria let her lure float on the surface of her fishing pond, watching Tommy and hoping he would take the bait. She enjoyed watching his face light up.

"That's funny. I thought you were serious at first. You're friends?"

"Yeah. We worked together for a short time. I was hoping to drop in and surprise her."

"She would've been here, but called in with a babysitter problem."

Nick gazed at Maria with interest as he spoke the question she had assigned him.

"Tala? Is that ... wait. What'd you say was her last name?"

For the plan to work, Maria could not speak, but if she remained silent too long ...

"Caylao. Tala Caylao."

"That's it, Tommy." Nick's eyes flared open as his cheeks and the corners of his mouth rose upward.

Twenty

1

Like her older brother, seventeen-year-old Augustina "Tina" Erbi possessed a willful streak. Tina, in contrast to Ari, employed slathers of honey-coated charm, or when she deemed necessary, a little fib to evade parental constraints. She had engineered a plan based on the latter strategy, so that she could attend a movie with a boy she had kept secret from Emilio and Rosabella.

Because this was a school night, Tina told her parents that she would be studying and staying over with a schoolmate, Cecilia. Tina had advised Cecilia to lie to her parents in kind. The girls smuggled out makeup and evening wear and hastened to the downtown Carnegie Library, where they slipped into a restroom to make their preparations. With one last look in the mirror and at each other, Tina and Cecelia began the six-block walk to the theater.

A passerby watching the young women strolling hand-in-hand would have espied a study in contrast: Tina's high, round bosom and straight waist accentuated a tall, svelte, female version of her father's physique. Her high cheekbones, artist-sculpted face, and onyx-flecked jade eyes replicated her mother's genealogy. Cecilia's figure mirrored the hourglass shape much admired by men earlier in the decade. Both

137

wore flapper cloches over their bobbed hair, Tina's a radiant sable and Cecelia's a platinum blonde.

Tina wore a knee-length, faux-*Poiret* twill wool coat over her peasant-style cotton dress. Although Cecilia also wore a light wool coat to ward off the evening chill, hers fell just below the calf and was crafted in a simpler style. Her periwinkle dress had an asymmetrical hemline that flounced well over her knees.

As the girls neared the corner of Fourth Avenue and C Street, they saw Primo Tacchino and his younger brother Carlo pacing in the alcove of a stairwell leadingto Bernard's, a women's apparel store that occupied the second floor of the nine-story California Theatre building. The two teens giggled at the sight of the boys' twelve-year-old sister lurking behind her brothers. Once again Mrs. Tacchino had required her sons to let Donatella tag along.

Primo puffed on a cigarette, while Carlo buried his hands in his plus fours. Primo, the taller of the two, had donned a silk tie and tweed sport coat, his brother a bowtie and argyle sweater. Both boys wore their inky-black hair slicked back. Donatella wore a plaid dress, high-top shoes, and patterned long stockings. Carlo elbowed his brother in the ribs when he saw Tina and Cecilia approaching. In response, Primo flicked his cigarette to the ground and stepped out of the alcove's shadow. Tina glided next to Primo, placed her hands on his shoulders, and stood on tiptoe as she kissed his cheek and whispered into his ear.

"Does your Mama know anything about the movie Dona is about to see?"

As Tina stepped back, Primo shook his head.

"It will be a good primer for her though, no?"

They continued their conversation as Primo led Tina toward the theater's entrance. Cecelia, Donatella, and Carlo fell in behind.

"I think it might be a little raw for someone Dona's age."

"I suppose you're right." Primo grew silent and stared off into the night sky; then his face brightened. "Let's have Carlo and Cecilia sit in front of us with Dona, so they can shield her eyes during the racy parts."

Tina wrapped an arm around Primo and drew nearer.

"Double good idea, Primo. They'll be blinded to any risqué scenes that may unfold *behind* them, as well."

Primo bought tickets at a freestanding booth designed to reflect the Spanish Colonial Revival architecture of the building. Carlo and Primo then ushered their dates into the lobby, ignoring Donatella, who fell in behind. Tina sensed a chill from head to foot each time she entered the movie house, which the newspaper where her father worked had declared "the cathedral of the motion picture" and "an enduring contribution to the artistic beauty of the entire Southland" when in it opened two years earlier. The lobby featured an array of murals on its walls, the 2,200-seat auditorium's ceilings had been embellished in gold leaf, and ornate sculpted frescoes graced the walls.

The foursome and their charge made their way to an upper section of the balcony. As the evening progressed, Tina concentrated on G. W. Pabst's lurid melodrama, *Diary of a Lost Girl*. Tears trickled down Tina's cheek as she watched the heroine—a corrupt pharmacist's naïve daughter—being raped by her father's assistant. Primo, his left arm draped over Tina's shoulder so as to allow him to cup her breast, heard Tina's sniffles and handed her his handkerchief. By the time the "lost girl" gives birth to a child that she leaves with a midwife when she escapes home, Primo had begun walking his fingers along the inside of Tina's leg. Tina moaned, leaned in closer, and kissed Primo.

He then advanced their snuggling and kissing, sliding his hand beyond the terminus of her gartered stockings and tracing his fingertips along the edge of her step-ins. In turn, Tina kissed Primo more fervently while running a hand over his chest. Primo repositioned his left arm, so that he could slip his hand into her bra. As he did so, Tina undid his fly.

"Shit, Primo," Tina whispered in Primo's ear as she clasped him in hand. "Your dong is so fucking hard. It's like a baseball bat."

October 30, 1929
Wednesday, 6:00 a.m.

2

The next morning, Tina awoke to ungainly quiet. No sounds emanated from the kitchen, where Rosabella should have been preparing breakfast for Emilio, Ari, and Tina. No defiant cries or knocks on the bathroom door arose as her father dueled with his son for the right to use the facilities. Throwing back the covers and donning her robe and slippers, Tina heard a muffled baritone voice, speaking in clipped tones. *Who could have come to their home at this inconvenient hour?* she wondered.

The staccato voice gained clarity as Tina walked down the hall to the parlor, where her father, mother, and brother huddled next to the wooden, cathedral-style radio. That morning's *Sun* lay open and discarded at their feet. Her family's funereal countenances were explained by a newsman's words that, despite crosstalk from the ether, could not be mistaken:

> Ladies and gentlemen of the radio audience, this is Wade Douglas. I'm standing at the foot of the New York Stock Exchange, where this morning confusion is spreading through the concrete canyons of this city's financial district. That rumble you may hear in the background is actually emanating from thousands of panicked stockholders, who have massed here after the Dow Jones fell 13 percent yesterday. As we reported earlier, more than sixteen and a half million shares were traded in the selling frenzy. The paper fortunes of many Americans have dissolved into thin air overnight. These events, coupled with the dramatic losses over the past week, will surely touch upon every man, woman, and child within the sound of my voice.

Twenty-One

1

Two men stood apart from the others on the observation deck at the stern of the *Bahia Belle* as it churned through Mission Bay on one of the steamer's regularly scheduled cocktail cruises between the Bahia Hotel and its sister property, the Catamaran Resort.

Most of the approximately 120 guests aboard the 190-passenger Victorian-style paddle wheeler gathered on the two interior decks, each of which had been outfitted with wooden paneling, oak and brass railings, cast iron staircases, red velvet curtains, and etched glass. The celebrators chatted about the skyline, imbibed drinks, and listened to live music.

At the stern's rail, an older gray-haired man and his companion, a Los Angeles-based Catamaran Resort guest, drank scotch and smoked. The older man puffed his third Nazionali, drawn from a pack he had slipped in the pocket of his Hawaiian shirt. He leaned against the rail, placing a deck shoe–clad foot on the lowest rung. Despite a daytime high in the low seventies, a cool breeze generated by the boat's forward motion slapped his shirttails against his cotton chinos. His companion, attired in an oversize T-shirt with three-quarter sleeves, sweat pants, and sandals, clung to the older man's side. The tall, wiry brunet with spa-conditioned and tanned skin drew rhythmically on a Montecristo Especial No. 1.

"Yah got down here damned quick, Sal," the old man croaked.

"T, you really know how to get Flipper and Pete's attention." The younger man's speech rolled from his lips at a tempo a used-car salesman might envy. "What's the stupid son of a bitch up to?"

The old man shrugged, took a sip of scotch, and turned his head toward the softer-spoken man.

"Maybe da *sminchiato*'s developed a death wish. I hear da pen can do dat to yah when yah been in awhile."

"Smeen-chato?"

"Jesus, Sal. Spend less time on the goddamned beach, so's yah can learn da native tongue. *Sminchiato*: idiot."

The more senior of the two scanned the passing shoreline and exhaled a puff of Italian cigarette smoke. The younger, more agile Salvatore Caputo took the old man by his shoulder and brought him face-to-face.

"Are you calling me an idiot?" Puffy, blue snakes creased Sal's face as he reddened from neck to forehead.

"Let go, yah *chooch*. *Sminchiato*: It means I was callin' Vito an idiot, *not* you."

The color drained from Sal's face, replaced by an olive-hued blank slate. He moved his gaze to the skyline before speaking again.

"If I got it right, the asshole lit a flame under a hot little dish and some pipsqueak that used to generate the daily fish wrap. Flipper says I should follow your orders and put an end to it." Sal looked over both shoulders and then back at his gray-haired partner. "Does it matter which one I hit first?"

The old man flicked his cigarette butt over the rail. His body stiffened.

"Let's try a li'l sugar before we get to dat. That's why I asked for you. Yah got da art of persuasion. Yah know what I mean?"

"Sure. Sure. Then what's the plan?"

"With Vito pining away in his secluded castle, ain't much chance of gettin' to him again. Da muckraker'd sing sweeter'n Frankie, if we went to him directly, and da hot li'l tomatah—she's an unknown commodity right now, just like the barkeep."

The old man leaned over the rail again, using his lower arms to support him. Sal took a puff from his cigar, then mirrored his companion's stance. The old man spoke into Sal's ear in a coarse whisper.

"I'll keep an eye on da writer; you scope out da slant-eye and hot-assed parakeet." He took a folded sheet of lined paper from his pocket and slipped it into Sal's hand. "Dis gives you all da info you needs. Put in a few days of footwork; then we'll compare notes and decide how best to deal with dis situation."

"Whatever you say, T. As I said, you're calling the shots."

"Good that you remember dat, Sal."

July 1, 1990
Sunday, 11:30 p.m.

2

Pulsating spray buffeted Nick's back as he stood in the shower ruminating about the previous week's fruitful research and the rarity of a relaxing weekend he had just been afforded.

On Tuesday, in response to Nick's earlier request and with a recently supplied last name, Buck concluded a background check on Tala Caylao. Nick learned she had no arrest record nor any known run-ins with the law, which boded well—at least on the surface—for her veracity, should Tala provide an alibi for Vito. In addition, Buck's research on Chesa failed to uncover any criminal history.

Also during the week, Nick conducted an additional background investigation into LA and local mob bosses at the time of Bompensiero's murder, their roles at the time, and their current whereabouts. He found no connection between them and Tala.

Michelle and her children returned from Zach's continuing tour on Wednesday, and she was able to confirm over dinner Friday night with Nick and her sister that GDE had no recent dealings with the Teamsters' funds. Her assistant, however, had discovered records of several land deals Louis Gallo made in the early to mid '60s. Acquisition and construction money for most of the purchases from this era had been ponied up by the Teamsters, and Erbi Realty had served as the broker.

"I almost couldn't believe my eyes," Michelle reported to Nick, "when I discovered my dad had dealings with the Erbis. What's worse, I think, is that they may have used the deals to wash mob money."

Early Friday, Nick dropped into *The Journal* and paid respects to his former associates. He told them that he had just arrived in San Diego to conduct research to support a new novel he was working on, which, he thought, wasn't an outright lie, if not the whole truth. He used the opportunity to scan the catalog files and microfiche morgue in *The Journal*'s basement. During two hours holed-up in the paper's morgue, Nick came upon a catalog entry referencing Vittorio "Vito" Erbi. The pall of fog that had obscured Nick's memory vaporized.

"That's it," Nick heard himself say out loud. He dropped the card back in place, thumbed through the microfiche index to locate the proper corresponding reel, and spun the tape forward through *The Journal*'s 1983 issues until he came upon the crime analysis he wrote in April of that year:

> Confidential sources and file research indicate organized crime has been active in the region at least since Prohibition and as recently as 1983, when Jackie Presser allegedly secured the services of a local mob enforcer to ensure that Presser became vice president of the Teamsters Union "one way or another."

> Now, with the death in Kansas City of current VP Williams, Presser has been awarded the position he coveted.

> Sources also claimed that a San Diego company known as Erbi Realty fronted bootlegging, numbers running, influence peddling, and other illegitimate operations for members of the LA, Las Vegas, and Chicago mob for several decades.

Although the founder, Emilio Erbi, and his son, Ilario "Ari" Erbi, were never convicted, records indicate that the District Attorney and the San Diego Police Department kept close tabs on the firm and individual Erbi family members for close to 20 years.

A reliable source indicated that the Erbi Realty founder's grandson, Vittorio "Vito" Erbi, had been a runner for organized crime locally until his arrest and conviction in 1980 for the murder of former San Diego Mafia boss Frank Bompensiero. The source said he knew for a fact that the youngest Erbi had been the trigger man.

Carlo Tacchino, Nick's confidential source for the story, had been the one to detail the criminal activities of the Erbis. *What was it that Carlo had told him a little over a week ago? What I know 'n' what I don't ... that's my business this time, Nickie. Let's just say it's personal.*

Nick jotted a few more notes and made plans to stop in at the Central Library before arranging a second meeting with Tacchino.

Digging through that pile of detritus will be a royal pain in the ass, he thought, *but if I find evidence of bad blood between Tacchino and the Erbis ...*

Saturday Nick spent the morning catching up on correspondence and talking to Laura. In the afternoon, he went body surfing and strolling along Tourmaline, the couple's favorite beach haunt. Later that evening, he dropped in at Pitchers, hoping to find Tala at work. He had been disappointed to learn that she had taken a week's vacation and would not be returning until after the Independence Day holiday. He had hoped to give Maria and Michelle a positive report when he met them Sunday morning for a planned trek into San Diego's East County with Michelle's two children.

On Sunday morning Maria and Nick had stood in a restaurant parking lot in Ramona, where the group arranged to meet for breakfast. Nick's cell—a used Motorola MicroTAC he had purchased after committing to the investigation—rang. It was Michelle telling him she had developed a sinus infection and apologizing for not being able to join them. Nick then contemplated aborting the outing.

I don't want to give Maria the wrong impression by suggesting just the two of us go on as planned, he thought as he signed off with Michelle, *but what reason do I give for not completing the big scenic tour I promoted?*

He opted for what he considered cowardice and asked Maria what she wanted to do.

"Why fuck-up our day," Maria responded, "just because my sister crapped out on us."

After a full breakfast at Ramona's Old Telephone Booth, Nick and Maria journeyed to Julian, where they window-shopped before motoring southeast on Highway 79, down the backside of the mountains and on to Lake Cuyamaca. They stopped at the lake, took a long hike, and bought Cokes and trail mix, which they consumed on a leisurely drive along Highway 79 southward to I-8, then westward back to San Diego. They had burgers and beer in Hillcrest near Maria's apartment, where he dropped her off.

Nick cranked off the shower as he concluded his recollection of the week's events.

All in all, this wasn't such a bad weekend, Nick thought, *even though I struck out contacting Tala. And, what a pleasant surprise Maria's company turned out to be. Just like hanging with an edgier, Bohemian version of Michelle.*

Twenty-Two

June 3, 1930
Tuesday, 4:10 p.m.

1

Tina pressed her back against the wall that separated the California Theatre's projection room from the dank storage room where her brother told her to meet him. With the temperature outside creeping up to eighty and the humidity rising, Tina felt like she had entered a sauna. Her clothing clung to her body, and mascara streaked her cheeks. Her hand shook as she removed a cigarette from her lips and exhaled with an audible moan. She cast the butt to the ground, crushed it with a shoe, and stepped to the bare window that provided the only light in the room. Tina glanced to the street below and worried that Ari had blown her off.

Ari—whose youthful peccadillos included sneaking into the theater for free, lifting candy, and when the opportunity presented itself, pilfering the cash register—suggested the meeting place inside the California in response to his sister's telephoned plea.

How ironic, Tina thought, *that Ari would choose to rendezvous in the theater where Primo and I ...*

The sound of feet shuffling out in the corridor brought her back to the present. Ari rapped lightly on the closed door as he turned its knob. He scanned the corridor before reclosing the door behind him and then turned to face his sister.

"Jesus Christ, Tina, you're looking like a bug-eyed Betty. What's all this hush-hush shit about?"

Tina embraced her brother, then looked up into his eyes.

"I've really fucked up, Ari."

Ari pushed his sister to arm's length. As he did so, Tina stared into eyes that reminded her of her father. *In fact*, she thought, *Ari is so much like Papa—if you took away Ari's beer belly and broom-like, sorrel moustache.*

"Hey, a deb don't use that kinda language."

"Oh, Ari. I'm ... I'm pretty sure I'm knocked up."

Ari dropped his arms to his side. Tina watched him digest the meaning of her words. Ari staggered back, his lips curled, and his dusky topaz eyes raged.

"You're pregnant?"

"I've been with a boy. Several times since before Thanksgiving, and it's been six weeks since I last ... you know."

"Who did this to you? I'll kill the bastard."

Tina's shoulders dropped and her body quaked. She turned away from her brother's fury, slinking to a nearby window and staring out. Tears that had been welling in her eyes rolled down her cheeks. Ari stepped forward, clasped his sister by the shoulder, and turned her around to face him.

"I need to know who forced himself on you, Tina."

"It ... it wasn't ..." Tina met her brother's glare; then cast her eyes downward and mumbled. "I'm the one who ..."

"Who what?"

Tina pressed her body against the wall and cowered, as she looked at her brother again.

"Who wanted to do it."

"*Troia*." His slap seared Tina's cheek. "My sister the fuckin' slut."

Tina felt Ari's blow and condemnation rip her as surely as a ragged knife. She collapsed to the floor sobbing.

"*Madre di Dio*," Tina wailed. "What am I to do? What is to become of me? I thought you would help me."

In response to her outburst, Ari knelt by her side, took her in his arms, and brought her to her feet. He ran his hand through her hair as she cried uncontrollably into his chest.

"I'm sorry, Tina. I didn't mean what I said. Does the kid's father know?"

"No, I didn't ... I don't know what to say to Primo."

"Primo Tacchino? That little ..."

"Please, Ari. It's not his fault."

Ari looked away from his sister and then paced the room. Tina sat cross-legged on the floor, where she rested her head in her hands. Her brother stood before her now and placed a comforting hand on her shoulder. When she raised her head, he lifted her to her feet, and embraced her.

"I will find a way to protect your honor, sis. Give me a few days to think this through. In the meantime, keep this our secret."

June 4, 1930
Wednesday, 10:00 a.m.

2

Emilio hunkered over his desk in a dreary cubicle at the rear of Erbi Realty with his collar unbuttoned and tie loosened, executing a money draft in the name of Fred King for an amount five times that of which he had stolen from the grocery store in Spokane over twenty years prior. A bare bulb, suspended on a cord from the ceiling, lit his efforts. Before taking his seat on a wheeled but unpadded wooden chair, he had secured and locked the metal door, which bore a sign that said Private—Knock Before Entering. He placed his pen on the desk, checked the document for accuracy, and allowed his face to reflect the pleasure of finally repaying—with significant interest—the ill-gotten bounty that had funded his and Rosabella's escape to San Diego.

He set the draft aside for posting and turned his attention to a cursory review of Erbi Realty's financial health. He had not been surprised when, in a town advertised as the "the ideal home city," sales of residential properties his company represented continued at a steady if not hot pace following Black Tuesday. These legitimate transactions, however, constituted only a baseline for his growing financial empire. His major achievements appeared in a second set of books, unrelated to Erbi Realty.

He turned his attention to these records now and gave thanks for the association with Mulock, which had afforded opportunities to engage in profitable but illicit lines of trade that he chose to keep secret from his Rosa. Income from these operations dropped rapidly the first few weeks after the crash. But gamblers, convention sponsors, industry magnates not dependent on the stock market, hard-timers who had lost everything and counted on luck to rescue them, and losers, who sated their melancholia with booze, rapidly resumed their old daily habits.

Emilio pored over his books until he heard a rapid knock, delivered in a practiced cadence. He rose from the desk and strode to the door, where he unlatched the lock and ushered in Ari, whose arrival had been anticipated. They embraced before Emilio returned to his place behind the desk. Ari secured the door and then claimed the lone remaining chair in the room. He waited without speaking as his father continued to scan his records. After a few moments, Emilio closed his log and secured it in a desk drawer which he locked with a key that he returned to a vest pocket.

"How did the business go this morning?" Emilio used both hands to remove his reading spectacles, which he folded and set on his desk. His question came in anticipation of receiving the fruits of that morning's collections—a chore Emilio entrusted to his son, who had demonstrated cunning, aptitude, and a maturity that had been lacking only a year or so previous.

"Real good, Papa." Ari withdrew from his coat pocket an envelope stuffed with currency. "I had to put the squeeze on Jenkins. Little shit cried in his beer about needing his cash to feed his kids."

"Rough stuff?"

"Nah. I just had to remind him that no one held his arm behind his back when he got in." Ari's eyes brightened and dimples creased his cheeks as the corners of his lips rose. "Of course, I was bending his arm when I reminded him of the consequences of welching on his debt."

Recently, Emilio had expanded his business to incorporate a numbers game as an adjunct to ongoing bootlegging operations and had brought his son into his confidence. Their legitimate realty company continued to operate as an independent front for washing illicit cash for themselves and their mob connections. Despite having no formal affiliation with *La Cosa Nostra*, the Erbi business distributed a healthy cut of its take to the LA family. "The price one must pay the piper," Emilio had told Ari, "if we want to march in his parade."

Emilio slipped the cash from the envelope and added up the take in his head. As he did so, he noted Ari's demeanor, which he had learned to read as precisely as his hand-entered numbers. He turned to secure the cash in a floor safe, and then wheeled around to query his son.

"What is it, *caro mio*?"

"What do you mean, Papa?"

"Ari, you know I always can tell when you are worried about telling me something. Did a collection go badly?"

"No, Papa. It's not that." Ari tugged his cap from his head and kneaded the bill with both hands.

"Then what?"

"I hate to bother you with this, but I got a problem."

"I am here to help solve it, *figlio*. What is it?

"T ... my ... a young girl ... someone I know real well ..." Ari looked at his hands briefly and then his head bobbed upward. "She ..."

"Drank from the baptismal fountain? Swallowed the watermelon seed?" Ari started as Emilio rose from his seat and stood next to him. He relaxed when his father patted his shoulder. "How important is this young woman to you, Ari?"

"Very much, Papa."

"Not what they call the 'quickie'?"

"No, Papa. I mean ..."

Emilio put a finger to his lips and stepped back from Ari, resting his weight against his desk. Then he shook his head.

"How many times have I told you to wear the raincoat if you were going to be foolish enough to get your *pistola* wet?"

Ari's face flushed as he shifted ramrod straight in his chair.

"No, Papa, I didn't ... I'm not the father. No ... No way. Hell, I don't even have a girlfriend."

"Then who is this?" Emilio stared at his son, whose face turned wan as he examined the cap he rotated slowly in his hands. Emilio emitted a heavy sigh, made his way back to his chair, and dropped like dead weight. His shoulders slumped forward. *"Beata Vergine Maria Madre di Dio.* You can't mean our beloved Augustina is ...?"

Ari continued to look downward and away as a second rush of color came to his face.

"Che cazza?" Emilio pounded the desk. "Do you know who did this to my Augustina?"

"Yes." Ari continued to find difficulty meeting his father's eyes. "I'm pretty sure it was Primo Tacchino."

"Did he force himself on her?"

"Tina is no *sfogliadell'*, Papa, but she insists that she initiated their ... ah ... intimacy."

"So, then, they are in love?"

Ari came to his feet, staring at his father with heat roiling in his eyes.

"Your daughter gets knocked up by some Sicilian scum, and you ... you ... talk of love. What the fuck? We need to make that fuckin' prick pay."

"Gesù Cristo, Ilario. Sit down and do not speak again to your father in that tone. We must think first about your sister."

Ari slumped, thumping the chair's arms with his hands as he did so, his eyes blazing like solar flares, his mouth curving in a snarl.

"I don't care what you say, Papa. I swear on our family name I'm going to kick that *capa di cazz*'s balls into his mouth."

Emilio took a deep breath and exhaled slowly. He drummed his fingers on the arm of his chair and muttered in Italian under his breath.

"What is done is done, *caro mio*. You must trust that I know about this kind of thing. We must think of Tina's honor now."

Emilio broke off his thought, appearing entranced by a cobweb looping from a corner of the ceiling to the dangling light bulb's cord. Despite his apparent inattentiveness, Emilio sensed Ari continued to seethe. Yet Emilio remained in reverie until Ari cleared his throat.

"I think the time has come," Emilio said without emotion, "for you and your sister to meet your grandparents in Spokane."

"Visit our grandparents?" Ari looked to Emilio as though he had just seen a Martian. "The ones you and Mama have never discussed in our presence?"

"The philosopher Giordano Bruno wrote many, many years ago: *Time takes all and gives all.*"

"What the f—"

"*Stagitt', figilio*. Considering your sister's situation, I think the time has come to overlook what has been taken." Emilio ran a hand through his slicked-down hair and pushed back in his chair. "I hear about a businessman who operates a bootleg operation in Spokane. He also is said to be very civic-minded. Arranges aide for young women."

"But Papa ..."

Emilio raised a hand.

"I hear associates as far away as Chicago and Vegas use the kind services this Mr. Commellini offers to the *gumad* and girls like your sister. They go to Spokane; they stay a little while; they come home like from vacation. *Capesce'*?"

"Yeah, but Nanna and Nanno ..."

"Yes, I will need to work on your mother's parents, but leave that to me. In the meantime, wait a few days. Then you and your sister come to Mama and me—when we are together. Say you want to meet your grandparents. During the summer recess."

"Okay. You put on a show for Mama and then reluctantly decide it's the right thing for us to see our grandparents, despite whatever bad blood has passed among the four of you. What if Nanna and Nanno don't want to see us?"

"Trust me, Ilario. I will work this out for the honor of our family and Augustina."

"And what about Tina? Shouldn't *she* be punished?"

Emilio paused, then sighed deeply.

"Take your sister to the woodshed? Think, Ilario: giving up the *bastardo* ... that will be punishment enough."

Twenty-Three

July 6, 1990
Friday, 2:05 p.m.

1

M aria, attired in summer dress, high heels, and thong, heard Naomi greet her two o'clock appointment as she sat on the toilet peeing. She flushed, freshened her makeup, and brushed her hair as Naomi escorted the customer into the rub-and-tug's largest bedroom. Maria felt no compulsion to hasten. She knew her appearance would not be required until Naomi had collected the gentleman's cash, advised him to disrobe and lie prone on the massage table, and then cover his buttocks with a towel that lay folded at the edge of the bench.

She was thankful for her client's timely arrival, as her appointment would afford Maria an opportunity to gather her composure and put further distance between the next time she spoke to Naomi and what occurred when Maria arrived for work just after the noon hour. She had found the front door locked, which was odd for Friday—one of the busiest days in the massage industry. After unlocking the door and entering, she saw no sign of Naomi. She kicked off her heels and padded into the hallway. Then she heard a series of low moans emanating from the rear bedroom.

Beyond the open door, Maria espied Naomi lying naked on the massage table, touching herself. She ignored an impulse to step away, choosing to watch the pregnant woman pleasure herself. Maria fixed her gaze on Naomi and, after a few moments, sensed her own arousal mounting. She gasped when Naomi shifted her position and caught Maria in an act of voyeurism.

"Oh, God, Naomi. I'm so sorry." Maria's face glowed pink. She took a step back.

"Hush, honey. I should have closed the door." Naomi rolled to a standing position and gestured at Maria to approach. "As long as you're here, I really could use a massage. Okay?"

Maria lingered before approaching. When she arrived within arm's length, Naomi met her gaze, slipped her hands under the straps of Maria's dress, and lowered them over her shoulder. The frock dropped to Maria's bare feet. Naomi looked into Maria's eyes.

"Isn't this what we both want?"

Satisfied with her preparations, Maria exited the restroom, tapped on the closed bedroom door, and entered. Although Naomi had dimmed the room's light before she left, Maria had no trouble discerning a naked, slender-built man—clean-shaven with a minimal amount of body foliage and a head bearing a well-groomed mop of brown hair. As she glided toward him, her client rolled on his side, letting his towel slip away as he affected a Burt Reynolds *Cosmo* pose *sans* a discretely placed arm.

"Good afternoon. I'm your masseuse, Maria." She gazed into the middle-aged man's face without acknowledging the sizable erection he had begun to stroke. "Why don't you just lie face down, so we can get started?"

"Nice to gain your acquaintance, Maria," her client said as he scanned her from head to toe before obliging her request. "I'm Salvatore, but my friends call me Sal."

Once at his side, Maria retrieved the towel and placed it over his buttocks, where—pursuant to city red-light abatement regulations—it was required to remain at all times. She then strode to a cabinet that stored fresh towels and various lotions, oils, and talc, keeping the muscularly toned man under constant view—a security measure she had learned the hard way while working in San Francisco.

"Would you prefer talc, lotion, oil, or my favorite: a blend of lotion and light oil that I've been warming over a candle?"

"Your favorite is now mine."

Maria dribbled some of her concoction into the palm of her hand. As she glided back toward the table's side, she noted her client's deep tan, square jaw, full lips, and high cheekbones.

"Would you like your massage soft, medium, or hard?" She rubbed her hands together; then applied light pressure to her client's shoulder blades with her fingertips.

Sal raised his head from the well of the massage table and gazed at Maria with anthracite eyes.

"I'm in need of a little *stress relief* this afternoon. So how about running those lovely hands slowly and softly *all* over my body?" He winked, then returned his face to the table's face port. Maria initiated her therapy with firm, light strokes along his upper back and shoulders. He uttered a low moan in response to her touch.

"You *do* have wonderful hands. Been doing this long?"

"I'm a licensed CMT with a few years of experience."

"Up in San Francisco, right?"

Maria's hands froze.

"Don't stop now, sweetheart," Sal said as he raised his head up to look at her. "Is there something wrong?"

Maria feigned a smile, shook her head, and resumed her kneading while regaining her focus.

"I'm fine. I just thought I was going to sneeze."

"Got an allergy? Different allergens down here than up north, huh?"

"Why do you keep referencing the Bay Area as though I'm from there?"

"You are, aren't you?"

Maria drew her hands down his back, pressing in an outward motion and hoping as she did so to distract Sal from his line of questioning.

"Came back to see relatives, I bet. Any interesting ones?"

"Pardon?"

"Oh, I just have an interest in people's ties to a community, especially if they've had long ones. Yah know, like in law or land development."

Maria felt her stomach muscles tighten and a flush flow upward through her body. She stepped away to gather more lotion and oil in

157

her palm. She moved to Sal's right side, concentrating her efforts on his lower back. In the interval provided by her journey, she discerned her safest course in response to Sal's eerie line of conversation would be to continue the session without revealing her trepidation.

"Your inquisitiveness makes you sound like a PI, cop, or attorney working a case. I'm guessing lawyer."

"Closest to the latter, I guess, but I'm totally off duty. You usually that good at scoping your clients?"

"In your case, it wasn't too difficult. Cops and dicks don't show up professionally groomed or wearing expensive clothes like the ones I saw neatly folded on the sofa when I came in."

"Point taken, Maria." He lowered an arm from the tabletop and caressed Maria's leg from calf to thigh. She tensed, but didn't protest.

"What kind of law do you practice, Sal?"

"Corporate ... before I earned a position with an income to justify the wardrobe." As Sal spoke he walked his hand higher on Maria's leg. When she did nothing to dissuade him, he palmed her bottom.

"Is your company located in San Diego?" She moved to the foot of the table, gliding her hands along his legs and, in the process, avoiding Sal's further examination of her *derrière*.

"Not really. I travel a lot for business."

Maria chose another tack.

"You must work out a lot." Maria brushed her fingertips over his calves. "Your body is quite well-toned."

"I find that having a little muscle is very helpful in my profession. Unfortunately, my business requires that I use every advantage to convince careless people to discontinue behavior that will prove disadvantageous to their health."

"Now you sound like a doctor." Maria tried to keep her tone light as she struggled to comprehend the intent of the threat she perceived.

"No, Maria my dear. I'm no doctor, but I do know how to deliver stiff medicine to ... let's call them my *patients* ... when they misbehave."

As he spoke, Sal traced his fingers along the crease between her torso and leg. Maria strode to the cabinet to retrieve additional lotion and curtail Sal's further intimacy.

"I think it's time to stop talking, Sal, so you can concentrate on relaxing," she told him as she took a post at the foot of the table and began massaging the soles of his feet.

Her efforts to this point had consumed about thirty minutes—moments that seemed like hours to Maria. She moved now to Sal's left side, delivering a series of chops from calf to thigh. Sal again let his arms dangle from the table, sweeping his left hand from her calf up to her bottom and then around to her stomach. As he intensified his efforts, Maria guided her hands over his posterior, then shifted to his right side, where she performed an encore of her most recent strokes.

She then asked him to roll over, adjusting his towel as he did to ensure the resulting pup tent sheltered his mast. She raised his left arm. As she undertook a series of motions to relax it, Sal lifted his right hand to her shoulder, then walked his fingers down her neck and bodice so that he could cup a breast.

"Lots of women go braless these days, but few pull it off with your panache."

Jesus Christ, Maria thought, *if only I could yank this creep's hand off my body and bite down on it until he bleeds.* Though she considered stepping away and ending the session, she knew doing so could jeopardize her job and the much-needed income it generated. *If this weirdo is actually a legitimate client, as unlikely as that seems, he'll be expecting at least the happy ending Naomi's Swing ads subtly promise, and is likely to raise holy hell with her if I don't oblige him.*

"Just to confirm," Maria purred softly, "you're not a cop or connected to law enforcement in any way?"

"Absolutely not, I assure you." Sal shifted his head to make eye contact while simultaneously tweezing her nipple between thumb and forefinger.

"You mentioned early on that you needed some *stress relief?* Maria emphasized the last two words as she lowered his arm and began caressing his chest. "What *exactly* did you have in mind?"

"*Everything.*" Sal raised himself to a sitting position, facing Maria, and began unbuttoning her dress. She clasped his arms and, with a motion as smooth as her touch, lowered them back to his sides.

"I offer full service only to regulars, Sal. For today though, I can make you feel real good in other ways."

"Hmm." Sal cupped his hand and mimed a piston movement, then raised it to his mouth, where he feigned sucking his thumb.

"How much you got for that?" She flashed "fuck me" eyes and drew her mouth into a pout before speaking again. "You know, the larger the number, the greater the satisfaction."

"Will you be getting naked, too?"

"That depends."

Maria scanned him from eyes to crotch—pausing as she tugged his towel to the floor; then swept her gaze back to his eyes. Her mouth formed a lopsided, upward arc, revealing dimples on both cheeks.

"My friend here," Sal said with a nod toward his penis, "would really like to explore those gorgeous lips, so how about sixty?"

Maria remained expressionless—a small challenge, because she would have gladly accepted thirty dollars and a quick conclusion to the session. She then glanced toward his clothes.

"Oh, sure. Up front. I get it."

As Sal rose from the table to retrieve his wallet, Maria unbuttoned the rest of her dress, exposing her breasts, taut stomach, and silk thong as her garment dropped to the floor. When he returned with her fee, she asked him to lie faceup on the table and, once he had complied, joined him, straddling his upper legs with her knees. She then leaned forward so that her breasts brushed against his chest and lowered her lips to his ear. She licked the lobe and sighed, so that her warm breath filled his ear, then brushed her breasts and nipples like bird feathers down his chest and over his firm stomach before capturing his erection in her cleavage. While stroking his penis between her breasts, Maria employed her fingertips to caress and pinch his chest.

She then rose up, straightening her arms and setting the palms of her hands next to his head. The motion supported her weight while she allowed him to caress breasts and nibble her nipples. She feigned a moan in response to his touch and allowed him to slip the crotch of her thong aside as she took him in her hand and began stroking him.

2

A sculpted wildcat flanked by busts of its brethren denoted the entrance to the Golden Lion Tavern, a downtown fixture since 1906 that endured Prohibition, several moves, a return to its original location, and then a devastating fire. In the 1980s, Michael Mihos Construction converted the Ingle Building tavern into a restaurant, retaining and restoring an impressive stained-glass cupola composed of eight unique murals that surrounded a roman-numeraled clock.

This evening Maria huddled with Nick under the dome at a table near a large plate glass window facing Fourth Avenue. She sat with ankles locked, rubbing the back of her neck with one hand while wielding the other to churn a spoon through her black coffee. Her face turned ruddy as she bit the corner of her bottom lip and then cleared her throat.

"I've never been so ... so fucking freaked in my life." Maria spoke in a high-pitched, rapid stutter. "I could barely ... hardly keep my act together. I think he ... well, I'm worried he caught on that I was ... was maybe ... on to him."

"Did he say or do anything threatening?" Nick leaned in closer to Maria as he made his query.

"Not anything specific, but his overall demeanor was just ... just so creepy. Do you think we should call your friend Buck?"

"I don't think we've got enough."

Maria's coffee spoon clinked against her cup and fell to the table. Nick observed a discernible quake traverse her body. He placed his arm over her shoulder and drew her nearer. She rested her head on his shoulder.

"Maybe, Maria, we should just drop our investigation before ..."

"No." Maria bolted upright in her seat. "I may be frightened, but I'm not ready to cave to somebody's silly mind game."

"We've been going at this pretty intensely for nearly a month. Why don't you take a break tonight? I can meet with Tala."

After a frustrating encounter with Tala at Pitcher's while Maria was at work, Nick had been surprised to receive a subsequent call on his cell. Tala had undergone a change of heart and agreed to meet that evening at her home.

"No way, Nick. Besides, I feel safer at your side than alone in my apartment."

She raised a hand to his forehead; ran her fingers through his hair; then tilted her head upward. Their eyes met, and Nick dipped his head. Over the shortening distance, her lips sought connection with his. Nick cradled her face in the palms of his hands, impeding her further progress, and shifted back in his seat.

"Maybe we should order some appetizers or dinner and strategize our approach with Tala before we head up to Mira Mesa."

July 6, 1990
Friday, 8:35 p.m.

3

After exiting the northbound I-15 ramp, Nick steered his black rental along a circuitous route through Mira Mesa's streets. Maria's disclosure and Nick's misgivings about being tailed intermittently over the past few days, a fact he had chosen not to disclose to Maria, had provoked the meandering course Nick undertook to the Caylao residence.

Tala had reported to work that day for the first time in nearly a week and was tending bar only a few hours when Nick dropped in. He took a place at her station, ordered a beer, and engaged her in light conversation. As Tala tended to her duties, Nick sat back in his chair, so he could scrutinize Vito's potential alibi: a svelte woman in her early forties with bolts of silver lightning highlighting otherwise luxuriant sable hair—coiffed short enough to expose earlobes adorned with silver studs shaped like rose blossoms. Her oval face bore a symmetrical flat nose and high cheekbones, moon-shaped, deep irises stained in a hue akin to dark pumpernickel, and full red lips that unveiled rows of pearls when she smiled.

To this point, Nick and Tala had exchanged first names, and Nick had told her he was a professor at Reed with long-time connections to San Diego. When she returned to his table to see if he would like another draft, Nick clasped her hand.

"Before you place that order, I wanted to ask … well, I think we share … or shared … a mutual friend: Vito Erbi."

Tala's lips clamped like the shell of an oyster responding to an approaching sea turtle. She lowered her chin, cast her eyes downward, and scratched her forehead with French-manicured fingernails. Her eyes flared like twin, roiling cumulonimbus moments before a storm.

"What is this about?"

"You know about Vito's present circumstances, right, Tala?"

The barkeep shifted her eyes upward and sideways. She bit her lower lip. Nick raised his arms from the table, pinching his elbows inward to his waist and rolling his palms upward with fingers spread.

"I'm trying to *help* Vito, Miss Caylao. Our research strongly indicates that Vito willingly took a fall for reasons he hasn't made clear. He's implied that you know where he was at the time of the shooting."

Tala brought her hands to her face, perching her fingertips at the bridge of her nose, covering it and her mouth. Her eyes darted around the bar.

"That was a long time ago," she said in a voice so soft Nick had to lean toward her. "What good would anything I might know do now?"

"Depending on what you know, we could gain a new trial or maybe even have the conviction overturned outright," Nick said.

Tala pulled her hand from Nick's grasp, and took a step back.

"You could free an innocent man who may rot in a cell for the rest of his life."

Tala glanced around furtively one more time before responding.

"I … We were … We cared for each other very much." Tala sighed, her body quivered, a tear pooled in one eye before tracing a rivulet down her check. "He was … is such a nice man. I wish … but I can't."

"Why?"

Tala wrung her hands. Perspiration beaded on her forehead, and dark stains formed crescent moons under her armpits.

"I must get back to work." Tala stepped away, strode past the bar, and disappeared behind a swinging door that led to a storage room.

As Nick rose to exit Pitchers, he noted a tanned, fit man seated within eavesdropping distance of Nick's conversation with Tala. He held a full beer mug in one hand and a folded copy of the early edition of the *Trib* in the other, which he appeared to be plumbing voraciously.

There's something about that guy beyond his out-of-place Hollywood coif and natty attire that doesn't add up, Nick thought as he passed him by. *Could he be the asshole that needs lessons in how to tail someone discreetly in traffic?*

Nick had allowed an extra twenty minutes before Maria and he were due at Tala's home so that he could survey the neighborhood and, if necessary, employ the additional time to shake anyone that might be following them. Trashcan Sinatras intoned about being long in the tooth and short on wisdom on 91X as Nick turned left from eastbound Dewsbury on to Draco Road, which extended all of about two hundred feet.

He planned to take a left on Gemini and then a quick right on Pegasus, the street where Tala lived, but stopped short and pulled to the curb. A cadre of blue, red, and orange lights flashing atop SDPD patrol cars and fire department emergency vehicles blocked the Gemini-Pegasus intersection. Nick killed the Lumina's engine and lights and told Maria to wait inside. He slid from behind the steering wheel and sauntered toward a huddle of SDPD officers that appeared to consist of a crime scene investigator and two traffic cops. As he neared the group, a potbellied sergeant Nick did not recognize from his former police beat stint stepped toward him.

"Please get back in your vehicle, sir," the uniform drawled with a hint of Texas in his voice.

"We're on our way to visit a home on Pegasus," Nick said, gesturing toward Maria sitting in the Chevy, as he spoke. "What happened here?"

The traffic officer spread his legs wider and placed his hands on his hips.

"An accident, which is still under investigation, as you can no doubt tell. I suggest you and your companion find another route, as we may be here quite a while."

"I'm a freelance reporter affiliated with *The Daily Journal*," Nick said, standing his ground and acknowledging to himself what he considered a minor stretch of the truth. "Detective Buck Jarrett in Homicide can vouch for me."

The traffic cop rubbed his protruding stomach with one hand as though he was assessing the progress of his dinner's digestion, and then placed his arms akimbo.

"Damned ambulance chaser, huh?" The officer removed his cap with the same hand he had been using to massage his girth, walked the fingers of the other through his butch-cut blond hair, and then replaced his hat. "Hit and run. One soul, female, DOS, apparently lived in the neighborhood. Got a witness that claims a white late model bore down at high speed as the vic entered the northbound crosswalk."

"Got a name or description of the victim?"

"Appears to be of Asian descent. You can get details from the blotter after we're finished here."

The sergeant turned away. For Nick, the coincidental facts lined up like dominoes about to topple. He gave the first tile a push.

"One more moment, please, officer. Was she carrying any ID?"

"Yes," the cop said over his shoulder.

"Officer, I was supposed to meet someone that lives in this neighborhood that could fit the vic's general description. Her name's Tala, Tala Caylao."

The sergeant stopped and turned back to Nick.

"And your relationship to Ms. Caylao?"

"Business, officer. We think she may be an alibi witness in an old murder case we're investigating."

Without any change in an expression that had remained as unreadable as a doctor's prescription, the towering potbelly walked his gaze over Nick, peered into the Lumina for a moment, and then looked back at Nick.

"Sir, would you and your lady friend please come with me? I'd like you to speak with the chief investigator on scene."

4

The old man sat at the breakfast table, dunking biscotti in black coffee and scanning the morning *Union*'s B section, when his attention was drawn to a headline on the second page. The story under it detailed a hit-and-run that occurred the previous evening in Mira Mesa. He read the article carefully before folding the local news and setting it down on the table. Freeing his cane, which had been hooked over the back of his chair, he plodded to the kitchen wall phone, dialed the Catamaran Hotel, and asked to be forwarded to Sal's room. On his pick-up, Sal sounded groggy, as though he had just been wakened from a hangover. The old man didn't wait for Sal to speak.

"Yah see this morning's *Union*, Sal?"

"Huh? What? Just a minute."

The old man heard Sal set the phone down; the sound of labored steps crossing the room; a door opening and then closing; the rustling of newspaper.

"You'll find something of interest in da B section. Read it, get dressed, and meet me at the little coffee shop down by the Old Trieste on Morena at eleven."

"Jesus, T. I just woke up. Had a late night." Sal cleared his throat. "What's the big rush?"

"We had a business plan, Sal. Looks like you cashed in a blue chip dat we'd agreed to hold a little longer."

"Something had to be done quickly, T. She was about to ..."

"Not on the phone, Sal. I'll see you at eleven. Be there on time." He slammed the receiver into its mount and cursed.

Silver tongue or no, he thought, *I shoulda known da* cazz' di merda *would pull somethin' like this.*

166

Twenty-Four

August 11, 1930
Monday, 8:40 a.m.

1

Tina had become accustomed to living in conditions she likened to being crammed into one of the sardine tins Primo packed at Sunset Seafoods. Her thoughts turned to him now, as they often did, while she applied makeup at a sink in the twelve-foot-square SRO she had let in Spokane's Commercial Block building on West First. She and thirty-three other residents, all of whom were single or widowed, and equally divided among men and women, lived in separate rooms. Each living area had lath-and-plaster walls; a twelve-foot ceiling; an internal window facing the hallway, perhaps intended to provide additional light; a sink; an armoire; a small armchair; and a bed.

Why has he not answered my letters? she pined as she dressed for work as a part-time waitress at Skeeter's lunch counter, located on the ground floor two stories below her. *Has he found someone else? Would it be different if he knew he was about to become a father? Should I have told him?*

As she troubled over Primo, she caressed the growing orb of her stomach and sighed, then picked up a comb and dragged it through her tresses. Her thoughts drifted on as she pondered the multiple vicissitudes that redirected the course of her life over the last three months.

Shortly after their conversation three months ago, Ari learned that his father had been contemplating Albert Commellini's abortion facilities as the way to address Tina's situation. The Depression notwithstanding, his father told him, the cash register had sung with good cheer for Commellini's burgeoning empire. The success of an importing company, grocery store, restaurant, exclusive club, hotel, and apartments paled in contrast, however, to the Spokanite's lucrative bootlegging operations. Emilio had told Ari that Commellini had earned a reputation for being generous. He had opened a soup kitchen for those beleaguered by the Depression and—of relevance to the Erbis—operated an abortion service for mobster molls, mistresses, and unwed daughters.

Ari felt no compulsion to reveal all this information to his sister, when on the Monday following his discussion with Emilio, Ari pulled up beside her in his '27 Nash Roadster with the top down and called out.

"Would the lovely kitten like to rest her plates?"

"I'm not flat-footed like you, Ari, but I'll take a ride." She tossed her schoolbooks onto the two-seater's passenger-side floor as she stepped in and closed the door. "Wanna go by Walker Scott for a soda?"

Ari shifted the Nash into gear and rolled away from the curb. His eyebrows flattened and his eyes squinted as he gazed over at Tina.

"We need to talk—in private." He paused briefly. "Let's take a drive to Papa's pier. We can talk on the way, and I'll treat you to a white cow when we get there."

The Erbi family referred to Pickering's Pleasure Pier in Pacific Beach as their father's, even though Emilio's only connection had been to join fellow realtor Earl Taylor in convincing Ernest Pickering to construct the attraction at the foot of Garnet Avenue. Out of curiosity, Ari had done some asking around and learned that Taylor and Erbi had conjured the attraction risk free. Picking bore the financial and operating burdens as a lure for buyers to purchase homes the two had for sale in the area.

"Kippy, Ari." Tina clapped her hands, and then settled back on the bench seat. So what's shakin'?"

"This is serious, sis." Ari glared at Tina as he spoke. "You asked for my help. Well, I've got a plan."

"What is it?"

"After your graduation, you and I'll be takin' the rails to Spokane, where we'll meet our grandparents."

"Are you nuts?"

"Hear me out. In a couple of days, we go to the folks and convince them we want to meet our grandparents. You do a little sob-sister bit about wanting to know who they are before they die."

"Shit, Ari. What on earth would convince Papa to fork over the Benjamins for that, let alone agree to let us go? Christ, he's apt to fucking kill us right on the spot."

"Primo teach you to talk like that, too?"

Ari's reprimand evoked a punch in the arm from Tina.

"That's a shitty thing to say, Ari. Stop this car. I'm getting out here."

"Calm down, sis, and put a zip on that foul mouth before I take some soap to it. Don't think for a second I wouldn't."

Tina balled her hands and huffed loudly, then turned her head to stare out the passenger side of the Nash.

"I've already talked to Papa, but you let on, and this whole plan to save your skinny little ass goes up in smoke. You do as I say, he'll follow the script. As for the money, Mama will be told that I've saved up some dough to cover the cost."

"But Papa's paying the tab? Why would he do that?"

"Sometimes, sis, you can be so dense. Do you think he wants you paradin' 'round town carryin' a watermelon or—worse— embarrassing the whole family by poppin' out a li'l *bastardo*?"

"You ... you mean ... he wants me to have an abortion?"

"Now you're catchin' on, kiddo."

"I ... I don't think I can do that."

"Come on, sis, what are the alternatives? I mean really."

Ari took satisfaction in his ability to ultimately persuade his sister to see things his way, but bowed in admiration at the mastery of his father's performance when Ari and Tina approached their parents about going to Spokane.

Holy shit, Ari thought as he watched his father wring his hands and blather with apparent disapproval. *You'd think he had trained at his revered* Teatro La Fenice. *And the fruit didn't fall far from the tree with the way Tina played her part, convincing her mother that she wanted to meet her aging grandparents before they died.*

Ari continued to watch his sister and father bring the curtain down on their one-act play. With tears welling in his wife's eyes, Emilio made a show of softening to his wife's unspoken plea and "grudgingly" agreed to grant his children's request.

Once they arrived in Spokane, Ari and Tina stayed with Giuseppe, Augustina, and their maiden aunt Gabriella, working odd jobs and helping with housework. Then, as planned, they received a letter from Emilio that fabricated a tale about the need for brother and sister to return home immediately. The dodge allowed Ari and Tina to implement the thorniest part of the scheme.

At the train station on the day of their scheduled return trip to San Diego, their grandparents and aunt offered tearful embraces, kisses, and prayers for a safe journey. As Ari focused on what surely would be a final good-bye to his grandparents and aunt, his sister, in accordance with their plan, slipped through the central aisle of several passenger cars and stepped from the train on the opposite side.

The plotted course had been for her to be met by a caregiver in Commellini's employ while Ari traveled back to San Diego to return to work and help his father reveal to Rosabella the real purpose for her children's trip to Spokane. On the train ride south, Ari devised a final act for the family performance. This part of the script, however, would remain his secret.

August 14, 1930
Thursday, 5:10 p.m.

2

After working her shift, Tina purchased a few necessities and dropped by the post office before climbing the stairs to her quarters in the Commercial Block building. As she hastened to her room along the six-foot, wainscot-treated hallway, her fingers tore at an envelope posted from San Diego. The corridor's gaslights and third-floor skylights illuminated the correspondence that bore her mother's delicate script. A shiver coursed through her body, and her fingers trembled as she began to read. *Finally*, she thought, *word from home*—the first since she had written home explaining her decision to continue her pregnancy to term.

As she approached her door, a flood of nausea enveloped her. She rushed to the common facilities, braced her hands on the edge of a sink and endured a series of dry heaves that brought heat and perspiration to her face. She began disgorging waves of bitter bile. Tina would have collapsed to the floor had another resident not entered the ladies room and rushed to her side. Her fellow building tenant, a graying woman in her late fifties, dug a handkerchief from deep within her purse, moistened it with cool water, and drew it over Tina's forehead. She then guided her to a toilet seat and made Tina rest until color returned to her face.

"Lordy me, child," the woman exclaimed after administering motherly care for several more moments. "Let me help you to your room. Do you have someone …?"

"I'll be fine, ma'am. Thank you so much for the kindness."

"Think nothing of it, dearie. What room are you in?"

"I'm in 312."

"That means I'm just around the corner from you. Room 324. My name is Mrs. Pettigrew. Now, don't hesitate to call on me if you need anything at all."

"Thank you again, Mrs. Pettigrew. I'm Tina, and I'm sure that under different circumstances, it would be a much greater pleasure to make your acquaintance."

After entering her room and closing the door behind her, Tina collapsed on her bed. She lay atop the covers and succumbed to sleep and a fitful nightmare:

Mama. Papa. Please, don't stare at me that way. I can explain.

Primo. Please, Primo, tell them that you love me. Please, why do you turn away from me?

Ari? Is that you? What are you doing here with that knife?

"It is the naked, gleaming truth, Tina, that I will use to avenge the loss of your maidenhood."

No, Ari, please, you must not harm the baby.

Primo, I knew you would return. But why do you have a blade in your hand, too?

"Because Ari and I have made a pact to save your honor."

Stop. Please stop, Mama. Papa. Please. Please help me.
Oh, no. Not you, too? No, please, please, no ...

Tina snapped awake in darkness, drenched in a cold sweat. She cradled her bloated stomach, exploring her abdomen in the certainty that she would discover a tattered and bloody womb. She sighed with relief when the round firmness of her belly proved she had only been dreaming. Lying still and breathing heavily, Tina gathered herself and then padded to her sink for a glass of water. She had filled the glass and taken a few sips, when she noticed her mother's correspondence crumpled near her feet.

She retrieved the letter, made way to her chair, and inhaled in anticipation of the castigating prose she expected to find. *Will these words be the last I ever read of yours, Mama?* she wondered. *Am I cursed forever in your eyes?* Tina pressed her lips together. Her eyes roiled as though they had become boundless depths of murky seas. Her brows arched like rafts weathering the turbulent seas below. She began to read:

Cara mia. It has taken too long to find the words to write this letter. You must believe my silence until now means the worst for you. When your brother returned with your news, fury consumed your Papa and me. No parent wants to receive such information about a daughter, especially in this way. And then to find that you are bearing this child on your own.

I am still angry, but not in the way you might think. Why would you so disrespect us and endanger yourself and the baby by relying on the care of strangers? You disappoint me terribly with your lack of trust. We had so many talks about the need for you to come to me if you were ever troubled.

As time has passed, I realize that maybe I am at fault as well. I should have let you know that I, too, had been a frightened young girl who, when facing her parents' scorn and rejection about my condition, ran away. Did you not question the story we gave you about why your Papa and I left Spokane?

You have made a horrible mistake, and I wish you had acted more wisely. Your Papa and I, however, cannot and will not treat you the way your grandparents treated us. Please come home as soon as your condition will allow. We must speak together with the young man responsible for your condition and make this right.

Twenty-Five

January 10, 1931
Saturday, 3:20 a.m.

Tina felt her first contraction shortly after lunch. She initially blamed the soup she had eaten—a spicy, tomato-based broth served without meat because it was Friday. By early Friday evening, her water broke. Her contractions soon became less sporadic and more intense. Twinges of panic rushed through her as she realized she had made no plans for the birth of her child. I am such a childish fool. How could I have not made plans? By the time she thought of Mrs. Pettigrew, the intensity of pressure against Tina's cervix had risen. She hurried to room 324 and rapped frantically at the door.

"Coming. Coming." As Mrs. Pettigrew spoke, Tina heard the woman's steps approach the door. "Hold your britches on."

"It's me, Mrs. Pettigrew. Tina. Please, I need your help."

When Mrs. Pettigrew opened her door, Tina quaked.

"Lordy. Lordy, my dear girl. You come in here right now and lie on my bed. Have you a doctor or midwife?"

"No. No. I'm so stupid for not ..." Tina began sobbing.

Mrs. Pettigrew wrapped her arms around Tina, calmed her, and led her into her room.

"You just lie here and take deep breaths now. Okay?" She grabbed a sweater from a nearby rack and pulled it over her shoulders. "I'm going to fetch Vittoria, the midwife that lives on the second floor. I'll be right back. Don't worry, honey. We've got time."

As Friday night became Saturday morning, Tina's contractions decreased in interval as they rose in strength, lasting for as much as a minute. Vittoria wiped away the perspiration gathering on Tina's forehead with a cool towel, and Mrs. Pettigrew held her hand while carrying on a softly spoken dialogue intended to reassure. Tina became increasingly exasperated and cried for relief from the seemingly unending spasms. She felt strong rectal pressure and the need to push. She grunted, then held her breath. Vittoria admonished her about the need to keep breathing.

At first Tina would moan or grunt, but as the need to push intensified, she began to scream. Vittoria moved into position to receive the emerging child. Something was wrong. The baby's bottom was presenting. Tina was becoming hysterical, but from the expression on Vittoria's face, Tina could not have realized that the midwife also had become apprehensive. Later, after giving birth, Tina learned from Vittoria that a complete breech could have resulted in disaster for the baby and Tina, and at that point in her delivery, no time remained to rush Tina to a hospital or call for a doctor.

Tina heard Vittoria explain, without comprehending what she said, that the baby needed a little help to complete its journey. As Tina's midwife employed her hands to examine the exact state of breech, she asked Mrs. Pettigrew to restrain Tina, who had started thrashing.

"Thank the Lord," Vittoria sighed. "The baby's legs are folded up against its body—what is called a *frank* breech. This is a good sign that increases our chances of turning the baby into head-down position and delivering it safely."

At 3:20 a.m., Saturday, January 10, 1931, Tina—on the verge of exhaustion—found the energy for a final push that delivered a repositioned, healthy boy. As she took her son in her arms, she smiled, thanked Mrs. Pettigrew and Vittoria profusely, and knew at that moment the name she would give her son.

Twenty-Six

July 9, 1990
Monday, 9:50 a.m.

1

When approached on Broadway near Fourteenth Street, the three-year-old SDPD headquarters ascends like a triad of offset monoliths stacked seven stories high. The scored façade, outlined in white, bore wide swaths of pale blue running horizontally beneath large obsidian-tinted windows. Like an afterthought, a splash of Trolley red draped the entry, set back at an angle so that the corners of the floors above created an external, triangular foyer.

Clad in summer-weight clothing, Maria, Michelle, and Nick strode across a sunlit plaza that already radiated heat destined to peak in the low eighties. As they neared the front doors, the trio passed a red sculpture Nick had described during his reporting days as "modern Tinkertoy." Once inside, Nick informed the receptionist that the group had arrived for a meeting at ten with Buck Jarrett. They were directed to modular, spaceage seating bathed in electric-blue surfaces, where they waited until Buck personally greeted them and then escorted his guests to his division's quarters upstairs. A pitcher of ice water and glasses had been set out for them on a large table in an austere meeting room that reminded Nick of a setting not dissimilar to one in which he had spent an uncomfortable early evening in 1987 being grilled by Buck's compatriots about the death of Holly Damkot.

Buck's booming voice jolted Nick out of his reverie about that day, the demise of Holly, and the selfish sexual deviant he had been only a few years ago—and still was if he didn't remain constantly on guard.

"Unfortunately, as I indicated on the phone when we set this meeting, SDPD has very little additional information from what you learned on scene, Nick."

"I'm sure the three of us would appreciate a full briefing anyway, Detective," Michelle said as she briefly panned left and right to gain Nick and Maria's acquiescence.

Buck picked up his glass of water and drank, set it back on the tabletop, clasped a thin file placed face down before him, and opened it.

"What you know already is that a late model white sedan was observed rounding the corner at Hyades Way and then traveling eastward at high speed on Gemini. A witness could provide only a partial plate that hasn't led us to any specific vehicle or driver. Our witness further claims the driver appeared to purposely bear down on Ms. Caylao as she entered the crosswalk at Gemini and Pegasus, as she was walking north from the southern curb of Gemini. The ensuing impact threw the victim over the vehicle's hood. The driver continued eastbound without hesitation, turning south on Black Mountain."

Maria edged forward on her chair and nibbled at a fingernail before speaking.

"What have you learned that we don't know?"

Buck looked up from his file at Maria, giving her a flash of snowy white through upturned lips.

"Of course, Ms. Gallo." Buck set the file down. "Our investigators located a neighbor who claims to have seen Ms. Caylao at the Mira Mesa post office around eight in the evening. They allegedly conversed for a few moments—light, neighborly discourse apparently. The witness reported that he saw Ms. Caylao deposit a letter into an exterior post box near where they spoke."

"So the working theory," Nick interjected, "must be that she was returning from the post office when she was hit. I know the area a little bit and would guess that would have been about a half-mile walk."

"That is our assumption as well, but I wouldn't run with that just yet."

"Did anyone your men have spoken with notice anyone suspicious in the neighborhood in the days prior?" Nick reflexively pulled his pipe from his shirt pocket and tucked it into the corner of his mouth.

"Not so far, Nick, but by that *I-know-something-you-don't* look you've got plastered on your face, I assume you have some knowledge to share."

Nick met Buck's raised-eyebrow gaze with slightly widened eyes and closed lips that suggested a thin smile.

"Maria and I suspect we were being tailed in the days before our planned meeting with Tala. Assuming someone *is* keeping tabs on us, he or a partner could be the perp. He's an amateur when it comes to surveillance, but definitely well-trained in avoiding observation that would let us ID him."

"This may not be related," Maria said, "but I had a client come into my spa around the fourth. He seemed odd, asked a lot of questions, and creeped me out."

"Do you remember what he looked like? Any distinguishing features?" Buck took a pen from his pocket and clicked it open.

"I'd say he was about six-two, on the thin side, but with a muscular upper body. Expensively dressed and professionally groomed—pedicure, manicure, salon hair—and I would guess he's a tanning parlor aficionado. He said his name was Sal, but I wouldn't give it any weight considering … well … the circumstances under which we met."

Buck caught the drift of Tina's insinuation, but chose not to pursue the details. *No need to do Vice's job for them anyway*, he thought.

July 9, 1990
Thursday, 2:40 p.m.

2

Carlo Tacchino sat against the back wall of Tony's Trattoria on the east side of India Street in Little Italy, rubbing detritus from his eyeglasses with a cloth napkin. He was accompanied by Sal and the

LA mob's second in command, Carmen "Flipper" Milano, who'd flown down earlier in the day. Carlo placed his spectacles back on his globular nose, and then sipped an espresso while intermittently puffing on a Nazionali.

Holy Mother of God, Carlo thought as he passively observed his guests. *What sins have I committed that I gotta take this rant? And worse, from a fat slob more than a decade my junior. Little shit woulda been stepped on like a bug, 'cept for his pedigree.*

Flipper, hair slicked back on his balding head, pot-bellied, and shabbily dressed in a collarless white shirt and cheap slacks, had been disbarred as an attorney and was broke when he decided to hook up with his eldest brother, Pete, boss of the LA family, who was serving a six-year sentence for various crimes. Flipper, who drew only a six-month sentence during the same trial, had assumed a role at the table as a go-between for Pete.

"Carlo, I don't like the way this mess is playin' out," Flipper said as he rolled a fork of spaghetti on a soup spoon. Carlo suppressed a cringe as Milano stuffed his mouth and chewed with abandon, then quaffed a half-glass of Chianti before speaking again.

"You really shoulda ordered more, Carlo." Flipper gestured with his fork toward Tacchino's empty plate. "At least you didn't fuck up on picking a restaurant. This is just like Mama used to make."

Flipper tugged a cloth napkin from his lap and pawed at his mouth before continuing.

"Like I was sayin', Carlo, Sal here tells me snuffin' the slant-eye served a good purpose, but now—as of this mornin' right, Sal?—the three fuckin' musketeers paid a visit to the cops."

Veins like magenta snakes rose and squirmed across Carlo's forehead and down his neck as his smoldering eyes bore bullet holes into the *stuppiau* that sat to his right. He blinked before shifting a softened gaze at Flipper; wrinkles gathered near his mouth; his lips parted with ambivalence.

"*Chepreca!* This is the true shame." He paused briefly for emphasis. "But of course we wouldn't be facing dis problem if the woman hadn't been whacked in the first place."

Flipper waved his arm in a brushing motion.

"That's piss down the toilet now."

"So what's the plan, Flipper?"

Milano nodded to Sal, who pulled a cigar from his jacket, and then moistened and lit it. He took a long puff, allowing the smoke to roll through his lips like wispy clouds wafted by a light sea breeze.

"The investigator and the slut have been hanging together a lot lately. Wouldn't be difficult to imagine them being together in the wrong place at the wrong time."

Carlo ripped his napkin from his lap and slammed it to the table.

"Are you mad?" Carlo looked to Flipper for a sign of concurrence.

"Relax, Carlo." Flipper set his spoon and fork down and wiped his face with the napkin that had rested on his lap. "Pete knows you've been kinda fond of the kid over the years—which I gotta tell you gots us all scratchin' our heads a little—but that's for another day. No question, Carlo: We proceed calmly and rationally. Right, Sal?"

Sal glared at Carlo as he nodded accord. Carlo ignored Sal's pejorative expression. He raised his arms outward with his palms up.

"So what is it den you askin' me to do?"

Flipper, who had reclaimed his fork with intent to laden on more pasta, sighed and set the fork across his plate. He picked up his Chianti glass, swirled the remaining contents, and emptied the glass.

"That brings us to the nub of my visit."

Flipper looked to the side and dropped his chin, displaying a disproportionate number of bottom teeth. The rest of his face remained devoid of muscle contractions, and no wrinkles gathered at the corner of his eyes. The faux look of cheer placed Carlo on edge.

"You've been a fine and reliable *fratu* for many years, *amico*. Pete has told me often how much he respects you, and ..."

"Da shit's dribblin' down your chin, Flipper. Spit it out."

"Please, Carlo, we mean this with all respect." Carlo winced as another faux smile lit the sloppy fat man's face. "Sal clearly understands the lay of the land, and a man your age deserves a little time to enjoy life without all its complications. Maybe take a trip to the ol' country, aye?"

"*Vaffangul'*, Flipper, and the fuckin' horse you rode in on!"

"*I-malano-miau, Tacchino. E mi conosc'*?" Flipper barked in retort.

"Well, believe it. And, yes, I know who I'm talkin' to: a *gavone* with an asshole as big as his mouth."

Flipper smirked and sat calmly, but Sal shot to his feet.

"Apologize, you old fool."

Carlo remained seated and waved Sal off as though he were a bothersome fly.

"At least *now*, yah understand da native tongue."

"Sit down, Sal. For Christ's sake, we're in a public place." Flipper scanned the restaurant's patrons with a shrug and a sheepish expression before directing his attention back to Carlo. "And mind your tongue, Carlo. It's done. Accept Pete's decision and generosity with grace."

Flipper nodded to Sal, who placed a hand inside his seersucker jacket and extracted an envelope filled to capacity and placed it in front of Carlo.

"Pete wants you to have this with his thanks and wishes that you find many fine things to spend it on."

Carlo pushed the envelope back at Sal.

"*Numu fai shcumbari!*"

"No need to be embarrassed. Take it. You earned it."

Carlo retrieved his cane from the back of his chair, employing it as leverage to assist him to his feet.

"Please, express my gratitude to Pete next time you pay him a visit in prison," Carlo said as he shuffled away, leaving the envelope on the table.

Flipper shook his head and shrugged. As Carlo hobbled away, he heard Sal's unintended stage whisper and his boss's response.

"That old *gabbadost'* shouldn't get off that easy. You want me to rub him, Flipper?"

"Perhaps, in time, Sal. Just keep him close. In the meantime, I think you should treat *yourself* to a rub while you talk some sense into that little masseuse."

Twenty-Seven

1

Tina clutched two-month-old Vittorio to her breast and held her brother Ari's hand as the afternoon train steamed toward San Diego's Santa Fe depot. Multiple transfers and a two-and-a-half-day trek had exhausted her. Now she steeled herself for a reunion with her parents, thankful that Ari had taken time from work to serve as her escort on the trip home.

When the train was about an hour away from the station, she handed her son to Ari and made her way to the women's room of the Pullman, where she grappled for balance while changing into a fresh outfit she had chosen in the hope of being presentable when she stepped to the platform: black midcalf-length skirt, white shantung blouse, striped jersey waistcoat, and black Walk-Over heels. She thought it complemented Ari's double-breasted, herringbone, charcoal suit.

Now Tina lightly wrapped Vittorio for the outside air, which remained in the high seventies despite the time of day. As she made these preparations, Ari rehashed the story Emilio and he had constructed to protect her honor:

While she and her brother were visiting their grandparents in Spokane well over a year ago, Tina met a Northern Pacific railroad detective ten years her senior. It was love at first sight. Fearful that grandparents and parents alike would disapprove of her relationship with a cinder dick more than half again her age, Tina kept her marriage secret. After dating a few months, they were married in a civil ceremony, and Tina quickly became pregnant. Just prior to Vittorio's birth, Tina's husband died under suspicious circumstances when his body was crushed between two railcars. With her husband dead and not wanting to upset her elderly grandparents, the sorrowful widow decided to come home and live with her parents.

Tina peered out the Pullman window as Ari completed his summation of the fabrication. Her eyebrows knit and slanted inward, causing a crease to gather at the bridge of her nose. She twisted her mouth to one side and puckered her lips.

"I get it, Ari," she huffed. "I'm not a wheat just landing in the big city, but did my *husband*'s death need to be so melodramatic?"

Tina moved her gaze from the passing scenery to her brother, who shrugged as she responded.

"Hey, sis, cut me some slack, huh? I read a story in *Black Mask*, and it seemed plausible."

"My life: a pulp magazine tragedy." Tina rolled her eyes and blew air upward from the corner of her mouth. She grew quiet, then peered down at her son, whom she cuddled in her arms and began caressing.

Ari picked up a two-day-old newspaper that had been left on a seat across the aisle and leafed through it lethargically. Tina offered Ari a controlled smile and then glanced away, turning her head downward as she did. After a few moments of contemplation, she raised her head, her eyebrows camped closely over alert eyes and her lips pressed.

"Please tell me again exactly what you told Primo."

Ari crumpled the newspaper into a haphazard fold and tossed it across the aisle. His face reddened. He choked back a groan and worked his mouth into a thin upward curve.

"You gotta get over him, Teen. He's moved on."

"I just can't believe he could act so coldly."

"What can I say? The guy's a shameless egg, and you're better off without him. I mean, did he ever respond to any of your letters? Absolutely not."

"But ..."

"Trust me. It's going to be just fine." Ari propped up Tina's chin with a loosely coiled fist and gave her a wink. "I know several guys that would die to take you out ... even with the kid."

Tina gently removed Ari's hand, grasped her son close to her, and stared out the rail car window, shielding Ari from the sight of tears gathering in the well of her eyes like dewdrops perched on a petal.

With Tina apparently appeased, Ari allowed his thoughts to drift to the days and weeks ahead and how he would have to redouble his efforts to make sure Tina never learned the truth about Primo. *Will she ever understand what a brother must do to save his sister's honor?* Ari then allowed self-adulation to bathe his ego as he recalled the events of that late afternoon almost a year ago:

The Tacchino brothers—like most young Italian boys of the time—had dropped out of school and taken full-time employment with the Sunset Sea Food Company, a fish market operated by the Bregante and Ghio families and located near the foot of Market Street. Ari had taken a post nearby as their work day neared completion and watched Primo and Carlo finish hand-trucking fresh fish from the docked seiners into the market building, where they gutted and scaled the catch for sale. He had been studying the brothers' end-of-shift habits and knew he could rely on them to walk an undeviating course homeward.

Just as Ari had anticipated, the boys strode along Atlantic Street—recently dubbed Pacific Highway—and proceeded northward about a mile toward their home on Belt, which lies between Atlantic on the east and the ocean on the west. He trailed them as they walked, listening to the boys chat about news that Anthony Bregante's daughter Catherine and her husband, Michael Ghio, would soon be expanding their chowder and seafood cocktail counter at the foot of Broadway.

"Da yah think dis means we'll finally get a chance to jump to da restaurant side of da business, Primo?"

"Who knows, kid? But it sure would be great, huh?"

As they entered the intersection of Atlantic and Ash, where Ari had instructed three toughs to wait for them, Ari drew nearer. He let them cross the street, then called out to them. When they turned at the sound of his voice, one of Ari's thugs jumped Carlo, pinning his arms behind him. At the same time, the remaining two toughs tackled Primo. Ari's goons wrestled the boys into a passageway between two buildings, where Primo's attackers began pummeling him with saps, fists, and boots, while the largest of the four men continued to constrain Carlo. In moments, Primo's face had been battered. Blood from his broken nose stained his torn shirt.

Carlo, straining to free himself, screamed for help, but Ari rushed to Carlo's side, grabbed the boy's cap, and stuffed it in his mouth.

"Shut your yap, you little *cazz'*, and watch," Ari snarled, before bounding toward Primo. "This is what you get when you stick your dick where it don't belong."

Primo's assailants yanked him by his armpits into a slumping stance. His head lolled sideways against his chest; his arms sagged; blood soaked his sleeve where his right arm had been broken; his knees buckled. Ari posted himself slightly toward Primo's right side, so that his brother's view would be unobstructed, and drew his leg back as though preparing to kick a field goal. After glancing at Carlo to ensure that he was watching, Ari drove his foot upward at full force into the eldest brother's groin. Primo's head whipped up. His eyes bulged and a deep groan exploded from his curled lips. Ari swung his foot into Primo's groin again and again. He grinned, stepped back, and then leered at Carlo.

"If you or Primo ever go near my sister or say a word about this to anyone ..."

Ari pivoted on his left foot and swung his right foot a final time. He then made a show of wiping his shoe against his pant leg and adjusting his cap.

"Rip him apart boys, and then leave what's left for his *piccolo fratello* to carry home."

Ari turned on his heel and ambled slowly southward on Atlantic.

2

On Tina's nightstand, the Westclock Big Ben ticked like a metronome, beating rhythm for her heart as she lay awake in her twin bed in the back bedroom of her parents' Second Avenue bungalow. Emilio and Augustina had spared no measure in rearranging the room for daughter and grandson. They filled the ten-foot-by-ten-foot space with a twin bed, nightstand, small dressing table, armoire, rocking chair, crib, and tender. The room also provided privacy because it could be entered only via the kitchen.

Hours earlier, Tina bathed and dried Vito, diapered him on the tender's closed back, and tugged nightclothes onto the squirming and giggling boy. She hummed a lullaby as she rocked him to sleep, then placed him into his wooden crib. With her son down for the night, she shrugged out of her travel clothes, allowing them to slip in a pile at her feet. From her valise, she extracted a gown and light robe, and then padded to the dressing table, where she brushed out her hair and, finally, fell into bed. Following an emotional reunion with her parents, enduring her father's veiled criticisms, caring for her son, and bearing the burden of a discomforting silence that soon fell over the home, Tina thought she would journey into deep sleep as soon as her head hit the pillow. Such had not been the case.

After tossing and turning and then staring at the ceiling with thoughts sweeping through her mind like wind-blown tumbleweeds, Tina threw back her covers and went to the kitchen, where she prepared a cup of hot tea. The six-room single bath floor plan afforded her direct access to the kitchen, which was separated from her room by a doorway that led to the backyard.

In the kitchen, she filled the teapot with fresh water and then set it on a modern electric range her father had purchased the previous year. While the water heated, Tina retrieved a teacup from a cabinet above the adjoining kitchen sink and then loose tea from a small pantry on the other side of the room.

When the tea had steeped, Tina vacated the kitchen with cup in hand and passed through the formal dining room as she made her way into the living room, set at the front of the home behind a large covered porch. She strode around the sofa, picked up a footstool that rested next to one of the side chairs, and placed it down near the fireplace, where she sat and stared into the still-glowing embers.

Tina sipped her tea for a few moments and then tiptoed—so as not to disturb her parents, whose room connected to the living room via a short hallway—to one of the white, mullion-clad front windows. Only the sounds of sleep emanated from her parents' room and Ari's, which lay at the opposite end of the hallway, past the bathroom. The wall clock pulsed with the rhythm of the large hand sweeping toward the small, its beat keeping time for the one thematic set of thoughts that continued to tick in her mind.

Primo still loves me. I know he does. He would adore Vittorio as soon as he set his eyes on his handsome son, Tina's inner dialogue told her. *I just can't believe what Ari has said about him.*

It was then that she acknowledged where her beleaguered reflections had been taking her.

One day very soon, she vowed silently, *I will leave Vito in the capable hands of his grandmother and pay a visit to the Tacchino family in Little Italy.*

Twenty-Eight

1

Nick wove through early rush-hour traffic up the Highway 163 grade toward downtown. As he slogged along listening to 91X, he silently praised his earlier decision to acquire the Motorola. Without that expensive concession to modern technology, he would have missed Laura's call.

He had been window shopping at Fashion Valley—mystified in his attempt to identify an appropriate anniversary gift for Laura—when he got her call on his mobile. She had received a message from the Dean's Office at Reed about a woman who related a story about how Nick had given her his business card and said it was urgent that he contact her about a letter she had received. He had been advising Laura daily about his investigative roller-coaster ride, so she grasped the significance of the information.

After he hung up, Nick placed a call to Star Bar, confirmed his suspicions, and then instigated a series of calls: first to Michelle to tell her about the letter and to obtain Maria's phone number at her place of work. The ensuing conversations, including a quick heads-up to Buck Jarrett, had resulted in the scheduling of a meeting at four thirty at SDPD headquarters. On the phone, Chesa's voice vacillated from rumbling with anger, to trembling, to a whisper. Fearing that Chesa might lose her resolve, Nick arranged for Maria to swing by the tavern on her way to the police station.

July 10, 1990
Thursday, 4:35 p.m.

2

Buck had an urn filled with strong coffee, an array of cups, cream, and sugar waiting in a conference room when first Nick and then Michelle arrived. Zach, fresh from tour, accompanied his wife. Buck welcomed them, refreshed acquaintances with Zach, and offered coffee.

"Who's watching the kids?" Nick asked after greeting his friends.

"Our regular babysitter, fortunately." Zach poured Michelle and himself a cup of the dark brew. "We're paying her a bonus for her willingness to rearrange her schedule at the last minute."

The small talk soon flagged as the foursome awaited Maria and Chesa. Michelle held hands with Zach and forced a cheerful expression. Nick claimed his empty pipe and gnawed on the mouthpiece as he paced the room. *They should be here by now*, Nick thought. *What if the sartorial thug got them?* The conference room's phone buzzed. Three sets of eyes turned to Buck as he picked up.

"Yes, I see." Buck's face remained a blank slate as he stared out a west-facing window. "You're sure? Positive ID? Damn it. Okay, I'll need about …"

Michelle's gasp interrupted Buck's train of thought. His gaze returned to the room, where he encountered an array of anxious faces. He placed his hand over the mouthpiece, shook his head, and mouthed: "No, no. Not them. Different matter."

"Of all times to get a goddamned flat." Maria groaned as she plopped into a chair. Chesa stood in the doorway until Nick approached her, took her hand, and walked her to an open seat. Her hands shook as she set her purse in her lap.

"You look like you both could use some coffee," Buck said as he introduced himself to Chesa and poured a mug each for her and Maria. "Cream or sugar?"

Chesa shook her head and clasped the proffered cup, fixing her gaze on its contents. Maria doctored her coffee with cream and took a drink, then reached into her purse, extracted a lighter and pack of cigarettes, and put one to her lips.

"Must you really, Maria?"

"Force of habit, sis, but at times like this, you might find taking a few puffs helpful, too."

Maria set her lighter and cigarette on the table and turned her attention to Buck as he began to speak.

"I understand you have something you want me to read, Chesa." Buck's voice channeled snake charmer. "Is that right?"

Chesa looked around, nodded, and steadied her hands on her purse as she opened the clasp and removed an envelope. For a moment, she clutched her charge as though it were a cherished family Bible and then passed it to Buck. Jarrett paused before brushing the envelope's flap open and looked at Chesa with a questioning glance. She dipped her head.

Buck withdrew a second envelope from within the first, scanned the scrawl on the front of it, and then read out loud: "Chesa: Open This Only Upon My Death." At the sound of Buck's terse spoken words, Chesa began to weep. Buck slipped his fingers into the second, unsealed envelope, removed and unfolded two sheets of wrinkled buff paper, and scanned them before looking up.

"You'll understand if I don't reveal the contents. This document may contain sensitive information related to the perpetration of a crime or crimes currently under investigation."

"Detective Jarrett," Michelle said with practiced courtroom demeanor. "After all of this, am I going to have to seek a court order to learn what Ms. Caylao wrote?"

"I'm sorry, Michelle. My hands are tied." Buck shrugged apologetically. "Besides, you know no judge will ..."

"Buck," Nick interrupted. "We could have read Tala's declaration without you."

"But you didn't." Buck raised his shoulders and opened his palms toward Nick. "I'm sorry, Nick, I can't jeopardize an investigation."

"Maybe not, Buck, but Chesa can tell us what it says, and if the media were to learn of Michelle's filing ..."

Buck straightened in his seat; his chest expanded like a linebacker sizing up an open-field runner.

"You wouldn't."

Nick leaned forward in his chair, enforcing his threat with a hard-set glare.

"When it comes to evidence, my friend, you *know* we've *both* done worse."

Buck and Nick locked eyes in a game of chicken.

"Wait a minute, you two," Michelle interjected. "Maybe there's a way to do this without endangering a potential case, a career, or a long-standing friendship."

Both men sat back and looked to Michelle.

"Detective, why don't you take a few moments to digest Tala's letter, and then you can paraphrase the contents for us without revealing sensitive information?"

"But Michelle ..." Michelle raised her hand at Nick before he could continue.

"It's a start, Nick." She turned her attention back to Buck. "What do you say, Detective?"

Buck rolled his eyes, sighed, and then raised his arms in a conceding gesture.

"Okay, okay, but do I have to do this in front of an audience?"

Michelle briefly glanced at the others before responding.

"Chesa certainly doesn't need to be dragged through this again, so I suggest Zach and I take Chesa wherever she needs to go. We trust Nick and Maria will convey anything of import to us later."

Michelle rose, not tarrying to field any objection, and led Zach and Chesa out of the room.

Buck set the two-page document on the conference table in front of him and rubbed his chin.

"That's the gist of it." His shoulders rose slightly as he gestured with his right hand, palm up, and shook his head. "Not exactly what we may have hoped for ..."

"Shit, I'm no attorney, but you can say that again—in spades." Nick huffed as he ran a hand through his hair. Maria leaned in toward Buck.

"But Vito told her how it came down, and ..."

"Unfortunately, Miss Gallo, Vito's explanation to Tala after the fact wouldn't stand up in court, *even if* this letter became admissible as evidence. It could be the truth, or it could be a fabrication to create an alibi after the fact."

"And the death threats?"

"Again ..."

"Probably not admissible in court." Nick withdrew the pipe he had been gnawing before speaking and leaned forward in his seat. "Let's put aside the legal process for a moment."

Buck sat back and crossed his arms over his chest. Maria looked attentively to Nick, who inhaled deeply before continuing.

"If we are to believe what Vito allegedly confided to Tala, he was suckered into riding to the scene in the Impala and asked by the driver to pick up an envelope from a guy standing out front of a Pacific Beach gas station, the same one where Bompensiero was rubbed out later that night. Tala says that before they learned of Frank's demise, Vito told her he feared something bad was going to come down, because a passenger in the car was a long-time enemy of the Erbis. We can assume the reference is to Carlo Tacchino."

"Why Tacchino?" Buck asked.

"It's a long story; details to follow as necessary." Nick paused for Buck's nodded assent and then continued. "Vito tells Tala he was dropped off at one of Gaspare Matranga's bars downtown, where he left an envelope stuffed with racket take in a designated drop box. Conveniently, he alleges to her that he didn't see anyone who would have recognized or noticed him, and when he returned to the sidewalk, his ride was gone. He tells Tala he took a bus home and didn't know anything about the hit on Bompensiero until he read the paper the next morning.

"We know from the record that as time passed, the public learned that the suspect leaving the scene and entering a black Impala wore clothes similar to what Vito had been wearing. He claims to have told Tala at that point that he thought he was being set up for the murder and why.

193

"His final major assertion involves a meeting with a *consigliore* at which he was informed that he was going down for the murder and to take it like a man or be fitted with cement boots. Tala claims that Vito told her the *consigliore* showed him surveillance photos of people close to him. We all can assume Vito understood the intended implication, if he chose to sing."

Buck interjected. "But what do we make of Tala's assertion that as squad cars pulled up to take him in, he told her he had lied—that he had gunned down Bompensiero?"

"We can assume that at least one of the pics held Tala's image," Tina responded. "He was trying to protect her. Obviously, if he had left her believing his original story—what I think was the truth—she would have fought to prove his innocence and in the process, placed herself in danger."

"All of which," Buck stated, "is hearsay and inadmissible under California rules of evidence."

"What about the beating and threats she says she got shortly after Vito was arrested?" Maria asked.

"By itself?" Buck shook his head. "I doubt anyone could build a factual foundation to allow its admission."

Maria sighed, and her face paled. She placed her head on Nick's shoulder; he put his arm around her.

"It's not over yet, Maria. I think I know what comes next."

Twenty-Nine

March 29, 1932
Sunday, 11:20 a.m.

1

Despite a sleepless night, Tina rose with energy and purpose for the day that lay ahead. She quickly cared for Vito's needs, bathed, and donned her best outfit. She had explained to Rosabella and Emilio that she planned to attend Mass with an old friend at Our Lady of the Rosary parish in Little Italy. They told her they were pleased that she would be socializing out of the house for the first time since she had returned to San Diego. She kissed Vito and hugged her parents before stepping out in high heels and a cloche to catch the streetcar south and then transfer to the route that would take her westward to Little Italy.

As she stepped from the rail car and strode toward the church, she wished she had worn a lighter outfit. Although the thermometer nestled in the high fifties, Tina's pace brought perspiration to her forehead and underarms. Her sweater clung to her lower back. As she neared Our Lady of the Rosary, Tina became apprehensive about entering.

What if the Tacchino family is not at Mass? she fretted. *Do I have the* coglioni *to just fucking show up at their doorstep?*

Because San Diego remained a part of the Los Angeles Diocese, an LA cardinal had appointed Sylvester Rabagliati as pastor of the parish in 1921, and Tina was pleased that the convivial priest continued to serve his flock. As she negotiated the six concrete steps that rose to the vestibule, she contemplated a congenial-if-brief reunion with Father Rabagliati, who customarily greeted his parishioners with a handshake or a hug. Much to her chagrin, however, Associate Pastor Bruno Abadia, a priest she found to be inflexible and irascible, stood at the entry.

As Tina neared, Abadia's eyebrows rose, but his eyelids lowered. His mouth opened slightly, and then a look of recognition came to his face. He withdrew his outstretched hand and cast a gaze at Tina that enveloped her like a winter breeze off San Diego Bay.

"Under the circumstances, I am more than a little surprised to see *you* here," Abadia said. "I pray you've made a good, honest confession recently."

Tina dropped her head and bit her bottom lip. She would have fled but for the gaggle of parishioners flocking up the stairs behind her, making withdrawal even more embarrassing than proceeding on into the nave—where she hastened to a back pew and withdrew a handkerchief from her purse. She lowered her chin and dabbed at her eyes.

Gathering courage, Tina raised her head. Despite the myriad of Masses she had attended inside the long, narrow confines of her church, she never ceased to be awed by its décor. Father Rabagliati had retained Venetian painter Fausto Tasca to craft nine colorful frescoes, including a large crucifixion mural above the altar and the Last Judgment in the rear of the church. Tina savored the fact that Tasca, who painted during the Mussolini era, had depicted fascist sympathizers among the damned in his portrayal of the Last Judgment. She focused next on four sculptures crafted by Romanelli.

Tina had been admiring each of the fifteen oversized stained-glass windows depicting the Rosary when she became aware of the grumbling, coughing, and shifting around of her fellow parishioners. The commotion alerted her to an unusual delay in the commencement of services. As Mass finally began, Tina searched the congregation for the Tacchinos and found all but Primo standing a few pews in front and across from her.

Where could Primo be? she thought. *Now, when Mass ends, I will have to approach his whole family. What should I say?*

With the service well underway, Father Abadia stepped to the pulpit, read a Gospel ordained by the Catholic calendar, and then bent to kiss the weighty volume. He cleared his throat, tugged a handkerchief from his rear pants pocket, and then dabbed at his mouth with the wrinkled rag. He looked over the congregation, paused for effect, and then began to speak.

"Good morning, my fellow children in Christ," Abadia began. "I apologize, my beloved brethren, for my tardiness. Something occurred earlier this morning that obliged me to delay Mass while I revised my planned Liturgy of the Word."

Abadia crossed his arms over his chest and peered at the congregation with motionless eyes hooded by knitted eyebrows. He allowed the anxious murmurs to float among his flock before speaking again.

"As the Bible expresses in numerous passages, and as we unfortunately know through our own community's experiences, all too often women selfishly employ their wanton guiles to seduce and entrap innocent, young Catholic men. This very morning, I espied such a woman, who dared reenter our congregation after a passage of some time."

Tina's face flushed and her body stiffened as the pastor's words slammed into her with the impact of cars colliding at full speed. Her hands began to quiver as the priest continued.

"I modified today's homily, because her actions brought to mind a passage from Ecclesiastes, which I paraphrase:

> She lied in wait in secret places
> At every corner she would sit.
> In the city's squares she displayed herself,
> And in the town gates she set herself,
> And there was none to stop her from whoring.
> Her eyes glanced hither and thither,
> And she wantonly raised her eyelids
> To seek out a righteous man and lead him astray
> And a perfect man to make him stumble.

"That such a woman would defy God's will, seduce an innocent young man, and then unashamedly bear a bastard child—yes, we know her story about a phantom marriage—is unconscionable in the eyes of our Lord. For her to parade unremorsefully amongst us without concern for the pain she and, we must assume, her brother brought upon a family of this parish: a brutal mutilation of a beloved son and his subsequent death. Such unremorseful behavior can be viewed only in the eyes of God as an unforgivable abomination."

At the reference to Ari and a "subsequent death," Tina's head snapped up. She covered her mouth with gloved hands, then wrapped her arms around her to stave off the chill that coursed like a lightning bolt up her spine.

No. That can't be. Was Father being literal? But how could he? Ari told me ...

At this point, Abadia paused, swept his eyes over the assembly again, and then rested his glare at the rear of the church in the direction of where Tina sat. Tina's first thought was to rise from the pew and rush out, but she fought the instinct for fear of drawing even greater attention to herself. As she continued to endure Father Abadia's scorn, she wilted, bringing her hands to her lips and tilting her head to one side as she did so. Her mouth opened and closed several times, implying she was attempting to articulate her thoughts. She then gulped, exhaled slowly, and shook her head. Abadia concluded his homily.

"Though instinctively we may be inspired to seek revenge against such despicable behavior, the Lord has taught us to resist such temptation. Likewise Our Lord also asks that we not retaliate against the sibling and a band of hooligans who viciously robbed this young man of his mortal coil before he had barely begun to undertake his life.

"If we are not to take our pound of flesh, then I humbly plea of our Almighty Father that He protect every man and every boy from the corruption of the flesh beset upon them by the charming guiles of coquettes and harlots, wanton women and wayward girls—such as she that is among us—who deviously employ their seductive skills to lure men astray or coerce them to conduct vicious behavior."

Recitation of the Lamb of God signaled the beginning of the Communion Rite. Most members of the congregation rose and assembled in two orderly rows that progressed toward the altar rail to receive the wafer that symbolized the body of Christ. Tina used this opportunity to slip out of the church.

A cool breeze blustered up Date Street from the bay, whipped around the State Street edifice, and shrouded Tina as she stormed down the vestibule stairs. She clasped her cloche to prohibit a gust from blowing it off and hurried southward along State toward the D Street rail stop, where she could board a car that would take her home. Had she glanced over her shoulder as she departed the church, she may have espied two young men following at a distance. She hurried on, her mind churning with bewilderment of what Ari could have done to Primo. As her pace quickened, she became less observant of the uneven surface that rose a few steps ahead.

"Shit," Tina exclaimed, as a heel struck a ragged edge of concrete, causing her to lurch for support against the wall of a closed retail building. Bracing herself, she raised her foot and discovered a broken heel. "Damn it. What else could ..."

At that moment, a hand swept over her mouth and another wound tightly around her chest. A second pair of hands and arms encaged her legs. She screamed and flailed as her assailants carried her to a dank recess between two buildings. The male who held her legs dropped them, pulled off her heels, and ripped off her silk stockings. His accomplice stuffed one of her stockings into her mouth and used the other to tie her gag in place.

Tina tried to twist away, but the second attacker froze her in place with a quick succession of punches to the stomach, face, and chest. She collapsed to her knees; her head sagged; rivers of mascara-laden tears rolled down her cheeks.

"What next, Carlo?" the slugger whispered.

"Ixnay da names, *chooch*," Carlo Tacchino barked.

"Yeah, sure, man. Okay if I have a little fun before you ...?"

"Holy Mother of God, you just left da Mass, *sminchiato*. What I gotta do is bad enough. Now, grab her arms and hold her down."

The black flecks floating within Tina's dark green orbs flared as Carlo pulled a box of matches from his pocket and struck the first one. Her muffled screams gurgled like a brook trickling through a dense forest. When she thrashed out and tried to rise, Carlo punched her in the jaw, then placed the flame against her cheek. Seemingly oblivious to Tina's writhing and muffled wails, Carlo struck more matches and methodically traced them along the contours of her face, neck, arms, and legs.

"You crawl home now, *sticchio,* and tell *la famiglia* to never fuck with da Tacchinos again."

Carlo nodded at his companion to let Tina go. Before she could rise, he kicked her in the groin, spat in her face, and dropped a lit match in her lap. Tina slumped to ground as consciousness ebbed.

Tina awoke in the dark, dazed and shivering, every part of her being screaming in agony. Despite the pain, she tried to rise, but crumpled to her knees. Only one thought filled her mind, a thought that drove her on hands and knees out of the bleak corridor: she must get home to Vittorio. She covered only a few feet before lapsing into darkness. Conscious again a few moments later, she dragged on, only to collapse yet again. Finally, Tina made it to the sidewalk, where passersby gasped and scurried away from the frightening site.

"Please help me," she begged. "My little Vito needs me."

April 3, 1931
Friday, 7:00 p.m.

2

"In nomine Patris, et Filii, et Spiritus Sancti," Father Rabagliati solemnly intoned as he initiated the Rosary by raising his right hand from just above his head down to his chest, then horizontally to his left shoulder, and finally to his right. The assembled mourners, among them associates of the Erbi family crime operations and their realty clients, Matranga and a few of his soldiers, family friends, and Tina's friend Cecilia, crossed themselves and chanted amen in unison.

A large group of parishioners that knew the family, including Thelma Bompensiero, who had come with her fifteen-month-old daughter, also joined the mourners. Frank would have accompanied his young family, but he was serving a sentence for a Prohibition violation that would take him to McNeil Island near Tacoma, Washington, the very next day. He would not be released for another year.

Copious yards and varieties of black fabric, styled into long dresses, shawls, jackets, trousers, veils, and women's hats, cloaked the huddled mass assembled in the front pew: Emilio, dark circles underlying bloodshot eyes, shoulders drawn in and down, sat closest to the aisle with his arm draped over Rosa, who wailed in anguish as the service for Tina began and blotted her tears with a handkerchief she had tucked in the sleeve of her dress.

Ilario knelt next to his mother, accompanied by his cousin Gabriella, who tended to young Vito. A sobbing fifty-eight-year-old Augustina knelt next to her eldest daughter, and Giuseppe Erbi, wearing all of his sixty-four years, sat at the end of the family pew with arms crossed and chin tucked against his chest. The Spokane contingent of family had hastily made train arrangements after learning of Tina's death, arriving in San Diego only the day before. Gabriella, who at age forty-two no longer bristled when referred to as a spinster, had immediately assigned herself to the care and well-being of her nephew.

Switching from Latin to Italian, Father Rabagliati formally initiated the rite, reciting the Apostles' Creed. This prayer, jointly recited by the congregation with the priest, was followed by a litany of approximately sixty devotions initiated by Rabagliati and completed by the attendees. The priest then read one of the Sorrowful Mysteries and recited two more prayers before concluding with a sign of the cross.

At the conclusion of Rabagliati's service, those in attendance that chose to approach Tina's open casket cued in a single row for the visitation. The Erbi family remained in their pew until each of the mourning and morbidly curious, determined to examine whether the mortician had successfully camouflaged her wounds, stood or knelt before the mahogany coffin, lined with virginal white satin crepe and embossed with a sunray design in the corner of the head cap panel.

A casket spray of gladioli, carnations, and roses in shades of pink and purple lay at her feet, and a cornucopia of ostentatious floral arrangements surrounded her, all having been provided by Matranga and his LA boss Frank Dragna, who a year ago had replaced Joseph "Iron Man" Ardizzone as capo. Dragna had been feeling generous after recently completing a peacemaking campaign with the National Crime Syndicate on the East Coast to atone for a conflict among branches that his predecessor had caused.

Following tonight's service, tomorrow's funeral, and hours lapsing into days that bled into weeks of mourning, the family would agree that Gabriella should move in with her sister and brother-in-law to serve as surrogate mother to Vito. They also decided that Giuseppe and Augustina would return to Spokane, sell their home, and relocate to San Diego, where they would live with the extended Erbi family in a roomy, two-story Craftsman home in Mission Hills.

April 14, 1931
Tuesday, 10:15 a.m.

3

Ari sat at his father's desk at the rear of Erbi Realty with his elbows propped on the desk and his hands covering his face. His hair— usually neatly slicked back—fell disheveled to one side. He promised his father, who remained at home comforting Augustina, that he would evaluate the state of their legitimate and illegitimate business, the latter of which had been entrusted to one of Matranga's associates in the Erbis' absence.

On the realty side of the ledger, the Depression continued its drag on construction. However, just prior to Tina's death, Erbi Realty had landed a contract to represent Cliff May. May, born in San Diego in 1908, began as a young man building Monterey-style furniture. By 1931, he had established an office in Vista and started working as a designer and builder of homes in the area.

A review of the books Ari cared most about revealed a modest dip in income from numbers, protection services, and bootlegging. He could not discern whether the contraction could be attributed to the lagging economy or lack of family oversight.

On his first day back to the office since his sister's funeral, Ari found it difficult to concentrate or care. Figures on the ledger pages bled red with images his mind painted of the cruelty his sister had endured on the day of her death. His head began to reel; his stomach churned.

Nothing, he thought, *will ever fill this hole in my heart.* Ari sat back and rubbed his eyes. His mind returned to the one thing, the *only* thing that might balance the ledger of his sister's legacy. *I must be patient and bide my time*, he thought. *At the right moment, I will honor Tina's memory with Tacchino blood.*

Thirty

April 23, 1937
Friday, 10:35 a.m.

1

Five-year-old Vito clung to Gabriella's hand as they entered Marston's, but he broke loose when they passed the toy department, an attractive nuisance from his aunt's point of view. Gabriella had dressed Vito in short pants, knee socks, and a two-button jacket and promised him a milk shake at one of downtown's luncheon counters if he behaved while she shopped for cosmetics at San Diego's first department store.

Before Gabriella caught up with him, Vito had become mesmerized with a revolving searchlight airport, priced at a dollar, an expensive new Marx Toys offering.

"Look, look, Zia." Vito had switched on a battery-powered searchlight, standing nearly a foot tall amid two hangers. Three steel aircraft were displayed on the toy's almost two-square-foot tarmac. "I can make the light go 'round. Can I have it?"

"*Caro mio*, it's too expensive, and I already promised you a milk shake."

"Please, please!" Vito used a chubby hand to grasp the larger of the three transport planes. "I have to have it."

"Come now, Vito. I just need to buy a few things, and then we must go. We still need to go to the library, and then I have a meeting to attend."

Vito threw himself on the floor and began yelling.

"You're so mean. I'm going to tell Zitzi Ari."

Gabriella's face reddened as she scanned the department and noticed the stares they had attracted from other shoppers passing through. She bent over and took Vito by the hand.

"Stop that. You're causing a scene, and I don't care what you tell your uncle."

Vito pulled away.

"Then, I'm gonna have Nanna and Nanno buy it for me." Vito stuck his tongue out, got to his feet, and scurried beyond Gabriella's reach.

In the intervening years since his mother's death, Vito had developed a willfulness that befuddled Gabriella. Yet she could hardly blame the motherless child, who charmed his doting uncle and grandparents into fulfilling his every want. Despite the challenges of raising young Vito, Gabriella had gained new vitality since relocating to Southern California. She had made several friends; joined a women's gardening club, the fruits of which blossomed in the Erbi yard; and become an avid reader.

She wished Vito's great-grandfather had fared the transition from Spokane to San Diego as well. She knew her father missed his companions, customs, and surroundings, and it troubled her that he had become grumpy and had been drinking and eating in excess. Though it had pained her greatly, she was not surprised when he died of a sudden heart attack in the fall of 1934. Her mother, Augustina, who had been of frail health when she relocated, seemed to Gabriella to adjust more readily. Augustina had gushed to Gabriella about how she enjoyed San Diego's year-round temperate climate. But in early 1935, she contracted consumption and spent the remainder of her days in a sanitarium.

Gabriella took umbrage with her nephew Ari for not devoting more time to Vito. Ari, she thought, had become consumed by oversight of the Erbis' business since taking command of her brother-in-law Emilio's operations, and she worried about the veracity of disparaging rumors being spread that Ari had begun establishing ties to a Las Vegas branch of the mob.

I would think my brother-in-law would take Ari to the woodshed, she reasoned, *if he knew that his son was entangling the family in syndicated crime operations. But* Dio mio, *what if Emilio is aware, is encouraging Ari's activities? Could such connections explain my brother-in-law's ascent up San Diego's civic leadership ladder?*

Although possessing less stature than the Erbis, Carlo Tacchino had come to appreciate a career in the life that manifested wads of cash, shiny autos, and fast women for an enterprising, obedient soldier. During the day he worked as foreman at the cannery. But when called upon, he undertook lucrative assignments for friends of friends of made men. In this role, he exhibited a willingness to abide orders without question and employ his talents with fire in creative ways that brought him to the attention of the Commission, an assembly of the major mob family leaders that controlled organized crime nationally.

Despite his cozy relationship with the mob, Carlo Tacchino fretted that Emilio and Ari would hide behind their greater influence and plot to avenge Tina's death. In anticipation of such a countermove, Carlo had gathered a loyal group of thugs that accompanied him wherever he went.

No matter what scheme da Erbis craft, Carlo assured himself, *ain't nobody penetrates my human shield. Da Erbis can never touch me.*

As confident in his safety as he had become with his goon squad surrounding him, Carlo had failed to consider that an Erbi might plot a less direct course for revenge.

April 28, 1937
Wednesday, 2:05 p.m.

2

Donatella, Pasquale, and their year-old daughter, Angela, strode from their seats at Lane Field with the rumble of nearly eight thousand fans echoing in their ears after the Padres had trounced the rival Oakland

Oaks 18–3. Pasquale held Donatella's hand while cradling Angela in his other arm. Carlo's sister had met Pasquale, a sailor from New York stationed in San Diego who, after completing his navy stint, relocated permanently and asked for Donatella's hand in marriage.

With Primo's death, Donatella had grown close to her brother and depended upon him for guidance. As Carlo doted on his sister in return, she was happy that he had taken an immediate liking to the rail-thin, quick-witted Italian boy and used his connections to obtain his brother-in-law work as a short order cook in a Little Italy café. Donatella married Pasquale Belsito in June 1935, and when she became pregnant a few months after her wedding, Carlo lavished the couple with nursery furnishings, infant clothing, and baby toys.

Now, as the Belsitos exited the stadium, Donatella wished her brother Carlo, who had treated them with seats behind home plate, could have joined them. She knew Carlo, who had to work his shift at Sunset Sea Food, would have been thrilled to see the Padres win. Donatella had expressed little enthusiasm about attending the early afternoon contest and rolled her eyes when her husband bombarded her with facts prior to the game:

As they drove to the game, Pasquale told her, "The Padres' owner, Bill Lane, relocated the team from Hollywood just last year, making this only San Diego's second year in the Pacific Coast League.

"Can you believe how gorgeous this stadium is?" Pasquale asked rhetorically as they took their seats. "Can you believe the WPA spent $20,000 to build this gem right next to the harbor at the foot of Broadway?"

Donatella's attitude had changed by game's end.

"Now you seen baseball is not boring, aye, Dona?" Pasquale gave his wife a playful poke in the rib as he chided her for her prior lack of interest.

"Murder! I had no idea."

"You should learn to trust your husband. I told you the team was good. Jimmie Reese still has spunk and that southpaw Hebert throws some heat. And, that Hoover High kid, Ted Williams, is going to burn up a lot of pitchers."

"He's number 19."

"Yah, that's him."

"I think he's cute as a bug's ear."

Pasquale dropped Donatella's hand and shifted his daughter to his other arm.

"Hey, you're a married woman. You can't be talking like that." He gave her a playful jab in the upper arm.

"I didn't say I wanted to share a honey cooler with him." She batted her eyes. "You know you're the only man I want to hug and kiss."

Pasquale handed Angela to Donatella and opened the passenger door of their '32 Ford sedan, another gift from Carlo. He walked around the car, got behind the wheel, and started the maroon Ford's V–8 engine. He engaged the car in gear and steered southward on Harbor Drive toward the canneries, where they had told Carlo they would pick him up for supper at their home. Pasquale concentrated on the road, which had become partially obscured by fog drawn in by the unusually cool afternoon weather, while Donatella doted over her daughter. He failed to notice a pea-green-and-dark-blue Chevy roadster pickup approaching from behind.

Donatella screamed and the couple pitched forward when without warning their sedan's rear bumper was jolted by the truck. The Belsito car shuddered and slid toward the right edge of the roadway, allowing the Chevy to pull alongside. Before Pasquale could fully regain control, the pickup's driver wheeled his truck into the side of the Ford, slowed, and then regained speed, using the rapid acceleration to ram the car's left-rear quarter panel and force it to tumble from the roadway into the harbor.

April 28, 1937
Wednesday, 5:30 p.m.

3

As soon as he received news of a vehicle accident involving his sister's family, Carlo rushed to the hospital. Pasquale, Carlo had learned, had managed to escape the family's car as it plunged into the harbor, but nearly succumbed as he dove repeatedly into the frigid water, attempting to rescue his wife and daughter.

Not knowing the full extent or any details of the accident, Carlo ran into the emergency ward lobby and buttonholed a doctor and police officer he heard speak Pasquale's name as he charged by. The officer calmed Carlo down and led him to a seat in the hospital's intake area, while the doctor consulted briefly with a member of his staff. A nurse and an orderly with hot coffee quickly joined the officer and Carlo.

"What's happened to my family?" Carlo cried repeatedly. The orderly handed Carlo the coffee and departed.

"Mr. Belsito is your brother-in-law?" The officer inquired as he stood over Carlo. Carlo nodded.

"Mr. Belsito and his daughter, your niece, suffered only very minor injuries. They are fine, and you will be able to see them shortly."

Carlo tensed in anticipation of the officer's next statement.

"I'm sorry, Mr. Tacchino, but Mrs. Belsito, your sister, did not survive the incident."

Carlo's scream reverberated within the room and echoed into the general waiting area. He turned to the nearest wall, pounding it with balled fists and cursing in between wails of anguish. Carlo had to be subdued by the attending nurse, the officer, and two orderlies, who managed to settle him into a chair.

"How did dis happen? Why would Pasquale drive his car into the harbor?"

"Why don't we take a few moments to regain our composure before ..." The nurse stopped short as Carlo raged to his feet and pushed her aside.

"I've got a fuckin' right. I gotta know now," Carlo boomed, his face tightening and skin reddening.

"Please sit down, Mr. Tacchino." The officer stepped closer as he spoke.

"I'll do that when you answer da question."

The policeman glanced at the nurse and shrugged.

"Okay, you get back in the chair and calm down, and I'll tell you what we know."

Carlo stammered, ran his hands through his hair, then meekly sat.

"Witnesses at the scene," the officer began slowly, "and Mr. Pasquale report that your family was driving southward on Harbor Drive when their vehicle was forced from the road by an older model pickup that sped away after making contact at least twice."

"Some *bastardo* ran dem off da road?" Carlo clenched his fists and bolted to his feet.

"Please, Mr. Tacchino. If you can't control yourself, then I can't continue."

Carlo blustered, sighed, and then sagged into his seat.

"That's better. Apparently Mr. Belsito escaped the vehicle and dove several times under the surface. He reported finding his daughter, Angela, floating just outside the front passenger window. He got her to the surface, left her in the hands of a gathering crowd, and then continued diving.

"Mr. Belsito said when he reached the car again, he found Mrs. Belsito attempting to free herself through the open passenger window. He reached for her arms and pulled, but her foot had become entrapped. Mr. Belsito said he motioned for her to move back from the window—I would imagine an extraordinary effort considering an intuitive compulsion to do just the opposite.

"He said that once he had succeeded in entering the vehicle, he grappled with her trapped foot and freed her. At this stage, he said, Mrs. Belsito was no longer struggling. Witnesses reported that Mr. Belsito burst onto the surface gasping for air with his wife slung over his shoulder.

"Again, Mr. Tacchino, I offer my condolences. Mrs. Belsito did not regain consciousness."

Before the officer had completed his account, Carlo suspected who had been responsible and why. He also knew instinctively that neither the truck, if and when found, nor any other evidence would be tied back to the perpetrator.

Even if da cops do figure dis out, he thought, *I ain't gonna sit 'round waitin' for da courts.*

October 27, 1937
Friday, 4:45 p.m.

4

Carlo Tacchino, clad in black from head to foot in recognition of his continued state of mourning, trod the rear fire escape of Erbi Realty as stealthily as a tomcat tailing an unsuspecting rat. He removed his shoes at its apex before sliding through a window at the end of a hallway that contained the Erbi Realty offices. He had spent several days casing the space, memorizing the Erbis' daily routines, the contents of the office, the furniture and its composition, the locations of electrical fixtures, the source of heating, and the existence and direction of any drafts. Early in the day, he had ensured that the window through which he gained entry was unlocked.

From his reconnaissance, he knew Ari and his father would stop working early, as they did every Friday, in order to engage in a low-stakes game of pool. Emilio's passion for the game required that a billiard table be located within spare office space. Carlo placed an ear to the door.

"But for your Mama, the wonderful woman she is," Carlo heard Emilio say, "I would call you a cheating son of a bitch."

"I don't cheat, Pops. Face it. You're just losing your touch."

"*Vaffangul'*, you little shit. How much do I owe you this time?"

"Not enough to break the bank."

"Fine. I'm going home to Rosa. We can settle later."

"Sure thing, Pops."

Carlo moved down the hallway and out of sight and waited, knowing from his reconnaissance that Emilio would be pulling on his suit jacket and grabbing his hat before departing. He heard the office door open and steps that would be Emilio's pad down the hall. He waited a few moments, and then stationed himself next to the door, knowing that Ari would be exiting Erbi Reality at exactly 5:05 p.m.

As the handle turned and the door began to swing inward, Carlo lunged, using his weight and the force of the heavy, wooden monolith to drive the unsuspecting Erbi backward. Ari moaned, stumbled, and fell back, hitting his head on a desk. Carlo pounced, dropping both knees on Ari's upper torso. Ari grunted as air hissed from his lungs. He thrashed his arms as Carlo brought his gloved hands to Ari's throat. With little or no oxygen left to fuel his struggle, Ari quickly succumbed.

Carlo didn't bother to ensure that Ari had died. He doubted that he had. Carlo wanted Ari to suffer long and painfully as he descended into the hell he had earned. He employed his skill with arson to set the scene, relying on his knowledge of the innumerable ways to ignite a fire, camouflaging his effort so that an ensuing inferno would appear to have been ignited by an electrical short, faulty furnace, bare wire, or improperly stored chemicals, and the manner and speed in which flames spread depending upon myriad conditions, such as environment, temperature, or man-made accelerants.

The twenty-four-year-old removed Ari's jacket and hat, placed them back on the coat rack, and repositioned an unconscious Ari in his seat next to the desk. Carlo then removed from his own jacket pocket a bottle filled with a highly flammable but difficult-to-detect liquid and splashed the contents on Ari's trouser cuffs and the floor. After slipping a cigarette from a pack resting on Ari's desk, Carlo lit it with one of Ari's matches, and let it drop to the floor next to Ari's feet.

Carlo waited for confirmation that his work had been properly implemented. He watched Ari's body twitch and convulse and heard Ari's scream. He scanned the room for any minute piece of evidence that he may have left inadvertently, and then stepped out the door, closing it softly behind him.

Thirty-One

July 12, 1990
Thursday, 12:25 p.m.

1

Nick wondered if it was sheer coincidence that Carlo Tacchino had chosen to meet him at John Tarantino's Italian and Seafood Restaurant on North Harbor Drive. He knew from his previous time in San Diego that Tarantino, a fifty-nine-year-old native of San Diego's Little Italy, had enjoyed cooking for celebrities, including comedian Jerry Lewis and columnist Walter Winchell. Another notorious figure who had considered Tarantino's his favorite was Frank Bompensiero.

Prior to requesting a meeting, Nick returned to the library, where he scoured every available resource for additional connections between the Erbi and Tacchino families. The tedious effort of pawing through the card catalog, scrutinizing the vertical files, and scanning microfiche until his eyes burned, generated little in solid evidence. But he had discovered reports of incidents containing one or both of the surnames that fact-checked back to relatives of Vito and Carlo. Standing alone, his findings meant little.

Nick thought, *The accumulated record of over fifty years of suspicious incidents, however, can't be mere coincidence.*

Dottie, the restaurant's long-time manager, stopped by the table to inquire how Nick was doing. *No doubt,* Nick thought, *she wonders why I've been nursing a cup of coffee and leafing through* The Union *for nearly twenty minutes.* He glanced at his watch. *Make that twenty-five minutes.*

Turning back to his newspaper, he skimmed an article reporting that Saddam Hussein had used his Revolutionary Day speech to complain to OPEC about Kuwait allegedly stealing oil from an Iraqi field near their shared border. As he read that Hussein had threatened war, Nick became aware of a minor commotion just inside the restaurant's entrance. Nick's face reflected the question mark that floated in his mind as a healthy-looking, tall brunet in his early forties, wearing khaki slacks, canvas boat shoes, and a gold-buttoned navy blazer assisted his portly companion through the entry.

Carlo's cane clattered against the glass entry as he swung his girth through the door and plodded toward Nick's table. A trademark Nazionali, burdened with substantial ash, dangled from the corner of his fat lips. His companion, who Nick immediately recognized as Maria's client Sal, followed behind; his face revealing a why-the-fuck-do-I-have-to-be-here glaze.

As Carlo approached, Nick rose to greet him, simultaneously allowing his lips to part and rise slightly upward as he extended his right hand. The old man, who appeared to Nick to be wearing all of his seventy-seven years, waved off the proffered handshake; choosing instead to cock his head side-to-side and wink. Nick shrugged, accepted a milquetoast shake from Sal, then returned to his seat.

Sal's unexpected attendance led Nick to conclude that Carlo should select the tune for their ensuing three-party waltz. Wan-faced and struggling for breath, Carlo fell into a seat directly across from Nick, hooking his weathered, wooden cane on the table's edge. His companion grunted as he sat between the two.

"Dis here's my associate from LA, Salvatore Caputo." Carlo spoke in a gravelly whisper. Nick noticed that Carlo's hands were shaking. His face looked chalky; behind dusty lenses, his matte-finish, coal eyes projected ambivalence. "Sal, dis here's Nick Lanouette."

Nick nodded. Sal's menacing ebony eyes suggested no apparent response as his gaze drilled into Nick's forehead. The waitress arrived with glasses of water, dealt the menus that had been tucked under her arm, and ticked off a list of nightly specials. Nick paid little attention.

Regardless of its quality, I doubt I'll be savoring whatever I order, Nick thought.

Sal's eyes moved in sync with the rhythm of the young, full-figured waitress's sway as she sashayed from the table. Carlo's attention followed Sal's.

"*Che bella bombella,* aye, Sal?"

Nick detected sarcasm in Carlo's tone. Sal snapped his head back to face Carlo and Nick.

Even though the slick bastard seems to be calling the shots tonight, Nick surmised, *maybe Carlo's got the power to embarrass him for ogling instead of minding the business at hand.*

"Nice ass and legs, all right," Sal said flatly. "If *this* business doesn't drag on too long, maybe I'll invite her into the men's room and treat to her to some fresh salami."

Carlo's eyes flickered in Nick's direction before he cast them downward and stared at his hands. Nick glanced at Sal and then returned his attention to Carlo.

"I didn't realize we were going to be a threesome, Carlo." Nick picked up his mug and sipped his coffee.

"Carlo's getting on in years, Mr. Lanouette, as you know," Sal responded in Tacchino's stead. "It seems lately *some* people been having a little trouble understanding him when he speaks, so I'm here to translate, as necessary."

"That so, Carlo?" Nick continued to focus on Carlo. "Can Sal here shed some light on the bad blood between the Tacchinos and Erbis dating back several decades?"

"It's outta my hands now, son. I've been let out tah pasture, and Sal here's been made my shepherd."

Sal glared at Carlo and cleared his throat.

"As I believe Carlo has indicated clearly in the past, you should drop this cloak-and-dagger preoccupation with Vito Erbi. These types of obsessions, as I'm sure Carlo told you, often lead to troubling health conditions."

"Is that a threat, Sal?

Sal looked as though his Italian mother had just accused him of stealing from the cookie jar.

"Mr. Lanouette, what an unkind thought." Sal's expression morphed; his lips curled, one thick eyebrow arched higher than the other, and his eyes cast frozen ropes. "I never threaten, Nick. I've always found 'or else' to be so superfluous."

July 12, 1990
Thursday, 3:00 p.m.

2

Maria perused a magazine as she sat at Naomi's desk in her apartment-*cum*-massage parlor. She agreed to "hold down the fort," as Naomi called it, while Naomi went to an appointment with her ob-gyn. No massage clients had been scheduled, and walk-in traffic had been sparse, so Maria assumed she could leave the phone unattended for a brief bathroom break. She secured the lock on the screen door before entering the restroom and closing its door behind her. Just prior to flushing the toilet, she heard scratching noises coming from the front of the apartment. She assigned their source to a mangy cat that Naomi had fed a few times without considering long-term consequences.

Maria stood before the bathroom mirror, feathered her hair with her fingertips, applied a fresh coat of clear lip gloss, and arranged her breasts so as to enhance her cleavage. Satisfied that she had achieved the desired affect, she opened the door and noticed that the screen door was ajar. *Great*, she thought as she crossed the living room area to secure the screen. *The damned lock must be broken.*

As she reached out to close the door, a figure coming from the kitchen entered her peripheral view. Before she could register that someone had broken in, a gloved hand swung in front of her face and covered her mouth while a second hand and arm enwrapped her waist. She bit hard on the gloved fingers and screamed, both to no avail. She felt faint; her mind became cloudy and her vision surreal.

Having successfully employed a doctored glove to administer chloroform, Maria's assailant dragged her body into the front bedroom and bound her feet and hands with duct tape acquired from a small duffle bag he had carried with him. He then stuffed her mouth with a handkerchief secured with tape as well and retraced his steps into the living room, where he locked the screen and front doors. Satisfied that he wouldn't be interrupted by surprise, Sal Caputo strode back to the bedroom, knelt by Maria's side, and withdrew a 'Nam-era SOG from its ankle sheath. He put the blade to the duct tape that bound her feet and hands, and tugged off her shoes, layered floral skirt, and thong before lifting her over his shoulder and delivering her in a sitting position on the massage table. He held her against his upper torso as he pulled her bustier and bra over her head and tossed them to the floor.

Sal admired Maria's braless breasts as he positioned her face up on the table, restrained her arms above her head with handcuffs taken from his bag, and then bound her upper torso to the massage table with nylon cord. Next he spread her legs, binding each individually to supports at the foot of the bench. Stepping back from his work, he took a moment to survey Maria's body, scanning downward from the dark nipples that crowned each pert mound to her flat stomach that rose and fell in rhythm with her shallow breathing, and then to her uniformly sculpted, inset navel—an element of female anatomy he found particularly erotic when adorning a svelte woman's torso.

He paused at this point, withdrew a cigar container from his shirt pocket, and slipped out a prepunched Montecristo. He closed his eyes, savored the intense, slightly spicy, sweet notes, and then ran his tongue along its circumference. After lighting his cigar and relishing the smoke's mingling of sweet and bitter wooden accents, Sal turned his attention back to Maria. As he waited for her to awaken, Sal walked the gloved fingers of one hand across her stomach, combing them through her groomed pubis and then tracing the outline of her vulva as he continued to puff on his Montecristo.

Maria floated on a puffy cloud, enveloped by the aroma of burning wood and spice. She felt mounting sensual arousal stimulated by caresses of her genitals and a tongue dancing over her nipples. She moaned; her eyes flickered. A smile came to her face as she imagined the attentiveness of her last real lover. She raised her arms to envelop him, but something was wrong. Her arms would not obey her command. Her legs refused to move. Her vision cleared, and as cognition returned, her brows arched and her eyes snapped open. She pulled her chin in and her head down; felt her face flush, then turn ashen. She screamed, but emitted only a gurgle.

"Such a shame that you awoke when you did, Maria." Sal's facial expression encapsulated Brueghel's depiction of lechery. "We were both having such a good time."

Maria wriggled, straining against her bindings and whipping her head from side to side.

"Relax, honey. I mean you no harm *yet*."

Sal unbuttoned his shirt and let it fall to the floor. As he unbuckled his trousers, Maria's eyes dilated like a camera lens advancing to f/2 aperture. Her body quaked. Sal continued puffing his cigar intermittently as he removed his shoes, socks, and trousers. By the time he removed his briefs, Maria could see he had become aroused.

"I know that sweet cunt of yours is drooling now that you've caught sight of my manhood." He shifted his smoke to the corner of his mouth as he spoke. "But unfortunately, business has to come before pleasure."

Maria once again railed against her bindings while vocalizing gurgles and gasps, noises that would have been screams were she not gagged. Sal stepped to the edge of the table.

"You and your new boyfriend are so fucking dense I apparently have to spell this out." Sal took a draw from his Montecristo before continuing. "Make no mistake, my little *putana*. I'd rather just finish you off right here and now and be done with all this shit, but ..." Sal shrugged his shoulders. "My orders are to give you and that writer pest one more chance.

"So here's how it's coming down. You sashay that tight little ass of yours back to Frisco, never look back, leave Lanouette behind for me to ... shall I say 'care for,' and you're free to do what the fuck you want with the rest of your life."

Maria shook her head frantically and bucked against her restraints.

"Yeah. That's how I hoped you would respond."

Sal paused. His eyes widened and his lips parted, revealing an upper row of teeth. As he continued to leer at Maria, he rolled his cigar between his fingers; then tucked it between his lips again and inhaled.

"Assuming you feel the necessity, it's up to you to convince Li'l Nickie to take his nose out of ... my *family's* affairs. You succeed, and he can go back to his wife in Oregon or shack up with you in Frisco for all I care. Of course, I don't give a shit how you do it. Maybe you buy him off with a chunk of the illicit income you derive from this place. Or ...”

Maria shifted her head and froze Sal in focus. He met her scorn with a beady gaze and subtly upturned lips, a facial expression her father might have described as a "shit-eating grin."

"You could rely on your talents. I'd happily arrange to snap some shots of you and the kid in flagrante delicto. Once that ball-and-chain of his sees what he's been up to ... well, you catch the drift."

He took a long drag on the Montecristo; a cloud of smoke rose slowly to the ceiling.

"Changing that arrogant bastard's mind won't be easy though, will it, Sweet Meat? We both know he'll insist on plowing forward no matter how you try to dissuade him. If you tell him about our chat today or give any inkling about your real motivation for abandoning Vito Erbi, he'll go running to the cops for help and protection."

Sal sucked hard on his cigar, exhaled, and took interest in a ribbon of smoke that rolled over Maria's face.

"Please understand that if either of you go to the cops, you'll be in my clutches before SDPD can dispatch a single patrol car."

Maria closed her eyes and turned her head away. Sal shifted his gaze down the length of her body and back to her face, placing his left hand on her right breast and massaging her nipple with his thumb. Her cool, damp skin tightened as she squirmed under his touch.

"To be honest, I really hope you don't succeed. These little games we keep playing are worse than jacking off." Maria heard Satan channeled through Sal's ensuing chortle. "Besides, as you may have guessed, I can make the Marquis de Sade seem like a harmless pantywaist."

Sal mounted the massage table, kneeling between Maria's legs.

"Now, open wide, Sweet Thing. I ain't leaving without a piece of your skinny little ass. Consider it down payment on the price for your foolish perseverance."

Thirty-Two

January 12, 1952
Saturday, 7:00 p.m.

Giovanni Rosso pushed back his plate and set his fork to the side. He and his wife Leonora had joined Rosabella and Emilio for dinner at the Erbi residence, a once customary social evening that had waned in recent years. Emilio blamed their friendship's deterioration on Giovanni's discomfort with Emilio's increasingly obvious involvement in criminal enterprise.

Ironically, Emilio thought as he eyed his friend, *I bet it is those very entanglements that prompted Giovanni to suggest this get-together.*

Emilio turned his gaze to his wife as Giovanni addressed her.

"Rosa, your meal was once again wonderful, but I swear you'll be the death of me. Whenever I eat your cooking, I can't stop stuffing myself."

"Stop that, Giovanni." Rosa waved her hand in a disarming gesture. "You eat like a *piccione*. Here, let me serve you more pasta."

"Please, Rosa, I'll bust."

Leonora patted her husband on the shoulder and gestured to her plate.

"Truly, Rosa, your food is marvelous as always, but if this is eating like a bird, Gio and I will soon grow to be flying elephants."

"But you haven't even had dessert yet," Rosa protested. "I made chocolate chip *cannoli*."

Emilio perused his guests' faces and then turned to Rosabella.

"Rosa, maybe you and Leonora should clear the table while Giovanni and I have a little chat. You two can join us in the living room when you're done. By then our guests will have digested their dinner and made room for coffee and cannoli."

Without waiting for a reply, Emilio nodded to Giovanni, rose in his chair, and excused himself from the table. He approached his old friend, who had stood up as well, placed an arm over his shoulder, and led him out of the dining room to an overstuffed sofa. Emilio sat in an armchair directly across from Giovanni and offered him a cigarette from a gold case. Emilio lit the smoke Giovanni had selected and then his own.

"Now, *caro amico*, what is it I can do for you?"

Giovanni shifted his weight, took three rapid puffs on his cigarette, then set it in an ashtray. He gripped the arms of the chair and met Emilio's gaze.

"Milio, I hate to bother you about this. It's just that I have a very close associate—you may have heard of him, Joel Morse, a distributor to taverns of sodas, fruit juices, and snacks."

"I see. This is about Gold Enterprises, no?"

"I'm sorry to trouble you, but ..."

"Nothing you might ask, my friend, is trouble."

Giovanni nodded and smiled thinly.

"You know, Milio, since Bompensiero, Fratianno, and their associates established Gold Enterprises last year, union members like my friend Joel that have depended on their distribution contracts with the bars can no longer making a decent living. I know Gold has relied on your financial acumen and civic connections, especially your ties to the mayor, so I thought perhaps you could have a word with Frank or Jimmy."

"What is it, assuming I had any such say, that you would want me to tell them, Giovanni?"

"Joel Morse is a good, hard-working man, Milio. A fine husband with a growing family to feed." Giovanni took a drag from his cigarette. "He's also a strong supporter of the union."

"Ah, yes, always the unions, aye, my friend?" Emilio stood and walked to a curio cabinet. "I feel like some port. You'll have some with me?"

Giovanni nodded and continued the conversation as Emilio secured two small tumblers and tipped a large pour into both. As he returned to his chair, he handed Giovanni a glass, sat back and took a sip, and then reached for his cigarette.

"My concern, Milio, has always been for the little guy, you know that. Have you forgotten how we met?"

"Giovanni, please, you hurt my feelings. You know I've always shared your interest in workers' welfare, but the time for unions is over, especially here. I bet your friend has been paying dues for years and years, and look what that's come to."

"But Milio ..."

"No *but*, my friend: you know my employees—none of them unionists—earn a comfortable wage, and we take care of them and their families' welfare, when needed."

"At what price, though?"

"Far less than Mr. Morse's dues, you can be sure." Emilio took a sip of port and raised a finger to advise Giovanni he had not completed his thought. "And, look at me. Look what a little hard work and dedication can do, if a man puts his mind to it."

"You can't compare yourself and what you've done ..."

"Don't, my friend. Besides, what makes you think I can be of the help to this Morse fellow and his family?"

Giovanni stiffened, set his glass down, and leaned in toward Emilio.

"Milio, really?"

"And, what does that mean?"

"Come on, Milio, we go back too far for you to play that kind of game with me." Giovanni waved his arm and scanned the room. "You think I don't know how you earned all of this ... or about your questionable connections?"

"Gio, *amico mio*, you are ruining a fine evening among friends."

"Friends? Friends don't ..."

"Friends don't run their mouths about things they don't understand."

223

Leonora had finished a funny story as the women entered the room. Their giggles trailed off as they noted their husbands' demeanor. Giovanni stubbed his cigarette into an ashtray and bolted to his feet.

"Thank you so much for the wonderful meal, as always, Rosa." He strode to Rosabella and gave her a kiss on the cheek and a hug. "Leonora, please grab your coat. Unfortunately, we must take our leave."

"But you haven't had dessert yet," Rosabella protested. "What has happened here?"

"I'm truly sorry, Rosa." Giovanni turned his attention to Emilio, who also had risen from his seat. "I can't believe what you've become, Milio. I've closed my eyes to piles of dirty laundry you've accumulated over the years, but this cuts it."

As Giovanni and Leonora exited the Erbi home, tears came to Rosabella's eyes. She turned to her husband.

"Emil, what has happened?"

"It's nothing, Rosa. Gio has become a *Communista*. Marx has made him a foolish *culorosso*. We have many other good friends with better manners."

Thirty-Three

1

Vito Erbi sat at his desk in the offices of Erbi Realty, which Emilio and Vito had relocated to the new Clairemont Village Shopping center, located near the elder Erbi's new home on Takalon Street less than half of a mile southwest of the office. A framed photograph of Vito's uncle Ari rested on his desk. He scanned the morning newspaper while waiting for Emilio to return for a meeting his uncle had requested.

In the aftermath of the fire, Emilio moved his business temporarily to a second downtown location. During this time, Vito continued to be raised by his Zia Gabriella and doted upon by his grandparents. As a gift for his grandson's twenty-first birthday, two years earlier, Emilio invited Vito to assist him in relocating the business in a new part of the city and to join Erbi Realty as a junior partner.

Vito had just completed the sports section when his grandfather entered carrying a grocery bag. Based on Emilio's demeanor, Vito thought, he could just as well be meeting with an undertaker. Without a word, Emilio gestured for his grandson to join him in his office, where Emilio removed a bottle of Chianti from the grocery sack, retrieved tumblers from a side table, and poured them each a glass.

"What is it?"

"Please, Vito, *sedersi*. It is time you and I have a talk. You are a man now. There are things you must know. First, we *salud* your momma and Zitzi Ilario."

Vito shrugged, picked up his glass, and joined his grandfather in his brief toast.

"I am an old man now, *caro mio*, and the time has come for me to tell you things before I join your mother and uncle in heaven." The corners of Emilio's lips curled slightly upward. His eyes glistened as he took his grandson's measure. "You have earned the right to know why your mother, your uncle, and also your father were taken from you before you had the years to understand."

Vito rolled his tumbler between his hands. An eyebrow shot up, he wrinkled his nose, and his mouth raised upward on one side. Emilio raised his glass to his mouth, finished its contents, and then revealed the truth.

"You're telling me that Ari killed my father, that ... that the Tacchinos killed my mother and uncle?"

Vito's jaw thrust forward and his head dropped. Fire raged in his eyes as his eyebrows lowered and his lids tightened. His mouth fell open, and then he jumped from his chair and threw his glass, which shattered when it hit the office floor.

"And ... and I'm a fucking Tacchino myself?"

"Please, *caro mio*, sit down. We need to discuss this calmly, like gentlemen."

"Not *like* gentlemen, Nanno. I'm a fuckin' half-breed, but I have the balls to do what is necessary to honor my mother, as you should have done years ago."

Emilio rose, moved to Vito's side, and placed a hand on his grandson's shoulder.

"*La vendetta è un piatto che si gusta freddo, figlio.*"

Vito pulled away.

"What the hell does that mean?"

"My boy, you forget your Italian?"

"No, I understood the words. Some old country saw about not seeking revenge in anger. You've certainly had plenty of time to cool off, and what have you done?"

A sharp, flat hand rap burned Vito's cheek.

"Don't be a hot-headed young fool. You think my loss ... yes, it is mine, too ... no longer gives me pain every day? I have lost both my children over this *follia*."

"This ... this craziness, as you call it, you've known about all these years and done nothing?"

"We must obey our faith, Vito. Revenge can be taken only by our Savior. Come sit down. Let's finish our talk."

Emilio led his grandson back to his chair and then sat on the edge of the desk to be close.

"Now, *caro mio*, what would you have me do? Carlo is a made man surrounded by security thugs and with strong connections to LA and Chicago. You think you or I can just rub out Tacchino and walk away? What is done is done, Vittorio. Let things be.

"Your grandmother and I ... we suffer much, yes, but I have learned one simple truth: *Chi campa senza conti, muore senza canti.* Concentrate on making the money, boy. That will make for the sweet, winning song; *un canto* made sweet by wealth and power that someday we can use to drown our enemies."

Vito held his tongue ... for now.

December 8, 1954
Wednesday, 9:00 a.m.

2

Emilio stood before a mirror at his sink, shaving in preparation for a meeting Vito and he would have with C. Arnholt Smith later that morning at Smith's Westgate-California Tuna Packing Company. Snagging Smith as a client would be a major triumph for Erbi Realty, and Emilio greeted the opportunity enthusiastically, especially because Vito, whom Emilio noted had been keeping his distance since their argument, had been responsible for luring Smith's interest.

Emilio's own research revealed that Smith came to San Diego as a child from Walla Walla, Washington, and left high school in San Diego to become a grocery clerk. After that brief stint, he became a messenger for the Bank of Italy. By 1933, Smith had amassed enough savings, combined with money loaned by his older brother, to buy a controlling interest in the United States National Bank. That same year, he also acquired the California Iron Works, which had been established in 1905 as a small machine shop and foundry.

By 1949, Smith had changed the company's name to the National Steel and Shipbuilding Company (NASSCO) to reflect its expansion into ship construction. Now that Smith had developed a shipbuilding behemoth that rivaled Campbell Industries and had become owner of the Westgate-California Tuna Packing Company, Emilio had been told that Smith wanted to turn his attention to civic projects and real estate.

Emilio, even at an advancing age, kept many channels of communication open, and through these links had become aware that Vito had been nurturing an independent source of contacts. Through this network, Emilio learned of Vito's backdoor efforts. Rather than confront Vito about his independent streak, Emilio chose to wait for his grandson to approach him about this new business opportunity.

December 8, 1954
Wednesday, 11:15 a.m.

3

Smith, a slim, well-tanned man of some physical stature, sat at a conference table within his offices wearing his characteristically cheerful mien along with trademark Buster Brown shoes and brown suit. Several business associates surrounded him. Smith regaled his guests with anecdotes about his business acumen and accomplishments. Emilio considered the small talk an inevitable prelude to the meeting's true purpose.

"Gentlemen, let's talk some business, shall we?" The dark-haired entrepreneur's mouth revealed a picket fence of glossy white.

Assessing Smith's mannerisms along with the pomp on his head, high forehead, large ears, long nose, and cleft chin, Emilio considered the man to be a bit of a prig. Despite his reservations, he respected the money and power Smith had amassed. Emilio and Vito leaned in as Smith continued.

"First, I want to remind you of the waiver you signed a few moments ago. Nothing—I mean absolutely nothing—of what we discuss here today leaves this room. Understood?" Smith's wide-set eyes paused on each individual in the room as he recorded their nods and oral assents.

"I have been conducting negotiations to purchase the Padres. If I am successful, and I expect to be, I can't have *my* team playing in that termite resort down at Lane Field." He now directed his attention to the Erbis. "I need you two gentlemen to represent me in the acquisition of a new site in Mission Valley.

"If you accept my offer, you will head a front company seeking to purchase the land. If the landowner were to learn that I or one of my holdings had an interest, the acquisition costs would skyrocket. Once we have the land, we can provide the city and the team with a structure that is clean, modern, and classic in its simplicity."

Smith spent the next several minutes detailing his plans, confirming individual assignments, and answering questions. He scanned the room for any additional comments or queries, took a sip of water from a tall glass sitting before him, and then made a sweeping gesture encompassing all in attendance, except Emilio and Vito.

"Now, if you don't mind, boys, I would like to spend a few moments with our new land acquisition partners."

Once the room had cleared, Smith asked the Erbis to move closer. He spoke in low, firm tones.

"Don't get your hopes up too high, men." Smith's eyes twinkled and his mouth turned characteristically upward. "I don't intend to pay you any more than the going rate for your real estate services. However, I know that building my Westgate Park in the heart of what some local officials consider a pastoral Eden will be as controversial as hell.

"I expect to encounter a number of cold shoulders down at City Hall. This is where I understand you or some of your associates could offer some assistance for which I would pay—in cash, of course—quite handsomely. I've been told on good authority that you and your colleagues possess the professional resources to apply appropriate inducement to bring any reluctant city councilmen to our side."

Thirty-Four

July 13, 1990
Friday, 4:00 p.m.

1

Michelle left her Mercedes with a valet in front of the La Jolla Regency, anticipating a relaxing weekend with her family. Just one last meeting, she thought, as she stepped inside the hotel and walked toward Michael's Lounge, where her assistant had told her she would be meeting with a potential financier for an upcoming GDE project. Her interest had been piqued by the gentleman's unwillingness to disclose the source of funds or the party he represented.

Based on the self-portrait he had painted for Michelle's assistant, the potential investor had not arrived yet, so she settled in an armchair to the side of the bar and ordered a glass of Pinot Noir for herself and an hors d'oeuvre to share with the financier. She withdrew a notepad and pen from her purse and started jotting a weekend grocery shopping list.

"Good afternoon; Ms. Gallo, I presume?"

Michelle glanced up from her notepad, bemused by the grandfatherly man who stood before her: stout, senatorial white hair combed back on the sides and top, bushy eyebrows floating over large horn-rimmed glasses. He carried a cane and wore a pale blue suit, white shirt, black-and-blue striped tie, and black shoes. Not at all the person her assistant had described.

"Mr. Tarno?"

"It's Tacchino actually, Michelle, but you may call me Carlo." Tacchino pulled out a chair and sat facing her.

"Forgive me, Mr. Tacchino ... Carlo. I thought I was meeting with a Cal Tarno, whom I was led to believe was much younger." Michelle offered her right hand.

"It is nothing. Sometimes I don't talk too clearly on da phone." The waitress approached, and Carlo ordered a Syrah, then continued. "Of course, I knew who you was as soon as I come in da room. I have an eye for da tall, beautiful Italian women ... with business acumen, of course."

Rather than clasp her hand in a shake, Carlo lowered his head and kissed the back of her hand.

"Another beautiful day in paradise, yes, Michelle?"

"Wish I had more time to enjoy it."

"Ah, time. Don't we all wish we had more?" Carlo paused to sip the wine their server brought, using the interval to contemplate his next words. "Runnin' GDE, raisin' two children, and keepin' tabs on da musician: not enough hours in da day, no?"

Michelle's right eyebrow popped upward on her forehead. The corner of her lips displayed a faint upturn.

"You seem to have me at a disadvantage, Mr. Tacchino. You've done your homework, a pleasure I've been denied."

"I've known about you and your family for many years, and I gave your assistant no way for you to learn about me or my business. I hope you've taken no offense."

"None taken."

"Good. Good. You see, Michelle, I had da pleasure of being in your father's company many times." Noting Michelle's stiff reaction to his reference, Carlo quickly added, "I know his problems must have caused much difficulty. Please accept my sympathies."

"Exactly how did you know my father, Mr. Tacchino?" Michelle spoke with an edge in her tone.

"Carlo, please." Tacchino tipped his wine glass toward Michelle and smiled. "I only knew him through shared business associates."

"I see."

Michelle put her glass to her lips and savored the wave of alcohol. They sat quietly for a few moments, taking each other's measure.

"Maybe we should discuss the business you had in mind, so we can get the weekend in paradise started."

"Of course. Of course. You depend mostly on CalPers retirement investments to fund your projects, yes?"

"Once again, you've done your homework well."

"It's my business … on behalf of the da investors I represent to know dese things. Although I regret dat I can't give names, I assure you they're most reputable and experienced investors, who'd be able to bring fifty million dollars to the table under the right conditions."

"That's impressive liquidity. Why GDE?"

"It is, I fear, a little big-headed of me, but I brought you to their attention. Business, like life, it sometimes is like da little raft on da mighty ocean. The fate of people, many very close to us, depends on the decisions we make. Some fortunate; some we regret."

"And the conditions?"

"Minor details." Carlo made a pretense of pausing and taking a swallow of wine. "GDE, with you at its helm: you've steered a smooth course. My associates, however, believe your ship is in peril because of recent actions taken by others on your behalf. My associates offer their guidance and funds simply to buoy your ship before any harm arises."

"A foreboding picture from one who has often been on the seas himself?"

"My family was in da tuna business many, many years ago."

Michelle glanced toward the bar area, feigning interest in a group of noisy vacationers that had just arrived. Carlo's demeanor and message, combined with her intuition, sparked a frightening scenario in her mind. She opted to play the hand she had been dealt, as weak as it was, and call Carlo out. She turned her gaze to him as she spoke.

"Your past may explain the nautical nature of your cautionary tale, but do I correctly sense a quid pro quo or … forgive me, a masked threat circling like a shark below the surface of your allegory?"

"Now, *I'm* offended, Michelle. I'm here simply to offer help and a little advice." Carlo removed his glasses, rubbed the indentation on the bridge of his nose, held the spectacles up to the light, and— apparently satisfied that the lenses were not smudged—slid them back in place. "As I recently pointed out to our mutual friend, Nick Lanouette, our choices *always* have consequences."

"Your advice couldn't be clearer, Mr. Tacchino." Michelle grasped her purse from the foot of her chair, selected enough cash to cover their bill, and placed it on the table. "I thank you for your time and interest, but I don't think I can accept your investors' conditions."

July 13, 1990
Friday, 8:00 p.m.

2

Shortly after slogging through the last stack of records and files in his possession, Nick began calling known associates of the Erbis, Tacchinos, and Frank Bompensiero. If he failed to receive a return call, he slated a future drop-in. Acquaintances, friends, and family members, including those involved only tangentially in organized crime—if at all—proved reluctant to break the unwritten code of *omertà*. A few shared anecdotes and remembrances revealing personal traits and habits of little interest to cops, courts, and journalists.

Today Nick decided the time had come to walk in Frank Bompensiero's final footsteps. Before embarking on his journey to Pacific Beach, he leaned against the headboard of his motel bed and sipped from a cup of in-room brewed coffee while he summarized his findings and assumptions to date:

Frank Bompensiero: Ruthless hit man. Garrote, and later, gun weapons of choice. Approached job as dedicated soldier, not driven by personal vendetta. Received no compensation for unquestionably following orders from LA capos. Devoted husband who, unlike most of his ilk, never cheated. Doting father, caring son, loved and admired by those who came in daily contact.

Jack Dragna: LA capo, 1931–56. Frank's benefactor. Appoints him de facto capo of San Diego. Rewards his fidelity with Gold Rail, first of several bars Frank ultimately owns. Jack dies. Frank falls out of favor with successors (DeSimone, Licata, then Brooklier), seeks transfer to Chicago family. Subsequent loss of respect, status, motivates Frank to become an informant?

Potential Conspirators:

Jimmy Fratianno: LA caporegime, 1953–56, government witness. Would kill his own mother, distrusted Frank, yet incorporates him into trucking front when Bompensiero is released from prison in 1960. Why did Frank go to work for Jimmy? Jimmy likely knew about hit, might even be the gunman.

Acquitted threesome:

Dominic Brooklier: LA capo, 1974–84; *Lou Dragna:* caporegime, 1960s–80s; *Sam Sciortino:* underboss, 1974–79. All three charged with obstruction of justice relating to Frank's murder, all three acquitted. Had motive. Brooklier probably gave the order, might have been triggerman himself, but not likely. Dragna and Sciortino, through LA family status, had to have prior knowledge.

Shooter(s):

Carlo Tacchino: SD soldier, 1913–?. Long-standing family feud motivates disdain; not known to use firearms of any kind. Unlikely Carlo pulled trigger, but probably abetted any frame-up. Would need LA family clearance? Easily accomplished as way to take heat off? What's Carlo know he's not telling?

Salvatore Caputo(?): Mystery man, likely using an alias. Not admittedly known by anyone queried, but get impression some people recognized his description, if not "current" name. Why does Carlo seem to defer to him? Superior family rank? Is he the shooter? If so, why risk going public now?

Brooklier, Dragna, Sciortino, Fratianno, Caputo: Take your pick.

Erbis:

Vito and family: Outsiders with fringe connections to LA and Vegas family organized crime. Feud with Tacchinos dates back to Vito's mother being impregnated by Carlo's brother. Interviews, clippings imply multigeneration retaliations.

Vito, a two-bit crook, lacks street smarts of grandfather—Italian immigrant and bootlegger—and uncle Ilario "Ari," who influenced Vito. Lowlife son of a bitch with some redeeming qualities; may deserve prison for minor role in organized crime. Little if no evidence of hot temper or violent behavior. What would his motive have been? Huge payout? If so, what happened to the money? Why would

Frank's enemies hire a nonmade man, non-Sicilian with no known hit experience to do the job?

When Nick finished his summary and a second cup of coffee, he folded his notes into a shirt pocket and prepared for his drive to Pacific Beach. Now he stood at the security gate of the four-story, twenty-four-unit condo complex at 4205 Lamont, a building distinguished by its potbelly wrought iron deck rails that overshadowed a residential neighborhood constructed prior to World War II.

At around eight o'clock on the evening of February 10, 1977, Frank—as suggested by evidence collected by Nick—would have exited unit number 7, on the third floor. He probably rode the elevator to the street, lit a cigar, and strolled two and a half blocks, crossing to the other side at Reed or Thomas Avenue, in order to reach the Arco station at the southwest corner of Lamont and Grand. There he most likely entered a phone booth at the rear of the lot adjoining a paved alley. He wore dark green slacks, a short-sleeved white shirt, and a rusty brown cardigan. *Probably not unlike the one Carlo Tacchino wore that afternoon we met at the bay*, Nick thought.

Although it didn't play directly into his investigation, Nick wondered who Bompensiero had planned to call that night or whether he had completed the connection. He figured Frank did not want to use his home phone, probably because he assumed it had been tapped by the Feds for whom he had been acting as an undercover informant. He would have known that the FBI had been listening in on several occasions in the past.

At that moment, Nick recalled a particularly poignant paragraph he had gleaned from a book he came across while doing research:

> When he walked out on the street that evening to go to the Arco station, skies were clear. You could see the stars. Temperatures were in the midfifties. Lights were on in the small houses along Lamont Street. Television sets glowed from windows. People were watching *The Waltons* and *Mobil Oil Presents*. Bompensiero dialed whomever he dialed. They did or did not answer. He turned then, and started walking south on Lamont, back toward [his condo].

Before he approached the phone booth himself, Nick assessed the station's surroundings: a small convenience center with a liquor store, cleaners, and a donut shop operated across Grand; a 7–11 was situated catercorner to the Arco, and another service station operated across Lamont to the east. He walked to the front of the phone box and peered across the alley at the stucco and modest wood-trimmed home with a partial second floor tacked on just behind the fireplace chimney about midway back of the first floor.

Windows in the front east- and north-facing corners of the addition would have afforded an opportunity for the lone witness to peer down directly at Frank as he made his call. *Had the witness said she was drawn to her window by a popping sound?* He tried to approximate her view from the far side of the alley. *The gunman would have hidden here, probably behind the tall fence that demarked the station's southern boundary.* The shooter, who apparently had waited until Bompensiero finished his business, shadowed the old man southward for about a block, until he stepped off the curb at the alleyway between Thomas and Reed.

That means the witness could not have seen the actual hit, Nick surmised. *Might she have become confused, placing the popping noises she heard to a time just before Vito left the station instead of after?*

The first .22 slug entered the back of Bompensiero's balding head. Three more shots were fired in rapid succession, all hitting Frank high above the ear. When the police arrived at the scene shortly after the shooting, they found the victim, four shell casings, a partially smoked cigar, part of Frank's eyeglasses, and three dimes.

When Nick returned to his car, he noted that Michelle had left a message. *Guess I should get in the habit of lugging the phone with me,* he thought to himself. He had not acquainted himself entirely with what he considered to be a cumbersome system of having to dial to retrieve messages. As he knew he would be seeing her the next evening, Nick chose not to call back.

Thirty-Five

December 17, 1954
Friday, 12:20 p.m.

1

As Vito drove north this morning, he made two pledges to himself: Never to be anyone's bagman after today, and to die—if he must—venerating his mother's soul. Following his spat with Emilio two weeks previous, Vito had continued to roil whenever his thoughts turned, as often happened, to Emilio's lassitude when it came to defending his family's honor. His grandfather's cowardice, as Vito perceived it, would not be the legacy Emilio would bestow upon his grandson.

Vito decided his first step would be to separate himself from Erbi Realty and step out on his own. He had begun a few months earlier, fishing for associations unrelated or unknown to his grandfather.

This trip, he thought, *is the last I make as errand boy for my grandfather.*

Twenty minutes after delivering an envelope stuffed with the LA capo's share of the Erbis' San Diego take for the past two weeks, Vito tooled his virgin-white '53 Vette Roadster into a parking slot in front of Simon's Sandwiches, located across the street from the May Company department store at Fairfax and Wilshire in LA's Miracle Mile. With no plans for the rest of the afternoon, he decided to visit his favorite LA fast-food diner for a quick lunch and then Christmas shop at nearby May Company.

He shut down the Chevy's six-cylinder Blue Flame and studied a menu featuring spaghetti, chili, hamburgers, and barbeque displayed at the top of the full-length glass panes of the circular building. Vito weighed the option of a twenty-cent pork sandwich against his favorite, barbequed beef, as a tall, svelte carhop approached. Her shoulder-length, yellow tresses flowed freely beneath a bell captain hat color-coordinated with her uniform slacks and long-sleeved, vee neck top.

"Hi there, handsome. I love your machine." While the buxom blonde scanned the lines of his car and the bright red interior, Vito eyed her full lips and the contours of a blouse that accentuated a pair of breasts that strained against her bra. "What is it?"

"A Corvette."

"I've never seen one before."

"That's probably because they just came out last year, and Chevy only made three hundred of them."

"Cool. You're a lucky cat. It's gorgeous."

"Just like you, sweetheart." Vito winked and his lips parted into a wide, upward curve. A rouge hue blossomed on the carhop's cheeks.

"I bet you say that to all the girls. Now, what can I get you?"

Vito ordered the barbecued beef and a Coke, then intently ogled the pendulum sway of the blonde's ass as she strode away from the Vette. As he waited for his order to be delivered, Vito mulled over the brief conversation he had with Pauli, one of Jack Dragna's soldiers, an acne-faced, enterprising young henchman with an immaculate duck's ass do and shiny suit.

Pauli bemoaned the LA crime family's recent loss of stature and predicted that the local syndicate would focus more on prostitution, pornography, and the sex trade as a way to revive their declining empire. When Vito, scheming to make his own mark, expressed interest, Pauli regaled his experience as a procurer of women for pornography and prostitution on behalf of the *family*.

"Man, there's tons of cabbage to be made, and best of all, yah can sample the produce without cutting into the take. I mean *somebody*'s gotta make sure the goods is fresh."

"I'd love some of that kinda action."

"Cat, ain't nothin' like charmin' some babe, 'specially if she's underage. Imagine how easy it would be to lure a little high school paper shaker with a car like yours. Give the dame a ride, slip her some juice or something stronger, and then take her back to your place. Get her tipsy, put her in the right mood by showin' her one of those new split-beaver flicks, and then tell her how she could put the dishes in the flick to shame—if, of course, she's got the right body hidin' under her cheerleader outfit."

Vito raised an eyebrow and smirked.

"You sure it works just like that, Pauli?"

"Trust me, man, works eighty, ninety percent of the time, especially if you lets it drop that yah have a connect to the film industry. Then yah just leaves it there. Let her stew on it awhile. Maybe say somethin' like: 'Gees, what'm I thinkin?' You don't have no actin' experience, and your keepers probably give yah a big weekly allowance.'"

"Pauli, you're so fulla shit."

"It works for a guy like me. Think how easy it'd be for a Big Daddy like you. Once yah get her loose and naked, yah tell her yah wanna take some shots y'all need to promote her. If she's hot and willin,' pump her once or twice, and then make her your bitch, or yah can ship her ass up here to us. Either way she'll be camera- or street-ready in no time and, if she's good, a sweet cash cow."

"Sounds like a lotta time and trouble. She could go to her old man or the cops."

"She ain't spillin' to no one once yah remind her of the pics yah shot. Besides, yah just do that with the ones yah wanna fuck. Anything else yah just dope-up, rope-up, and ship up here or out to Vegas. You should chat up Hollywood when you get back down to San Dee. Yah knows him, right?"

Vito chuckled now as he sat in his Vette outside Simons. *No way I'd fall that low,* he thought. He placed an elbow on the convertible's door and propped up his chin with his hand as he watched the carhop stroll toward him with his food. *Then again, might not be a bad way to earn some easy cash. And come to think, I could use a ruse like that to settle an old score.*

"Here you go, honey. I hope you're hungry."

Vito washed his eyes over the carhop's body, soaking up the curves without attempting to conceal his interest. *Maybe I should give Pauli's seduction scheme a little spin and see what I get*, he thought.

"I'm always ready, sweetheart … to eat."

The blonde's cheeks flushed again. She diverted Vito's attention back to his roadster.

"I just can't take my eyes off your car."

"You like cars? Fast cars?"

"You kidding, hon? I'm the only girl in a family of three older brothers. One's a stock car racer; the other two build hot rods. And my father's an auto mechanic. I *have* to love 'em."

"Would you like a ride in this?"

The carhop's eyes brightened; her mouth opened; then her expression became somber.

"But I can't just leave work, and … well, I don't even know you."

"My name's Vito, Vito Erbi. My business is in San Diego, but I'm up here pretty regular to meet with associates. What's your name?"

"Greta."

"As in Garbo, huh?" Vito shot her with a finger pistol and a wink. "Well, now we know each other. What time do you punch out?"

"Oh, I don't get off until three thirty."

"That's perfect. I've got some shopping to do across the street, and the car needs a wash anyway. How 'bout I meet you here at three thirty then?

"Well, I …"

"Come on, Greta, I can tell by that look in your eye you just can't wait to tell your father and brothers about the great ride I gave yah."

"Well, actually, I could *show* them, if you would be kind enough to give me a lift home. It's only a couple of miles from here."

"My pleasure, hon."

"You're such a smooth talker. I'll call my brother and tell him not to pick me up. Wait till he hears why."

2

Hollywood and his sex trade associate rendezvoused with Vito at the Gold Rail Steak House, as had become their custom over the last few weeks. This evening the plan had been for Vito to be escorted by the duo on his first red light fishing expedition. Without informing his grandfather, Vito had made contact with Hollywood. As Pauli had predicted, the soldier heading up San Diego's sex-trafficking operations recognized the skills Vito possessed for recruiting young women.

During their first two meetings with him, Hollywood and his associate, Fast Frankie, had taken measure of Vito's capabilities over cheap drinks at the downtown bar owned by Bompensiero, his nephew Louis, and Jack Dragna's son. The twenty-five-stool bar was situated at 1028 Third Avenue near C Street, and in the heart of an area renowned by some as the "sailors' entertainment district" and others as "neon row."

No steak or food of any type was served at the Gold Rail, despite a legal requirement to do so. Vito had heard via word on the street that Bompensiero earned a reasonable profit from legitimate bar operations and supplemented that by skimming bar proceeds, which provided tax-free income. According to rumor, the bar became his reward for dedication, obedience, and the willingness to kill when and as ordered despite never receiving a dime from the mob for his work.

Vito also learned that Bompensiero, known to be a loving husband and father with a reputation for working over husbands that beat or cheated on their women, had no taste for the sex trade.

Guess it doesn't bother him, though, Vito thought, *if pimps, panderers, or other trade operatives frequent his establishment.*

To date, Vito's mentors, skilled in the art of *family*-style pandering, had briefed him about the type of young women he would be suborning for purposes of their various levels of clientele.

"Your highest-priority acquisitions," Hollywood had instructed him, "need to be nubile, naïve girls with good looks, hot bodies, and—ideally—a *Lolita* appeal. These babes, if they make the grade, get pimped to wealthy VIP clientele, who pay top dollar, 'specially for young virgin types. We pimp addicts, alcoholics, street urchins, and older girls through various mob outlets or just put them out to walk the streets. They're like chump change; but it can add up."

"Youse ain't gotta worry about breaking 'em in to the game," Frankie added. "We seen to that."

Frankie had a penchant for cheap suits that draped his skinny rail like a wet blanket, and he seldom wore a hat. Vito learned in an aside from Frankie's business partner that the young, wan Sicilian had gained his moniker from his resemblance to Sinatra and a propensity to ejaculate prematurely when given the opportunity to break in a new prospect.

Hollywood, his aptly branded associate, led the threesome this evening out of the Gold Rail and south on Third to Broadway. In contrast to Frankie, Hollywood carried himself like a quarterback and asserted a befitting confidence. He stood six feet two with a wavy, rust-hued and Brilliantined coif, scrubbed denim eyes, and a movie-poster face that he packaged in a dark, bespoke suit, silk tie, dress shirt, highly polished brogues, and a Stetson.

"While we're on Broadway, let's stop off at Cindy's," Hollywood said, then explained to Vito: "We've groomed a helpful *associate* there, who turns girls our way."

As they strolled down Broadway, Hollywood told Vito that Cindy's strip joint shared ownership with a pizza parlor on Fifth Avenue, where women served pizza to a lunch crowd during the day and then stripped at Cindy's at night.

"Yup," Frankie chimed in. "Yah might say both places specialize in stuff dat's great for eatin' out."

As they entered Cindy's, Vito and Hollywood doffed their hats and waited to be greeted by the on-duty manager. They exchanged introductions and Hollywood asked after Delilah, a club veteran who filtered potential prostitutes to the syndicate. They stood in the foyer a short time before Delilah joined them.

Hollywood and Frankie exchanged hugs with Delilah and introduced her to Vito. With his arms draped around her torso so that his hand firmly cupped her ass, Hollywood charmed the stripper with compliments about her appearance and abilities. He explained that Vito would be joining their business.

"Sugar, anytime my pal here, Vito, comes by," Hollywood said in a baritone that could have been professionally trained for radio, "you make sure he gets the best scouting tips *and* service."

The dishwater blonde—with more miles showing on her than a late forties Nash Rambler, Vito mused to himself—nodded at Hollywood, winked at Vito, and stepped to his side. She scanned the room for evidence of onlookers, then raised her skirt and guided Vito's hand inside her G-string.

"Ooh, handsome, as you can tell, you make me wet just looking at you. You be sure and come around whenever you like."

Frankie, who revealed little interest in the matters at hand, cleared his throat before tapping the stripper on her shoulder.

"You seen any more candidates like dat little brunette yah steered our way last week?"

"No, Frankie, but if Vito's stopping by from now on, y'all can bet I'll be extra vigilant."

"Vagi-cunt?"

"She means she's going to be watching out for us, Frankie." Hollywood slipped a money clip from his front trouser pocket, extracted a sawbuck, and tucked it deep into her cleavage.

"Thanks as always, sweetheart."

After departing Cindy's, the trio ambled down Broadway to Fourth and then east on F Street. As they walked, Frankie and Hollywood assessed the streetwalkers they passed. Hollywood explained that the girls that worked up and down Broadway and Fourth, Fifth, Sixth, and Third Avenues typically failed to measure up.

"Like Hollywood says earlier, we's got no interest in 'em if they's streetwise, drugged-up, or gots attitude," Frankie explained. "Da young and innocent—now we's talkin' real value."

Hollywood advised Vito that were he to encounter a potential candidate on the street, he should "bring her in."

"If you get any hassle from her pimp, do what you gotta do, but only if you've hooked a babe. No need to draw unnecessary attention to yourself or strong-arm the handler if she's lacking quality."

On F Street, they passed the Hollywood Theater, a burlesque venue owned by Bob Johnston and his wife Frances, that later that night would be featuring veteran Janne Cafara.

"It's a shame she stops at pasties and G-string," Hollywood lamented, "but her looks brought in shiploads of randy sailors after the war, and she's still worth a peek and a poke."

"Early on we'd go after da strippers," Frankie told Vito. "But Bob and Frances, da owners of dis place, keeps a tight rein. 'Sides, the gals tends to be a little older than we likes."

Clearly, Vito thought, *Frankie's forte can't be procurement. He couldn't woo a tuna into a seiner net.*

They continued their stroll within a roughly twelve-block brewing cauldron of burlesque theaters, strip joints, flophouses, brothels, bars, tattoo shops, greasy spoons, and rundown hotels. When they arrived at one of the latter, the Golden West at the foot of Fourth Avenue and G Street, Frankie ushered them through the double doors fronting on Fourth.

They strode about twenty yards through an entry hall, lined on either side with armchairs, sofas, and floor lamps, before descending five steps to a lobby dominated by a wooden-and-glass front desk that resembled an oversized bank teller's cage. The enclosure housed spaces demarked by overhead signs, declaring Information, Cashier, Mail Keys. Two paneled skylights dominated the ceiling. A wide corridor to the left opened to a row of phone booths, stairways along the east and west walls, and a second hotel entry fronting on G Street.

"You a history buff, Vito?" Hollywood doffed his hat to a young woman that passed by, then looked to Vito.

"Not so much, but I take an interest on occasion."

"This should be one of them, then. She doesn't look like much, but this three-story baby was unique when it was built. John Lloyd Wright—yeah, that Wright; his son—designed it for old man Spreckels and had it constructed in 1913 of concrete and steel. Pretty unique approach back then."

When they reached the front desk, Hollywood and Frankie nodded to staff, then ushered Vito through a wide corridor to their right. They passed through a lounge and slowed as they neared the far wall at the end of the front-desk enclosure. They stopped at this point and greeted a slim woman in her late forties, who had been working in an inner cubicle.

"Good evening, Margie." Hollywood tipped his fedora. "We dropped by to check on business and introduce you to our new colleague, Vito, here."

Margie set down her pen, rose, and glided toward them on three-inch black-and-white heels. A scarlet sheath dress clung to her columnar figure.

"Good evening, gentlemen. Come on in."

She unlocked a hinged portion of the wood-and-glass cage and stepped aside to allow entry. Hollywood introduced Vito before hanging his coat and hat on a nearby rack. Vito doffed his hat in greeting, while Frankie removed his suit jacket and hung it. As Margie and Hollywood stood chatting, Vito assessed the plain-faced woman. She had pinned her long blonde hair into rolled bangs in the popular pompadour style, daubed on a heavy application of rouge, and framed her wide mouth with bright red lipstick.

Frankie rejoined them while Hollywood made his way to Margie's workstation.

"Margie here helps da girls learn their manners and takes care of paperwork for us," Frankie told Vito. "Looks like Hollywood's all business as usual. How's 'bout you gives me the key to the dormitory, Margie, so's I can show Vito round while youse bring H up to speed."

Key in hand, Frankie led Vito out and toward the back wall, where a locked door was identified by an overhead sign that read: Men's Dormitory. The dorm, intended as single-night accommodations for working men, had been commandeered by the mob at an attractive rate to the hotelier. Frankie unlocked the door, allowing Vito to enter first, and then employed the key to lock them inside. Once Vito's eyes adjusted to the dim lighting, he staggered as he scanned the scene before him, then gathered his composure in an attempt to mask his revulsion.

He espied nearly a dozen women in their late teens and early twenties lying in various states of undress on ten cots bearing filthy linens and ragged blankets—four within the confines of an approximately fifteen-by-fifteen room, with another six in a larger, connected space to the rear. The occupants were confined to their beds by leather straps or chains that restricted movement to only a few feet. One girl sat naked on the floor, pawing gruel from a dog bowl. An overflowing bedpan lay nearby.

The stench of urine and vomit, the rancid smell of perspiration, and the odor of sweet opium smoke comingled in Vito's nostrils. As he studied other permutations of the dank chamber, he saw that the bare walls bore a Rorschach pattern of unrecognizable stain and splatter. Pipes of various types, discarded needles, tie-offs, and spoons littered the musty carpet.

Frankie stood next to Vito.

"As yah can see, whats we gots here ain't prime beef." Frankie waved his arm in a gesture encompassing the two rooms as though they were a tenant farm pasture. "Hollywood works his charms with the quality talent. Thems that gots it never seen this place. They gets kept in proper style.

"At the next level, the brighter cunts with some potential, they only needs a short stay before theys understand what's best. We shifts them to nicer hotel quarters, where they gets three squares, a private room for entertaining clients, clothing, and girlie-type things."

"And, the others?" Vito asked.

"It's left to me mostly to break the ones that's left. They ends up working the streets, unless they's hooked so bad they ain't worth a dime or gots attitude like that saucy, brunette bitch over there. Whatever happens to them happens."

As he spoke about the brunette, Frankie gestured toward a disheveled child Vito guessed to be underage sitting cross-legged on her bed, head down, writing intensely with a nub on a scrap of paper. Her matted, brown hair flowed like an unruly rat's nest over her shoulders; dark circles underscored puffy eye sockets; and tearstains marred her cheeks.

Frankie strode over to the girl, yanked the pencil and paper from her hands, and shoved her against the wall. She stared as in a trance at the ground, quivering as she clutched a fragment of sheet against her naked, skinny frame. Frankie hovered over her, waving the fragment of paper in her face.

"What do yah think you're doin'?" He had planted his wiry frame within a foot of the trembling rag doll. Red-faced, he jammed his arms akimbo and barked at her when she didn't respond. "Stop da bullshit and look at me, yah li'l bitch."

When she didn't obey his command, he grasped her by the chin and pushed her head against the wall. As her head lolled to her chest again, he buried his fist in her solar plexus. When she wailed and bent in a spasm, he jerked her head up again and slapped her face. She pressed the opposite cheek against the wall. A rivulet of urine dribbled down her legs.

"Yah knows da rules, whore," he screamed. "No letter writing. No notes. No messages to anyone."

Vito's stomach churned, but he stood frozen in place, knowing that to intercede would not fare well for him or the urchin. By the time he had returned to Vito's side, Frankie had regained his composure and asked Vito to join him as he conducted his bedside inspections. Like a doctor making rounds, inspired by debauchery rather than care, he made a gesture of checking the young women for overdoses, open wounds, and their general condition.

At each occupied cot, while inattentively assessing a ward's well-being, he drew his hand across a breast, tweaked a nipple, caressed a naked bottom, or walked his fingers along or into an unwitting women's vulva. Once he had completed his tour, Frankie led Vito to the exit, keyed open the door, and let Vito out.

"Now, if you'll excuse me, I've gotta go give dat brown-haired rag a lesson."

As Vito left his companions later that evening, he drove to the nearest bar, ordered a double Rittenhouse rye, and asked the tender to leave the bottle. His head hurt; his stomach tossed. He chugged the double, then refilled his glass three fingers deep. Disgust over what he had just witnessed and allowed to occur warred with the plan he had devised to avenge what the Tacchinos had done to his mother and uncle.

Do I have the balls to do the Tacchino babe that way? he silently queried. *Does anyone deserve to see the inside of that fuckin' torture dungeon even if it's to settle a score?*

As his time at the bar grew in reverse proportion to the bottle's remaining contents, Vito's thoughts circled back to his grandfather's admonition. *La vendetta è un piatto che si gusta freddo*, Emilio had said, advising him to concentrate on making money instead of waging a vendetta in a fit of anger.

No one now, not even Nanno, could accuse me of going off half-cocked, Vito thought as he brought his glass to his lips. *Taking down that hot-looking Tacchino babe—like shooting two pigeons with one bullet. But does anyone deserve that hellhole I just cased?*

Vito set down his glass, withdrew his wallet from his trouser pocket, and flipped its clear plastic passcase to the last folder. He stared at the fading, dog-eared photo that had been transferred from a scrapbook to his first passcase and then to every new one since: a teen nymph decked in a frilly party dress. He could discern her blush even now in the old sepia tint.

He continued to gaze at his only photo of his mother, grabbed the bottle, and sloshed another tug of rye into his glass. He emptied the glass in a single swallow, savoring the sear at the back of his throat and the char in his stomach.

January 19, 1955
Wednesday, 9:55 p.m.

3

Vito parked the stolen panel truck at a meter on First Avenue slightly north of Broadway and killed the engine. The location offered him a vantage point for espying arriving Greyhound buses, their departing riders, and—most importantly to him at the moment—a depot employee completing her shift. While he waited, Vito leafed through the January edition of a new men's magazine that had debuted in December. He occasionally took a furtive sip from a paper-bag-wrapped bottle he cradled between his legs.

Over the last two weeks, Vito had devised ploys like those he used on the Simon's Sandwiches carhop to lure women into the sex trade. He relied on charm and guile—never force or brutality—to seduce likely candidates to turn those he perceived to be uninhibited, enthusiastic in bed, and eager to use their bodies to make a living. He had dismissed or avoided any girl he deemed likely to need breaking at the Golden West dormitory—until this evening.

Vito continued to monitor the Greyhound station as he tugged on his concealed whiskey bottle and admired the svelte-figured, full-breasted, naked beauty of Margie Harrison, who the copy accompanying the centerfold declared had been distinguished as the first "Playmate of the month."

Ain't no Monroe, but I'd pump her, Vito thought as he ogled the centerfold from wavy black locks that coiled down to her shoulder to large pink areolae to flat stomach, long legs, and firm, round ass.

He glanced up and noticed his target exiting the bus plaza and walking toward the van. He slipped the *Playboy* under his seat, took a long pull from his bottle, and exited the truck. He wore an olive drab delivery uniform, replete with jaunty cap that he pulled low on his brow as he ambled to the rear of the vehicle and opened the back doors.

Vito busied himself with feigned work until Angela Belsito, Donatella Tacchino's daughter and ticket counter employee for Greyhound, hurried by, her head down, concentrating on the short walk home. Vito grabbed Angela from behind, muffling her wails with his hand and brandishing a sharp blade before her eyes.

"Not a peep, babe, or you'll bleed out right here and now."

He dragged her into the vehicle, closing the doors behind him as he entered. Once he had her bound and gagged, he opened a tool bag and withdrew a heroin-loaded syringe. Angela struggled wildly against her constraints. Vito watched dispassionately as her comely face contorted and her eyes bulged like sapphire moons as he tied off her arm and injected her. With less satisfaction than he had anticipated, he removed her clothing, exited the truck, and returned to the driver's seat.

Perspiration beaded on Vito's forehead and accumulated in his armpits as he steered the truck along downtown streets for the next twenty minutes. His head ached. Sips from his whiskey bottle became gulps. The fire in his gut fed his need for vengeance. Yet his resolve wavered.

I would be condemning an innocent child to sickening brutality, he thought, *but I won't be taking her life. Is that better or worse than what they did to Mama and Ari ... and me?*

A salty, putrid taste filled his mouth. His stomach rolled like a ship being ravaged by a stormy sea. He pulled the truck to the curb, staggered to the sidewalk, fell to his knees, and spewed bile, booze, and hate into the gutter. When it was over, he rested on his knees as though in prayer, wiped his mouth with his shirt sleeve, and shuddered. Before rising, he made the sign of the cross, and then lumbered back to the driver's seat.

He struggled to picture his mother's face and contemplated what his life might have been had hers not been taken. He thought of his grandfather's admonitions, and then he asked himself what his uncle would counsel were he here to guide him. Then his mind went blank. At Fifth and B Street, a block from where Vito had emptied the contents of his stomach, the panel truck turned north on A Street. A right toward Sixth Avenue came next. Then followed a mile course north to Juniper. The vehicle entered Balboa Park, traveled eastward toward Eighth, and journeyed south through a wooded area.

The truck lights went dark, and a few yards later, the vehicle rolled to a stop in a poorly lit, wooded area of the park. A figure clad in a dark uniform stumbled from the passenger compartment to the rear doors, opened them, and stepped into a cubicle that on an ordinary day might be laden with laundry or bread or delivery packages. He hovered briefly this night over the sole contents that lay on the truck's bed.

Over a period of several hours, Vito cowered over the bound and bruised girl. Vexed by his inability to trigger the rage necessary to sexually humiliate his defenseless captive, he finally extracted a second syringe of heroin from a bag in the rear of the truck, tied off Angela's arm, and then slammed the needle repeatedly into the vehicle's panel. With rivulets of moisture scarring his cheeks, Vito returned to the driver's seat and drove the panel truck to the Belsito residence, where he gently lifted Angela and left her bound at her doorstep. He drove a short distance to Our Lady of the Rosary, parked the truck, and entered the shadow-filled church, striding rapidly to the devotional area.

Vito knelt before the mostly unlit votive candles, slipped change into a coin slot, took a match, struck it, and lit a candle. He then bowed his head and made the sign of the cross.

"Nanno, I light this candle for you. I should have listened. Forgive me, Nanno. Forgive me, Jesus."

Thirty-Six

July 14, 1990
Saturday, 11:20 p.m.

1

Zach Watson raised his shot glass and proposed a toast to his sister-in-law in celebration of her thirty-fourth birthday. He and the three other members of his band had completed a set as the BellyUp's warm-up earlier in the evening and then retreated with Maria, Michelle, and Nick to the VIP seating area in a loft above the north side of the stage.

As Chicago blues and electric guitar music legend Harvey Mandel took the stage, Zach ordered two bottles of Jack Daniels along with ice-filled tumblers and shot glasses for his party. They drank heartily and conversed with good humor as they watched Mandel's mastery. After "the Snake" left the stage and Zach's bandmates had departed, Zach apportioned the second liter's remains in four glasses.

"Here's to great music, great booze, and great friends and family." Zach took up his glass.

Although toasted in an altogether different manner, Nick retained enough cognizance to note the small circle's lack of enthusiastic response. Earlier in the evening, before inebriation dulled his senses, Nick perceived an uncharacteristic sullenness in Maria. And Michelle, whom he also had monitored, sat quietly, often staring off as though

253

her thoughts had taken her far outside the confines of the BellyUp. Nick could not imagine the source of Maria's pique. She had been acting strangely even earlier in the day. But he knew why Michelle had been so distant all evening. She had called him again that morning and asked him whether he knew a man that identified himself as Carlo Tacchino:

"Carlo? Of course, but how would you know him?" Nick responded when queried on the phone.

Michelle gave Nick the details of her meeting with Tacchino. When she completed the recapitulation, she and Nick agreed to meet at Maria's apartment while Zach and his band prepared for their gig. Michelle had pleaded with Nick to keep Zach in the dark about these recent events. She told Nick that Zach needed to focus on the band's BellyUp show that night, so she would wait until Sunday morning to bring him up to speed. Nick convinced Michelle in return that he had to contact Buck and arrange protection for Maria, Michelle, and her family.

As they huddled in Maria's apartment that afternoon, Nick noted Maria's disengagement—until he expressed his intent to confront Tacchino. He also had gained an equally unexpected response from Michelle.

"I never gave into this kind of intimidation when I was reporter, and I'm not about to now."

Maria bolted to her feet as Nick vowed to proceed.

"You ... you can't." Catching herself in midoutburst, Maria reclaimed her seat. "It's just gotten too weird. In fact, instead of calling the cops, I think we should just give this whole thing up."

"Talk about weird, you've been acting strangely since Nick and I got here. And, you didn't say a word, let alone object, when we decided to seek Buck's help."

"I'm sorry, it's just ... I mean ..." Maria fussed with her hair, shifted in her seat, then took a pack of cigarettes from her purse and lit one up. "I've always thought that Vito, deep down, is an honorable man, and I want his son to meet him on the outside. From what you've told me about him over the past several weeks, Nick ... and now this threat ... maybe it's best if we just leave things as they are."

Michelle stood, took several paces, and squared to confront Maria.

"You've known from the beginning, sis, that Vito's no Sir Walter Raleigh, but you insisted it wasn't right to have an innocent man serve the rest of his life in prison. And before you object, yes, I was the least enthused about getting involved. I agreed to go along, because my legal training requires me to take my clients as I find them and provide the best defense I can, especially if I believe—as I do now—that they didn't commit the crime."

"Did I miss something, you guys?" Zach set his glass down without completing the toast. "I thought this was a birthday celebration, not a wake."

Nick, sated with beer and an abundant share of Jack, came to the inebriated conclusion that the burden had fallen on him to brighten the mood.

"Guess we're jush a trio of party poopsers. Wow, Zachie, that gives me an idea. Lesh band together 'n' play some lowdown blues. We can call ourselves The Parsley ... The Parshy Pooshters."

A playful jab glanced off Zach's shoulder. The momentum of his swing caused Nick to sway sideways. He grabbed Maria's knee in order to right himself. Maria neither reacted nor spoke, except to cast her eyes downward. Michelle rolled her eyes in exaggerated fashion for her husband's benefit.

"It seems like we've all had a little too much partying already." Zach rose. "We should just call it a night, I guess."

"Yeah, and I'm really tired from a tough week." Maria reached for her purse as she spoke.

"See, Zach. Like I shed: the Party Poopers Band." Nick rolled in his seat in Maria's direction. "Come on, Maria, one more to another year. We'll split Chelle's glass three ways."

Michelle tapped Nick on the shoulder.

"I think that's enough, Nick."

"Huh." Nick channeled an Alfred E. Neuman shrug. "'In retrospect, it becomes clear that hindsight is definitely overrated.'"

"It's okay, sis." Maria placed a hand on Nick's arm. "Actually, Nick, you're kinda funny when you're loaded."

"Nah, I'm jush coppin' ol' *Mad Magazine* lines and puttin' it on a little for the show."

"Nick?" the sisters queried in unison.

"All right. But if so, then I'm only *two* sheets to the wind."

July 14, 1990
Shortly before Midnight

2

Maria and Nick had arrived at the BellyUp in separate vehicles. In consideration of his questionable condition, Maria promised Zach and Michelle that she would drive Nick to his place and help him retrieve his car in the morning. The foursome shared hugs, kisses, and handshakes, and then Maria guided Nick to her Tempo. Nick passed out in the passenger seat—his habit drunk or sober—as Maria steered toward his place, stopping first in Solana Beach for hot, black coffee for them both. Her head throbbed, but not because she had imbibed like the others. She dared not—not while her mind whirled with the lurid recollection of her rape and Sal and Carlo's separate threats.

Nick and Maria sipped coffee as she drove south from Solana Beach on the southbound I-5 and exited onto I-8 eastbound. Nick, true to his character, dozed off before he finished his brew. Maria continued a short distance, intending to exit at Hotel Circle, which led to Nick's room, but then switched her foot from the brake to the accelerator and goosed the throttle. She continued east to Highway 163 South and then to University Avenue, where she turned left and steered toward her City Heights apartment. She kept her eyes focused on the road, opting not to risk a glance at Nick for fear she would lose her resolve.

Maria parked her car behind the apartment complex and turned off the ignition. A quiver slithered snakelike up her spine. She whimpered, but then steeled herself. *Compartmentalize, Maria*, she silently reminded herself. *You must do this. There are too many lives at stake besides your own.*

She awakened Nick, exited the driver's side, and strode to the passenger door to help him out of his seat. She took his hand as he stepped away from the Tempo. He shook his head, ran a hand through his hair, and teetered.

"Where are we?"

"I brought you to my place. I didn't think you were in any shape to be on your own."

"Oh ... ah ... but ..."

"It's okay. You can sleep on my sofa."

Though unsteady, Nick navigated his way to Maria's door and inside, where she flipped on the wall switch and directed him to her sofa. She then made her way into the kitchen, where she poured Jack over ice: a double for Nick, a watered-down one for herself. She delivered the drinks and sat next to Nick.

"Whoa, girl. I think I'm pretty loaded already."

"We don't have anywhere we need to go, and you've earned the right to let your hair down a little. Relax."

Nick gazed foggy-eyed at Maria and then at the bourbon in his hand.

"Oh, fuck. Why not?" He raised his glass and took a deep swallow.

Silence filled the room. Then Maria initiated a new line of conversation.

"I've been doing some serious thinking about Vito, Nick." Maria placed a hand on Nick's knee as she spoke. "Ever since Tala was killed and that creep came to my place of work, I've gotten more and more frightened. Now, this Carlo thug shows up. I think we should just stop while we're ahead."

Maria stared into Nick's eyes and grew silent. Nick sat upright again and leaned toward her. She thought his expression made him appear as though she had hit him in the face with a pail of ice water.

"What? What are you sayin'? You do realize ... damn, my head's spinnin'. Don't think I need any more of this." Nick set his glass on a nearby coffee table. "You know how closhe we are to ... to provin' Vito didn't off Bompensiero, right?"

Maria shifted her eyes upward and to the left.

"I just think I've taken advantage of you and your time for too long, and I'm worried that we've stirred up something that should have been left alone." She paused and took a sip from her glass. "Nick, I want to pay for your flight back and give you a stipend for all your hard work."

Nick shook his head, lifted Maria's hand from his knee, and held it.

"That's crazy. I chose to get into this, and now ... may I trouble you for some black coffee?"

"Sure thing, Nick." Maria went to the kitchen, retrieved the bottle of Jack, and microwaved a cup of instant. On her return, she handed the coffee to Nick and poured them each a fresh glass of whiskey.

"Now, where were we?"

"You were being a gentleman and accepting my offer of payment."

"Ah ... yeah ... right. I mean ... no. I don't need to be paid. The first book's royalties fronted my costs, and I'll write off the expenses of my work here when I publish."

Maria pulled her hand away and ran it through her hair. She cast her eyes downward and sighed before speaking again.

"It's ... It's just not right. When you asked in the beginning whether I understood the possible consequences, I was being selfish in thinking only about what might happen to me. I never dreamed I would be putting your—or anyone else's—life at risk. Nick, please, just book a flight as soon as you can and go home to Laura. I was wrong to bring you into this."

Nick's right eyebrow shot upward and a crease formed between it and his left brow. His nose wrinkled, and his mouth rose at the left corner.

"You don't really think I would do that, do you? I've come way too far and gotten in way too deep. It's just not in my makeup to throw in the towel without getting to the bottom of this."

"Nick, please, listen to me." Maria placed her hands on each side of Nick's face, forcing him to meet her gaze. "I can't say why ... well ... let's call it a woman's intuition, but I know this is going to end badly."

Nick clasped Maria's hands and held them in his lap.

"You've never faced these kinds of threats before, but they were part of the job description when I did investigative reporting. I've still got my press credentials and good contacts. No one's going to mess with me." He paused. "I understand how you feel, though. Take a few days for yourself; play with your niece and nephew or take a relaxing trip somewhere. I'll handle it from here."

Maria dropped her gaze to the floor and nibbled at a fingernail. She began bouncing a leg as though it were a piston energizing her heart and mind. She felt a chill as the scene with Sal and the advice he had given came to mind. Those thoughts bolstered her resolve, and her career had equipped her with the skills she would need now, but her growing affection for Nick made blackmail and its likely consequences to his marriage—even if it was to save his life—seem horribly selfish.

"I'm not going to persuade you no matter what, am I?" Maria didn't wait for Nick's answer. With a shrug and the faintest of smiles, she raised her glass and gestured to Nick to do likewise. "I guess all that's left is to drink to your safety."

She coerced Nick into finishing his whiskey while she removed his shoes and socks. "So you can relax," she told him. She slipped off her shoes as well, lit two large candles that sat on an end table, and stepped to the front door to extinguish the overhead light. She padded to the kitchen to replenish their drinks. This time, she poured a double for herself as well. She left the drinks on the counter and strode to her bedroom, where she rummaged through her closet for a cheap Kodak she had picked up at a yard sale and tucked it under her arm so that she could carry their drinks.

With the camera pinched to her side, she gave Nick his drink and sat down again, allowing the Kodak to slide quietly to the floor, out of Nick's view. She knelt in front of him and massaged his feet and spoke softly.

"Does this feel good?"

"Magical."

"You've become special to me, and I'm ready to do anything that makes you feel really good."

"As long as we're letting our emotions hang out ..." Nick took a long drink, put his glass down on the coffee table in front of him, and inclined toward Maria. "I've enjoyed our time together, too. When this is over, I'm going to miss you."

Nick bent forward, clasped Maria by the shoulders, kissed her on the cheek, then released her and sat upright. He reached for his glass and took a gulp.

"I'm sorry. You ... must think I'm such a cad."

The knot in Maria's stomach turned tighter. She rested her hands palms down on his knees so that Nick would not see how they were shaking.

Can I do this? If I don't, Nick's a dead man and that sadistic bastard is likely to harm Michelle and Zach. And, the devil knows what Sal will do to me before he …

"A cad? Of course not, Nick," she purred. She rose higher on her knees, pressed herself between his legs, and kissed him on the lips.

"No, Maria. We can't." Nick clutched her upper arms and gently pushed her away. "It wouldn't be right. Even if I weren't married or your sister weren't my best friend, there'd always be a question tormenting us. You know the nature of my addiction. Neither of us dare tempt that genie."

Maria glanced downward as though in thought, got to her feet, and sat beside Nick on the sofa. She gazed into his eyes and ran a hand through his hair.

"I've learned," Maria forged on. "I've … I've learned that nothing else matters in that moment when two people find each other despite all odds. Just as we have."

Maria withdrew her hand, slipped her blouse over her head, and reached back to undo her bra. She leaned in and kissed Nick with open, moist lips. Her tongue sought his. Nick put his hands to Maria's shoulders, but before he could push her away, she slid them to her breasts and then unbuttoned his shirt.

Maria sensed Nick's resistance eroding like a rain-sodden cliff slowly slipping onto an adjacent shoreline, the terrain that composed his willpower weakening. His arms fell to his side. She pushed onward, massaging his neck, shoulders, and chest, and resisted his waning attempts to deflect her advances. She drew his shirt down over his arms, pressed her bare breasts against his chest, and sighed warm breath into his ear.

They pawed, grappled, and kissed before tumbling to the carpeted floor. Maria traced her tongue along Nick's lips, pierced an imaginary veil between their open mouths with urgent prodding. She knew she was about to sweep away Nick's tenuous footing on her imagined landslip. They lay on their sides when Maria leveraged Nick to his back. Their passion intensified as Maria straddled him. She reached for him, forgetting the camera, took him into her hand, and directed his tumescence to her.

As she guided it along the edge of her moistness, Nick—as though flayed by a charged wire—tore himself away and rose to his knees.

Maria lay on her back adjacent to him, her chest rising and falling in unison with his. Once she caught her breath, Maria rolled to her side and rested on an elbow. Tears rolled down her cheeks.

"Nick. Oh, God, Nick. Fuck. I'll never be able to make up for this."

Nick grabbed his shirt, worked it around his privates, and sat crosslegged next to Maria.

"No. This was my fault. I know I shouldn't drink like I did. I got way outta line."

Maria sat up, mirroring Nick's position while allowing her knees to touch his. She buried her head in her palms.

"Nick, you don't understand," she mumbled, and then drew her hands away from her face as she raised her head. "I've done something horrible—even worse than this—and an innocent woman has died because of it. Now, *we're* in danger, too, all because of me."

Thirty-Seven

July 16, 1990
Monday, 1:25 p.m.

1

With Maria standing close behind, Nick cracked open the hotel room door and scanned the corridor. Satisfied that no one lurked in the hallway, he gave Maria a hug, and admonished her not to leave the room under any circumstances, or open the door to anyone unless she knew who it was. He tapped the outside of his jacket just under his left armpit, as he took the stairs to the ground floor and walked out into the afternoon sun. Reassured that the holstered pistol remained discreetly in place, he turned his thoughts to the meeting he had set with Carlo for two this afternoon.

After Maria had revealed the details of Sal Caputo's threats, Nick convinced her that they could not safely remain in Maria's apartment, and they needed to arm themselves—at least until SDPD could afford protection for them, Michelle, and her family. Well before dawn, they walked in shadows to University Avenue and hailed a taxi downtown, rode the Trolley, making three separate transfers separated by short jaunts through buildings with open access, and then registered together under aliases for a room with double beds at the Gaslamp District's Horton Grand Hotel.

With little sleep and no breakfast, Nick escorted Maria at ten that morning to a Hillcrest gun shop, where they selected a two-inch Smith & Wesson snub nose .38, ammo, and a holster for him, and on the advice of the sales clerk, a five-and-a-half-inch, polymer Grendel P10 for her. It weighed only fourteen ounces, carried ten rounds in the magazine and one in the chamber, and could be readily concealed in her purse. They spent nearly two hours in the store, determining what weapons they should buy and taking instruction in their use and general firearm safety.

Nick then left a phone message for Buck, while they gobbled burgers and fries at a nearby Jack in the Box. After lunch, they undertook a circuitous route back to the hotel, where Nick showered and then placed a call to Carlo Tacchino. In his call to Buck, he chose not to tell him about their purchases, his planned encounter, or where to find Maria. He knew Jarrett would nix the meeting and attempt to get to the hotel before Nick left. Nick figured he could give Buck the information on Maria's whereabouts while on the way to meet Tacchino.

To reach his car, Nick headed east on Island Avenue, crossed it and then Fourth Avenue, and walked north on Fourth to the metered, diagonal spot where he had parked. Just a few paces up Fourth, he spotted a black-and-white blocking his exit.

"Shit, I forgot to plug the meter," he muttered to himself. He remembered then that Maria had stuffed it after an exaggerated process of dislodging coins from the bottom of her purse. *Maybe Buck sent a car. Christ, no, you idiot. You played it cute and thought you'd tell him after you left the hotel.*

As he neared his black Lumina, an officer exited the cruiser and approached.

"Hello, officer. Something wrong with the meter?" Nick made sure the officer's eyes followed his as he verified that the meter displayed a green flag.

"Is this your car, sir?"

"Yes ... yes, it is. I mean it's my rental."

"Would you step to the rear of the vehicle, please."

"What? I'm parked between the lines in a legal space, and the meter has plenty of time remaining. Is there something wrong with the car?"

The officer made a show of placing his right hand near his holstered service revolver. Nick ignored the gesture and took a step toward the Chevy's front door.

"It would be unwise to resist, sir." The officer flicked his holster snap, breaking leather. "You really don't want to make serious trouble for yourself, do you?"

Something's way wrong, Nick told himself. He had an urge to bolt, but feared being taken down in a hail of bullets.

"I guess I have no choice." Nick glanced at the cop's nametag. "Officer Pettiman."

"That's more like it." As Nick neared the rear of his vehicle, the back door of the patrol car swung open.

"What the …?" Nick swallowed the rest of his question. When he looked over his shoulder to ask it, his gaze was met with the barrel of the officer's pistol aimed at his head.

"Get in; quickly, or I'll be writing a report that I had to use lethal force to detain you."

Nick nodded, then swung his body around the open door of the screened rear compartment. Sal Caputo sat on the far side of the cruiser with his pistol aimed at Nick.

"Please, Mr. Lanouette, join me, although I *do* wish we were meeting under more pleasant circumstances."

Nick's first thought was to reach for the pistol tucked under his armpit, but he knew he would be dead before he could get off a shot. Sal's trained eye caught a telling movement.

"Officer, before the gentleman enters, would you please be kind enough to see what he finds so valuable inside his coat?"

"Please, step back, sir, and place your hands on the top of the car. Slowly, now. No fast moves."

The officer conducted a patdown, discovered the S&W, and withdrew it from Nick's holster.

"Good call, Mr. Caputo. Look what our friend was carrying."

After securing Nick's snub nose in his waistband, the officer dedicated himself to a more thorough search and then, placing his hand on Nick's head, guided him into the backseat.

"Pettiman, come around to my side and hand me the kid's piece. It might come in handy." Sal beamed as he spoke.

After the officer closed the door on his side, Nick became aware of a stationary figure sitting in the front passenger seat.

"Carlo!"

Tacchino cocked his head in the direction of Nick's voice.

"Yah really should've taken da advice, Nick. I warned yah more than once; even told yah it was outta my hands da last time."

"Carlo, how could you?"

"No choice, kid. Seems my phone got extra ears now."

Carlo turned his head away, slumped in his seat, and looked out the front passenger window.

"Where are you taking me?" Nick asked Caputo as the officer opened Sal's door and slipped him the S&W. Pettiman closed the door and sauntered to the driver's side, where he entered behind the wheel.

"Not far, and I'm sure you'll find it very comfortable."

Fuckin' asshole, Nick thought as he bore his eyes into Caputo's face.

"You'll never get ..."

"Save me the bothersome clichés, Nick. It'll make us both sound like amateurs."

Nick thought of Maria. *When will she realize I've been gone too long? Will Buck pick her up before she panics and does something stupid? How could I be dumb enough to tip off this madman that I was packing?*

The police cruiser made its way south on Fourth one block, turned right on J Street, executed a second right on Third Avenue, and following a final right turn, pulled in front of the Grand Horton Hotel and stopped.

"This is where we get out, Nickie." Caputo, Nick realized, was wallowing in pleasure at Nick's expense.

"What the hell is this?"

"Our friends from SDPD saw you and the babe enter the hotel earlier, bright boy. Doesn't take much brainpower to figure this is where you've set up your love nest. How convenient."

"You're dumber than you look. We just ate lunch here is all. Maria is long gone, Sal."

"Look who's calling the kettle ... Didn't you get that we've had eyes on the place since you got here?"

"I don't believe anything *you* say, shithead."

Caputo rapped Nick on the side of the head with the butt of his Beretta.

"Watch your tongue, *stupido*."

"Or what? You're going to kill me?"

"Please, Nick, listen tah Sal and don't make any more trouble for yah and da young lady." Carlo had shifted his head so that he could peer into the backseat. "Let's go inside peacefully and come tah a reasonable solution to our mutual problem. Yah have my word no harm will come tah da girl or yah."

From his position in the rear seat next to Caputo, Nick caught the beady glance Sal shot at Carlo.

"Okay, you two. Enough brotherly love. We're going to attract attention sitting out here like this, so be smart and listen to Carlo, Nickie."

July 16, 1990
Monday, 2:05 p.m.

2

Caputo had turned a desk chair in the hotel room so that its back faced the bed, where Maria and Nick huddled together. Nick had taken Carlo at his word, realizing that resistance would not deter his abductors from searching every room of the Horton Grand until they found her. The police officer—if he really was one—had been instructed to wait in the foyer as Sal prodded Nick to the staircase. Carlo trailed the pair.

Caputo sat now with his arms resting on the back of the chair, menacing his hostages with a Beretta M9 clutched in his gloved left hand. Nick found little irony in the fact that he had just learned about Caputo's weapon of choice earlier that morning: short recoil, semiautomatic, fifteen-round staggered box magazine with a reversible release that can be positioned for either right- or left-handed shooters.

Carlo Tacchino, using his cane for additional support, leaned against the door just to Sal's right. He also wore gloves. His face had turned uncharacteristically wan, and Nick could see perspiration gathering on his forehead and in his armpits. He blinked and seemed to be having trouble keeping his eyes focused in any one place.

"Now, let's get down to business." Sal slipped his right hand into his coat pocket, removed a suppressor, and snapped it into place on the Beretta. "Let's start with you two lovers getting undressed."

Maria's eyes widened. Her body stiffened as she pushed her shoulders back and straightened upward on the bed. Nick rose to his feet, but Caputo jabbed him in the midsection with the butt of his pistol, causing Nick to fall backward.

"Sal, stop. This ain't ..."

"Shut up, old man. You wouldn't be here at all, if I didn't need you. Now, Carlo, move down the wall a little, so I can keep you in sight."

Nick watched Caputo scan the three of them as though satisfied that he retained control of the room. Caputo nodded and then began his yarn.

"Let me tell you a story. We all love good mysteries, don't we? Our tale begins with our young lovers going at it like rabbits, when Carlo bursts into the room, firearm in hand."

"Salvatore, are yah mad?" Carlo had found his voice again, but Caputo ignored him.

"It seems Carlo's received orders to silence the two of you—a most believable plot line, thanks to the diligent footwork the two of you have done in town, not the least of which was piquing SDPD curiosity. But I digress.

"A gun battle ensues. Fortunately, a cop—a part played by someone you recently met—is downstairs. Hearing the shots, he comes rushing to the room only to find ... well ... you get the rest."

"It'll never work, asshole." Nick barked, surprising himself with an authority in his voice that belied his physical state. "You can't shoot Carlo with the same gun you use on us, and it'll take SDPD five seconds to see through your pretend cop."

"Jesus Christ. I'd fuckin' beat you silly right now, if it wouldn't fuck up the plan. Let me spell it out for you, Nickie." Sal tucked his hand inside his coat and, this time, withdrew Nick's snub nose. "Originally, I *did* have somethin' else in mind, but this little *pistola*? Sal waved the S&W as he spoke. "It answers your first question. And, Pettiman? What makes you think he's not a duly sworn officer of the law? SDPD is relatively clean, but you of all people should know we've bought more than a few of San Diego's finest over the years."

Nick turned his gaze to Carlo, whose olive skin had blanched to a shade almost as white as the hotel room wall. He looked as though he would collapse. His knees and cane quaked simultaneously.

"Mr. Tacchino ain't going to be of any help to you today."

"There is one thing." Nick raised his hand as though he were in elementary school responding to a teacher's inquiry. "Carlo, who really shot Frank Bompensiero?"

Sal cackled with forced laughter.

"If we knew, you really think we'd tell you?"

Carlo cleared his throat and spoke in a whispered rasp.

"Your boy, Vito, didn't do it, Nick. He was framed. Like I told yah, it was personal."

"Enough of this crap." Sal rose to his feet, pointing the Beretta at Nick and Maria with his left hand and Nick's pistol at Carlo with his right.

"Wait." Maria raised her hands to eye level, palms forward. "Didn't you want us naked?"

"What the fuck?"

"You're a smart man, you know I'm stalling, because I don't want to die." Maria slipped a strap of her tank top over her shoulder. "On the other hand, I also know what you like."

"You fuckin' *putana*. You almost make me wish I didn't have to take you out. I love tail with your kinda spunk." Caputo returned to his seat. "Go ahead. We got time for a little show ..."

The blow from Carlo's cane crashed down on Sal's head. Stunned but conscious, Caputo twisted and fired at Carlo with the S&W. As Carlo slumped to the floor, Sal swiveled, leveling the Beretta at Nick. Three sharp reports echoed like cannon fire in the hotel's confined quarters. Nick saw Sal stagger backward and fall. Then he looked back in wonderment at Maria. Smoke wafted through a black hole in her purse. Nick could tell she still clutched the P10 she carried inside.

"I ... I did it. I got the bastard. Twice." Maria's face slackened and drained of color. Wide-eyed and open-mouthed, she turned her head to locate Nick, who had scrambled toward Carlo as she fired at Caputo.

The hotel door crashed open.

"Maria! It's Pettiman!"

Maria raised her pistol. Pettiman, lurking in the doorway like a digitally distorted Max Schreck vampire, pulled the trigger on his service revolver. Nick cringed, awaiting a sear of lead ripping his flesh. Blood and flecks of brain matter splattered his face and clothing.

In the silent din that follows ear-shattering gunfire, Nick could feel his heart pounding like a drum. His mouth dropped open, then snapped shut. He gulped and closed his eyes. The room thumped like an anvil struck repeatedly with a sledge hammer. His head spun. When he opened his eyes, Pettiman's body lay bullet-riddled in the doorway. Uniformed officers filled the room, and Buck Jarrett stood over him, blocking Nick's view of Maria. Buck extended an arm as Nick wobbled to his feet and tried to reach Maria.

"That can wait, Nick. Let's take a little walk down to the foyer. I noticed a sitting area as I came in."

Nick thought he nodded an assent. As he planted his left foot, a lightning bolt raced up his leg. He struggled to assemble cogent thought, but his mind's eye refused to cooperate. Like a looping newsreel, Maria's final moment flashed repeatedly before him, and then he lost consciousness.

Thirty-Eight

1

He *strolls along the harbor in front of Anthony's Fish Grotto ... passes the twin-mast Star of India and the Berkeley ... gazes out over the ocean. Laura approaches, breaks into a run, wraps her arms around him ... they kiss. She disappears in a wisp of fog. Carlo limps into view, tips his cane, tells him a joke ... in Italian? ... vanishes as a familiar voice calls to him. He turns, Maria stands before him, covered in blood. He races to her ... collapses in a heap at her feet ... rises to his knees and stares at his scarlet-stained hands.*

A voice sounding like the rumble of an approaching train echoed in his ears. Then the words became more distinct.

"Nick, over here, on your other side."

"Huh? Someone call?" Nick rolled onto his back, away from the hospital room window. "Who's there?"

"It's me, Nick—Buck, along with your nurse and one of my fellow officers."

The nurse moved to Nick's bedside. She took his pulse and then his blood pressure.

271

"I'm your nurse, Sheri Fruin. You're at University Hospital, where the doctors successfully operated on your foot. Do you recall being shot earlier today?"

"Shot. Shot? Oh yes—left foot."

Nick twisted his head in Buck's direction, where the detective's blurry image came into view. Nick rubbed his eyes, and could now clearly see Buck sitting on a chair at his bedside. A uniformed officer stood behind Buck, leaning against the doorjamb.

"His vitals look fine, officers," Nurse Fruin said as she unraveled the Velcro cuff from Nick's arm. "He's all yours, but please keep it brief. Say ten minutes?"

Buck dipped his chin and turned his attention to Nick. The uniformed officer unfolded a note pad that he retrieved from his belt and stepped closer.

"I'm getting real tired of saving your scrawny white ass, pal. That said, how's the foot?"

"Don't feel a thing."

"Good for now, but after the trouble you've caused, I hope it soon hurts like hell." Buck clasped Nick's shoulder and allowed the corner of his lips to ascend. "Nick, if you're up to it, we need to take your statement."

Nick's eyes wandered around the room, wobbled, and then refocused on Buck.

"Maria?"

Buck shook his head. "I'm sorry." He paused before continuing. "From the incident scene, it looks like Maria saved your life before Pettiman got there. Can you confirm that she was Sal Caputo's shooter?"

Nick nodded.

"I need you to speak for the record, if you can, instead of gesturing."

"Yeah ... yes. I can't believe how cool she handled her ..." Nick went silent. He flicked a tear from the corner of his eye. "Carlo?"

"The old buzzard got winged. He'll be fine, and he's talking like a magpie. He claims plans had been in the works to clip Bompensiero as far back as '75 and that the order came from the LA capo himself. He says he's pretty sure who the wheelman and shooter were, but can't ... or won't ... name them. He's coughed up enough to clear Vito Erbi."

"That's good ... I guess."

"You guess?"

"Not sure his ass was worth the price." Nick sprung upward using his forearms on the mattress to brace his upper torso. "Wait. How did you know where ...?"

"Maria called soon as you left on your foolhardy mission. She was rattled and worried as hell that you'd get yourself killed. We sent units to her place, your place, and Tacchino's. When she told me where she was and how you had admonished her not to open the door to anyone she didn't know, it made sense for me to be the one to check on her."

"Pettiman?"

"Dirty and very dead; and you're welcome."

"Oh, Christ, yes. If you hadn't come along when you did ..."

"Do I have to say it ... again?"

"I told you so? No, I'm cured, Buck, lesson learned."

"I'll believe it when I see it. Now shut up and let me do my job."

July 24, 1990
Tuesday, 11:20 a.m.

2

Maria's body lay at her burial site in a simple wooden coffin festooned with a bouquet composed of Scarlet Knight Grandiflora roses. Laura wrapped her arm around Nick, who wavered on his crutches, as they stood behind Michelle and Zach, who sat in a single row of chairs. Buck and his wife also accompanied a small group of mourners assembled at the Old Catholic Cemetery in Mission Hills just north of Little Italy. Steve and Donna Molina had flown from the Bay Area with Maria and Vito's son, Evan, who sat next to Michelle. Much of Michelle and Zach's week had been consumed with contemplation about becoming the boy's legal guardians, a process, they realized, that could not be undertaken out of a sense of mere obligation and one that would need to be coordinated with Vito Erbi, if and when he was released from prison.

Vito remained in MCC awaiting a court hearing that would determine whether he would be retried or set free. Buck had informed Nick that Vito had been offered an opportunity to attend the services accompanied by police guard, but declined. Vito also had been advised as to why Maria had become so dedicated to his cause.

Nick dabbed at his eyes with a tissue. With the exception of brief moments of elation when Laura arrived from Oregon on Tuesday, Nick had cycled through anger, tearful outbursts, and depression. He had clung to his wife for physical and emotional support.

As the priest completed Maria's burial rite, Zach rose and turned to the knot of bereaved attendees, thanked them for their expressions of sympathy and love, and encouraged them to select a rose from Maria's bouquet as a memorial remembrance. Nick and Laura approached the coffin, stood silently for a moment, and then each clasped a scarlet bloom, stepping away to wait in the distance. Zach guided Michelle to her sister and wrapped his arm around his wife, while she ran her hand slowly along the coffin's wooden surface. Nick watched in anguish as Michelle's shoulders rose and sank in shudders.

He felt like a voyeur and had to avert his eyes. He stared off. Along a distant tree line, he observed an old man leaning on a cane. He had removed his glasses and was wiping his eyes with a yellowed handkerchief. Nick then watched him totter away.

After several moments at the burial site, the immediate family, including Evan, the Molinas, and the Lanouettes, made their way across the cemetery lawn toward their cars, which were parked at the curb of Washington Circle. Nick and Michelle embraced.

"All the lost and wasted years without her, then to share so little before losing her again," Michelle said as they broke their hug. She held Nick's hand and wept. "What purpose could God have had in mind for this?"

"You know, Chelle, I'm the last one to answer questions about any kind of deity. I do believe, however, that we come to life without preordained destiny and, like Maria, often pass too young for no seemingly justifiable reason. In between, our challenge is to find our own purpose. Some find it easily. Some never do. Others, like Maria, wrestle unfathomable demons before they catch hold of a fire that ignites their journey like a rocket soaring beyond the stars. Then, when the journey is accomplished, the purpose met, no further reason remains for them to soar. We are left to contemplate the prematurely spent rocket and ask why, knowing that there really isn't an answer."

"Nick. My God. That's the nicest, deepest thing I've ever heard you say."

"Chelle, you don't think that bullet's turned me into a marshmallow, do you?"

Michelle's eyes brightened; a thin smile softened her face.

"No, I'd never hurt your feelings that way. You know you'll always be my favorite arrogant asshole no matter."

Afterword

One of the primary characters within this novel migrated from southern Italy to Boston and on to Spokane, as did my paternal grandfather, who—like over two million Sicilians and southern Italians—fled hunger and a devastated economy between 1901 and 1910.[1] They, like both of my Calabrese grandfathers, undertook perilous journeys in order to seek their fortunes in the United States.

As a native of Spokane and a long-time resident of Southern California, I have observed civic leaders and local media artfully craft images of my birthplace and San Diego that belie troubling and sometimes treacherous parallels between the two, despite obvious differences in lifestyle, climate, geography, and population. Many residents of San Diego and Spokane consume, with little or no question, a travel brochure fantasy of Potemkin villages that obscures a shared history of Italian migration, labor unrest, Prohibition era intrigue, governmental corruption, and organized crime activity.

During my early twenties, I became intrigued by a series of magazine articles describing La Costa Resort outside of San Diego as a safe harbor for *La Cosa Nostra*. When mafiosi visited the resort or—to a lesser extent—San Diego generally, it was understood that their grudges, guns, garrotes, and knives were to be checked at the door. In 1977 that protective shield failed in singular fashion, when a successful hit took the life of Frank Bompensiero, LA crime family boss in San Diego, mob executioner, and undercover FBI informant.

Growing political awareness and admiration for then Supreme Court Justice William O. Douglas, who resided in Washington State and attended Whitman College in Walla Walla, awakened my interest in the Wobbly movement. The Wobblies (Industrial Workers of the World) attracted numerous migratory workers, among them a teenage

---

1   Immigration statistics from Advocates for Human Rights, Energy of a Nation: Immigration Resources, http://www.energyofanation.org/wave_of_italian_immigrants.html, accessed March 30, 2013.

Douglas, who worked with IWW members during harvest season and referenced them deferentially in his 1974 autobiography.

This work seeks to seamlessly interweave fictional characters—including a cast introduced in *Falling Down: A Tale of Addiction, Betrayal, & Murder*—within the fabric of historical events, weather conditions, culture, and locales during eight decades of eastern Washington and Southern California history.

In some cases, events or sequences thereof have been altered to facilitate character interaction. Any errors in the description of historical facts or events are solely those of the author.

Jerkwater Town grew from seeds of inspiration planted by my brother, Donn, who strove from an early age to collect, save, and understand the importance of family history and culture. Like the fruit that never falls far from the tree's branches, my nephew and Donn's oldest son, Anthony, shared his father's interest in family roots. In response to a query from Anthony, I prepared a compilation of genealogical photos, art, historic documents, and letters—a task that inspired *Jerkwater Town*. Unfortunately, Anthony died in a traffic accident before I could share the family compendium and this novel with him.

Extensive refinement and improvement of this work arose from the dedicated critique, extensive evaluation, and keen editing skills employed by my wife Jane, who has always been my anchor, muse, and greatest love; son Brian, an accomplished and published technical writer; and son Matthew, whose clear-sighted approach to life always offers creative stimulus.

Finally, in an era in which almost any writer can publish, not every author benefits from dedicated, professional publishing and editing services such as those provided by the iUniverse team, including Kimberly West, Kathi Wittkamper, Caroline Benton, and Stephanie Miller, whose guidance and advice is greatly appreciated.

Notes

Although this novel's fictional characters interact considerably with factual events and places, I have employed certain liberties when deemed necessary to advance the storyline:

- Although similar gatherings in approximately the same numbers occurred in Spokane in 1909, the reference in chapter 5 to about a thousand angry workers assembled on Stevens Street on September 6, 1909, is fictional.
- The three-story Colonial Hotel, cited in chapter 7, housed a brothel on its second and third floors, but hairdressers—not a restaurant, billiard parlor, and saloon—occupied the first floor.
- The chapter 9 description of the Pennington Hotel lobby and staircase is a fictional recreation, and in chapter 10, the lumberman and the order in which speakers came to the podium are the author's creations.
- Nick is neither a relative of the fictional Vito nor an attorney representing Mr. Erbi, so he could not have gained visitation rights at the Metropolitan Corrections Center, as described in chapter 10. Descriptions of the meeting room and access thereto, as well as the location and details of Vito's cell in chapter 2, are fictional.
- In chapter 12, the daily practices of Joel Barnes King and the description of his grocery store's interior are fictional. Likewise, the interior descriptions of the Khyber Pass restaurant and Pitchers in chapter 18 have been altered from how they appeared in 1990.
- The Star Bar described in chapter 14 is factual relative to its 2013 appearance and, therefore, does not accurately depict conditions in 1990. The interior description of the San Diego jail in chapter 15 also is fictional.

- Although civic leaders did acquire the services of Charles Mulock for the referenced American Legion convention in August 1929, and Frank Bompensiero had been convicted at the time of a Prohibition infraction, the luncheon that occurs at the U. S. Grant Hotel in chapter 17, as well as the subsequent meeting in fictional suite 209 of the hotel, is not based on any factual premise.
- The California Theatre storage room in which Tina informs her brother of her pregnancy in chapter 21 does not and did not exist, at least not as described herein.
- Whether a representative of the alleged Commellini abortion clinic would have met arriving "clients," as set forth in chapter 23, is pure speculation on my part, as is the description of the services such a clinic provided.
- Although the description of the Commercial Building in chapter 23 is mostly accurate based on researched documentation, liberties were taken within the layout of Tina's room, the format of the U-shaped hallways, and the unit numbers.
- The layout of San Diego Police Headquarters above the first floor, as described in chapters 25 and 27, is fictionalized, as are all references to SDPD policies and procedures.
- There is no record indicating that Carmen "Flipper" Milano visited or ate at Tony's Trattoria on India Street, as fictionally depicted in chapter 25. The description of the railcar interior in chapter 26 also is fictional.
- Although I have heard similar philosophy spoken within the context of a Catholic Mass, Father Abadia and the contents of his homily presented in chapter 28 are the author's fictional creations.
- The Marx Toys' searchlight airport toy described in chapter 29 may or may not have been available for purchase at Marston's.
- The interior description and menu selections made by the characters eating at John Tarantino's Italian and Seafood Restaurant on North Harbor Drive in chapter 30 and serving portions referenced are fictional.
- In chapter 32, the description of the realty office being at the Clairemont Village Shopping center is a creation of the author. Although the meeting with C. Arnholt Smith depicted

280

in this same chapter attempts to accurately describe him and his character traits, no such meeting occurred, and there is no evidence that Smith sought outside influence to obtain City Council permission for his construction of a new Padres facility in Mission Valley.

- Although similar treatment of young women—and girls as young as eight years old—has occurred within San Diego at other locations according to published reports, no such activity or organized crime operation—as alleged in chapter 34—has been linked to Golden West Hotel. The events depicted at this location have no bearing in fact. The author wishes to thank hotel management for providing access to its Men's Dormitory, so that it could be physically described.

- Harvey "the Snake" Mendel appeared at the BellyUp in Solana Beach on a different night close to the time described in chapter 35. The depiction of his performance and activities within the club are the author's creations.

- The description of the interior of the Horton Grand Hotel in chapter 36 has been modified for purposes of this work.

F. James Greco
Encinitas, CA

References

Anon. "Laying Out the Case: Spokane, WA: Spokane Police Abuses Past to Present," July 19, 2007, updated April 1, 2010. http://spokanepoliceabuses.wordpress.com/abuse-laying-out-the-case/.

Anon. "Historic Hotels of America: Montvale Hotel, Washington, DC," accessed November 8, 2012. http://www.historichotels.org/hotels-resorts/the-montvale-hotel/history.php.

Anon. "The People History: 1930s Homes Including Prices," 2004, http://www.thepeoplehistory.com/30s-homes.html.

Bauder, Don. "Story Behind the Scene." San Diego, CA: The *Reader*, September 10, 2008.

Bennett, Kelly. "In the Gaslamp, a Bed and a Sink and History." San Diego, CA: *San Diego Voice*, August 1, 2007. http://www.voiceofsandiego.org/housing/article_6609d7a2-deae-5323-8d89-aa32537067a2.html.

Bergman, Lowell, and Jeff Gerth. "La Costa—Syndicate in the Sun." United Kingdom: *Penthouse Magazine*, March 1975.

Boydston, Cassandra. "The Creole Palace (San Diego)." Seattle, WA: BlackPast.org., University of Washington, accessed November 2, 2012. http://www.blackpast.org/?q=aah/creole-palace-san-diego.

Bryant, J., et al. "The History of Modern Pornography." Hillsdale, NY: http://www.porno-graphyhistory.com/.

Burns, Emily. "Vintage: Crystal Pier." San Diego, CA: *San Diego Magazine*, August, 2013.

Crawford, Richard. "First Library Building Quickly Outgrew Its Space." San Diego, CA: *San Diego Union-Tribune*, May 24, 2008.

_____. "The Way We Were in San Diego, Westgate Park: Home of the Padres." Charleston, SC: *The History Press*, 2011.

Crawford, Richard W., editor. "A Village Within a City." San Diego, CA: The *Journal of San Diego History*, Vol. 41, No. 3, Summer 1995.

Davis, Mike, Kelly Mayhew, and Jim Miller. "Under the Perfect Sun: The San Diego Tourists Never See." New York, NY: *The New Press*, 2005.

Dippling, Caroline. "San Diego Native Recalled for Generosity as Restaurant Host." San Diego, CA: *San Diego UT*, August 5, 2010.

Dodge, Richard V. "San Diego's 'Impossible Railroad'." San Diego, CA: *Dispatcher*, June 29, 1956.

Dotinga, Randy. "SD's Prohibition Scandal—From Hooch to Hoosegowe." San Diego, CA: October 10, 2011. http://www.voiceofsandiego.org/this_just_in/article_f4068a76-f38d-11e0-b8f7-001cc4c03286.html.

Dowler, Jeff. "Carlsbad Homes—A Unique Neighborhood along the La Costa Resort Golf Course." Carlsbad, CA: *Solution Real Estate*. http://activerain.com/blogsview/319000/carlsbad-homes-a-unique-neighborhood-along-the-la-costa-resort-golf-course.

Engle, Nancy Arlene Driscoll. *Benefiting a City—Women, Respectability and Reborn in Spokane, Washington, 1886–1910*. Gainesville, FL: University of Florida, 2003.

Frammolino, Ralph. "El Cajon Blvd. Neighborhood War on Hookers Is Paying Off." San Diego, CA: *Los Angeles Times*, March 15, 1987.

Gelfuso, Louis. "Los Angeles Crime Family Crumb Bum." Los Angeles, CA: *Hollywood Goodfella*, August 29, 2008. https://af11.wordpress.com/tag/louis-gelfuso/.

Hammar, Richard. "Playboy's History of Organized Crime." New York, NY: *Playboy Magazine*, July 1974.

Hensley, Herbert C. "Mutton Chops, and a Round." San Diego, CA: The *Journal of San Diego History*, Vol. 2, No. 4, October 1956.

Hunt, Thomas. "The History of Organized Crime in the United States." Middlebury, VT: The American Mafia, 2011. http://mob-who.blogspot.com/2011/04/brooklier-dominic-1914-1984.html.

Hutson, Lorie. "Mother-Daughter Team to Revive Commellini's." Spokane, WA: The *Spokesman-Review*, December 15, 2010.

Innis, Jack Scheffler. *San Diego Legends: The Events, People, and Places That Made History*. San Diego, CA: Sunbelt Publications, Inc., 2004.

Jenkins, Logan. "Labor Day Has Wobbly History in San Diego." San Diego, CA: *San Diego Union-Tribune*, September 1, 2008.

Kalez, Jay J. "This Town of Ours ... Spokane." Spokane, WA: Lawton Printing, Inc., 1973.

Kizer, Benjamin H., "Flynn, Elizabeth Gurley (1890–1964)." Seattle, WA: History Link.org Free Online Encyclopedia of Washington State History, May 7, 2005. http://www.historylink.org/index.cfm?DisplayPage=output.cfm&file_id=7309.

Kragen, Pam. "Mad Scientist—El Bizcocho's Imaginative New Chef Ryan Grant is Crazy Like a Fox." Escondido, CA: *North County Times*, July 1, 2010.

Landis-Stewart, Susan. "History of the Hotel Spokane Silver Grill." McLean, VA: *USA Today*, accessed November 20, 2012. http://traveltips.usatoday.com/history-hotel-spokane-silver-grill-100739.html.

Larson, Thomas. "The Good Shoemaker and the Poor Fish Peddler." San Diego, CA: The *Reader*, August 8, 2005.

Lindsey, Robert. "Hearing Nears on $63-Million Libel Suit Involving Coast Resort." New York, NY: *New York Times*, November 10, 1975.

Logan, Ron. "Stolen Innocence—Human Trafficking in San Diego County." San Diego, CA: *East County Magazine*, April 9, 2012.

MacPhail, Elizabeth C. "Shady Ladies in the 'Stingaree District' When the Red Lights Went Out in San Diego—The Little Known Story of San Diego's 'Restricted' District." San Diego, CA: The *Journal of San Diego History*, Vol. 20, No. 2, Spring 1974.

Mandel, Harvey. "The Snake's Biography." Crested Butte, CO: http://www.harveymandel.com/biography.html.

Martin, Jonathan. "Legendary Dining in Its Storied Past, Commellini's Restaurant Has Been a Gathering Place for Spokane's Elite, Famous, Notorious." Spokane, WA: The *Spokesman-Review*, December 5, 1996.

May, Allan R. "Frank Bompensiero—San Diego Hitman, Boss & FBI Informant (Parts One & Two)." Cleveland, OH: May 15, 2000. http://www.americanmafia.com/Allan_May_5-15-00.html.

Miller, Arthur J. "Origins of a Wobbly Life." Chicago, IL: *Industrial Workers of the World*, accessed August 5, 2012. http://www.iww.org/en/history/library/AJMiller/Origins.

Moore, Judith. "A Bad, Bad Boy." San Diego, CA: *Reader Books*, 2009.

Morris, Desmond. *Manwatching—A Field Guide to Human Behavior.* New York: Harry N. Abrams, 1977.

Mundinger-Klow, Garth, MD, PhD. *Paying For It: Men and the Oldest Profession.* New York, NY: Ophelia-Olympia Press, 2009.

Noble, Holcomb B. C. "Arnholt Smith, 97, Banker and Padres Chief Before a Fall." New York, NY: *New York Times*, June 11, 1996.

Owen, Ryan W. and Forgotten New England. "Exploring New England As It Was, Boston's Immigrant Experience in 1900—Anticipation & Hope Amidst Confusion & Exploitation." New England, December 28, 2011. http://forgottennewengland.com/2011/12/28/bostons-immigrant-experience-in-1900-anticipation-hope-amidst-confusion-exploitation.

Potter, Matt. "Mafia Hunter." San Diego, CA: The *Reader*, December 17, 1998.

_____. "Mob Scene." San Diego, CA: The *Reader*, November 18, 1999.

Raugust, Dale. "Fanning the Flames of Discontent." Spokane, WA: *Washington Free Press*, September–October 2009.

Reider, Ross, and History Link staff. "IWW formally begins Spokane free-speech fight on November 2, 1909." Seattle, WA: History Link. org Free Online Encyclopedia of Washington State History, June 22, 2005. http://www.historylink.org/index.cfm?DisplayPage=output .cfm&file_id=7357.

Shanks, Rosalie. "The I.W.W. Free Speech Movement—San Diego, 1912." San Diego, CA: The *Journal of San Diego History*, Vol. 19, No. 1, Winter 1973.

Shelton, Keith. "Prostitution in Early Spokane." Spokane, WA: Spokane Historical, accessed November 13, 2012. http://spokanehistorical .org/items/show/204.

Silverado Rare Music. "Harvey Mandel & the Snake Band—BellyUp Tavern—Solano Beach, CA, August 16, 1990." Solano Beach, CA. http://silveradoraremusic.blogspot.com/2010/02/ harvey-mandel-snake-band-BellyUp.html.

Smith, Jeff. "The Big Noise—The Free Speech Fight of 1912 (Parts 1–8)." San Diego, CA: The *Reader*, May 23–July 11, 2012.

Thompson, Mary M., certifying official. Commercial Block National Register of Historic Places Registration Form. Spokane, WA: United States Department of the Interior, September 13, 1993. http://properties.historicspokane.org/_pdf/properties/property-1760.pdf.

Thornton, Kelly. "The New Breed of Federal Inmates." San Diego, CA: Voice of San Diego, August 1, 2010. http://www.voiceofsandiego.org/public_safety/article_b9459aba-9dd7-11df-9cba-001cc4c002e0.html.

Vann, Gene. "Coffee During the Great Depression." Denver, CO: Examiner.com, December 29, 2010. http://www.examiner.com/article/coffee-during-the-great-depression.

Waudby, Dr. June. "Contextualizing Vittoria—Subjectivity and Censure in The White Devil." This Rough Magic: A Peer-Reviewed, Academic, Online Journal Dedicated to the Teaching of Medieval and Renaissance Literature, accessed March 9, 2013. http://www.thisroughmagic.org/waudby%20article.html.

Wolf, Carlo. "Resort Rejuvenation." New York, NY: National Real Estate Investor, Marcy 15, 2006. http://lhonline.com/mag/resort_rejuvenation/.